SEAL
OF
SILENCE

DIXIE LEE BROWN

All rights reserved. No part of this book may be reproduced in any form or by any means without the prior written permission of the author, excepting brief quotes used in reviews.

Copyright © 2021 by Dixie Lee Brown
ISBN: 9798726087665

This book is a work of fiction. Any similarities to any person, living or dead, or any business or organization are purely coincidental.

To the extent that the image or images on the cover of this book depict a person or persons, such person or persons are merely models, and are not intended to portray any character or characters portrayed in this book.

DEDICATION

Dedicated to the men and women of the armed forces wherever you may be. Thank you for your service.

May God bless and keep you and your families.

ACKNOWLEDGMENTS

A huge thank you to Jodie Hughes, without whose help this first self-publishing attempt would still be in the planning stages. Jodie is my critique partner, which means she reads my manuscript when it is in its roughest, most deplorable condition and somehow manages to figure out what I meant to say and get me back on track. She also designed this gorgeous cover and basically held my hand while I tried to learn the ropes.

I could not have done it without you, my friend!

Many thanks to Yvonne Cruz who so graciously agreed to Beta read and give her comments, suggestions and honest opinions.

Your help was invaluable, Yvonne!

Thanks also to my fantastic sister, Dorothy Cail, and my amazing friend, Cindy Smith, who went above and beyond to help make SEAL of Silence shine. Thanks for offering your time and encouragement.

Your support means the world to me!

May we all have many more trips around the sun!

CHAPTER ONE

Thunder rolled through the foundation of the compound. Flakes of mortar and dust rained from the high ceiling. Jade flung her arms over her head. *An earthquake?*

Silence returned as though the world stood still. Leaning her weight on one shaky elbow, she forced herself upright on her thin sleeping mat. *Yes, Lord! Bury this vile place so deep not even the devil can escape.*

A chain, attaching her ankle to the wall behind her, dragged the floor as she swung around to peer at the faint strands of dawn stealing across the dark sky beyond the high window.

An explosion rumbled through the house, jerking the air from her lungs in a rush. More cracked plaster landed in her hair and pinged off her bare arms. The vibration slowly faded to a moment of calm before women's voices, sharp with alarm, raised to wake their sleeping children. Jade hugged her knees to her chest to stop her limbs from trembling with the sudden rush of adrenaline.

Men swearing and shouting joined the discord as a surge of running footsteps clattered on the staircase beyond her door. No doubt Mahaz and his soldiers were scampering for the rooftop. *What's happening out there?*

Repeated blasts of automatic gunfire drowned out the other sounds. Jade ducked and pressed as far into the corner of the darkened room as the chain would allow. When the bursts finally stopped, an eerie hush dulled the ringing in her ears.

Okay—not an earthquake. The compound is under attack.

Mahaz Bashara had no shortage of enemies. Syria's Sunni tribes that split from their clansmen and fought against ISIS had learned well the steep cost of disloyalty. Mahaz, high in the jihadist hierarchy, had given the order for their slaughter. Followers had murdered hundreds, yet survivors vowed revenge. They weren't the only enemies the monster had made. Any number of allied governments would love to get their hands on Mahaz for his crimes, including his role in the bombing of a French embassy that took the life of an ambassador in Islamabad a year ago.

Jade's heart hammered loudly in her ears. She had to hold her breath to listen for footsteps approaching her door. Chained, she had no chance of hiding from whoever was assaulting the compound. It was unlikely the force overrunning Mahaz's sanctuary would spare the life of an American prisoner. As bleak as her future looked, it could always be worse. The last thing she wanted was to be taken alive again.

Yet a pinprick of hope flared to life anyway. There was one chance in a million the U.S. military had come to call, and one chance was better than none. Besides, the enemies of her captors were, by default, her friends, weren't they? A measure of conviction took root.

As the minutes ticked by, her optimism slowly diminished. Periodic explosions kept her nerves taut. Perhaps they would burn the place to the ground, not bothering to search for survivors. She should have known better than to hope.

Mahaz had sworn an oath that she would die before she'd ever taste freedom again. If the battle turned against him, she had no doubt he would honor his vow. As his final act, he would take great pleasure in killing her. Revulsion twisted her gut, and she made a vow of her own. The animal who'd tormented, tortured, and raped her wouldn't achieve his final goal painlessly.

From the hallway, a short salvo of bullets splintered her thin, wooden door. Lead penetrated the flimsy barricade. Jade hit the floor, face down, and covered her ears.

The next instant, her door burst inward, shredding the casing where the lock had been. Three figures surged through the opening. Dressed in dark clothing that blended into the night, they gave no indication who or what they were. She couldn't mistake the outline of automatic rifles held tightly to their bodies. Night vision goggles covered their faces.

One of them turned his rifle toward her. "On your feet!" He spoke English, and she would have recognized that Brooklyn inflection anywhere. Another repeated the command in flawed Arabic, but she was already scrambling to stand as relief engulfed her.

"I'm an American. Please, help me." Her mouth had gone dry, and the words were barely audible.

"Captain McDowell?"

"Yes." *They know my name.* Tears she'd denied for eight long months welled in her eyes. Her rubbery legs threatened to collapse. She dropped clumsily back to her mat, afraid otherwise she'd confirm her weakness with a faceplant in front of her rescuers.

The first man lowered his weapon, removed his night vision apparatus, and hurried to her side. "Lieutenant Braden, ma'am, SEAL team four. We're here to get you home, Captain. Can you walk?"

Was she dreaming? She'd given up on being rescued months ago—had come to terms with dying a prisoner. When she could see no other option, she'd prayed for death to take her. The hope she'd squelched now flooded through her. *Home? Damn right, I can walk.*

"I might be slow, Lieutenant, but I'll make it. Just one hitch." She reached for the manacle attached to her ankle, and the chain clapped against the stone floor.

"Not a problem." The lieutenant grinned as he touched the comm device in his ear. "Toolbox, bring the bolt cutters." He rose to his feet and turned to one of the others stationed just inside the door, watching the hallway. "Griz, stay with her until Toolbox gets here. Then the two of you get her out and onto a helo."

"Copy that," Griz replied.

The lieutenant turned back to her and pointed to the ceiling. "How many?"

"I'd guess eight or ten."

"Sit tight. You'll be on your way home before daybreak." He and the third man slipped from the room. Though she listened for the sound of their boots on the stairs, she heard nothing.

Griz knelt beside her, took a penlight from his vest, and shined it in her eyes. "Bruises on your face. Incised wound on your upper arm. Any other injuries?"

"Nothing worth complaining about." Which, loosely translated, meant she didn't have time to enumerate them all. Although the green streaks smeared on his face made it difficult to guess his age, he seemed surprisingly young to be a SEAL. "Why do they call you Griz?"

"Would you believe it's because I'm warm and fuzzy?"

She smiled when he winked. Obviously, that wasn't the whole story.

A booted foot scuffed against the floor in the hallway. Apparently, Toolbox had arrived with the bolt cutters to free her. Instead of welcoming his teammate, Griz froze. The humor in his expression disappeared, replaced by the deadly seriousness of a well-trained warrior.

"Get down." He ripped his sidearm from his holster, swung around, and moved to shield her from someone he clearly considered an enemy.

Jade flattened herself on her mat, but not before reaching for the SEAL's rifle, propped against the wall beside her. She covered it with her body and the ragged edges of her blanket. A shot rang out in the tight quarters. Blood splattered her as the bullet grazed the inside of Griz's arm. He dropped to his haunches, swearing as his handgun spun out of reach toward the center of the room.

When Mahaz stepped into view, she went still. "You didn't think I'd forget about you, did you, Captain?"

Pulling herself up straight, she was careful to keep the rifle concealed from him. Hatred for the man simmered just beneath her skin. Memories of the pain and humiliation she'd endured at his hands made her long to remove the arrogant smirk from his face. She hadn't expected to be rescued, but she'd come so damn close, and the disappointment was a bitter pill. She returned Mahaz's glare with calm determination. Time for plan B. If the fates had decided she wasn't going home, one way or the other, her captivity ended today. No way would she allow the filth that stood before her to touch her again.

Regret sat heavily on her heart. Griz and his SEAL unit had been sent into harm's way to retrieve her. He'd suffered a bullet wound in the process. Unless the lieutenant or Toolbox arrived in the next few seconds, his chances of survival were no better than hers. His death would be on her head. For a heartbeat, she gave free rein to guilt, surprised she could still muster such an unselfish emotion.

Dumb move. Jade should have shut it down at once before regret cracked open an old fissure in her chest, and the memory of a sinfully handsome, larger-than-life man inundated her mind. Her heart broke as a vision of the person she'd once been kissed him goodbye on the tarmac at Al Asad before her five-hour mission had turned into forever.

She'd fallen hard for the guy the first time they'd met, and she'd wanted to see where their relationship would take them. With her track record in romance, chances were good she'd been headed for heartache. Maybe it was just as well she'd never see Navy SEAL James Cooper again.

Swallowing around the lump in her throat, she forced Coop's image from her head. She needed to focus on the man in front of her. Mahaz expected fear and submission, and she'd be damned if she would give him what he wanted this time. Rewarded with a hint of surprise and uncertainty in his expression, she smiled. "I was counting on seeing you one last time before you die."

He threw his head back and emitted a scornful laugh.

"Easy, Captain," Griz whispered.

A glance revealed blood soaking through the sleeve of his shirt, yet he reached slowly for the long knife on his hip.

"As much as I'd like to kill you here, in front of your would-be rescuer, I still have use for you. You're my ticket out of here. On your feet, Captain. You have one more service to perform." He motioned impatiently with the gun. "Stand up and step aside. I have no reason to keep your friend alive."

Delay was the only card left to play. She rolled to her knees and leaned on Griz's legs to leverage herself up the rest of the way, blocking the SEAL's upper body and knife hand from Mahaz's view.

Once standing, she rattled the chain. "You'll have to free me first."

Mahaz produced the key, tossed it toward her, and glanced nervously into the hallway. "Hurry," he growled.

Jade let the three-inch piece of metal fall through her fingers. It landed on the dusty, stone floor with a soft *clink*. Anything to buy time. When Mahaz scowled and took a step toward her, she bent and grasped the key, making eye contact with Griz.

"Get down, Captain." He mouthed the warning as he sat up partway and brought his arm back, the knife seeming to hang in the air.

She hit the floor. Time slowed like an old-fashioned movie projector. With trembling fingers, she forced the key into the lock at her ankle. It clicked open as Griz released the knife with a quick, controlled flick of his wrist.

Mahaz jerked toward the wounded SEAL, taking an additional fraction of a second to reposition his weapon. The blade slammed into his shoulder at the same instant his finger squeezed the trigger. Two earsplitting blasts shattered the eerie scene. His first shot went wide. The second hit the ceiling as he stumbled back with a roar. He struggled to catch himself while his gun hand flailed. As though on cue, the battle upstairs began in earnest.

Griz launched himself toward the man, but Jade already had the SEAL's rifle snugged to her shoulder. Hatred cloaked her in a haze of red. Only partially aware she'd pulled the trigger, a rapid burst of lead struck Mahaz's chest, throwing him backward. His body jerked grotesquely as each round found its target. He crumpled, lifeless, against the wall.

Griz crossed the room and kicked the weapon from Mahaz's hand, kneeling to check for a pulse. Then he stood and turned toward her, his eyes holding a hint of wariness. "Nice shooting, Captain. What d'ya say you give me the weapon?"

His voice snapped her from the bloodlust that still burned within her. With numbness stealing over her, she lowered the rifle and passed it to him. He continued to study her as though she might go off at any moment. Did he think she was crazy? Likely he was right, but she wasn't sorry Mahaz was dead. Nor did she regret being the one to snuff out his pathetic life. If that made her crazy, she'd earned the right.

Another SEAL, probably Toolbox, raced into the room, weapon raised and ready. The lieutenant wasn't far behind, stopping when he saw the dead body. With a frown, he assessed her, then turned to Griz. "What the hell? I can't leave you alone for a minute?" A grin tugged at his lips.

"We're clear, Waldo." Griz snickered and threw her a wink before retrieving his knife from Mahaz's body.

She straightened, standing tall for the first time in an exceedingly long while. She was going home.

"What do you mean *I can't go home?*" Jade heard the tremor in her voice, but a week of field hospitals and military transports had left her too tired to care.

General McDowell darted his cold gray gaze heavenward and heaved a sigh as though she was wasting his time. The general in charge of Middle East air combat—AKA *daddy dearest*—displayed no signs she meant anything to him other than a failed mission and the loss of a multi-million-dollar fighter jet. Jade stole a glance at her commanding officer, sitting beside her at the table, but Colonel Reiner directed his focus on the general.

What the hell's going on?

Colonel Mark Reiner had met the helicopter when it landed on the tarmac at Al Asad airbase in Iraq two days prior and stayed close by throughout her exhaustive medical examination. Not only had he been a buffer separating her from the questions of the curious and well-meaning hospital staff, but also a friendly face in a suddenly too-foreign world. If only she'd known then that having every bruise, cut, and broken bone cataloged would be the easy part compared to this debriefing overseen by her father.

"You knew how sensitive your mission was when you volunteered, Captain." Her father had aged physically, his sandy-colored hair predominantly white. His commanding presence, if possible, was even more uncompromising. He'd always been a hard man, but she'd expected some sign of emotion. Maybe relief that she was still alive. Even dispensing with her rank and calling her by name would have made her feel valued as his daughter. Instead, he acted as though she was nothing but an inconvenience in his schedule.

Glancing again toward Colonel Reiner, she caught his scowl and the red flush that darkened his features. Mark was a good guy, a respected officer, and a friend. He'd tried to warn her all those months ago. He'd encouraged her to reconsider in the final briefing with her father, earning the general's ire.

"The mission is top secret, Captain. Only you, me, and Colonel Reiner know the true nature of your assignment."

"That means—"

"It means if something goes wrong, the Air Force, the military...hell, the President will deny any knowledge of your unauthorized activities." The general's eyes held a zealous glow as he scrutinized her.

She understood the dangers. U.S. forces had, ostensibly, pulled out of Syria. Neither Assad, the Russians, or the Kurdish forces America had just deserted would welcome an intrusion into their air space. But the massive troop movements and the loading of large trucks at a known chemical weapons facility outside Damascus could have ramifications that would stretch far beyond Syria.

It's only a few pictures of the plant and any current troop movements—in, under cover of darkness, out and done.

"Consider the implications before you agree to this, Captain." Colonel Reiner had seemed opposed to her flying the mission from the start, not even trying to hide his misgivings from the general. *"I've got another pilot standing by to take the run. Just say the word. No one will think less of you for passing this one up, Jade."*

Did he have a premonition? The qualms, fluttering in her belly, almost got the better of her—

until she caught his meaning. It had been the one thing sure to make her stand and fight. The mission held additional risks for a female pilot. Men would always be men, and the colonel had a man for the job. Would she never be allowed the respect she'd earned—respect men were handed just for breathing?

Anger swelled within her and slammed her back to the present. Pride had played a hand in her fateful decision, but so had her unrelenting need to earn her father's approval. Even if she'd somehow managed to attain both, the cost had been too great.

Sitting forward, she folded her hands on the table. Across from her, the full array of medals on her father's dress uniform mocked her. She would never be enough to make him proud. A hint of contentment followed the realization she no longer cared.

She shook her head as she silently tallied all the wasted effort. "You were never there for Nicole or me. Your next mission was always more important than your daughters. I'll never live up to your expectations, and I'm done trying. I don't give a damn about you or the mission. You don't have a clue what I went through. So, let's cut the crap. I want to go home, and I need to call Coop."

Why wasn't he there? Foreboding clawed its way into her throat. She darted another glance at Colonel Reiner. "Does he know? Did anyone tell him I'm here?" If Coop knew how much she needed him, he would have come.

Mark shifted in his seat and glanced at her father. "No, Jade. Coop completed his service obligation two months ago and didn't reenlist. I haven't heard from him since he shipped out, but he said he was heading to Idaho. Going to meet up with some buddies and *raise hell* before he decided what to do with the rest of his life. I have his contact information if—"

The general cleared his throat, and Mark stopped talking. "That'll be all, Colonel. I'm sure you're anxious to get back to your command."

Mark hesitated a heartbeat too long before he pushed his chair out and stood. He pulled a card from his pocket and laid it on the table. "It was good to see you, Jade. Give me a call when you get settled." He met the general's glare with a bland expression that clearly said, *screw you* without uttering a word.

Was she the cause of the bad blood between them? Bracing for the worst, she expected her father to explode in rage over the colonel's insubordination. She was mildly surprised when the door closed behind Colonel Reiner without incident.

Her father took a file marked CLASSIFIED from his briefcase and spread it open on the table. "Now, as I was saying...an Air Force officer in an F-22 Raptor strayed off course due to instrument malfunction, encroached on Syria's airspace, and took enemy fire. That's the official report, Captain. Though the aircraft was severely damaged, the pilot *and crew member* landed at Incirlik airbase in Turkey."

"What? You can't just *report* away Andy's death!" A drone strike had injured her weapons system officer during the attack that took out her Raptor. Jade had initiated the ejection sequence for them both, but Andy was dead by the time she'd reached him on the ground.

The general continued to read, not looking up from the file. "First Lieutenant Andrew Moore later died from injuries suffered during the incident. Captain Jade McDowell experienced an emotional breakdown. She was granted an extended leave for personal reasons and honorably discharged six weeks later."

She had to force her gaping mouth closed. Her eight months of captivity didn't even rate a footnote in her father's version of history. How could he act as though none of it had happened?

General McDowell closed the file and rose. Turning his back to her, he strode to the windows overlooking the busy landing field of Al Asad. "The rest of your squadron, your family, and friends must believe the report. America's leadership within the Allied Command and the reputation of the U.S. Air Force depends upon your silence." He turned partway and fixed her with an emotionless stare. "My command and that of Colonel Reiner depend on it as well."

He faced the window again, and Jade heard his deep sigh. "The Pentagon was content when you were MIA and presumed dead. When we discovered your whereabouts, I wanted—well, let's just say not everyone was ecstatic."

Jade couldn't believe her ears. The top brass would have been happier if she hadn't come back from the dead. Clearly, her father shared their views. Anger and bone-deep disappointment welled within her, stealing what little strength she'd regained. "I'm sorry if I've complicated your life, Dad." Bitterness oozed from each word.

"No matter. We won't speak of this again. You'll attest to the accuracy of the official report and swear never to discuss the actual events with anyone—least of all this Coop person you were once involved with."

"What?" He couldn't be serious. She was in love with Coop. He'd never said the words, but he'd made her feel cherished. "Nicole...my friends—you're crazy if you think they'll believe your report! They'll know I didn't end up in Turkey with a mental breakdown or that I left the service and disappeared without contacting anyone for eight months!"

Her father turned slowly. The silence was thick with unspoken words as they stared at each other. When the truth dawned, Jade stood, pushing her chair back so suddenly, it toppled over.

"You covered it up! Everything. Of course. I should have known." Jade shook her head as disbelief turned to hatred. "How..."

General McDowell strode back to the table and closed the file that contained the lies her life had become. "Don't be so naïve, Captain. There's always a cover story. Your mission was classified. Your failure was unfortunate. You've suffered significantly, in ways that many people won't understand. Do you want the details of your captivity splashed across the front page of every major newspaper in the world? Your sister looking at you with pity? Your friends talking about you behind your back?

"Your Navy SEAL—he quit and returned to the

states thinking you were dead. By all accounts, James Cooper was a broken man. In a way, he deserted you and his country. If you go to him now, what will you tell him when he asks where you've been for the past eight months? If you tell him the truth, will it change the way he looks at you?"

Being rescued from hell was supposed to be the best moment of her life. Instead, she remained trapped in an alternate prison—this one made of lies. She needed air. Her stomach lurched as cold sweat broke over her skin. It was suddenly critical she get out of this room. Turning abruptly, she almost tripped over her upended chair and started for the door.

"In time, you'll see this is the only way to protect yourself and safeguard our great nation."

She reached the door and flung it open.

"Your country appreciates your sacrifice, Captain McDowell."

Jade rushed through the hallway, searching for an exit, oblivious to the people streaming by her. Alternating between her need to throw up and bawl her eyes out, she finally stepped out into the slightly cooler Iraqi dusk. She followed the metal siding of the building around to the back until all she could hear were distant noises, slid down against the wall, and buried her face in her hands.

As much as she hated it—hated him—he was right. No one could ever understand the nightmare she'd lived. No doubt, her friends would try to be supportive and pretend she was the same person she'd always been. Beneath it all, they'd wonder why she'd fought so hard to live. After all, wouldn't it be better to be killed trying to get away than to suffer such brutality? Or take her own life at her first opportunity? If only they knew how many escape plans she'd entertained, then rejected because they were nothing more than glorified suicide missions. Hope had been strong in the beginning. As time went on, she'd survived on sheer stubbornness.

People who'd never set foot in a battle zone would still judge and look at her differently—or worse, not look at all. Though they could never imagine what she'd been through, they'd assume, assign blame, and question how she could hold her head up in decent society.

Was that how Coop would react? Her Navy SEAL had been on the ground in Syria. His team carried out hundreds of covert missions. He would have heard the horror stories and probably seen atrocities firsthand perpetrated by the Mahaz's of the region.

Coop wasn't a SEAL anymore. He'd walked away from the military and his brothers-in-arms. Had he been broken, as Dad said? She'd known Coop was the one for her after their first date, but he'd always been clear that his job was his first love. If he'd thrown it all away because of her, how was she supposed to live with that guilt?

Had he loved her? Did he still?

Even if she refused to go along with the lies in General McDowell's official report and the gag order he sought to impose, she didn't have the first idea how to track down Coop. Colonel Reiner had said he had Coop's contact information. Mark would help, despite the general's orders.

Maybe it wasn't too late.

She could make this right.

It was too much. Tears welled, and she bit her bottom lip hard enough to draw blood. Anything to get her mind off the pity party she was throwing. Beads of moisture ran down her cheeks anyway. She was powerless to divert the wave of grief that erupted in an enormous sob or any of the chest-rattling ones that followed.

Jade hugged her knees tightly and buried her face in her fatigues, muffling the pathetic sounds of surrender.

Who am I kidding?

CHAPTER TWO

Two and a half years later

"Seriously? What do you think you're doing? You've got about half a second to remove your hand from my ass unless you'd like it back in a few more pieces than you started with."

Ah hell. Not again. Coop took off his sunglasses and squinted toward the checkout counter in the front of the small mom-and-pop grocery store where Derek had insisted they stop for a case of beer. Today's commotion centered around a loud, obviously irate female near the front. The dagger-sharp edge to the woman's threat made a believer out of Coop and managed to generate a subtle grin. *Sounds like the offender might have overbid his hand this time—quite literally.*

Halfway to the coolers in the back, his position left part of the confrontation shrouded in mystery. Unfortunately, that encompassed the area most concerning. Slipping his shades over the neck of his T-shirt, he hooked his thumbs in his front pockets and strolled closer. He stopped as the space around the cash register gradually filled with the broad shoulders of three home-grown boys, apparently intent on taking care of their own.

"Now, darlin', I didn't mean no disrespect. I was just bein' friendly. You folks got somethin' against bein' friendly?"

Damn it to hell! It was no surprise that Derek Waldon, Coop's partner for the day—for lack of a better term—was the voice on the other end of the disturbance. Nevertheless, it pissed him off to no end.

"I don't need friends like you or the rest of those snakes currently slithering around town." The words were clearly forced from between the woman's gritted teeth and followed by a punch or jab into what was likely Derek's gut if the whoosh of air from his lungs was any indication.

Couldn't happen to a nicer guy. Coop wiped away the grin that would only give him away and slid his sunglasses back on his face. As unobtrusively as possible, he maneuvered around the small cluster of onlookers to a spot close to the door where he could see what was happening.

Derek's smart mouth and penchant for intimidation had already resulted in three altercations in the short week Coop had been there. Damn wet-behind-the-ears kid, barely twenty years old, was determined to make a name for himself with the group of lowlifes who'd descended on the town. The fool was a menace to himself and everybody around him, headed for jail or an early grave unless he changed his ways. Coop had tried to explain the inherent risks in the kid's highhanded methods, but Derek was all about learning the hard way.

He straightened, one hand cradling his ribs with

enough care to prove the woman who'd landed the blow meant business. "Now, why'd you have to go and do that, pretty lady? I was just introducin' myself. Seems like you'd appreciate havin' someone around who could offer protection—you know—with everything that's goin' on in this town." The leer that accompanied his indecent perusal of the woman's body dragged a groan from Coop's throat.

"You're drunk, and you smell bad, and someone needs to teach you a lesson." The woman had stepped back, but she was wedged in the corner of the L-shaped counter and had nowhere to go.

She wasn't wrong but, drunk or sober, Derek never knew when to quit. He held his arms out to his sides and twirled in a slow circle. "Well, I don't see anyone here with enough balls for the job, honey."

A round of grumbles and mutterings came from the assembled spectators. The corners of her mouth hitched upward ever so slightly as the woman cocked her head to one side and held up one delicate hand to stop her would-be protectors. Full lips, shimmering with pink gloss, stirred the fabric of long-ago and teased the fringes of Coop's memory. Unfortunately, forgotten bits of yesterday weren't the only things brought to life by this sexy spitfire. Annoyed by his lack of self-control, he ignored the tightening in his groin and forced his attention back to the trouble at hand.

She was spunky. Coop had to give her that. Which was good because it was beginning to look like chivalry was dead in this hick town. So far, the three burly locals had made no move to jump in and help her, an eventuality he'd been counting on. *Hell, what's the matter with them?*

Not that she appeared to need any help. Tight blue jeans hugged her long, shapely legs. A little white tank top highlighted tanned arms with well-defined biceps for a woman. She either worked out frequently or worked hard at making a living. A floral tattoo that spilled over her right shoulder and halfway down her upper arm intrigued him with its intricate design and exotic colors.

Derek stood barely three inches taller than her, which put her somewhere around five-eight. Wisps of silky, dark brown hair had escaped from beneath a white baseball cap decorated with sparkly, pink paw prints. She'd pulled the brim low on her forehead. Coop couldn't make out her eyes in the shadow of the cap's bill, but her body language clearly said she wasn't giving an inch.

Her wide stance, with hands planted firmly on her hips, showcased her slim waist and corresponding curves. A soft laugh dragged Coop's focus back to her shadowed face. From nowhere, nostalgia from an eons-old recollection settled in the pit of his stomach as a familiar image invaded his mind.

No way.

The mountain of a man behind the cash register slammed the drawer shut, and everyone except the woman jumped and swung toward him. "You got this, JD? Or do you want me to call the sheriff?"

A slow smile curved her lips. Déjà vu locked Coop's sense of duty in an imaginary game of tug of war at the same instant Derek's hand fell to the hunting knife he carried on his hip.

Oh, hell no. Not today.

Derek wasn't going to start another fight over a woman. If in the process, Coop blew his cover with the malignant troupe of rednecks he was supposed to be surveilling, so be it. He pushed forward a couple of steps before her cold, precise words stopped him.

"I can handle this, Ryan." She leaned back against the counter, crossing her arms over her slim midsection, as though Derek was an unruly teen and she was the principal. "You don't happen to have your gram's equalizer behind that counter, do you?"

Ryan chuckled as he tossed something long and black across the worktop. Without a glance in Ryan's direction, the woman caught the KSG 12-gauge in her right hand, pumped a shell into the chamber with her left, and snugged the stock tight to her shoulder. It happened so fast; Coop almost overlooked the chill that slid up his back at the woman's softly sensuous and vaguely familiar voice.

So much for wondering why the townspeople gathered around hadn't jumped into the fray. A round of snickers and a general murmur of approval floated through the group. Everyone already knew the smoking-hot hellion could take care of herself—everyone but him and Derek. Again, a pinprick of something just beyond the reach of his finely tuned instincts jabbed him in the solar plexus.

He was missing something crucial. The certainty settled over him like a parachute after a sea landing, and he broke out in claustrophobic sweat. His powers of discernment hadn't failed him this miserably—ever. *What the hell?* With renewed interest, he shifted his total concentration to the woman who, seemingly, knew no fear.

"Are you threatening me?" Derek spread his phony incredulousness around the circle of onlookers, pausing long enough in his slow turn to make eye contact with Coop, then continued his public propaganda campaign. "I think the pretty lady is threatening me. I'm damn sure I didn't do anything to deserve getting shot. Maybe we *should* call that sheriff."

Facing away from the woman, arms wide in a gesture of total innocence, Derek took a step back, and the I-dare-you grin he always wore right before hell was likely to break loose finally got Coop moving again.

Damn it! His inability to shake the apprehension, which had the hair standing straight up on the back of his neck, had put him about two seconds behind. As he weighed his options and considered the likelihood she'd shoot, the dream-like quality of his movements seemed to mire him in quicksand. He could be sure Derek was feeling no such impediment. One thing Coop had learned about his partner in the past few days—his stupidity was only exceeded by his arrogance.

Derek finished his three-hundred-and-sixty-degree turn and suddenly lunged toward the woman.

In the next heartbeat, she answered Coop's question about whether she'd pull the trigger just as Derek grabbed the barrel and shoved it upward. A *boom* reverberated off the shelves and windows an instant before a load of buckshot spattered the ceiling above Coop's head.

There it was—the shit storm he'd come to

expect. The ringing in his ears added to the red haze of anger he was struggling to control.

Ryan leaped over the counter and stalked toward Derek, hands balled into fists. The other men seemed to take their cue from him and started moving in. Derek ripped the shotgun from the woman's grasp, swinging to the left just in time to slam the stock into Ryan's jaw. Whether accidental or intentional, Coop wasn't sure. The result was the same. Ryan dropped to his knees, shaking his head, even as the scariest damn grin Coop had ever seen bared the man's teeth.

One of the locals grabbed the woman's arm and tried to pull her from harm's way, but the stubborn female merely shook off his hand. Two others circled Derek warily. No one appeared to pay any attention to Coop.

Being outnumbered only seemed to shove Derek further over the edge. Anticipation shone from his eyes as he shifted the shotgun into position against his shoulder.

Involving himself in a fight with the residents went way beyond the scope of Coop's directive, but if he was right, this was going to end badly, whichever way it went. Luke, Travis, and MacGyver, his partners in the private security business they owned together, wouldn't be happy if their undercover operation went up in smoke because of his ingrained need to protect. They'd expended no small effort to create his foolproof cover. It wasn't likely the group of agitators masquerading as concerned citizens, who'd all but taken over the small town of Pine Bluff, would be as easy to dupe the next time around.

With the shotgun pointed at them, the two men backed off, but Ryan was rallying, his eyes, black with anger, fixed on Derek. The woman, to her credit, intercepted him before he'd gone two steps. "Not worth going to jail over, Ryan." She looked back and forth between the store clerk and Derek. "Nobody needs to get hurt here today."

Where was that bit of good advice when she was the one with the shotgun? Interesting. Yet Coop sensed that the woman didn't do anything merely by chance.

"I couldn't agree more." Pushing forward, he inserted himself between Derek and Ryan. "Graves said no more trouble. Remember? Hand the shotgun back to Ryan, and let's get out of here." Carl Graves, Coop's new boss and self-appointed leader of the armed militia ensconced in Pine Bluff's Main Street Feed Store, had tasked him with corralling the kid. It had proven to be a nearly impossible task, and he was damned tired of babysitting.

For the count of five, Derek glared at him, clearly reluctant to be the one to give ground.

With his back to the townspeople, Coop met Derek's gaze with the quiet confidence of a thousand overseas missions with his SEAL team. The jerk didn't have a clue how much trouble he'd be biting off if he continued down this path.

With a nervous twitch, Derek looked away first. "Hell man, it wasn't my idea to pull a gun."

Coop had to agree with him on that. Though clearly competent in using the weapon, the woman had only been asking for more trouble. He'd seen it happen too many times. A civilian with a knife or gun, trying to defend his family. Inevitably, his inexperience gets him killed, and there's nobody left to keep the insurgents from doing whatever the hell they wanted with the guy's wife and kids. He locked down the unpleasant memories, but not before the bile at the back of his throat triggered his gag reflex.

Anger darkened his mood as he accepted the shotgun Derek shoved toward him. He turned partway and passed it to Ryan, who grunted and laid it on the counter behind him. The other three men grumbled as they meandered toward the beer cooler in the rear of the store.

"I'm sorry for the trouble, miss. He's had a little too much to drink." Coop turned the rest of the way, ready to take one for the team if it would make up for Derek's surly manner. Instead, he stopped mid-sentence, the rest of his words drifting beyond his reach, as though waking from one of his damn dreams.

But it wasn't a dream.

Yet it couldn't be *her*.

She was close enough; he could have reached out and touched her if he hadn't been afraid she'd disappear in a puff of cloud, complete with angel wings and halo. It seemed like an eternity before she settled her contempt-filled perusal on him. Her chin tilted upward, banishing the shadows from her face. He could see her eyes beneath the brim of her ball cap. Violet blue. Eyes that had haunted his dreams many a night. Eyes he'd never expected to see again.

The ghostly vision drew back a step. Maybe Coop had reached for her—he couldn't be certain. Sure as hell, his brain had fried. Data was still going in, but nothing was coming out.

It's not possible. There's no way this woman can be her. After all, it wasn't the only time he'd seen someone who reminded him of her. For the first few months, he'd seen her everywhere. Waiting to cross a busy street in New York City. Getting off a bus in Paris or eating alone in a San Francisco diner. Only to realize it was some other woman.

He'd finally put that chapter of his life behind him because drowning in sorrow wouldn't bring her back. After more than three years, he shouldn't imagine her face—her slim, vibrant body—on random women.

No stranger had ever been the spitting image of her before, though. Her perfectly kissable lips always looked a little pouty. Long, dark eyelashes made her gorgeous eyes pop without the benefit of makeup. With just a hint of pink, high cheekbones made her look like the-girl-next-door when she wasn't even close. He could almost feel those long legs wrapped around his hips. No ink had adorned her body when he knew her, but it wasn't hard to get a tat. If he dared touch her smooth, olive-colored skin, would it still feel like the softest of silk?

Maybe he was finally going nuts because he wanted it to be her with every ounce of yearning he possessed.

No, she couldn't be the woman he remembered. He had to be hallucinating. Captain Jade McDowell hadn't made it home after the F-22 she piloted was shot down over Syria. He'd held on to the hope she'd survived, a POW in some Godforsaken desert stronghold. Until his SEAL team, minus himself, had positioned themselves to rescue her on a tip from a captured insurgent. Instead, they'd confirmed she and her navigator had died in the crash. The SEALs recovered their dog tags from the compound, but all they'd gotten from the inhabitants was a rambling dialogue about a mass grave somewhere in a hundred square miles of sand and scrub brush.

The team leader had given Jade's tags to him. He still wore the damn things around his neck.

The next couple of years had been the hardest of his life. He'd gone through all the stages of grief, and it'd nearly cost him his sanity. The last thing he needed was to go back there.

"Okay, we'll go as soon as the pretty lady apologizes for tryin' to shoot me and agrees to let me take her to dinner." With a sneer twisting his lips, Derek stepped forward, pushing Coop aside and making him itch to rearrange the kid's face.

The contemptuous laugh that escaped her lips said it all. Not in this lifetime. When hell freezes over, or maybe screw you, plain and simple. He couldn't have said it any better, and no way was he letting Derek utter one more slimy suggestion.

He turned in front of the would-be-tough-guy and shoved him back a step. "That's enough."

Derek slowly shifted his attention to Coop, his grin drooping as the full import of Coop's words sunk in. "Who the hell died and made you the boss of me? I'll decide when it's enough." With fists clenched, he took a swaggering step toward Coop.

Shit! The damn fool was testing his patience. Nothing would satisfy Coop more than to deck the SOB and shut him up. Unfortunately, that course of action wouldn't help him cozy up to Carl Graves and the others at the center of this takeover. It might get him thrown out of the party, but now that he'd drawn a line in the sand, there was no way he'd back down. It wasn't in his makeup to take any more of the crap the kid was dishing out, and he wasn't about to let him continue spouting off to the woman who reminded him so much of Jade. If Derek wanted a fight, he'd get one.

He widened his stance and waited for Derek to throw the first punch.

Suddenly, Ryan stepped into his peripheral vision, one meaty fist catapulting toward the side of Derek's head. As though in slow motion, the crushing blow landed squarely on Derek's jaw, whipping his head to the right, and he folded like a cardboard box, groaning on the floor.

The next instant, Coop was eye to eye with Ryan, whose angry scowl clearly said he had more where that came from if necessary. Coop grinned. "Thanks, Ryan. I owe you one. I've wanted to do that for about a week."

Ryan only grunted again and headed back toward the counter.

Soft laughter came from behind him, and Coop swung around. Slowly, he removed his sunglasses, hooking them on the neckline of his T-shirt in a motion that had become second nature. The woman went silent as she stared at him. The same disbelief that held him in its clutches skittered across her features, chased by apprehension. Something close to panic flickered in her expression before she locked it down. In its place, a fierceness he remembered only too well and a barely perceptible shake of her head warned him not to react...although that might have come a few seconds too late.

"Jade?" He whispered the name, even though his every rational thought argued the impossibility of finding her alive in this small-ass town he'd never heard of until a week ago. If the brief chink in her shuttered emotions, the slight hitch of her breathing, the slopes and angles of the face he'd committed to memory hadn't been enough, the shock in those violet-blue eyes was the final proof. She recognized him too.

A split second of uncertainty flashed across her face. A fraction of a second later, it was gone. Her chin jutted forward the slightest bit as her expression frosted over like an arctic stormfront. Her graceful hands settled firmly on her hips, and a contemptuous smirk pulled her lips into a sneer. "You've mistaken me for someone else. I don't know you, and I don't want to if you're a friend of the vermin holding this town hostage." Her words, delivered with the precision of a scalpel, dripped with disdain and unmistakably contradicted what he'd read in her eyes.

Any words he might have uttered died on his tongue. *It's Jade, but how?*

The question echoed through his mind, along with countless others. Where had she been all this time? Why wasn't he informed when they found her? She could have easily located him through military records, yet she hadn't contacted him. Had he meant anything to her? If she'd wanted to see him, she wouldn't have let him believe she was dead. She wouldn't deny she knew him now.

Somehow, miraculously, Jade was alive, but it was apparent she hadn't intended for him to find out. Ever.

Despair, as deep as any he'd survived in the months and years when he'd thought her dead, churned slowly through his gut.

Her disdainful consideration swept over him to Derek and back again. Clearly, she saw no distinction between them, pegging him as part of the group currently terrorizing the town. He'd played his role well enough to make people believe just that. Trapped by the need to maintain his cover, he couldn't explain why it appeared he was one of them. Not in front of Derek, Ryan, and the others in the store. He couldn't say anything to assure her he was there to help the town.

Did he owe her an explanation considering the secret she'd not bothered to share with him? Could he even trust her with the truth? Anger came from nowhere, burning through his veins. The darkness of betrayal wrapped around his throat and clawed at the façade he'd assumed.

"Just keep an eye on things and report in," Luke had said. Coop wasn't supposed to draw attention to himself. Chances were he'd already blown by that boundary, but he could salvage the rest if he got his head back in the game.

"My apologies, *ma'am*."

Her eyes narrowed slightly at his use of the military recognition for a female officer. It was no accident he'd chosen the word.

His gaze slowly traveled the length of her, and

he shook his head. "For a minute, I thought you were someone I used to know, but you're right—I made a mistake." Coop could discern the vindictive edge in his words and gladly turned away when Derek swore and staggered to his feet.

His partner's glare flicked over him dismissively to land on Jade. A frown scrunched his eyebrows together as he massaged his bruised jaw. "Well, pretty lady, you and your boys just made a big mistake. We'll be around town until Bueller's trial is over and justice prevails. It'll go easier for you if you learn to play nice."

One stride put Coop up in Derek's face. He placed his open palms on the man's chest and shoved. "I said that's enough. Shut your mouth, and let's go."

It wasn't only Derek who stoked his simmering anger. A ball of fire burned in his gut, a symptom of his life spinning out of control. Jade, letting him believe she was dead all those years. Coop, having to let her think they were on opposite sides in the conflict brewing in this town. Derek was just the one lucky enough to be in his sights. Coop pushed him hard again until the troublemaker turned and headed for the door, a stream of swearwords drifting over his shoulder.

Coop followed him out to the street, resisting the urge to glance back and see if Jade watched. If she did, would there be regret in her expression? Current revelations suggested she had none, and it would be best if he didn't turn to see her slapping high fives around the room as he walked away.

He practically dragged Derek across the street to

where his truck was parked, opened the passenger door, shoved the kid inside, and slammed it shut. Three years and a handful of months ago, his life had changed course in an instant when Jade died.

Now, everything had changed again—only this time, it was her coming back from the dead that threatened to topple the framework he'd struggled to rebuild.

Her subtle warning had made it obvious she didn't want him to let anyone know he'd recognized her. As though *she* was the one undercover. Since her wishes had coincided with his, he'd been happy to go along. But soon, she'd answer all of his questions.

She'd tell him to his face what she hadn't had the common courtesy to say at any time over the interminable years that followed her disappearance. She had cruelly and selfishly perpetuated the lie of her death rather than tell him straight out they were through. She wasn't getting off that easy. He'd make sure of that even if it killed him to hear her say the words.

Coop slammed the truck into gear and hit the gas, squealing onto the street.

CHAPTER THREE

Jade's hands shook uncontrollably, despite the tight fists they'd curled into at some point during the past few minutes. Unable to look away, she stared through the glass doors as his dark green Ram truck rumbled to life and pulled away from the curb across from Nic's Grocery & Deli—friggin' James Cooper behind the wheel.

"This is a disaster!" The words were barely audible, but she checked to see if anyone had been close enough to hear her anyway. Satisfied no one had, she slumped against the counter. Swiping a hand across her forehead, she closed her eyes and strove to calm the pounding in her head that had grown in equal proportion with her stress level. Last she'd inquired of her friend and former commanding officer, Colonel Reiner had said Coop was visiting some friends near the Canadian border. Who knew he'd be in a blink-and-you'll-miss-it town in Oregon, population less than two thousand?

Crossing his path was the one thing that was never supposed to happen. At stake were the national security of the country and America's leadership role in the world. Her sense of duty, combined with pressure from the Pentagon, had formed the perfect storm at the weakest point in her life. Her father's coercion had been the final insult.

Quickly, she tamped down the familiar bitterness that threatened to undo all her shrink's efforts on behalf of her mental health. Her dad was no longer a part of her life, and she was good with that. For a long time, she'd blamed him for the hardest decision she'd ever had to make. Walking away from Coop had been devastating. In therapy, learning that she alone bore the responsibility for her choice had nearly destroyed her.

Now that she'd come face to face with the past, how was she going to fix this?

She whirled around and braced her elbows on the counter to steady herself. Her trembling fingers covered her mouth as though keeping Coop's name from escaping would make it all go away.

Come on—get your act together. You can handle this. Jade mouthed the words of the mantra she'd adopted to save her life. She'd dealt with more daunting situations than this one. Today's unexpected reunion barely moved the needle on her gauge of horrific life events. Sad but true. Yet Coop had sauntered in and unraveled the past three years of her life without breaking a sweat.

She straightened and scooped some loose strands of hair back behind her ears, settling her ball cap more firmly on her head. Scanning behind the counter for Ryan, she located him just before he disappeared into the back room with a stack of deli trays. Jade sighed, grateful the altercation ended with no injuries. Was it possible she'd overreacted? Maybe, but she didn't like to be touched...especially by strangers.

The wannabe thug, with his walking, talking ego, hadn't concerned her. No doubt he considered himself a badass, but he'd have to work harder if scaring her was his goal. Coop was a different story. He'd changed, but she would have recognized him long before he turned to face her—if she hadn't been preoccupied. His handsome face bore hints of hardship, his expression serious now when a carefree smile had typically been commonplace. His size and demeanor were even more intimidating than she remembered.

His light blue T-shirt had peeked from beneath a worn and faded denim jacket. Failing to conceal the snug fit that stretched across his firm, muscled pecs, it gave ample evidence of his ripped abs before tucking neatly into his waistband. His blond hair still cut short, together with the Navy SEAL combat knife sheathed at his hip, made him a walking testament to the military life he'd loved so much. The aroma of worn leather had wrapped around her as he'd turned to follow the one called Derek from the store.

The moment he'd removed his sunglasses, the charade that was her life had crashed and disintegrated. The walls she'd erected to hold back the guilt, the shame, the regret had crumbled into dust. At that instant, she'd been transported back to Damascus, sweat running down her back from the blistering sun and the burqa she'd worn.

The flash of recognition in his eyes had yanked her back to the present with dizzying suddenness. Hurt and anger had darkened his features. Her name on his lips had condemned her. All because of the vow of secrecy she'd taken.

Now, however, the proverbial cat was out of the bag in the worst possible way. She'd felt Ryan's attention shifting toward her, obviously curious about her stunned reaction. Thank heavens Coop had picked up on her warning not to give her away. It wasn't only him she'd kept the truth from about her last mission. General McDowell had fed Ryan and Nicole the official story. Nic had never thought to question their father's alternative facts. Funny how the stigma of a mental breakdown—AKA, going batshit crazy—kept people from asking too many questions.

Whatever the reason, Nicole had respected Jade's privacy—or maybe her sister had been afraid the details that had, allegedly, driven Jade over the edge would be too much for her. Either way, avoiding the issue had worked for both. Ryan, however, had always looked at her as though he knew she was hiding something. Her brother-in-law would be happy to meet someone who'd known her back then, and she couldn't allow that to happen.

The irony hadn't escaped her. If she and Coop had returned to the states at the end of their six-month deployments, mere weeks apart, she would've been proud to introduce him to her family. No doubt he'd have charmed Nicole and Ryan as quickly as he had her, and they would've loved him almost as much as Jade had. However, fate had planned a different ending.

With a coldness she wouldn't have thought possible, she'd denied any connection between her and Coop and still managed to hold it together until he walked out of the store. All the more reason she still trembled as though her bones had turned to liquid silicone.

"You okay, JD?" If Ryan's worried frown was any indication, her act hadn't been as convincing as she'd hoped.

Go figure. Her brother-in-law knew her too well.

She stepped toward him and forced a smile. "I'm fine." She managed to sound almost believable, but his curious inspection didn't let up, and she scrambled for a change of topic. "I'm hungry. What do you have that's good today?" Some of the tension left her body as Ryan waved her over to the deli counter.

"I made potato salad, and I've got ham for sandwiches. Might be a slice of carrot cake left, too. And, for you, it's on the house."

"Sounds great." She didn't need to remind him her lunch had been on the house every day since she'd arrived in town three weeks ago. It was just one of the ways her sister and Ryan showed their appreciation, though it wasn't necessary. Jade would do anything for her big sister. "How's Nic doing today?"

Ryan's shoulders seemed to slump, and he exhaled slowly. "Physically, she's getting better every day. Emotionally, she's a wreck."

"Still afraid to go out by herself?" Worry for Nicole pushed aside Jade's problems, though the dread in her stomach hung on.

"Hell, I have to nag to get her out for a walk with me in the evenings." He paused while making her sandwich and held his arms out to his sides as though presenting himself for inspection. "Do I look like I can't protect her?" A frustrated sigh punctuated his question before he went back to his task.

Jade couldn't help smiling as she studied his bowed head. "Hey. When the zombie apocalypse starts, there's no one else I'd want by my side."

Her brother-in-law was a large man. Not in height so much, at five feet ten, but every square inch of his arms, legs, back, and chest rippled with muscles. And not those would-be muscles from lifting the same weights every day at the gym. Raised on a Wyoming ranch, he'd grown up tossing around hundred-and-fifty-pound bales of hay, building fences, and pushing stubborn and half-wild steers into a branding chute. Considering how much Ryan loved his wife, Carl Graves's flunkies, including Coop, should think twice before walking down the same side of the street as Nicole.

Ryan glanced over the top of the deli counter, humor sparkling in his eyes. "Hell yeah. It's you and me, JD, and Nicole if we can get her out of her room." He rolled his eyes and chuckled.

"Does the sheriff have any leads?" She'd come as soon as she got the news Nic had been in a car accident. Except, according to her sister, it hadn't been an accident.

"Sheriff Carlton knows who ran Nicole off the road as well as I do. Don't get me wrong—Lindy is a fine sheriff and a good friend. She's doing the best she can with no proof." He snapped lids on the containers he'd filled with her lunch and stacked them carefully in a paper bag, along with a Styrofoam box that probably held the last piece of carrot cake.

"Why isn't she calling for reinforcements? The state patrol? Or the FBI? What's she waiting for—somebody to die?" Jade frowned. Someone had died. Poor Jenny Bueller. Now Jade's sister had been caught up in the aftermath. She'd been hurt and left for dead. Thank God a local hiking group had found her in the crumpled remains of her vehicle at the bottom of a ravine between Pine Bluff and Baker City.

Someone had intentionally run her off the road, but when no evidence had surfaced to prove Nicole's claim, it was her word against that of Carl Graves. "What about the judge? Can't he petition for a change of venue? I'd like to see Graves pull this in Salem or Portland."

Pine Bluff was a small town with a depressed economy, hundreds of miles from a major population center. Reporters had found little newsworthy in an orderly group of protestors exercising their right to assemble peacefully. No one outside their small community saw it as the armed occupation it was.

"This isn't like the stand-off in Malheur County a few years ago, where the protestors took over a federal building. At this point, the FBI has no reason to get involved. The state troopers are aware, and they're monitoring the situation, but their hands are tied. To everyone outside our little town, Graves and his followers are champions of free speech and the second amendment. Meanwhile, he's counting on non-verbal intimidation and Nicole's so-called accident to keep the townspeople in line. So far, it's working." Suddenly, Ryan pivoted and flung a metal bowl against the wall behind him.

Jade jumped as the clatter echoed around the store. The other customers rubbernecked to see what was going on but lost interest once it quieted down. Ryan's frustration matched her own. He was right. Three-quarters of the residents had been frightened into silence and were simply lying low, waiting for it to be over. She dropped her chin and tamped down her rising anger. Her task was to help Ryan and Nicole get through the next few weeks. It would do them no good to lose her cool.

"Which reminds me—you watch your back, JD. That troublemaker strikes me as the type who might want some payback. Maybe you should spend your nights in town with us instead of staying out there alone. Might even be smart to shut down the kennel until things get back to normal around here."

"No." She shook her head. "It's tough enough starting a new business. We must stay open and honor the reservations on the books. Besides, that's why I'm here eating all your food."

She grabbed the bag he'd set on the counter and stepped back to free up space for John and Larry Ames and Vince Neilson. They reappeared from one of the aisles and placed their haul of frozen pizza, chips, and beer beside the cash register. Ryan rang up their purchases and accepted their money while the men took turns giving her a hard time about the new load of buckshot in the ceiling.

She hadn't been in town long enough to get to know more than a handful of the locals, but the Ames brothers and Vince were friends of Ryan and Nicole. They'd been furious about Nic being targeted and coordinated with Ryan to make sure she was never alone. The day Jade arrived, they'd gotten the idea she needed watching over too. They had time on their hands with their jobs on hold after the local feed store, owned by the man about to go on trial for murdering his wife, suddenly became temporary headquarters for the protestors. They'd started following her from the kennel to town or showing up at random times to make sure she was okay.

That had lasted a day…until Vince startled her while she was focused on an injured dog. She'd reacted instinctively. Though genuinely sorry for dislocating Vince's shoulder, the upside had been the trio deciding maybe she could take care of herself. They were now her friends too, and it felt good to laugh and return their good-natured ribbing.

After they left, Ryan closed the cash drawer, and his weary sigh seemed loud in the silence that descended. "Nicole decided not to testify." Ryan studied something below the counter, clearly reluctant to look Jade in the eyes.

"What?" Her sister couldn't have meant that. They'd spoken only yesterday, and Nic had been adamant that Lloyd Bueller wasn't getting away with murdering his wife. She'd vowed to testify, even though former state senator Bueller had hired his own army of gun-toting mutants to take over the town, putting pressure on the judge and witnesses alike. Her testimony would place Bueller in the county that day, proving opportunity, despite the fact he claimed to be two states away.

Jade recognized the fear and uncertainty her sister exhibited—not unlike her own after finally making it home, filled with anger and guilt. Post-traumatic stress disorder wasn't only a military condition.

A year of counseling had taught her enough coping skills to face brief forays into the real world, but the doctors had warned her she might never get better and, most assuredly, would never be the confident, capable person she'd once been. Then, on the first anniversary of her homecoming, Colonel Reiner had presented her with a furry, smelly, tongue-happy service dog who'd wormed his way into her heart and gradually brought her back to life.

"Nicole needs to see someone—a counselor. The sooner, the better." It hadn't been easy for Jade to confide in a stranger, but it was what she'd needed. "Also, you should think about getting her a dog."

Ryan raised his head, and surprise jolted her at the medley of emotions parading across his face. His jaw, set in stubborn determination, held a hint of shame, which no doubt accounted for him not knowing what to do with his hands.

"The thing is…I'm glad Nicole doesn't want to testify if it means Bueller and Graves will leave her alone. I can't lose her, JD." His pain-filled eyes pleaded for her understanding. "The DA threatened to subpoena her if she refuses to testify willingly. I don't know what she'll do if…"

Nervous tension fluttered in Jade's stomach as the same relief Ryan expressed flitted through her mind for a heartbeat. "He won't do that. We'll make him understand. We're not going to let anything happen to her." It was one thing to encourage Nic to testify, but something else entirely for Harold

Standish to wield his power as district attorney to force her compliance.

"She's the only one who saw Bueller in the county on the day of his wife's murder. Without her testimony, there's a chance he'll walk. Jenny Bueller kept to herself, and no one around Pine Bluff knew her well, but she didn't deserve to die. Not like that."

Jade winced. The official report listed Jenny's cause of death as blunt force trauma. The small-town rumors spread like wildfire and spoke of a blood-covered claw hammer, walls drenched in blood spatter, and a woman's face so mutilated the coroner had confirmed her identity with a DNA test. It was proof Bueller and his lapdog, Graves, were capable of atrocities.

"That doesn't mean I'm willing to take a chance with her life. We'll pack up and leave if it comes down to that." Ryan raked one hand through his thick, black hair. His helplessness was palpable.

Jade had been where he was now, and it wasn't a good place. It was easy to make bad decisions when backed against the wall. "She's lucky to have you, Ryan. She'll get through this. It might take a while, but she's tough, and she has us. Let's not get ahead of ourselves. We'll deal with Standish and his subpoena if it happens." She tried for upbeat and confident for his sake, but her usual positive attitude seemed to have gone AWOL.

"I shouldn't be unloading on you. You're doing enough already. Why don't you join us for dinner tonight? Nicole can boss you around for a few hours and give me a break."

Nic's crash had resulted in a broken wrist, a

concussion, and cuts and bruises all over her body. The car was a pile of mangled steel. Even though her injuries had kept her from the newly opened pet boarding facility's daily tasks, it could have been much worse.

Ryan couldn't take over the kennel and keep the store open too. Jade was preparing to start her own business in the fall, teaching self-defense and esteem-building techniques to girls and young women. Currently, her days were full of lesson plans and marketing campaigns—all things she could do on her laptop in Pine Bluff just as efficiently. So, when Ryan explained the suspicious nature of Nicole's accident, Jade had packed a bag, placed her eight-pound Pomeranian on his bed in the passenger seat of her Jeep Wrangler, and driven five hundred miles from the Oregon coast.

It'd never occurred to her she might end up in the same small town as Coop. Three hundred million people in this country, and she had to run into him. What were the odds?

Frustration vied for a chance to vent, but she quickly forced it into submission and folded the edges over on the bag of food. "Thanks, but Moose and I have plans tonight that involve a hot bath, a bottle of wine, and a good book. I'll take a raincheck, though." It wasn't exactly the truth, but he'd get all protective if he learned she was expecting one of Graves' men to drop by, even if she dared to tell him Coop was an old friend.

Ryan's laugh came from deep in his belly. "Damn, JD. I can't believe you named that little piece of fluff you carry around like a handbag after one of God's most majestic animals. *Moose!*" He wagged his head. "Mouse is more like it."

She clucked her tongue. "And you wonder why Moose doesn't like you."

They chuckled together, but when the sound faded, she still hesitated.

"Listen. Be careful, Ryan. Keep an eye out for those jerks. They're looking for trouble."

Her brother-in-law nodded slowly. "The drunk one is for sure. The other guy—I kinda got the feeling you two know each other."

She chuffed a laugh, a pathetic attempt at denial, but heat rushed to her face. "Don't be ridiculous. Why would you think that?" Instantly, she regretted her too-quick objection and defensive tone. Ryan wasn't an idiot.

He braced his arms on the counter and leaned toward her. A smirk lifted one corner of his mouth. "Well, for starters, he called you by your given name."

Unable to keep from squirming under his inspection, she turned away. Stepping toward the door, she held up the bag of food. "Thanks for lunch. Gotta get back to work." She could feel his curious scrutiny long after the door swung shut behind her.

It would be a mistake to tell him the truth—that she'd known Coop a long time ago, in another lifetime. That would open a door she couldn't afford to leave ajar. Ryan would grab ahold of that like a dog with a new chew toy. He'd ask more questions. Nicole would find out, and the cross-examination would begin. Before long, they'd be inviting Coop over for a barbeque and a trip down memory lane.

He'd undoubtedly be happy to disclose what he knew in exchange for answers to a few of his questions.

Hell no—that wasn't happening. Jade had locked away memories so deep; they would rip her apart if they ever saw the light of day.

CHAPTER FOUR

Coop knelt in the shadows alongside a stand of young fir trees on a gradually sloping knoll, affording a perfect view of the Pink Paws Kennel below. He'd only had to slip a twenty to the bartender at the Dirty Duck Tavern, on the outskirts of Pine Bluff, to learn the whereabouts of the dark-haired beauty with the violet-blue eyes.

He stood, stretching his stiff legs as he brought night-vision field glasses to his face and peered through the darkness. Jade had emerged from the small, two-level house at dusk and strode toward the kennel, probably to check on the dogs one more time. When she returned, the lights downstairs went out and, a minute or so later, the upstairs windows lit up.

He'd lost track of how long he'd been there, silent, watching for any movement that might indicate Derek was making good on his drunken threats against the *pretty bitch who'd tried to shoot him*. He'd been shit-faced when Coop dropped him off at his campsite. Hopefully, by now, he was out for the night.

What am I doing here, anyway? Did he need to hear her reasons, none of which would be good enough in his mind? She had moved on. He also had, but not by choice. This cluster was going to set him back months, whether or not he heard the rejection straight from her lips.

He lowered the binoculars and raked his hand through his hair. *Damn it!* He might as well get it done.

As he stuffed the night vision equipment in his backpack, slung it over one shoulder, and started down the hill, the porch lights blinked on, and the front door opened. Jade stepped outside, and though she couldn't possibly see him, she scanned the hillside and seemed to hesitate on the exact spot where he'd stopped and gone still.

After a moment, she glanced down, and a smile formed. Coop understood why when a little dog scooted through the doorway and pranced across the deck. She'd always been crazy for dogs. It was no surprise she'd gotten one.

Jade had changed from her jeans and T-shirt into a blue sweater over black leggings. Her shoulder-length hair looked wet, as though she'd just showered. She carried a bottle of wine and a wineglass in one hand with a book under her arm. A blanket draped carefully over her other arm, covering her hand. The skin on the back of his neck tingled.

Ah, smart girl. She was armed. The hand under that blanket held a weapon. He knew it, as surely as he stood there gaping. After the incident at the store today, she wasn't taking any chances. Derek wasn't going to catch her unprepared, and he wouldn't be expecting to face down an Air Force captain trained in combat tactics by the U.S. military machine. The possible ramifications brought a grin to Coop's face.

What if she'd armed herself because of him? He sobered. Did she know he was there? Or did she only suspect he'd come? Either way, he couldn't squelch the strange pride he felt watching her.

The little dog followed her to the porch's corner, where two Adirondack chairs sat on either side of a small wooden table. She sat and tucked the blanketed bundle carefully against the back of her seat. The other items went on the table. With a few twists of a corkscrew, the cork popped free of the wine bottle, and she poured herself a glass.

He moved closer, staying in the shadows. Guilt niggled at the back of his mind as he studied Jade. Damned if he didn't feel like a voyeur. Or worse, a stalker.

She carefully retrieved the blanket, minus the weapon, and wrapped it around her shoulders, pulling the edges of the improvised cloak together across her torso.

The dog ran down the steps, his toenails *click-clacking* on the wood. Snuffling through the tall grass at the side of the house, he found the spot he'd been looking for and, a minute or two later, bounded back onto the deck. He strutted in a circle at her feet, his attention fastened on her. She patted her leg, and the dog leaped onto her lap, burrowing in until only his snout and ears peeked from beneath the blanket. Jade smiled as she scratched the dog's neck, and Coop felt the warmth down to his toes.

It was good that the air currents were in his favor, or the little mutt would undoubtedly spoil his surprise. Coop stopped about thirty feet away, behind an overgrown arctic willow. Even though it was mid-

April, a slight breeze cooled the night air. It would have been peaceful if not for his rioting emotions. The sharp scent of pine wafted about him as he listened to the moans and creaks of the ponderosas standing sentry at the edge of the yard.

He crept a few steps closer and crouched beneath the branches of one of the stately trees. Much farther, and he'd be in the open, and any last-minute chance he had of changing his mind would be gone. His heart heavy, he settled in to wait a few more minutes to make sure she wasn't expecting company.

The furry little meatball whined, shifted positions, and settled again. Was the dog always restless, or did the animal sense Coop's presence?

Jade scooped up the book she'd dropped on the table and sat back, but not without furtively sliding her hand behind her where her secreted weapon rested within easy reach. It gave him solace that she was still as cautious and deliberate as he remembered, though why he should care was a question without an answer. One he couldn't afford to give too much consideration.

She nursed her wine while she turned page after page of her book. The meatball finally stilled, curled into a ball on her lap. After a few minutes, she threw back the edges of the blanket and held the cool wineglass to her cheek. Still, the little mutt slept.

It was almost nine when Coop took his next step toward the porch. Immediately, the diminutive watch dog's head jerked up, his ears erect. Though Coop had yet to leave the cover of low hanging branches, the little dog's focus seemed to lock onto him like a laser sight on a sniper rifle.

*****

A slight vibration against her ribcage was Jade's only warning before Moose lifted his head, and his low growl became audible. Continuing to grumble, he sat erect, peering into the darkness beyond the porch.

"Did you hear something, Moose? That's a good boy." She closed her book as she reached behind her for reassurance that her handgun still rested there.

It had been a long and emotional day. Her glass-half-full outlook hadn't reappeared after the shock of seeing Coop again, and it was only going to get worse. Though she'd known he would come, as the minutes crept by, she'd started to doubt. Even now, the possibility it could be someone else set off alarms in her brain, exacerbating the coil of anxiety that slowly unwound in her stomach. The 9mm was a precaution for just such an instance. Anyway, that was what she told herself, refusing to believe the man she'd known could present a danger.

Turning her face into the wind, she welcomed the cool night air, tinged with pine and freshly mown hay from a nearby pivot. The smells and sounds of the forest often soothed her. Currently, however, it was doing nothing to curb the butterfly wings fanning nausea in her gut. It'd started the moment she'd recognized Coop, and the memories she'd tried so hard to lock away had escaped their box. There was good reason for her apprehension. Living a lie was about to get exponentially more challenging.

What if she was worrying for nothing? Moose

often alerted her to wildlife passing within earshot. Or he could be reacting to her stress.

Maybe the last thing in the world Coop wanted to do was show up here. He had to despise her about now. What a lousy way to find out she wasn't dead. Come to think of it; despising was too civil. He must hate her...and she wouldn't blame him.

A groan rumbled from her as she uncrossed her legs and sat forward. Who was she kidding? He'd come. If she knew anything about Coop, she knew that.

Moose glanced over his back at her, his ears dropping into his I-love-you-Mom position. A brief wag of his tail made her smile before the dog refocused on the driveway.

It was pathetic and a little scary how much she loved this eight-pound hairball—how much she'd come to depend on him over the past year and a half. He'd be no help if her unannounced visitor meant her harm, but that wouldn't keep the little guy from trying. If trouble came around, she'd be the one protecting the dog.

Moose whimpered, and a nervous shiver accompanied the raising of hair on his scruff. Jade settled back in her chair, the handgun pressed against her hip, hidden to anyone who stepped onto the deck. It never hurt to be prepared for trouble, even if her instincts were right about who approached in the dark.

The anger and betrayal in Coop's dark brown eyes had been unmistakable at the store earlier, the instant after the shock of seeing her had fled. Her deception had hurt him, though that had never been her intention. How many times had she wondered if there'd been any other way out? She always came back to the same answer. He would've seen through her bullshit story in a heartbeat—recognized her lies as a personal betrayal. It would have destroyed everything they'd had. Worse yet, he might have started digging on his own and unearthed a truth so toxic as to endanger the United States, along with the truth about who she'd become. Either way, their relationship would have ended.

"I'm not armed, Jade." From the darkness, a man's deep, familiar baritone reached out.

His disembodied voice came from the left, just beyond the reach of illumination from the fixtures beside the door. Moose whirled toward the sound and barked fiercely. Obviously, he wasn't a fan of the stranger who'd sneaked so close without a sound. Stroking the dog to reassure him all was well, she gave herself a few seconds to steady her voice. She understood Moose's indignation. She'd never gotten used to how ghostly quiet the man could be.

Hoping he hadn't noticed how badly he'd shaken her, she leaned forward and spoke quietly to Moose until he ceased barking, then addressed the darkness. "*I* am...so, considering your friends nowadays, it'd be better if you didn't make any sudden moves."

He might have been out there, waiting, when she first came outside. No doubt he'd been watching for some time, studying the surroundings, taking inventory of places someone could hide and escape routes for when things went sour. Patience was a learned tactic. And once a SEAL, forever a SEAL.

He stepped into the light at the foot of the steps to her right as though he hadn't been fifteen feet away in another direction mere seconds ago. "You'd shoot me? After everything we've meant to each other?" Scorn was thick in his softly spoken words.

That was all it took to decimate her façade. Shame and remorse swamped her, and sweat broke out on her upper lip. What had made her think she was strong enough to pull this off? Clearly, she wasn't. Remaining calm and unaffected in the face of his disdain or standing unmoved before the only man she'd respected enough to let down her guard had sounded good in theory. Yet, with only a handful of words, he'd ambushed her practical application.

She straightened and firmed her jaw. Coop didn't need to know his first volley had shattered her confidence. Her reputation as a kick-ass squadron leader meant she never gave up. It'd been a while since *that* woman had made her presence felt. Nevertheless, that was who Coop needed her to be. The sooner he went back where he came from, convinced she'd dropped out of his life on purpose, the better it would be for both of them. If he hated her, that was the way it had to be because telling him the truth was unthinkable.

Moose jumped off her lap and approached him, sniffing the air. Coop glanced at the dog, and amusement tugged at his lips.

Making sure the blanket slid down to cover the gun, she got to her feet and faced him. "That depends on whether you've come as a friend or an enemy."

He climbed the steps, taking his time, his gaze locked on her. "Used to be, you wouldn't have had to ask."

"That's true, but the crowd you're running with these days hasn't earned any goodwill around here. I've never known you to come down on the wrong side of trouble before. So, tell me, did my eyes deceive me? Or are you really part of the armed occupation of this town?"

He took the last step onto the deck and turned toward her, still moving slowly, his hands at his sides. "I can see why you might think so, but things aren't always what they seem." He stopped ten feet away and leaned casually against the deck railing. "Take you, for example. I've thought you were dead for three years. How long have you been back in the States without thinking to let me know?" His stare bored into her, demanding an answer.

Irrational fear wound its sticky tendrils around her chest, causing her to work for each breath. Her throat convulsed as her mouth went dry. No amount of training, or counseling, or positive self-talk had prepared her for this moment. Of course not. *This* was never supposed to happen.

The need to defend herself was strong, but that wouldn't help either of them. Coup deserved as much honesty as she could give him, right up until he asked her *why*. Maybe if she maintained eye contact, he wouldn't guess how her insides were shaking. "I got my discharge papers two years ago."

Something that sounded like a snarl escaped his throat, and his eyes flashed fire. "I think I deserve to know why I'm just now learning you're alive."

She met his anger with a half-assed shrug, the indifference of which shocked even her. "You know how it works. The mission was classified, as were the results."

"I don't give a *damn* about the mission. I want to know what happened to *us*." A steely strand of danger permeated his words.

"It's complicated. You had your career. I had mine. I certainly didn't mean to hurt you." *Damn. Too personal. I'm making a mess of this.*

"Hurt me?" His sarcastic laugh mocked her. "You *broke* me. How could you think it wouldn't destroy me to lose you?" For the first time, grief showed through his scorn. "Your plane was shot down over enemy territory in Syria, for God's sake. I didn't know if you were dead or alive…or taken hostage by one of those bastards. Damn it, Jade! I'd have crawled on my knees over broken glass to get to you." He paused as though he was incapable of going on, then scrubbed a hand over his face. "We got a tip that you'd been captured, and my team was assigned the rescue mission. The commander made me stand down. Said I was too close to the situation. He was right. I'd have endangered the team." He turned and faced the dark parking area and forest beyond. "Do you have any idea how I felt, thinking you were in trouble and I couldn't do a damn thing?"

Silence chipped away at her forced callousness for what seemed like several minutes. When he turned back, his expression held defeat. "My team went in without me, confirmed reports from local villagers that you were dead, and brought back your dog tags. No one knew where you were buried." His voice broke on the last word. "Guess that's no surprise, considering…"

Jade looked away before he could see the shock she couldn't hide. The SEAL team sent to find her immediately after the crash had been looking in the wrong place. The military, including her father, had to disavow her. She'd known that going in, but it still stung that Colonel Reiner and the general hadn't found some way to provide accurate coordinates to the search team. They hadn't given her a chance.

It was also abundantly clear why her father had been adamant that she stay away from Coop. He'd have never bought the official story. He'd been on the ground. He knew too much, and he was too close. No, the general had been right to stipulate that he never learn what happened.

How had the rescue team obtained her dog tags? Her captors had taken her identification moments after her capture. Assad's forces would have had to plant them at a location where U.S. soldiers would search. The odds of them stumbling on that information were poor.

The further she went down that rabbit hole, the more conspiracy theories unfolded in her head. Someone had to have tipped off the Syrian government. Had somebody leaked top-secret, classified information to the enemy? A chill feathered over her skin. If so, they had to have known she was alive. Yet, eight long months had dragged by before Navy SEALs had come to get her. Was it possible they had deliberately left her there to die? If that was the case, why had there been a second search team eight months later?

She barely noticed the trembling that started in her arms and legs and worked toward her core. Her attention snapped back to the man in front of her. The sadness clouding his face nearly choked her, overriding her resolve. "I'm sorry, Coop. I wanted to—"

"That's bullshit! You could have found me. You didn't even try, did you?" He paced a small circle before fixing her with an accusing glare. "Nothing to say? Shit! I thought I meant something to you. You sure as hell meant something to me."

Suddenly, furious with herself, she clenched her fists so tightly her fingernails dug into her palms, the pain hardly registering. "You have no idea how hard it was to stay away. I couldn't..." Her words trailed off as he swung around and stared. Any sign of anger was gone from his features, replaced with a cheeky smirk that somehow conveyed he'd won. *Hit them with raw emotion, then goad them until they fight back.* How many times had she seen him use that technique with friends and strangers alike? Yet she'd fallen for it like a newbie.

She was done reminiscing. They couldn't go back. An oath bound her, and even if she could talk freely, allowing Coop to think there might be anything ahead for them was foolish and cruel. She couldn't tell him the truth and, unless he'd changed his ways, nothing less would satisfy him.

Anxiety assailed her with the force of a violent wind. She turned away on a gut-deep groan as cold sweat blanketed her skin. A tremor rolled through her with such intensity she gritted her teeth to keep them from chattering together. Her chest heaved, air cutting like a knife instead of relieving the ache in her lungs.

No, this can't be happening now.

Lightheaded, she lurched toward the deck railing, grasping for balance with both hands. Something scratched her leg, and she glanced down. Moose pawed at her leggings, whimpering. Brown eyes stared into hers.

The panic attack had come from nowhere, sneaking up on her with no warning. She hadn't had a PTSD event in over a year. Despite what the doctors had said, she'd wanted to believe she'd beaten it. What a reality check that was. And the trigger stood behind her, silently watching her fall apart.

Nausea followed quickly behind the dizzying spin of her world. Leaning her hip against the deck railing, she closed her eyes and fought the disorienting fog that shrouded her brain. As though from far away, Moose barked and growled, his claws doing a frantic tap dance. She needed him. Where was he?

His little feet were on her leg, but she couldn't let go of the railing that stabilized her long enough to scoop up the dog. Coop said something, but the words were jumbled as though they came through a long, dark tunnel. Her shaky legs would surely give out if she didn't find a way to force air past the giant lump in her throat. Frantic to sit, to hold on to Moose, to be alone with the familiar, she felt along the railing toward her chair, nearly upending the small table, wine and all.

Then Coop was beside her, his arm around her waist, holding her up. Moose growled and barked once before scampering out of his way. Coop pried her fingers from the railing and led her to the chair she'd occupied when he arrived. He helped her sit on the edge, wrapping her abandoned blanket around her shoulders. A smile quirked his lips as he reached for the handgun he'd uncovered in the chair by her hip. After checking that the safety was on, he laid it on the table with the wine. Then he disappeared from her line of sight, reappearing to place Moose on her lap.

The dog immediately snuggled against her chest, occasionally licking her chin as though to remind her he was there. Threading her fingers through his fur, she buried her face in his thick coat and closed her eyes. Coop knelt beside her chair, one hand on her knee and the other stroking her arm. The smell of cinnamon and masculinity surrounded her. It should have stoked her alarm to have him so close, but instead, it brought an odd sort of comfort.

After what she'd done, she didn't deserve comfort from him. Far from it. One look at his face had confirmed the hell she'd put him through. However right her reasons had been, they didn't justify her total lack of honesty and respect. Long-buried emotions bombarded her. The longing to unburden herself was intense. The line between duty and integrity blurred. Would it have been so wrong to confide in him? Wasn't sacrificing eight months of her life and her self-respect enough?

The warmth of Moose's small body nestled in her lap was a lifeline, drawing her home. Except, home was suddenly an uncertain and scary place. The touch of Coop's hands warmed her, his presence forming a shield to stave off the rest of the world until she was, once again, able to do it for herself. She felt protected and vulnerable at the same time.

It was impossible to track the passage of time. It could have been only seconds or hours until Jade's heart rate slowed, and she was able to breathe normally, but when she opened her eyes, he was still watching her.

A relieved smile settled over his chiseled features. "Feeling better?"

She nodded, though she wasn't positive it was true. The aftermath of one of her events felt a lot like a hangover, sometimes leaving her reeling for hours. Clutching Moose closer, she silently cursed her luck. Shame burned up her neck and into her cheeks. Coop had seen her at her worst. Maybe now he'd understand she wasn't the woman he'd once known.

A self-effacing laugh hissed from between her teeth. "I'm sorry you had to see that. You should probably go now. I'd like to be alone."

Instead of standing and moving away, he reached out and gently stroked her cheek. Unable to stop herself, she turned into his warm caress. Nor did she protest when he leaned closer and brushed his lips over hers so softly it might have been her imagination. When he pulled away and searched her face, leaving her bereft of his warmth, a moan escaped her throat.

"I'm not going anywhere." His hand at the nape of her neck slowly tugged her toward him until he whispered her name a hair's breadth from her lips, sending a shiver through her taut muscles. When he slanted his mouth over hers and gently melded them together, the spark was instantaneous.

She jerked involuntarily and broke the connection before she could control her reaction. Coop leaned in again with infinite tenderness, planting small kisses from one corner of her lips to the other. He moved slowly and deliberately as though afraid he might break the spell.

Her heart galloped at full tilt, and something inside her whispered to end this before it was too late. But she was incapable of stopping the train, hurtling rapidly toward disaster. She wanted this, had missed this. Coop's familiar touch, his scent, and the heat of his body leaning into hers stole the objection from her tongue.

Images filled her mind, and she savored them. Him naked, between her thighs. His talented mouth bringing her to the precipice with sweet torment. Her screaming his name as he drove her over the edge. He'd never failed to take her breath away as he filled her, stretching her until she took all of him, then moved within her, taking her back to the very heights from which she'd soared only moments before.

She felt the dampness between her legs and the painful tightening of her nipples as she strained forward to press against his chest. Her sudden return to the present brought confusion and terror, quickly followed by guilt and self-loathing.

"No. We can't—" Jade pushed him away, and he immediately released her. "We can't go back. It's over."

Coop still crouched at the edge of her chair. "Why?" He studied her carefully until she couldn't take it any longer and looked away. "Oh, I get it. I guess I should have asked if you're married or have a boyfriend."

The pain in his voice cut through her like a knife. "It's not that. There isn't anyone else." It probably would have been kinder to let him think there was another man, but she couldn't lie anymore.

"Then why?" Anger tinged his voice.

"I'm sorry. I shouldn't have let it...us get out of hand. I don't want to hurt you again." She examined her hands, still clutching Moose. Anything to keep from meeting his eyes.

The silence stretched for long seconds. Coop sat back on his heels. "There's so much I don't understand, but I want to. I want to know what happened to make you disappear from my life without a word. I get that you don't want to talk about it, and I won't push you to do anything you don't want to do. When you're ready, we'll talk it out, just like we used to. What's important is that you're here and you're okay. Damn, I've missed you, Jade. Missed holding you—being with you." His voice broke, and he paused for a heartbeat. "I know you must have had a good reason. Whatever it was, it won't change how I feel about you. It'll be okay. I promise."

If only it were that simple. Even if she told him, her words would wipe the smile from his face. Forever. He'd never want to look at her again. If telling him what had happened on that last mission, and after, was the price he demanded, it was a price she couldn't pay.

She shook her head as she pulled back, leaving the security she'd only imagined. His smile faded, his hands slid away, and he stood. A muscle in his jaw flexed as confusion, hurt, and anger contended in his expression.

Jade refused to look away as she prayed for strength to do what she knew was right. "I *am* sorry, Coop, but my reasons are my own. I don't want you here. Please leave." Her chest ached until it felt as though the agony would crush her. It was everything she could do to move Moose aside and stand facing him. There was no way to fix things.

He straightened. Thirty seconds ticked by slowly. "Okay. If that's what you want."

It's the way it has to be. She longed to scream the words to the heavens, but she wouldn't compound her mistake by giving him a reason to think she could change her mind. It wasn't fair to him, and she wasn't sure she could get the words out anyway.

He started down the steps, then swung back. "Let me give you a little advice. This town is a powder keg, and it will get worse as the trial begins. You tromped all over Derek's pride today. Don't turn your back on him."

His inspection swept over her once before he turned away, descended the steps, and disappeared into the darkness as soundlessly as he'd come.

CHAPTER FIVE

Way to go, dumbass. What the hell did you think would happen?

Her deliberate disappearance spoke for itself. Coop had known better, but her mask had cracked, and the regret that blazed in her eyes had ripped his heart out—despite spending the afternoon agonizing over her cavalier dismissal at the store. He had to keep reminding himself that she had intended to drop out of his life. Trying to believe her scam was anything other than what it appeared to be was a fool's endeavor.

How in the hell did a dead United States Air Force officer appear out of nowhere and get home without anyone the wiser? It couldn't happen without help from people in high places.

Like a general.

Coop had come to despise Jade's father without ever meeting the man. Every wistful memory she'd shared of growing up smacked of how badly she'd craved his approval. She'd loved and respected him, but the picture she'd drawn for Coop revealed an absentee father who completely missed her childhood, was never there for any of her special moments, and never remembered a birthday.

Not choosing the Air Force as her career, training to become a fighter pilot, or being promoted to captain had been enough to earn his nod. 'Work harder, and you might make colonel someday,' had been the general's only acknowledgment of her success. Still, not a word of censure had ever crossed her lips within Coop's hearing, but her stories had forever tarnished his image of the great General McDowell.

Her commanding officer, Colonel Mark Reiner, had to be in on it too. Lying to Coop's face while calling to check up on him—pretending he gave a damn. And Coop's SEAL team? Did Travis, Luke, and MacGyver know and keep it from him? All nagging questions with no answers.

He glanced over his shoulder, but a twist in the road hid the house he'd just left. A lot of good talking to her had done. He knew less now than he had before.

If there'd been a tree within reach on his walk to the end of the winding driveway, it was likely he'd have plowed his fist into the bark with three years' worth of misplaced grief egging him on. He reached his truck, parked alongside the county road leading back to Pine Bluff, grateful he'd at least avoided a busted hand.

The damn woman isn't worth the aggravation.

Yeah, right. If that was true, why couldn't he stop thinking about the feel of his arm around her waist? He could still smell her familiar scent, ginger and jasmine, a blend he'd bought for her in the off-limits outdoor marketplace near the base. Why was his heart still beating a hundred miles an hour even though she'd twisted the knife in his gut?

Because she's alive.

Despite her blatant betrayal, Coop now had something he'd lost three years ago.

Hope.

His step felt lighter, even though she had mercilessly shot him down. If she thought, even for a second, he'd let her get by without explanation—well, that shit wasn't happening. He had top-of-the-line technology at his disposal, and he knew the right people. Hell, he could hack into any system in the world if he wanted.

He'd find out what she didn't want him to know. In the process, if he learned his friends had been in on it, he'd get some much-needed payback on his way out the door.

Coop started his pickup and shifted into drive at the same time he spotted the single headlamp blink on a hundred feet down the road. He felt the growl of the Harley rumble through his chest.

Derek waiting alone in the dark was precisely what Coop had dreaded. Possessiveness flared to life within him, even though Jade had made it crystal clear she wanted nothing to do with him.

He rolled up beside Derek and slid down the window. "Kind of off the beaten path, aren't you?"

Derek's cocky grin never wavered. "Saw you headin' out and thought I'd tag along. You sly dog. You wanted Miss Shotgun Annie all to yourself." He made a show of glancing at his watch. "Judging by how early it is and that scowl on your mug, you must have struck out." Snickering, he revved the bike.

"That obvious, huh?" Coop forced a grin, though

he might bite a hole through his lip to keep from saying what was really on his mind.

"What she needs is a real man. I bet she'll be happy to see me." Derek eased the bike across the white line, and it settled into a rough idle. "See you in the mornin'." He gave Coop a mock salute.

Hell no. The smart-ass kid wasn't getting within a mile of Jade. Coop's anger flashed hot as he opened his door and planted one boot outside the truck. It didn't matter why he was mad enough to chew nails right now. It was Jade, and despite the way she'd deceived him, he wasn't going to stand by and see her hurt. Or worse. Not today.

His cell phone vibrated in his back pocket. At almost the same instant, Derek reached behind him and dragged out his phone. His leer disappeared, evidence the message hadn't fit into his plans for the night. Coop glanced at his screen. Sure enough. A text from Carl Graves waited.

Mandatory meeting—30 minutes.

Carl wasn't a man who wasted words or time. This meeting wasn't likely to be good news for the town.

Coop returned the phone to his pocket, stepped toward Derek, and got in his personal space. "Hands off the woman, Waldon. I was here first and, as far as you're concerned, I've staked my claim. She's mine until I lose interest, and I protect what's mine. That means she's off-limits to you. Any questions?" He didn't want to know how fired up Jade would be if she'd heard his rhetoric, but Derek only understood two things. Power and the pecking order. For now, Coop held sway in both areas, and he could tell his edict hit home by the flicker of anger in Derek's eyes. Hopefully, it would be enough to keep her off his radar for the time being.

Coop stared him down until Derek gave in, turned the bike toward Pine Bluff, and sped away.

Graves was in deep conversation with his right-hand man, Ethan Trudell, outside the town's feed store, where the rest of the troops were gathering. It was apparent, from the dark glares they gave Coop and Derek as they walked by, whatever they were discussing wasn't for the second string. With Derek following close behind, Coop found a seat in the second row. The kid slumped into the one beside him, his anger apparently forgotten.

Graves had cleared the warehouse's backroom to make enough space for a mismatched collection of folding chairs and a rickety table. It looked as though someone had tried to sweep up some of the dirt covering the wooden floor in a thick layer. The air was heavy with dust, mixed with the smell of molasses. Thirty chairs, arranged in three rows of ten each, faced the table.

Nearly twenty men already waited there. The skin on the back of Coop's neck tingled as he glanced around at the men's faces. There were three new arrivals since this morning. Word-of-mouth spread quickly in these sparsely populated counties in eastern Oregon. The district attorney of Baker County appeared determined to proceed with the trial, even in the face of an armed insurrection.

Lloyd Bueller, former Oregon state senator and a man accused of murdering his wife, was your typical good-old-boy. Golden in the minds of his friends, whether he killed his wife or not, Bueller had called local acquaintances to join Graves' hired guns in Pine Bluff.

One of the newcomers was a local who sat in the last row with his cowboy hat, boots, and worn Wranglers. The other two were a different type. Confident, boastful, and carrying concealed weapons, they gave credibility to the reports that had brought Coop there. Claims that Bueller had hired help to stoke the fires of discontent. On a tip from the Circuit Court Judge Leland Holcomb, the FBI had engaged PTS Security for recon. Coop had volunteered to go undercover and keep the feds apprised of the heat level simmering in the public square.

The conversation dropped in volume when Carl and Ethan strode into the room. Both men stepped behind the table, and Ethan picked up a folded sheet of paper. "Thanks for coming so quickly. Jury selection begins tomorrow morning."

A rumble of dissention made the rounds while Ethan waited for them to quiet down again. "This is good news because now we can finally start to make a difference." He held the paper up for all to see. "I've got two lists. One names the townspeople who'd make good jurors, and the other is a list of people we don't want anywhere around our friend, Lloyd."

A cheer went up, which Ethan and Carl encouraged with a smile. Coop tried to ignore Derek's enthusiasm for the proclamation as the man joined in with the others stomping their feet on the worn, wooden floor. It was clear Graves took pleasure in riling up the unpredictable crowd—just what Coop didn't need.

Graves held up his hand for quiet. "From this point on, we're going to be more visible. Starting tomorrow morning, I need all of you out on the streets in groups of three or four. You'll cover the grocery store, the library, the diner, or anywhere else the residents hang out and visit with their neighbors. I want them to be talking about you and worrying about why you're here in their town. Intimidation is the order of the day, boys. We want them scared and eager to have this trial over and done with so things can get back to normal around here." He paused until he had every man's attention. "I'm only going to say this once, so listen up. No one gets hurt."

Ethan darted a glance to Graves as though not expecting the stipulation and started a chorus of *boos* that swept around the room.

Graves smirked and waved his hand for silence. "For now, that's an order. If anything changes, you'll be the first to know."

Coop's glance landed on Ethan at that moment and caught a side view of the sneer that transformed his demeanor from able-bodied assistant to common thug. Something about the guy made the hair stand up on the back of Coop's neck.

"Okay, you heard the man. In the meantime, there's a problem. A witness who's being unreasonable." The members hung on Ethan's words with an enthusiasm that didn't bode well. "Nicole West believes she saw Lloyd here in Pine Bluff the day his wife died. We've presented strong arguments to the contrary, but Ms. West persists in her belief. She and her husband, Ryan West, have managed to confuse a few of the citizens and turn them against our cause."

Coop sat straighter. *Ryan? Common name. It could be a coincidence. Ah, hell, what are the odds?* Jade and *her* Ryan had declared war on the armed militia that had caused havoc in their town. *Snakes*—that's what she'd called them. She'd also seemed quite well acquainted with the Ryan he'd met today. If he was the man Ethan was talking about, there was a good chance Jade knew Nicole West equally well.

I've got a bad feeling about this.

Graves stepped in front of the table. "Ms. West was injured recently in a regrettable accident, and she's recuperating, resulting in her sister coming to visit and taking over the operations of the Pink Paws Kennel just outside of town."

Ethan referred to the sheet of paper he held. "A JD McDowell. No idea what the JD stands for, but I've heard she's a pretty thing." He grinned in Derek's direction.

Coop tensed. *Well, hell. This just keeps getting better.*

He looked to his left, and his stomach soured at the lecherous expression on Derek's face as he basked in the attention from the higher-ups. Dragging the smart-mouthed jackass from his chair and breaking his damn jaw wouldn't solve anything, but it would sure as hell make Coop feel better.

"We had a run-in with the bitch this afternoon." Derek jabbed his thumb toward Coop. "She knows her way around a shotgun, but she needs to learn her place." He glanced over his shoulder and snickered. "You should ask Coop about her. He knows her better than I do. He just came from the kennel." By the grin he sported, Derek was a man who knew he'd just gotten even.

That explains his sudden BFF charade. Why the hell didn't I break his damn neck when I had the chance?

As everyone's attention homed in on Coop, he regarded Graves with his best poker face.

Graves' eyes narrowed. "Fraternizing with the enemy?"

Damn it. Derek's penchant for gossip was likely to land Coop in a confrontation he couldn't afford to lose. It would be a mistake to show weakness in this crowd. Stretching his long legs out in front of him, he crossed them at the ankles. "I wasn't aware she was the enemy at the time, but hell yeah. I go after what I want. Is that a problem?" He returned Graves' stare unflinchingly.

Everyone in the room waited, noise suspended on what their leader would say next. There were a few uneasy seconds of alpha-male posturing between Coop and the man in charge. Then Graves cracked a smile. "Now, there's something we can use. It's genius. If she does stick her nose where it doesn't belong, she won't be expecting the hammer to fall from your hand. For now, just keep doin' what you're doin'. In fact, the closer you can keep her, the better."

A muscle flexed in Coop's jaw as his teeth clenched, but he managed a slight nod.

Graves turned back to the group. "The rest of

you stick around until Ethan assigns you an area for tomorrow. Don't forget what I said. We don't want to see any of the good townspeople get hurt."

"Not yet, anyway," Derek said in a low voice, followed by a belly laugh. "Oh, and if you need any help with that pretty lady, you can call on me." A nasty leer twisted his lips.

If Coop spent one more second looking the kid in the face, he was going to lose his shit. This operation was officially in the toilet. He pushed to his feet and stomped out the front door. Once he hit the cool night air, he stopped and took several deep breaths, letting his fury subside further with each exhale.

It was time to call in reinforcements. The right state of mind to do the job successfully had disappeared about the same time he ran into Jade. How the hell was he supposed to get anywhere near her? Graves' veiled threats against her and her sister hadn't escaped him. He couldn't protect her and her family under the circumstances, spread out like they were.

With anger smoldering just below the surface, he started his truck and headed for his room at the roach motel two blocks off Main Street. It was, by far, the worst flea-infested dive he'd ever stayed in, and that included every Arab and Afghan shithole he'd fallen asleep in when he couldn't keep his eyes open any longer. There'd be no regrets when his partners sent someone to replace him. He couldn't get out of this town fast enough.

A few minutes later, he unlocked his room, stepped inside, and closed the door behind him.

Already pulling his handgun from the shoulder holster he wore, he strode toward the bed and placed it on the bedside table. He'd lied to Jade about being unarmed. Pine Bluff under siege wasn't the right place to suddenly stop packing heat. Besides, he didn't think for a minute she'd believed him.

It was hot and stuffy in the room, and he jerked his shirt off over his head, tossing it on the unmade bed. He wanted to check in with his partners, but he could spare five minutes for a shower to scrub away the frustration of spending the day with Derek. More pressing, he needed to remove the last traces of Jade's seductive fragrance still clinging to his skin and clothes. The soft, delicate smell had always been synonymous with wildflowers as far as the eye could see, sunshine and cloudless blue skies. Back then, that's how he'd thought of her. His too-good-to-be-true. His happily-ever-after. It turned out he'd been a damn fool.

He growled and stalked to the bathroom. Cranking the water on as hot as it would go, he stripped off the rest of his clothes and stepped under the steaming shower. The needles of water jabbed the tense muscles of his shoulders and back as he braced his arms against the wall. When it started to cool, he quickly shampooed his hair, lathered up, and scrubbed himself from head to toe as though he could wash away the history along with the grime. Yet, freshly shaved, wet hair combed and wearing clean jeans, low on his hips, and nothing else, the memories still haunted him.

He retrieved his phone from the bed, dialed, and strode toward the front window to peer between the filthy curtains at the deserted street.

"Hey, Coop, how the hell are you?" Travis' familiar voice grounded him.

The members of his SEAL team had known Jade back then. They'd cared about her because Coop did. They'd stayed with him around the clock after the team had brought back confirmation of her death. He wouldn't have survived if not for Travis, Luke, MacGyver, and the rest of his team.

Uncertainty washed over him. Travis wouldn't lie to him. None of his brothers-in-arms would. He'd trusted each of them with his life on too many occasions to count. They were rock solid.

No, *he* was the problem—hallucinating—imagining an encounter so real, it'd given him a hard-on. It'd been nearly two years, but he used to see Jade in all his old haunts. Fear ricocheted through him. Maybe he'd finally slipped the last few feet into his worst nightmare come true—the one where PTSD ruled.

"About time you checked in." MacGyver's was the next voice he heard.

"In case you can't tell, you're on the speakerphone." Luke always tried to keep their check-in calls on topic. He was a stickler for protocol, but after enduring six months as a prisoner in Afghanistan and nearly dying during his rescue, he could do anything he damn well wanted to, as far as Coop was concerned.

"Things are starting to move here. Jury selection begins tomorrow, and Graves is in full intimidation mode." Coop plunged right into his report, shoving aside the disturbing questions regarding his tenuous grasp on reality. "He has a list of prospective jurors he considers unacceptable. He hasn't said what he'd do if anyone on his blacklist gets tapped, but you can bet he won't stop at only threats. And there's something else."

Coop stopped abruptly, not sure if he'd intended for that to slip out. Pushing the curtain aside, he braced one arm against the window casing. He had to tell them about Jade and her sister. Didn't he? If he was hallucinating, they needed to know before he screwed up this operation. It would likely be the end of his involvement with PTS Security. His partners would never completely trust him again. Hell, he wouldn't trust himself either. If, after all this time, he'd relapsed into the world of gun battles, incoming missiles, and dead people walking, that would be the final blow.

The silence from his friends in their San Diego office was deafening, and he could imagine them exchanging glances, waiting for him to continue.

"What is it?" MacGyver's voice was wary with concern.

As hard as Coop tried to put his emotions aside and stick to the facts, the words to explain what he'd seen—who he'd talked to, if only in his head—eluded him. In frustration, he pivoted away from the window and started pacing.

"What aren't you telling us?" Luke's worry seemed to crackle over the distance, but his voice remained calm and steady.

Again, Coop tried to snatch the words streaming through his mind and force them out in some kind of intelligent form, but only garbled sentences and swearwords made it into the realm of hearing. Yep, they'd think he'd slipped a cog for sure.

"Slow down, Coop. You know we're here for you, right, buddy?" Travis sounded like he was right on top of the mic.

He and Travis were tight. The man had stood by him through worse than this in the beginning. His friend would give him the benefit of the doubt.

"She's here, Travis. It's Jade."

The silence was like a vacuum. Maybe Travis hadn't heard him. His words had been barely above a whisper, yet it felt as though he'd screamed them from deep in his soul.

They must have heard him. Seconds ticked by, during which he could count his own heartbeats. Then everyone started to talk at once.

"Naw, you saw someone who looked like her. You know that, right?" Travis was the first to draw blood, and his buddy's confirmation of Coop's fears set him back a step.

"Have Blake get the helo ready." Luke must have been talking to one of the others. "Hey, man, we'll be there in a few hours. We'll get to the bottom of this."

"That's right. You just sit tight." MacGyver sounded as though he was moving farther away from the phone. Probably the one tasked with getting Blake out of bed to pilot the helicopter.

Coop listened to their incredulous, guarded comments for a few seconds before he simply couldn't take it anymore. Everyone had their breaking point, and this was his.

He only had one more thing to say. "Yeah, you

should probably come. This town is in big trouble. Me—I need a drink." He ended the call while they were all still trying to apply logic to the most improbable of events. He finished dressing and left the motel, headed for one of several bars on Main Street. Hell, maybe he'd hit them all before he was through.

CHAPTER SIX

Peaceful sleep was not an option. Jade's past, made up of disjointed memories and moments of pure terror, had breached her seawalls. Angry waters boiled around her. Blackness swallowed her as she went under.

Jade concentrated as she lined up the bank shot that would sink the eight-ball. At stake was her title as the 847th Squadron Pool Shark and the ten dollars she had riding on the outcome. The exact instant she tapped the cue ball, someone let out a whoop as the door flew open, and a boisterous group of men joined the Friday night crowd inside the MWR.

The cue ball jumped, spiraled sideways, and bounced off the rail two inches to the left of where she'd intended, missing the eight-ball entirely. A chorus of groans from those watching, who also had money on the game, nearly drowned out the new arrivals. Security Specialist Jacobs quickly cleared the table, accepting his winnings and the accolades of his friends. Jade returned her pool cue to the rack on the wall, congratulated the winner, and returned to her table as a new contender stepped forward to challenge the reigning champ.

Colonel Reiner was chatting up Lieutenant

Delgado at the table where she'd left her friend sipping iced tea three games ago. Jade took her seat, smiled, and raised her glass in greeting. "Thanks for keeping Andrea company, Mark."

He smirked and winked at Andrea, who smiled and blushed. "My pleasure. Sorry about your game. You should know better than to let someone distract you when you're going for the win."

Jade shrugged and glanced toward the table where the newcomers had settled, high-fiving and clinking bottles of non-alcoholic beer. SEALS. Not one of them less than six feet tall and built like they trained all day, every day. Their desert fatigues carried no insignias. They didn't have to. These men were recognizable by their self-confidence, the camaraderie they shared, and the go-ahead-make-my-day glint of warning in their eyes. Hard men. Capable.

A celebration seemed to be underway. A tingle of exhilaration ran through Jade as she observed their interaction.

Suddenly, one of them caught her watching, and his lips moved, but she had no idea what he said or even who was on the receiving end. His hair was blond and cut short, with a rough growth of whiskers shadowing his face. A grin curved his sensuous mouth as he held her gaze. One by one, his three buddies noticed her staring. As though someone counted to three, they all raised their bottles and saluted her simultaneously.

She couldn't help but laugh, then raised her glass in response. While they tipped their bottles up and drank, she forced her attention back to her companions. They hadn't noticed her preoccupation. Their conversation was low and intimate, and Jade felt every bit the third wheel.

She set her glass down more vigorously than necessary and cleared her throat. "Early day tomorrow. I'm calling it. You kids have fun." Jade pushed her chair back and started to rise.

"Was that our fault?" The deep voice beside her table gave her a jolt.

"What?"

"The game. Were we responsible for you losing?" The blond SEAL stood close enough she could have reached out and touched him. His chocolate-colored eyes were rimmed with long, dark lashes and filled with warmth and humor.

"Um...no. I lost fair and square—although your untimely arrival might have had some small effect on the outcome."

His grin widened. "I'd like to make it up to you."

"No need. Anyway, I was just leaving, so I'm not sure how you would." She stood to say goodbye to her friends, but when she swung toward them, her movement morphed to slow motion. Her friends' faces shimmered and disappeared one by one as though they'd beamed back to the Enterprise. Silence settled over the empty rec room.

"I have a couple of ideas." The SEAL still stood at her elbow, his laugh soft and suggestive.

Unfazed by the abrupt change of scene, she smiled. "I bet you do. Thanks, but as I said, I'm leaving."

"Then let me walk you."

"Look, I don't know you."

He stuck out his hand. "I'm Coop. My friends will vouch for me."

A shiver ran up her arm when their hands touched. "Jade. I don't know your friends, either. And I don't sleep around, so you're wasting your time if—"

He held up his hands. "I don't do one-night stands, but I'd like to get to know you."

In the blink of an eye, they were outside, walking along a dimly lit path toward her barracks. She shivered again, this time from the chill of the night.

"You're cold?" He slipped his arm around her shoulders and drew her close to his side. "You have the most beautiful eyes."

She peered at him, and he leaned toward her, brushing his lips across hers gently. Desire pooled low in her stomach.

He pulled back. "Is it okay if I kiss you?"

Turning into him, she raised on her tiptoes and ran her hands up his chest to his shoulders. He caught her around the waist, pulling her closer, as he lowered his head. When their lips touched, fireworks exploded in the night sky. Something jolted awake within her—something that recognized him as her soulmate. His kiss was hungry, dangerous, yet she wasn't afraid. She felt as though she'd known him all her life.

He backed her up until she came to a hard stop against a building that hadn't been there a second ago. Then he lifted her off the ground, and she wrapped her legs around him. Every inch of his thick erection pressed against her core.

In a flash of light, the night shifted, and she was

alone. The heat of Coop's presence barely a wisp of sensation. Her entire body vibrated with the roar of a fighter jet engine. The power surrounded her as she raced down the runway, one with the aircraft, and rose above the earth. It was a feeling she loved. It made her genuinely happy—but something was wrong this time. Emptiness formed an ache in her chest.

A blast of bright light illuminated both sides of the aircraft, and the Raptor shuddered with the impact of the drone's rocket. From the rear seat, Andy swore until a bevy of alarms drowned him out. Smoke filled the cockpit with a gray haze. Jade's controls were useless; they were going down. Fear chilled her as the earth spun beneath them, closer and closer.

"Andy? We're going down! We have to eject! Do you hear me?" Silence. Panic engulfed her chest like molten lava.

Routine kicked in. Go through the checklist. Radio their location. Dump the fuel. Initiate the ejection series.

Alarms blared.

Jade bolted straight up. Her heart pounded. Her cotton tank and boy shorts clung to her, damp with sweat. Eyes wide and body tense, she waited for the impact. Her jet, dropping at a hundred feet per second, would disintegrate upon meeting the unyielding surface hurtling toward them.

She examined the dark corners. Something wasn't right. Where was she? Her bedroom? The softness of her thick cotton sheets against her bare legs startled her. The moonlight through the window lit up her surroundings.

Not the inside of a fighter jet. Not going down in enemy territory. Not this time.

Finally able to breathe, she dropped her face into her hands, and a groan rasped through her throat. *It was a dream.*

The nightmares weren't unusual, but it'd been months since she'd awoken with a weight the size of Mt. Everest bearing down on her chest and the fight or flight reaction hardwired in her brain. First the panic attack—now this. She'd hoped she was getting better.

Coop had upset her delicate grasp on reality.

His sudden appearance, with his rock-hard abs and rugged appeal, had been a stressor she didn't need. To be fair, running into her had probably disturbed his status quo as well. Was he also having trouble sleeping?

She dropped her hands into her lap and raised her head. Where was Moose? Her pint-sized service dog was missing in action. It was his job to plaster himself as close to her as he possibly could and lick her in the face, nudge her and, generally, be a pain in the ass until her vitals went back to normal. She'd had to go it alone this time.

Moose lay at the foot of the bed, ears perked up, all his attention focused on the open doorway. Instantly, Jade was wide awake, and the back of her neck began to tingle. Whether her body was still reacting to the dream or she was just now noticing the heavy silence that hung over the rest of the house, there was only one way to proceed.

She threw back the covers and reached beneath

her pillow for the 9mm. "Moose, chill," she whispered. The dog barely acknowledged her as the hair on his scruff stood on end. He'd heard something. She'd learned not to argue when it came to Moose's super senses.

"Stay." Sliding her feet off the edge of the mattress, she landed lightly on the carpet. Her firearm gripped in both hands, she glided toward the staircase just beyond her small living area. Descending the stairs, she winced at each creak of the boards. Every few steps, she stopped to listen. Despite the gloomy silence that greeted her, she proceeded cautiously. Moose had never steered her wrong.

She was two steps from the landing when a heavy *thump* on the deck out front froze her in midstride. A string of muffled profanities propelled her down the rest of the steps to the nearest window to peer out the blinds.

"What the…" She dropped the wooden slat back in place and leaned her forehead against the wall. Her respite was short-lived, though. Lighting up the face of her watch, she groaned. It was three ten in the morning. What was he doing on her front porch?

She strode to the door, unlocked it, and jerked it open. Coop sat on the top step, his back to her, holding his head in his hands. His pickup, parked out front with the driver-side door wide open, appeared empty. It seemed he was alone, yet she crossed the deck toward him with a cautious step.

"Do you know what time it is? Why are you here?" Apprehension magnified the irritation in her voice.

He dropped his hands and turned his head toward her.

Her heart thumped a couple of beats as her gaze swept over him. "What happened to you?"

For a moment, he didn't say anything, just searched her face with one glazed eye. The darkening bruise on his cheekbone, his other eye swollen partway closed, and his lip, split open and bleeding, skewed his lopsided grin. The result was his ghoulish appearance in the moonlight.

He clambered to his feet without the grace or coordination she remembered and shoved his hands in his pockets. "Hey, gorgeous." His speech slurred, and he winced slightly as his grin stretched his injured lip wider.

Of all the things he could have said, he'd chosen the one greeting that had always made her feel special. It was so familiar, so bittersweet, so Coop. Sadness for the life she'd missed out on settled like dense fog around her shoulders. If only that last mission hadn't gone so horribly wrong, everything could have turned out differently. Better. Maybe she wouldn't be trying to feel through a layer of grief right now.

But the mission had sucked, and there was no going back.

She tamped down the regret that lay like a slab of granite in the pit of her stomach. Familiar voices whispered at the fringes of her mind. They would never let her forget. She was damaged goods, defiled, ruined beyond redemption.

He deserved better. At least the man she'd known back then would have demanded better. Yet, he sided with a band of criminals against good people like her sister and Ryan. The Coop she'd known would never have associated with that vermin. "Things aren't always what they seem," he'd said the last time he stood on her front porch. Maybe she should give him a chance to explain. Would he call *quid pro quo* if she asked why he was consorting with those criminals? Probably, and she had nothing she was willing to trade.

"Aren't you gonna invite me in?" His tall frame swayed as his heavy-lidded eyes slowly blinked and focused on her open door.

Now, there's a bad idea. Coop had been drinking—that was new. Jade sighed. She could send him on his way, but she'd be doing the people of Pine Bluff a disservice by allowing him to drive in his present condition. In addition, he was injured. An ice bag, a couple of butterfly bandages, and a place to sleep it off would be the good-Samaritan thing to do.

"Did your friend, Derek, do that to your face?"

He snickered. "Derek is most definitely not...my...friend." He leaned toward her, nearly losing his balance in the process. "I kinda had it comin', though. The jackass just kep' pushin' my buttons. I shoulda let it go, but..." He bent his head and looked her directly in the eyes, continuing in a conspiratorial whisper, "...I might've had a li'l too much to drink."

Jade coughed to hide the laugh that sputtered from her despite the nerves that still stretched tight throughout her body. "You think? Since when do you get drunk, anyway?"

Coop straightened with a smirk and a shrug. "I

don't. Might've been the problem."

He'd appeared sober when he'd visited a few hours ago. Now, he was shitfaced. *That probably had nothing to do with running into me. Sure.* Another sigh escaped. "Come on. I'll make some coffee and fill a bag with ice while you wash the blood off. Then you can sleep on the couch." She jabbed a finger into his chest. "Just so there's no misunderstanding, that's all I'm offering."

He shoved his hands in his front pockets and stepped back as though her tap could actually move him. "*What* makes you think I want anything else?" His injured lip made his grin lopsided, but it still melted some of her apprehension.

"Right." Jade turned and strode toward the door, waiting for him to enter behind her before locking the deadbolt. "Up the stairs, across the living room, take a right, and you'll hit the bathroom. Beware of the dog."

He laughed without turning around. "That little meatball you had on the deck earlier? That's a dog?"

Why was everyone picking on Moose? "Hey! My house, my rules. If the dog doesn't like you, you'll be the one leaving."

He disappeared into the bathroom, muttering something she couldn't quite make out. Even drunk, his alpha-male presence filled her second-floor hideaway above the kennel office and made her super aware of the self-assurance he wore like a mantle. Goosebumps broke out on her arms. Her random acts of kindness were going to get her in trouble someday.

Moose trotted out of her bedroom, stopping to smell around the bottom of the closed bathroom door, then continued to where she stood in the kitchen, watching the stream of black coffee fill the carafe. She leaned down to scratch her buddy's ears. "That's a good boy. I don't care what anyone else says about you. I still love you to pieces." Moose accepted her declaration by flattening his ears against his head and spinning in a circle at her feet. She chuckled and reached for his treat bin to reward him for being so cute. *Nope, not spoiled at all.*

After a few minutes, Coop reappeared and pulled out one of the wooden stools at the breakfast bar dividing her small living room from her even smaller kitchen area. The blood was gone from his face and hands, but it didn't improve his haggard appearance much.

She poured two cups of coffee and set one in front of him. "So, why were you fighting?"

His lip was still bleeding, and he dabbed at the gash with a wet washcloth he'd carried with him from the bathroom. "Derek can't keep his trap shut...and I had just enough Jack Daniels to think I should give him a hand with that."

"How'd that work for you?" Jade circled the counter and took the cloth from him while handing him a pouch filled with ice for his eye.

"Granted, I wasn't at my best but, if you think I look bad, you should see that asshole?" His one contusion-free eye sparkled with amusement.

Reaching for his hand, she guided the ice bag to his cheek, none too gently.

"Ouch!"

"Don't be a baby." Jade managed to sound annoyed despite the grin she was determined to hide.

She pressed the washcloth to his cut lip and held it there through the glower he gave her.

"Why were you drinking?"

He looked at the countertop and wrapped his large hand around his coffee cup. "Do ya' really need to ask?"

Crap. "Was the fight about me too?"

He shrugged. "Don't men always fight over women?"

"I haven't noticed guys needing much of a reason. I'm sorry you got involved in the altercation at the store and that it caused problems between you and your non-friend."

An awkward silence settled over them, and he lifted his head to focus bleary eyes on her. "Hell, I'm not sorry, Jade. If I hadn't been there, I'd still be thinkin' you were dead."

His intense perusal continued, filling the room with unspoken questions. Caught between her raw emotions and the naked sorrow reflected in his expression, she fought the onslaught of guilt that pulled in two directions. The overpowering urge to reach out and touch him—to comfort—ballooned unbearably.

For a moment, she let herself play *what if.* What if she could make Coop understand? What if she could somehow steal him away to the world that still inhabited her dreams and let him experience the bone-deep cold, the hunger, and the paralyzing fear that even now ate away at her self-respect? Know the deprivation of everything familiar. Bear the loneliness. Be crushed by the absolute hopelessness until the specter of death was welcome.

It would never work. Coop was a man of worth—a SEAL. He'd *never* give up, never compromise. Not like she had.

She'd held out as long as she could. At first, she'd fought her tormenter's every vile touch, every abuse. Above all, Mahaz had wanted to break her—wanted her submission. She'd sworn she'd die before she gave him what he craved. Easy enough to say, but she hadn't been strong enough. In the end, death had been too far beyond her reach.

Shame clung to her like the stench of rotting corpses. Spinning around, she dropped the cloth on the edge of the counter, grabbed her coffee cup, and retreated to the sink.

His low voice followed her. "Whatever your reason to stay buried, I'm glad you're alive. Nothin' you say will ever change that."

Never say never. Jade snapped her mouth closed on the scornful retort that would only make things tenser between them. Leaving her half-full cup in the sink, she pushed away from the counter. "I'll get you a blanket."

In her room, she pulled the extra bedding from the top of her closet where Nicole had left it in case Jade got cold. Snatching a spare pillow from her bed, she returned to the living area. "I'm sorry—the couch isn't all that comfortable, but it'll have to do."

He turned away from the window where he was standing. "It'll be fine. It's a hundred times more inviting than the bed in my motel room." He took the blanket and pillow and pivoted toward the couch. "Thanks for letting me stay and for the ice and the coffee. I shouldn't have come—not sure why I did.

Sorry if this situation makes you uneasy. I promise I'll be gone before you get up."

She should have been grateful for that, but a sudden sense of loss was wreaking havoc on her emotions. "If you're staying until the trial is over, I'll probably see you around town." How was she going to handle that?

He shook his head. "I have to meet some friends in the morning, but then I'm heading home."

"You're going home?" She could have kicked herself for parroting him.

"I thought it'd be a good idea under the circumstances."

"Oh. I suppose you're right." It would be for the best. Life would eventually go back to the way it'd been before she'd run into him. That was what she wanted. *Right?* "Well, I'll say goodbye then."

He nodded but continued to study her until she forced herself to turn and retreat toward her bedroom.

"Jade?"

She stopped, twisted partway, and looked over her shoulder.

"Is there any reason I should stay?"

Yes. Tears stung the backs of her eyes. She'd known what seeing Coop again would do to her. That was one of the reasons she'd chosen the cowards way out instead of facing him. The feelings she'd had for him back then hadn't been buried as deep as she'd thought. No—she didn't want him to go, and one word from her might convince him to stay. She scanned his battered face, his feelings for her evident there. Hopeful. Loving. Resigned. He expected her answer to be no, but he'd put himself out there anyway. Even now, he was giving her another chance.

Doubts crowded her mind, but she tried to push them away and concentrate on his face, a smile playing at the corner of his mouth. Would he stay if her answer was maybe?

Another memory pushed to the surface. A man with dirty hair and dark skin wore a black shirt and camouflage pants, and a hood covered his head and most of his face. The *balaclava* concealed all but eyes that held disdain, contempt, and cruelty—so much cruelty. She looked away from Coop as though complying with an unspoken command. One of many orders she'd heeded in her attempt to stay alive. One compromise had led to another and another until she'd gone so far, she couldn't come back.

Despair gripped her. With a slight shake of her head, she continued toward her bedroom. "No, none that I know of."

She barely got the door closed behind her before grief overwhelmed her. Wounds reopened and started to bleed. She stumbled blindly to the bed and placed her 9mm on the nightstand. Dropping onto the mattress, she curled into a tight ball as though that could somehow protect her heart.

Regret was transient as anger took over—rage that had no outlet since the man in the balaclava was dead. Killing him had been the single most satisfying thing she'd ever done. It'd freed her from captivity, but the events she'd set in motion had already condemned her to a different kind of prison.

There was no sleep for the morally compromised.

Jade rubbed her eyes and rolled onto her back. Three hours had crawled by since the last time she'd glanced at her watch. Dawn was creeping over the mountains, and she hadn't slept a wink.

Stuffing a pillow over her head, she groaned. "It's going to be a long day."

Thankfully, she had plenty of chores to keep her busy. She'd get up and be ready to go when Coop left. It would soon be time to feed the dogs and clean their kennels.

Suddenly, she shot straight up in bed. "Moose?" He always slept with her. Where was he? She cursed the closed bedroom door that would typically be open if she hadn't had a guest. Certain the dog would have scratched and whined to gain entrance; anxiety began to tug at the edges of her mind. Had he somehow gotten outside where the woods were full of predators? Had she been that distracted by Coop?

She rolled from the bed, and three strides brought her to the door, where she paused to search for calm amidst the panic growing within. She reached three in her numerical journey to five. "The hell with it." She yanked the door open and barged into the other room.

Moose wasn't asleep on the other side as she'd hoped, and fear thrust her toward the stairs. Halfway there, she spotted the dog curled against Coop's bare chest on the couch. One of his large hands rested on Moose's back as though he'd fallen asleep stroking the dog. Moose lifted his head, lowering his ears in greeting, accompanied by a pathetic swipe of his tail.

"You little traitor, you." She couldn't help smiling at the picture they presented—the big, tough SEAL cuddled up with the tiny dog. *Too bad I don't have my camera.*

"You're up early. Everything okay?" Coop's raspy voice startled her, though it shouldn't have. He'd always been a light sleeper.

Relieved that Moose was safe, she tried to sound nonchalant. "Just wondered where the dog had disappeared to."

"You left so fast; you slammed the door in the meatball's face. I would have let the little guy in, but I figured you'd seen all you wanted of me. Anyway, he finally came around, and we got acquainted." Coop rolled to his back, stretching his arms above his head, leaving his muscled chest and sculpted abs in plain sight. Moose jumped down and lay on the carpet beside him.

She tore her gaze from his bare torso, refusing to acknowledge the heat that wound through her veins. "How's your head this morning?"

He groaned. "I think a marching band moved in while I was sleeping. What the hell was I thinking?"

Jade issued a short laugh, skipping the obvious answer. "At least your eye isn't as swollen this morning. How about some coffee?" She strode to the kitchen counter and poured out the remains of the previous pot.

"Naw, I promised you I'd be out of here before you woke up." He pushed himself forward and swung his feet to the floor—too fast, apparently. He spent the next couple of minutes holding his head in his hands.

She started the coffee, then shook out some aspirin from the bottle, filled a glass of water, and padded to the couch. When Coop finally glanced up at her, she held them out for him.

He accepted the pills with a puzzled expression, downing them and the whole glass of water before handing it back. "I'll just use the bathroom and get out of your way."

Yeah, good idea. "I could make you some breakfast before you go. Something nice and greasy might help the hangover." *What?* That was the last thing she'd intended to say, and he looked as surprised as she was. When he didn't answer right away, she rushed to fill the awkward silence. "You need to eat somewhere, but if you'd rather not—"

"Yes. I'd like that a lot." His expression refused to tell her how he felt about the invitation.

"Good. There are clean towels in the bathroom if you want to shower while I'm cooking." Now she couldn't stop herself from making it worse.

"Thanks. Sounds good. My motel has a serious shortage of hot water."

She felt his curious perusal follow her as she returned to the kitchen, not able to relax until the bathroom door closed behind him, and she heard the water running. *It's only breakfast. I'd offer the same to anyone who'd gotten hammered and beaten up. In another thirty minutes, he'll drive out of here, and I'll never see him again. Things will go back to normal.*

Right. Jade's life hadn't been predictable for a long time. Why would it suddenly start now?

Reaching for a large frying pan, she searched Nicole's cupboards until she located a deep bowl. Sausage, eggs, and pancakes with real butter should do the trick. She lined up the ingredients on her counter and started cracking eggs.

Sometime after the first half dozen, another noise grew louder than the shower. A car engine. It would be so like Ryan to come and check on her this morning. She glanced at her watch and frowned. It was a little early, even for her brother-in-law. The sound became harsher, rumbling like a freight train, or maybe a Harley. That couldn't be right. No one she knew had a bike. A warning bell jangled in her head, and she dried her hands.

The window where Coop had stood earlier gave her a full view of the driveway, his truck, and the approaching motorcycle. When the rider was even with the Dodge Ram, he braked, killed the engine, and removed his helmet.

Derek? The creep who'd tried to grope her at the store. The guy who'd busted Coop's lip while he was drunk last night. No way in hell was he welcome at her home.

She dashed into her bedroom, grabbed her handgun, and flipped off the safety. Then she hit the stairs at a jog, stopped at the front door for a moment before twisting the knob. The door only came open about three inches before it slammed shut again. Whipping around, she came face to face with Coop, towering over her, his hand firmly planted on the wood beside her head.

"What the hell are you doing? He might be your friend, but this is my home for the time being, and I don't want him here."

"I know. I agree, but let me take care of this. Okay? There are things you don't understand that make it dangerous for you to go out there alone. I'll tell you everything I know but let me get rid of him first. Please."

His stern expression convinced her he was telling at least part of the truth—that and her sixth sense, which was going crazy right now. "I'll back you up."

"No. Stay inside. Let me talk to Derek alone. I promise he won't bother you again. Okay?"

That was classic Coop. Chivalrous. Protective. Was he protecting her? Or the criminal element Derek represented? The problem was she didn't want to believe he was no better than them. She would never learn the truth unless she listened to what he'd promised to tell her. Standing mere inches from his shirtless body wasn't helping her powers of discernment either. The intensity in his dark eyes unnerved her, and she nodded her agreement reluctantly.

A partial grin rewarded her as he pushed her from his path. "That's my girl. Don't open the door."

She hurried to the nearest window and peered between the curtains as he strode toward Derek, his fingers hooked in his front pockets. His hair was still wet from the shower, and his clean, masculine scent lingered in the small office.

He hadn't been exaggerating. The biker looked like hell. He sported two black eyes, and the cautious way one arm guarded his side suggested a cracked rib or two.

Derek appeared to greet Coop as a friend, sticking out his hand—an overture not returned by Coop. As the two talked, Derek seemed to grow angry and even yelled at one point. Damn, she needed to hear what they were saying, but she could only catch a word now and then, usually of the four-letter variety. A tense moment later, Derek calmed down and looked as though he was listening. Coop's back was to her, so there was no way to gauge his anger quotient.

Soon, though, he turned and started for the house. Derek glared at his retreating back and even tossed an annoyed glance toward the office. The man was visibly upset, but after a few seconds, he straddled the bike, jammed his helmet on his head, and fired it up. Then he grinned and raised his hand, middle finger extended in an unmistakable gesture before he backed around and sped away.

Coop's mouth was twisted in a scowl when he walked through the doorway. "He's leaving."

She let out her breath slowly. "He won't be back?"

He hadn't yet looked her in the eye. "Not as long as I'm here."

"What?" Jade must have heard him wrong. "You said you were leaving…"

"Change of plans. I'm staying here with you." A sexy grin made a tentative appearance before sliding away to a hard-as-glass expression.

Who the hell does he think he is? Jade slammed her hands on her hips. "Over my dead body!"

DIXIE LEE BROWN

CHAPTER SEVEN

"That's a possibility I'm trying to avoid." Coop folded his arms across his chest and eyed the furious woman in front of him. She was clearly prepared to take him on, along with anyone else who got in her way.

"Forget breakfast. Get your shirt and get out." She whipped around and jogged up the stairs. Anger sizzled in her wake.

"Well, shit…that went well." Perhaps he could have been a bit more tactful. He turned the deadbolt and hesitated a moment while he rested his throbbing head against the wooden door.

Coop was stubborn, but he wasn't even in the same league as Jade. She was slow to reach the boiling point but, when she did, watch out. Fights had been uncommon, but neither of them would shy away from no-holds-barred arguments.

A flash of heat swept over his skin as his dick stirred with the memory of hard and fast make-up sex. Despite their occasional heated words, he and Jade had never gone to sleep angry. They'd always been able to talk it out until now.

Without trust and understanding, how would he convince her to let him stay? Times and temperature had changed in the intervening years. Maybe he should honor her request. Follow through on his first inclination and put some miles between him and this town. Forget he'd ever found her.

Yeah, like that would work. It wouldn't matter where Coop woke up tomorrow morning—he'd know he should be here—looking after her.

Determined to out-stubborn her, he climbed to the second floor. The kitchen was unattended. Cooking utensils and eggshells littered the counter beside the stove. The bathroom door was closed. When the shower started, he grabbed his shirt from the couch, where he'd tossed it after hearing the motorcycle outside, and finished dressing. The meatball kept one eye on him and one on the bathroom door.

Folding his blanket, he took it and the pillow to her room and laid them on the foot of her unmade bed. As he turned to leave, the photograph in its frame on the nightstand caught his attention.

The sucker punch to his gut was so unexpected, all he could do was stare. The water turned off in the shower, jolting him from his trance, and he circled the bed to grasp the picture. He and Jade, a few years younger, stared back at him. She in her flight jacket, him in his desert battle dress uniform. The photo had been snapped by one of his team members at Al Asad airbase in Iraq shortly after meeting her. An identical one rested in the drawer of his nightstand at home in San Diego.

Confusion magnified the familiar pain. *She kept it. Why?* Not in a drawer like he did because he couldn't bear to toss it out. If she'd wanted to be rid of him badly enough to let him think she was dead, why keep a reminder beside her bed? Last night, after he'd badgered her into defending herself, she'd admitted it had been hard to walk away from him, right before she stopped talking and refused to answer his questions. He'd blown off her statement at the time. If it was so hard, why had she left him hanging without a word? Now, the picture on her bedside table blasted his assumptions all to hell.

The shower door sliding open broke through his jumbled thoughts. He quickly returned the photo to its place and left the bedroom.

For the first time in many years, he was uncertain of his next move. Jade had told him to leave in no uncertain terms, but he'd be damned if he would. Not until he figured out what the hell was going on in her head. She owed him that much.

He flipped on the burner under a large frying pan, formed sausage into patties, and started cooking. Searching the refrigerator, he found mushrooms, cheese, and an onion. After chopping, dicing, and grating, he added the piles he'd made to the bowl of eggs she'd left on the counter. He turned the sausage, started another pan heating, and then poured himself a cup of the coffee she'd made.

Derek's appearance at her house this morning complicated things. After the jerk had mouthed off last night, his crude threats against Jade had made Coop boiling mad. The beating he'd given the guy should have dulled his anger and discouraged Derek, but Coop hadn't exactly been at the top of his game. Derek had come to apologize and get back on Coop's good side. The fact he was still spouting offensive suggestions made it clear how far Coop had missed the mark. All because he'd had too damn much to drink.

The phone in his back pocket vibrated, and he pulled it out with two fingers to view the waiting text from Travis.

Almost there. Meet at your motel?

His friends had made it clear they thought he'd lost his grasp on reality, seeing dead people again. They could have easily been right on that score. Hell, he'd almost believed it himself—always overthinking the problem. He'd been wrong, and so had they. Travis, Luke, and MacGyver needed to see Jade for themselves, and he wanted to witness the looks on their faces when they did. He leaned against the counter as he texted his reply.

Suddenly, the bathroom door swung open, and she stepped out, her skin so fresh and clean it glistened. Shiny, almost-black hair, still slightly damp, cascaded around her shoulders. She slid to a stop at seeing him. "You're still here."

He ignored the irritation in her voice. Returning his cell phone to his pocket, he poured half of the egg mixture into the smaller pan and turned the heat to a low setting beneath the sausage. After filling her coffee cup and adding cream the way she liked it, he pushed it across the breakfast bar toward her.

His fingers tapped out a mindless rhythm on the countertop as he studied her. "I'm making omelets—your favorite." The flicker of interest on her expressive face encouraged him to lay it all out for her. "We should talk, Jade. There are things you need to know."

Her eyes narrowed with a hint of suspicion. She tilted her head, and one corner of her mouth lifted as though she merely considered smiling. "Something smells good. You always made the best omelets." Her attention on the coffee cup, she advanced slowly toward the counter.

"Still do." He hid a smile as he pivoted back to his task. With practiced ease, he flipped the eggs, seared the other side, and slid them out of the pan to a waiting plate. He put two slices of bread in the toaster, forked a sausage patty onto the plate alongside the omelet, and pushed it toward her. With more flourish than necessary, he poured the rest of the egg mixture in the pan, caught the toast as it popped up, and passed it to her, along with the butter.

A grin spread across her features, sending a spark of amusement into the violet-blue depths of her eyes. Coop's heartrate flew into overdrive as his past collided with the future that was just beyond his reach.

"Still showing off your cooking skills to impress the ladies?" She slipped onto a stool and buttered her toast.

"Every chance I get." The truth was he hadn't cooked for anyone since…her. There was no sense going there and removing any doubt he was pathetic. He dropped more bread into the toaster, turned his eggs, and filled his plate with food. Hesitating, he waffled between eating, standing up, or taking the chair beside hers. When he did neither, she cast a curious glance in his direction and tipped her chin toward the empty seat.

"You said you wanted to talk…so I'm

listening." She swiveled her upper body to face him as soon as he was seated.

Maybe this would be easier than he thought if he could keep from screwing up. How much to tell her remained an open question. When she took a bite of eggs and *hummed* her appreciation as though the food rated right up there with the best orgasm she'd ever had, he opted to go with full disclosure. It was probably a lost cause to hope she'd reciprocate.

"Will you hear me out?"

"As long as what you tell me is the truth."

"Have I ever lied to you?" She was the deceitful one, but he'd gain nothing by placing blame.

As though she'd read his mind, her shoulders slumped ever-so-slightly. Her mouth full, she nodded and motioned with her fork for him to continue.

"The FBI hired my partners and me to keep an eye on the conflict brewing in Pine Bluff." He could feel her intense scrutiny as he chased his eggs around the plate, suddenly not as hungry as he'd thought. "That's why I'm here, putting up with a misogynistic dickhead when I'd rather break his neck."

A sound like a muffled snicker made him glance sideways toward her.

"I think you missed your best shot last night."

He was never going to live down his drunken brawl.

"Partners? Are there more of you?" She stopped eating and concentrated on him.

"We own a private security company. There are four of us, but I'm here alone for now." He held back on telling her she'd met them before. It would serve no purpose to scare her off prematurely. He paused to eat a few mouthfuls of food, hoping it would quiet his sour stomach and ease the pounding in his head.

She straightened and laid down her fork. "Why did the FBI hire you? Why didn't they send some agents? Isn't that what we pay them for?" Palpable frustration sharpened the tone of her question.

Coop took a swallow of coffee and studied her for the cause of her sudden irritation. Her mask was firmly in place, though, and her expression gave nothing away. "The Bureau has protocols they have to follow, which could escalate a situation like this. Besides, have you ever seen an FBI agent who didn't have *cop* written all over him?"

She snickered. "Good point."

"They're giving Graves a chance to end this peacefully, although, from what I've seen, he and some of his more ardent supporters are digging in for a fight. It's my job to call it when we've got enough evidence to put them away for menacing, jury tampering, or coercion. The agents will move in before anyone gets hurt."

"*Before* anyone gets hurt?" She huffed sarcastically, her eyes full of fire and contempt. "I guess you and the FBI aren't as good at your jobs as the people of Pine Bluff would hope."

"What the hell is that supposed to mean?" Why did her eyes glisten as though suddenly moist? He'd never seen her look so vulnerable before, and it was doing weird things to his insides. Tightening his hold on his fork, he fought the overwhelming need to reach for her and pull her close.

"When Graves' men were terrorizing my sister,

where were you or the FBI agents?" Her voice rose with each word. Suddenly, she pushed off her stool and turned her back, apparently not wanting him to witness her efforts to maintain control.

It was all he could do to remain seated.

"Carl Graves and his band of bullies ran Nicole off the road and left her for dead. Who knows what would have happened if a hiker hadn't heard the crash and gone to investigate? She broke her wrist and suffered a concussion, and she's having trouble dealing with everything emotionally. They'd just opened the kennel. Ryan couldn't take care of things here and run the store too. So, they asked me to come." A hiccup escaped, and she folded her arms across her chest.

Bypassing good sense, he followed her, turning her to face him. Ignoring her embarrassed protest, he tugged her closer. She made a half-hearted attempt to wiggle out of his grasp, but as his arms tightened around her protectively, she laid her head on his chest and leaned into him. For a few minutes, he held her as she cried soundlessly and nestled against him.

Before he was ready to let her go, Jade swiped away the tear tracks on her face and peered at him with a wet and chagrinned smile. "Sorry. I didn't mean to get you all wet." She brushed at a water spot the size of a baseball on his shirt as though the action could make it dry.

He stepped back as he reluctantly let her slip from his arms. "Don't worry about it. *I'm* the one who should be sorry. I didn't know about your sister, but now what Graves said last night makes a lot more sense. When did it happen?"

"Three weeks ago, right after Graves and his hoodlums arrived. Sheriff Carlton notified the state patrol and the FBI, but they did nothing. Are they waiting for Graves to kill someone?" She slapped her hands on her hips and studied Coop with an accusing glare.

He pressed his lips together. "I don't know, but that question will be at the top of my list when I talk to my FBI contact." He motioned toward the stools they'd left moments ago. When she didn't move, he returned to his breakfast and pretended interest in his food. Soon, he heard the rustle of her feet across the carpet before she appeared at his side and picked up her fork.

"No good can come of us getting along like this, you know." Her words came in a whisper as though she was trying to convince herself as much as him.

He couldn't argue with common sense, but he wasn't going to agree either. "Is your sister okay?"

She shrugged. "Her body will heal, but trauma leaves wounds no one can see."

Again, she avoided his glance. A chill went through him as certainty settled in his gut. Odds were she'd spoken from experience. Last night he'd noticed the knife scar on her upper arm. It had healed well, but she'd obviously tried to detract from it with the floral tattoo that spilled from her shoulder. It was fair to assume some of her emotional injuries still gaped open, raw and bleeding. And he was about to make it worse.

"I need to stay. Please don't fight me on that."

She laid her fork on her plate and turned to face him. "Why? I can take care of myself, and there's nothing here for you." She started to reach for his arm but stopped short and twined her fingers together in her lap.

Right. Jade didn't need or want him there. The last few years had left no doubt about that. For a few seconds, he allowed the pain to wash over him like a tsunami, but then the photograph on her bedside table appeared in his mind. There was a disconnect between the woman who'd pretended to be dead and the one who'd purposely kept their memory alive. If it was the last thing he did, he'd find out which one was the real Jade McDowell.

Determination hardened his heart, and he nodded in acceptance of her words—for now. "Graves tried to stop your sister from testifying once already. He won't quit now. He said as much last night in a meeting with all hands."

Fear pulsed in her eyes and her throat worked to swallow. "Ryan and I will make sure nothing happens to her."

"If you're talking about Ryan from the store yesterday, I don't doubt he can fend off three or four attackers, but there are a couple of holes in that plan." Coop got to his feet, carried their plates to the sink, and returned with the carafe of coffee. She shook her head when he paused over her cup, so he topped off his and set the carafe back in the coffeemaker.

"What holes?"

"Graves has at least twenty men and more are showing up every day. He already knows he'll have to take out Ryan to get to your sister. You're on his radar too. With you out here alone and Ryan and Nicole at the store in town, where do you think

Graves will send his army first?" He studied her over the rim of his cup as he took a swallow. "All of you are standing in the way of him getting what he wants, and, trust me, that's not a good place to be."

Like a trapped rabbit, she searched the room. Coop could almost see the ideas swirling in her head as she tried to figure a way out that didn't involve him staying in her space. The advantage was his. On his way back to the house after speaking with Derek, he'd followed the thread to its undeniable conclusion. She would, too, given enough time.

"You didn't answer my question. Why would you volunteer to stay after what I did?"

Mesmerized by her gorgeous violet-blue eyes, he strode slowly around the island until he stood beside her. "I don't know what happened to you, Jade. I'd like to, but the truth is you don't trust me enough to share that story with me, and you may never get to that point. There's one thing I do know, though. If I'd been there when it happened, I'd have stood between you and whoever hurt you or died trying. I wasn't there, and I'll never forgive myself. That's why I'm staying."

Moose jumped up from his spot overlooking the stairs and started barking. Two seconds later, Coop heard the unmistakable rumble of a helicopter.

The sound got closer until the air seemed to vibrate inside the building. Jade cocked her head, and a scowl furrowed her brow. "It must be Graves. If he thinks he's going to land that aircraft anywhere around here, he's seriously mistaken." She pivoted and rushed toward the stairs.

Coop went after her, catching her arm on the

first step. "It's not Graves. I wanted to tell you before they arrived, but they must have hauled ass getting here."

"Who?" Her nose wrinkled in that cute way he remembered.

"My partners. Friends. Members of my old SEAL team. I called them last night before I started drinking. When I still thought *you* might be a figment of my imagination."

Her expression softened.

He laughed. "You should probably know…they think I've lost my mind."

A playful smile broke through her guarded mask and lightened her countenance. "So, you brought them right to my doorstep so they could see for themselves. I assume I've met them before?" Her grin faded. "You realize they're not going to be any happier to see me than you were, right? They're going to hate me for hurting you. Not that I'd expect anything less." She glanced toward the bottom floor and crossed her arms, then dropped them just as quickly and straightened her spine. "Who are they?"

The helicopter's rotors slowed. Apparently, Blake was going to land in the parking area out front. The vibration of the displaced airwaves shook the house. Suddenly, the rotors picked up speed again. The aircraft lifted and buzzed so close over the top of the house, Jade and Coop both ducked, exchanging a questioning glance.

"What the hell?" He overtook Jade as she flew down the stairs and threw open the door. What had gotten into Blake? He had more experience flying helos than any five men. Why abort a landing so close to the house?

"In the back." She darted to the edge of the house, zipped around the corner, and froze.

He nearly plowed into her. A hundred yards away, smoke poured from a pile of wood shavings in front of a long wooden structure. The dense plume partially obscured the rose-hued lettering that spelled out *Pink Paws Kennel* under the eaves. Flames lapped halfway up both edges of the sliding barn door.

The helicopter landed hard a good eighty feet beyond the building, the whirlwind tugging the flames even higher. The pilot quickly shut down the engine while three passengers jumped out, fire extinguishers in hand.

It felt like twenty-five or thirty seconds elapsed while Coop registered the scene, but time and adrenaline sometimes played tricks on a person. It couldn't have been more than two seconds before Jade started moving again.

"Oh my God! The dogs!" Fear shredded her voice as she spoke to no one in particular, then raced toward the fire.

CHAPTER EIGHT

The kennel held twelve dogs. The mere thought of the building burning down around them forced more speed from Jade's legs. She wouldn't let it happen.

A lungful of smoke and ash particles set off a coughing fit that had her bent over, hacking up her guts. Her eyes stung and watered, nearly blinding her. She pulled the hem of her shirt up to wipe her eyes and cover her nose and mouth.

The fire had probably smoldered in the wood shavings for hours. A trail of material, the exact width of the bucket on the tractor, led to the three-sided storage shed a hundred feet directly across from the kennel.

The wind created by the helicopter's revolving rotors had fanned the flames, and they licked at the front wall of the building. One of the men from the aircraft rushed to where the fire had blackened the wooden doors and let loose with his fire extinguisher. Another man jumped onto the tractor, started it up, and rolled toward the burning pile.

A wall of flames and smoke obscured the entrance to the kennel. Frantic barking from inside got Jade moving again. Running full out, she leaped over the closest corner of the burning pile, landing six inches short of the concrete slab she'd hoped to reach. Her right foot broke through the top layer of shavings. Intense heat engulfed her as the flames lapped voraciously at the sudden injection of oxygen. Hurriedly, she jumped to safety, stamping her smoldering tennis shoe and slapping at her pant leg, ensuring that she wouldn't carry the fire closer to the dogs' confinement area.

Coop materialized from the billowing gray plume and landed beside her as she grabbed two leashes from the rack inside the door. "I'll get the ones on this side." He took the leashes from her and jerked a thumb toward the opposite wall. If he was as scared as she was, nothing in his calm voice gave it away.

His confident manner grounded her. *Get the dogs out. I can do this.* She forced her fear into submission. "There's a fenced play area out back. We'll put them all in there and move them later if we have to." She waited long enough to see him jump into action before she turned to her task.

The first kennel held a golden retriever named Rusty. The closest to the flames, he was fearful and skittish. With patience, she finally connected the leash to his collar and coaxed him to follow her to the next enclosure to retrieve his sibling. Both dogs in hand, she rushed toward the exit at the far end of the kennel, passing Coop on his way back to get two more dogs. His grin wrung a weak smile from her.

The man out front emptied his extinguisher. His companion on the tractor swept a four-foot path through the burning shavings, pushing them to a safe distance with the bucket and spreading them into a thin layer. The smell of gasoline swirled in the dust and smoke that hit Jade in the face as she walked the last two dogs to safety. Flames started anew along the bottom of the door, but the first man grabbed the kennel's extinguisher and knocked them down.

She wasn't surprised by the gasoline smell. The fire had to be arson, and she would expect the coward to use an accelerant. It wasn't hard to figure out who was the guilty party either, especially with Coop's disclosure that her sister was at the top of Carl Graves' blacklist. If they'd lost the kennel with the dogs inside, it would have devastated Nicole. What Graves and his bunch couldn't know was that Nic would have grieved for a time, but she'd have come back angrier than they could ever imagine. Her usually mild-mannered sister was bulletproof when she lost her temper. With one five-gallon can of gas, Graves would have guaranteed Nic's testimony and Bueller's conviction.

If Coop hadn't been there, or if his friends hadn't shown up in time to warn them, it could have been Jade's worst nightmare. Why hadn't the smoke detectors on either end of the building gone off? Had Graves disabled them?

Coop was throwing tennis balls for the dogs in the play yard but stopped the game long enough to open the enclosure for her. Freeing her two charges, she watched them run off, happily smelling the other animals. She blocked the sun from her eyes with her hand and peered at him. "Thank you doesn't seem like enough."

He tossed the ball again. "You're welcome."

Matter of fact. Unflappable. So like him. She would have given anything for a fraction of his courage. Today and three years ago. Jade brushed the painful thought away. "I should go help out front."

He glanced over his shoulder at the building. "Looks like it's all taken care of."

She followed his gaze. Four powerfully built men filed from the rear of the kennel and walked toward her. Even from this distance, she flinched at their scrutiny. Disbelief morphed to what she could only interpret as curiosity in one or two—unequivocal resentment in another. Sparks jumped between her nerve endings. Straightening, she braced for their condemnation. This was crazy. She didn't care what Coop's friends thought of her.

Liar.

A glance confirmed he wasn't going to stand with her for this. Not that she could blame him. He was the injured party, and no amount of regret on her part would undo that. He continued to throw the ball for the dogs, his expression inscrutable. She turned back to face the approaching men. Straightening her spine, she returned their appraisal. Being alone in unknown territory wasn't a first for her. It probably wouldn't be the last time.

Three of Coop's former SEAL team members and another man she didn't recognize stopped and studied her from twenty feet away. Travis Monroe, Coop's best friend, flanked by Luke Harding and Matt Iverson, bristled with antagonism.

The stranger was the first to approach and offer his hand. "Captain McDowell, I'm Blake Sorenson, formerly Lieutenant Commander in the Navy and

SEAL team leader. I had the privilege of meeting your father once under combat conditions. The general is a real American hero."

For some reason, shame crawled beneath her skin. Was it unfair to condemn her father for putting his country before his daughter? She grasped his hand. "Thank you, Lieutenant Commander. It's nice to meet you."

"The pleasure is mine, but I'm just Blake now." His grin put her at ease. "Perhaps we'll get time to talk, and you'll fill me in on what the old man is up to these days."

"Sure. Anytime."

Blake nodded, stepped around her, and continued until he stood beside Coop.

"Well, hell, if it isn't Jade McDowell in the flesh."

The scorn with which Travis delivered his sentiment made her wince. It was all she could do to stand firm as he strode closer. "How are you, Travis?" Her voice sounded small and weak, even to her.

He smirked. "If you were a man, I'd drop you right there."

Anger stirred. He might be Coop's friend, but he had no idea what brought her to the place she was now. He might not even have the stomach to listen if she told him. How dare he. How dare anyone.

"Don't let that stop you." Her sweetly dangerous words caused only a slight dilation of his pupils, but that was enough to know he hadn't expected her to stand up to him. She sensed Coop swing around to face them and couldn't help wondering if he was concerned about his friend.

Travis shook his head as though disgusted by what he saw, turned, and headed back the way he'd come. From the corner of her eye, she caught Coop's frown.

She forced herself to stand where she was because suddenly running didn't seem like such a bad idea. Luke and Matt, better known as MacGyver, exchanged a glance and started toward her. *Two against one. That's fair.*

Luke didn't stop until his arm went around her shoulders and pulled her in for a hug. Surprised, she didn't have time to protest. When he let her go, he looked her in the eye. "It's great to see you, Jade."

"That goes double for me." MacGyver pulled her sideways for another hug and kissed her on the cheek.

"It's nice to see a friendly face," she murmured.

"Don't worry about Travis. He'll come around." Luke tipped his chin toward Coop. "As soon as he does."

"Yeah. How's that going, anyway?" The corners of MacGyver's mouth curled upward, but he successfully held back the grin that was trying to break free.

"Not great. Coop has a right to be angry." She sneaked a peek at the big blond man still playing fetch with the dogs. "Thank you. If you hadn't arrived when you did, this could have been a disaster."

Luke turned to peer at the rear of the kennel, where nothing seemed out of the ordinary. "Probably not a good idea piling shavings in front of the door.

Spontaneous combustion is a killer under the right conditions."

She leaned over to brush the dust and ash from her pant legs. "If I'd left them there, I'd have to *let* Travis kick my ass. Besides, I smelled the gasoline. It wasn't spontaneous combustion. And it wasn't an accident. Somebody must have disabled the smoke detectors too." Did they think she was stupid?

"You believe someone started the fire on purpose?" Despite his question, MacGyver didn't look all that surprised. "Who?"

She studied him for a moment, but whatever he was thinking was hidden by his relaxed countenance. "The same man you're supposedly here to keep an eye on. Carl Graves—or one of his hired thugs."

Luke and MacGyver glanced at each other, but she couldn't read what passed between them. Tension wound her tighter as her suspicions went off the chart. Coop had been hanging with Derek when she ran into him. Derek worked for Graves and was a creep besides. Was Coop telling her the truth? She'd believed him, but what kind of an FBI agent stood back and let a civilian do the investigating?

That he might have been a part of setting the fire—of running Nic off the road—was not easy to swallow. Maybe that's precisely why she'd bought his story. She wanted him to be one of the good guys. After all, he did help her get the dogs to safety. But what if Graves had only meant to scare her? They'd managed that handily. The aircraft carrying Coop's friends had shown up precisely in time to alert her to the fire, averting the tragedy that might have been.

If Nicole decided to give her testimony, Graves

would try again. Maybe bring more than scare tactics next time. Is that why Coop said he was staying? Because she trusted him and he'd have easy access? Every part of her wanted to deny the suspicion taking root in her stomach.

"If you'll excuse me, I have to call my sister and let her know what happened. The kennel is her dream. I'm just helping out. She may want to call the owners of the dogs in case the fire makes the local news." The words tumbled off Jade's tongue like water over a dam. She forced her mouth shut to stop the deluge. Her nerves had taken a double hit with the fire and Coop's friends arriving, but it was no excuse to blather TMI to Luke and MacGyver. Whether or not they were Graves' stooges, they probably didn't care if clients decided to pick up their dogs early, but it would be a death knell for Nic's new business.

"There's coffee up at the house if you'd like." She shuttered her growing apprehension and gave Luke and MacGyver a welcoming smile. If Coop and his friends insisted on staying, she'd use the time to find out whose side they were on. With a glance toward Coop, she turned and strode toward the house, feeling their stares tingle across her back all the way.

She slammed the door and was halfway up the stairs before the skin on her arms started to crawl. Something wasn't right. Where was Moose? He never failed to meet her at the door, his little feet tapping out a rhythm on the hardwood.

"Moose? Where are you?"

Nothing. Could the dog have gotten outside? No,

she remembered closing the door in his face so he wouldn't be scared by the helicopter and run away. Maybe he was sulking somewhere. That wouldn't surprise her.

She swerved, changing course to the refrigerator, where a bag of Moose's favorite treats waited. He wouldn't be able to resist them, even if he was mad at her. Right now, with her mind in turmoil, she needed him to work his calming magic.

Skirting the island, where she and Coop had eaten breakfast, she started to pull the refrigerator door open. Simultaneously, she caught a glimpse of something moving on the floor where she was about to step. She jumped back and froze. Between the island and the kitchen sink, Moose writhed on his side.

As she watched helplessly, his tiny muscles contracted, straightening his legs and pulling his head back until his fear-filled eyes seemed to look right through her. She dropped to her knees beside him, recognizing the seizure that possessed him for what it was, though he'd never had one before.

"Moose? It's okay, bud. I know it's scary, but I'm right here. I've got you." She reached to touch him—comfort him—and still, he thrashed. For what seemed like several minutes, she crooned soft words as she held his head. Finally, his spasms released him, and he lay still.

Trembling so hard she had trouble making her fingers work, she gathered his limp body to her chest. Holding him close, she scratched him in all the places he liked and murmured his name, assuring him, or possibly herself, that he'd be all right. Gone limp in her arms, he didn't respond or even move. Not even a wiggle of his tail greeted her. He looked peaceful in sleep, but her gentle touch didn't rouse him, nor her more insistent nudges. What was wrong with him? Why wasn't he moving?

She laid his limp body on her lap and put her ear to his chest, but fear was thundering like Mt. Vesuvius in her head, and she couldn't hear his heartbeat. "Moose? Wake up."

Had he choked on something? Jade turned him and forced his mouth open. Nothing blocked his airway, and he was breathing, though shallowly. Tamping down her panic, she scrambled to her feet. Moose needed a vet, and the closest animal clinic was forty-five minutes away.

With dread twisting her insides, she ran to the bathroom for a towel to wrap around him. Keeping him warm had to be appropriate, right? *Where did I put the damn car keys?* She spotted them on the nightstand in her bedroom and rushed back to scoop up Moose in the towel. Clutching him to her chest again, she ran down the stairs, threw open the door, and collided with a wall of men.

CHAPTER NINE

Jade dashed through the office doorway and plowed head-on into Coop and MacGyver as they climbed the steps. Coop reached out to steady her, tightening his grip on her elbow as she tried to jerk free and dart around him.

"Let me go! I have to go!" She took a step back, refusing to look at him.

"Whoa! Hang on a minute. What's wrong?" Instantly on alert, Coop moved in closer, effectively boxing her in. MacGyver, Luke, and Blake had his back, concern rolling off of them in waves.

What the hell? He did a cursory examination. No burns or injuries were apparent—just a bundle of towels clutched in her arms. Her eyelashes fluttered rapidly, bringing his focus back to her face. Despite her efforts to ban them, tears welled over and rolled down her cheeks.

Shit! Something was wrong. As a woman and an officer in a man's world, she'd considered emotional displays a sign of weakness. In the time he'd known her, she'd rarely let down her guard, even when they'd been alone together. Holding her while she broke down this morning at breakfast had been unexpected and instantly awakened his protective tendencies. The only other times her sharp edges had softened was when she interacted with the meatball.

Ah, hell. Coop's focus dropped to the wad of terrycloth she held against her chest.

He brushed his knuckle along her jaw, dragging her attention back to him. "Jade? Give him to me." He reached for the bundle.

With a sigh that was no doubt half relief, she relinquished the towel, and he knelt as he peeled the covering from the tiny, unmoving dog. "MacGyver, need your help here."

His friend knelt beside him, gentle hands stroking the animal's chestnut-colored fur, examining him for wounds and listening to his heartbeat. "What happened, Jade?"

"He had a seizure…and then he just stopped moving." She dropped to her knees next to MacGyver, her mouth set in determination. "We don't have a vet in town. The closest is in Baker City, about 50 miles."

Clearly, it had taken a herculean effort to pull herself together, but Coop wasn't surprised. He was fully aware of how much strength resided within her.

"Do you have anything in the house he might have gotten into?" MacGyver didn't look up as he continued to monitor Moose.

"No. I'm always careful about what I leave within his reach." Her hand shook as she swiped it across her forehead.

"Get the helo ready." From behind Coop, Luke gave the order quietly.

"On it," Blake said as he broke into a jog toward the aircraft.

Luke moved to stand next to Jade, offering her a hand up. "Will you show me where you found him?"

She rose to her feet, and the screen door banged shut behind them as they disappeared inside the house.

"What do you think?" Coop glanced toward MacGyver.

"My bet is on poison, and, considering what just went down at the kennel, it was probably intentional. Hopefully, Luke will be able to find something. The vet will want to know what the dog ingested." MacGyver wrapped the edges of the towel around Moose again before scooping up the dog. "Time is wasting. We need to get going." As though in agreement, the helicopter whined to life as the rotors started turning.

Luke and Jade reappeared. Luke handed MacGyver an empty syringe with a printed label on the side. "Found this on the kitchen floor."

"Insulin." MacGyver tapped the plastic cylinder on his palm and glanced toward Jade. "Are you diabetic?"

"No."

"Is the dog?"

"No."

"Has anyone visited that might have left this?"

"No." Jade's face went deathly pale as her focus locked on Coop. "Did you know Graves was going to do this?" She slammed her hands onto her hips.

"Of course not, and we don't know for sure it *was* him." *Seriously?* "Do you think I'd turn a blind eye to anyone hurting the meatball…or you?" She didn't trust him, and the realization hurt, incensing him further.

She held her ground. "I haven't decided what to think about you...or your friends...or any of this. So, back off."

"Blake's ready to go." MacGyver interrupted the tense exchange.

With no small amount of effort, Coop buried his aggravation. He'd give her this one. She was distraught, lashing out at him because he was the closest scapegoat. But her suspicion of him wasn't acceptable, and it pissed him off. Despite her accusation, she wasn't the only target of his displeasure.

I'm going to rip out the bastard's heart! He silenced a growl of frustration. *Innocent until proven guilty—right?* Although he'd voiced doubt about Graves' guilt, he couldn't fault her conclusion. Who else could it have been?

For now, his focus needed to be Jade and getting the dog to a vet who could counteract the insulin before it was too late. Losing his cool would surely push her further away from where he needed her to be. He leaned close to her ear. "I'll find out if Graves was the one who poisoned the meatball."

She didn't take her eyes off Moose, but she gave a firm nod of her head. He had a feeling she'd been way ahead of him.

"Travis and I'll stay here and keep an eye on the home front." Luke glanced between Coop and MacGyver. "Keep in touch."

"Will do." Coop motioned Jade toward the helo. Her hands flexed into fists as she lengthened her stride to put distance between them. He sighed and reluctantly followed. If his presence on the flight would cause her additional stress, he should stay behind with Luke. The idea of leaving her alone to face the possible death of her service dog loomed like a climbing wall in basic training.

His decision was made for him when they reached the aircraft. MacGyver passed Moose to him and spoke quietly. "She's scared, bro. Going on the offensive is the only way she knows to react. You can relate. Right?"

MacGyver hopped in the front seat with Blake before Coop had a chance to tell him to mind his own damn business. He held the dog while she climbed into one of the rear seats and got settled, then handed off Moose and crawled in beside her. One look at her stricken expression and he was glad he hadn't snapped back. MacGyver was right. She needed his support whether she realized it or not.

The helicopter lifted off at a steep angle and gained altitude quickly. Blake circled and headed west, then pegged the craft at its top speed.

Jade held Moose's still form snug to her chest and whispered words of comfort as she caressed his tiny body.

Guilt pulled hard at Coop's conscience. Graves was an asshole, and she was undoubtedly correct about him being responsible for poisoning the dog. He should have expected the snake to pull something low to bully Jade and her sister. He should've been ready, and he damn sure shouldn't be nursing a hangover.

Meanwhile, he was back to square one. The cruel attack on Jade's dog had brought his integrity into question, and for that, if Graves proved guilty, he would pay. Coop's priority, however, was keeping her and Nicole safe, regardless of how uncomfortable Jade made things for him. What remnant of past feelings was responsible for his determination no longer mattered. It was the way things had to be for now.

Checking Moose's heart rate for the third time since they took off, he was relieved when it beat stronger. He covered Jade's hand, drawing her attention. "Keep talking to him. I think he's responding to your voice."

She turned her head toward him, hope springing into her violet-blue eyes. A tentative smile nearly appeared on her gorgeous lips before vanishing, replaced by sadness. Her mouth lingered close to his, and he could feel her faint breath on his face. He should've backed off, but her emotional exposure sucked him in like water through a sieve.

Instead of looking away, she returned his scrutiny, her eyes moist and red-rimmed but filled with the sparkle and fight he remembered. An ache started to throb in the center of his chest, making it difficult to swallow. When she caught her bottom lip between her teeth and bit down, the resulting look of innocence crossed with sinful pleasure hardened him in an instant and jerked him painfully back to reality. He shifted in his seat and averted his eyes as the heat of his desire rushed through him with a depth of possessiveness that brought him up short.

Disconcerted, Coop forced his emotions back under the iron-clad control that had become his salvation and glanced toward her again. A delicate red hue infused her cheeks, and she gave her attention to the dog, whose eyes were now open, though he still lay unmoving.

When the streets and buildings of Baker City became visible through the window, she suddenly leaned forward and pulled her cell phone from her pocket. Whoever she called was on speed dial and answered almost immediately.

She slapped one hand over her right ear and raised her voice above the rumble of the helicopter. "This is Jade McDowell. Is Doctor Prescott available?" The person on the other end must have heard the distress in her voice because within seconds she sighed, clearly relieved.

"Steve...it's Jade.

First name basis? How well does she know Doctor Prescott?

"Someone poisoned Moose, and he's been unresponsive for at least fifteen minutes. His breathing is shallow, and his heartbeat is steady but weak. *Please,* can you help him?" She tilted her head toward the window and twirled a lock of shiny, dark brown hair around her fingers.

Steve probably couldn't tell she was falling apart, but since the woman Coop had known had always been under control, this new side of her was playing one hell of a game with his head. By the glances he received from Blake and MacGyver, they were concerned about her too.

"We found an insulin pump on the floor."

Good. At least Steve was asking the right questions.

"*Thank you.* I owe you big time. We're about to

land a helicopter on your block. I'll see you in a few."

Coop's gut registered the irritation that filtered through him just below the surface. For a woman who'd only been in Pine Bluff a few weeks, she certainly seemed chummy with Doctor Steve from the next town over. She wasn't going to owe the man anything if Coop had his way. He'd make sure the good doctor received his payment—in greenbacks. And he damn sure wasn't leaving her alone with him.

Really? Jealousy? What the hell is wrong with me? She can pay the doc however she'd like. That's her business. Why did he care, anyway? She'd put him out with the trash some time ago, and just this morning, she'd made it clear whatever future they had wouldn't be together.

The veterinary clinic was on the south edge of town and, when Jade located the correct building, Blake set the copter down in an adjacent empty lot. Coop jumped out and turned to help her from the aircraft. Still holding Moose in her arms, she took off alone toward the rear of the clinic. He'd planned to accompany her in case things didn't go well and she needed someone, but it seemed she had no intention of needing him. He clenched his jaw and pushed down the prickly sensation of irritation.

A trim, dark-haired man in a white lab coat slammed through the clinic's back door and sprinted toward her. He barely looked at the animal she held before he threw his arm around her shoulders. With a familiarity that set Coop's teeth on edge, the doc led her inside the clinic. Anger darkened Coop's mood, and he turned away, stopping abruptly as Blake and MacGyver blocked his path.

"You okay, buddy?" MacGyver appeared concerned, but, beside him, Blake wasn't even trying to hide his shit-eating grin.

He eyed them both before returning his attention to MacGyver. "Why wouldn't I be?"

"No reason. Just checking. I wasn't expecting Steve to be so friendly, that's all." MacGyver turned toward Blake as though waiting for confirmation of his assessment.

Blake nodded. "Must be some history there. I understand you have a fair amount of history with her too."

Was there a challenge in his words? Coop bristled. He liked Blake, but he didn't know him as well as he knew Travis, MacGyver, and the others who'd been in his SEAL unit—who'd been there when her plane went down. Blake had saved MacGyver's life once on a mission gone wrong, and any friend of MacGyver's was a friend of his. But Jade was none of his business. There were boundaries, and Blake was getting close to crossing one.

"What's that supposed to mean?"

MacGyver stepped toward him. "Easy, Coop. We're both just wondering why you're still standing here."

"Right. Where should I be, exactly?"

MacGyver barked a laugh. "You're trying hard to deny what's written all over your face when you look at her. You know that, right?"

"You think you can read me, huh? Well, maybe you can, but I doubt that's giving you any clue to what's going on in my head because all I've got are questions. What the hell happened to her over there? Why didn't anyone contact me when she turned up? Why would she hide from the man who loved her?" His volume had steadily risen as the hurt and anger poured out until his voice broke and stopped his tirade.

Blake was studying the ground at his feet, and Coop almost felt sorry for him. Too much information. MacGyver reached in his back pocket and brought out a leather pouch.

"There's only one way you're going to get answers to those questions. But maybe you don't care. Either way, I'm just looking out for a friend." MacGyver tapped the pouch on the side of his leg. "I guess *I'll* take this to the vet, then."

"Shit!" Coop had entirely spaced the syringe. He ran a hand over his whiskered chin. "Give it to me." It was just the excuse he needed to check on Jade, but hell if he'd admit it to either of those asshats.

He grabbed the pouch from MacGyver and shoved it in his back pocket. Without another word, he turned and strode away, sure his friends were both smirking behind his back. *Damn them.* That was the one bad thing about having buddies who cared whether you lived or died—you couldn't get them to butt out even if you tried. The corner of Coop's mouth pulled upward in a grin. He wouldn't want it any other way.

The receptionist collected payment from a client trying to control a freaked-out standard poodle and didn't look up when he entered. Skirting the counter, he headed for the back. His disregard for protocol got her attention.

"I'll be right with you, sir. If you could just wait…"

He kept moving, only stopping when he heard voices behind a closed examination room door. One of them was Jade's. He rapped on the wooden surface but pushed it open without waiting for an invitation. Stevie-boy's startled gaze darted toward Coop, and his hands dropped from Jade's upper arms as he took a step back.

"Sorry to interrupt, doc." *Not.* Coop forced a stiff smile as he studied her face, curious about the splotch of color that spread to her cheekbones. "I thought you might want to see this." He opened the leather pouch and pulled out the syringe.

"Ah, good." Steve accepted the plastic plunger, with the needle still attached, and turned back to Jade. "We'll need to send this to the lab if you're going to file a police report. We should have the results tomorrow. The best news is he's starting to come around, so the dose wasn't big enough to kill him. We'll make sure he's hydrated and getting enough oxygen. Do some bloodwork to monitor his kidneys. He'll be comfortable and not in any pain. You don't have to worry." The doctor edged toward the door at the back of the examination room. "You can wait here if you like."

The half-assed grin Steve shot him clearly said the offer was only for Jade, which pissed off Coop. He closed the distance and placed an arm around her waist as he returned the doc's glower. "Let's go for a walk. Some fresh air will do you good."

"Yeah, you're right. I need to get out of here for a few minutes." Her eyes were vacant when she faced him, which was good because she probably didn't notice the scowl that quickly passed over Doctor Steve's face before he caught himself.

"Fine. I'll call you if there's any change." Steve gave her a strained smile as he turned to leave the room.

Yep. Blake's right. There is some history. Maybe Coop was in denial, but he couldn't see the woman he'd known falling for a handsy doctor—vet or otherwise.

She preceded him as they strode through the reception area, where the woman behind the counter fixed him with a distrustful stare. *Damn. These people need to lighten up.*

Once outside, Jade veered left toward a couple of livestock pens, one of which held a bay gelding with purple vet wrap covering his fetlock, securing a dressing of some sort around his right front hoof. Except for a flick of his ears, the horse ignored them.

Jade hooked her fingers over the top rail of the corral and laid her forehead against the metal. Coop turned to lean his back into the panel; close enough, he brushed her elbow. A wave of heat traveled up his arm and spread through his entire body. He jammed his hands into his pockets as though that would control his overpowering urge to pull her against him.

"How are you holding up?" He couldn't see her face, hidden by a sheet of silky hair. He reached out to tuck it behind her ear before he realized what he was doing and shoved his hands deeper into his pockets.

She didn't answer for the longest time, but she

finally lifted her head and examined his face. Determination shone through the redness of her eyes. "I'm sorry about what I said back at the house. It's just—I swear to God, if Moose doesn't make it, I'm going to kill that son of a bitch."

The intensity of her declaration sent a chill up his spine. He understood she wasn't easily intimidated. She was much more likely to respond by raining retribution on a man who wouldn't take it lightly. Unless Coop could talk her out of whatever crazy-ass scheme she devised. Short of that, he'd have to kick the shit out of Graves before she got to him. At the very least, he'd make sure she didn't go after Graves alone. "I'll be right there with you." His cover be damned.

She studied him for a few seconds, and whatever she saw must have satisfied her because she nodded once. "Thanks, Coop."

The loneliness in those two words slashed at his midsection, and he couldn't take it anymore. He reached for Jade and pulled her against him. She slid her arms around his waist, tucking her head under his chin where it'd always fit so perfectly. Damned if it wasn't like being home.

Too much stood between them. Coop ached with the knowledge that what they'd had was long gone. He still had this moment, and maybe he could earn back some of the trust Graves had cost him. "What is the meatball—about a year old?"

"Almost two."

"How long have you had him?"

"Since he was six months old." He could hear the smile in her voice as she warmed to the topic.

"Yeah? How'd you end up with him?"

She laughed. "Colonel Reiner gave him to me." Immediately, she tensed and lifted her head, searching his eyes. "This probably isn't something we should get into."

"Why?" He could guess why, and it took fortitude to swallow the bitterness that flared within him.

"I'm sorry I hurt you, Coop."

"Ah. You're afraid you'll hurt me more by talking about the life you led while I thought you were dead." If she only understood how impossible that would be. "Don't worry. There's nothing you can't say to me. Remember how we used to talk things out? That hasn't changed. It never will."

She closed her eyes for a moment, and when she opened them, she focused on his T-shirt, smoothing her hands over the Denver Broncos lettering and logo—and his pecs in the process. She seemed oblivious to his body's reaction to her warm strokes.

Tilting her head, she smiled. "Moose is a service dog, trained to wake me from nightmares. Mark gave him to me because he knew I was having difficulty adjusting to the real world. That dog pulled me back from the edge when I thought I'd go crazy. Now I rely on him far too much. I don't know what I'd do without him."

Did she ever dream of him? Coop's question begged an answer, but he'd gotten nowhere pushing her last night or this morning. There was no reason to think she'd be more forthcoming now, but at least she was talking. He dropped a kiss on the top of her head, thinking better of it after it was already too late.

Still, she didn't pull away.

"It's okay to depend on someone or something. Why do you think I still hang with my old team?" He grinned, relieved when she laughed.

"It's okay until the person or thing you've depended on isn't around anymore." She pushed away from him, turning to lean against the gate beside him. "I'm sorry. I shouldn't be crying on your shoulder. It's not your problem."

He noted the chill in her voice as the shutters keeping him from learning what was going on with her slammed back into place. "That's what friends are for."

"Friends, huh?" She studied his face. "Why are you so nice to me?"

"What *should* I do? Hate you?" He sensed her scrutiny as he turned to watch the two men in the adjacent bare lot, crouched in the shade of the helicopter. Hers was a fair question. He didn't know the answer. "Not likely to ever happen."

She tipped her head as though thinking that over and squinted into the midday sun. "It would make more sense. And it's what Travis would expect."

He grimaced. "That's not who I am. I could never hate you. Travis doesn't hate you either."

She snorted. "You could've fooled me."

"Surprised…pissed…scared about how I'd react to seeing you again—he's all of those things." Coop glanced down to the tips of his boots. "I put him and the rest of the guys through hell after you went missing. They covered for me with the commander daily. Hell, they saved my life."

His intense perusal locked on her again. "I know

you, and I know there had to be a damn good reason you disappeared. I hoped you'd trust me enough to give it to me straight, but I'll find out what you're hiding, one way or another."

Her chin lifted, and she stepped into his personal space. "Leave it alone, Coop. It's no one's business but mine." Determination mixed with despair in her eyes.

"Bullshit." Instant anger erupted with the expletive, and he struggled to reel in his temper. "It sure as hell is my business. How could you possibly think losing you like that wouldn't wreck me? When there was still a chance you'd survived, held hostage, I imagined every foul, deviant act I'd ever heard associated with those barbarians happening to you.

"Then, when they told me you were dead, I agonized over the possible ways it could have happened. Was it quick, or did someone torture you until you screamed as you did in my nightmares every night? I'd have gladly taken your place and died a happy man, knowing you were safe. My life stopped three years ago because I didn't know how to live without you. For a while, I didn't want to live. You wonder why Travis didn't greet you with open arms? That's why."

Great job not spewing vitriolic rage all over her. Even though Coop was aware he was heaping guilt on someone who'd suffered enough, he couldn't stop himself. "Now, when I've finally begun to put the past behind me, you come back from the dead. You don't want to talk about what happened. Fine. I don't need you to supply the answers, sweetheart. That's what I do for a living. But don't ever tell me it's not my business." A gut-deep sorrow flipped his stomach inside out as he strode toward his friends,

CHAPTER TEN

"Yeah? Good luck with that." Jade yelled the words as Coop retreated. It would be quite an achievement if he managed to flush out information the Pentagon, the Air Force, and her father had buried. Since when had Coop been the only one hurt? The need to follow him and make it clear he didn't have a monopoly on pain and loss warred with regret and an illogical yearning for one massive do-over. This time she wouldn't grab her flight gear and lead the final reconnaissance mission or be anywhere near a Russian drone strike that could shred the wing of her F-22, kill her navigator, and force her to eject in no-man's-land.

The official records had been altered, sealed, and a gag order put in place. Mystery shrouded Jade's homecoming to the point not even her sister had learned what really happened. There was nothing for Coop to find.

Her phone played a tune from her back pocket. Grabbing it, she glanced at the veterinarian's name on the display screen, worry overshadowing everything Coop had just thrown at her. She took a few steps toward the back of the clinic as she brought the phone to her ear. "How is he?"

"He's awake, and I'm pretty sure he'd love to see a familiar face."

A relieved laugh bubbled up, sticking near the lump in her throat. Blinking rapidly, she refused the happy tears forming in her eyes. The suffocating sadness that had enveloped her on the flight lifted somewhat, and the ache in her chest diminished. "Thank you so much, Steve." Her hand shook as she swept it through her hair. "I'll be right there."

She lowered the phone and peered across the bare ground to the helicopter, suddenly eager to share the news with Coop. His back was to her, and he appeared to be in deep conversation with MacGyver and Blake. None of them glanced in her direction.

Just as well.

She hurried to the back door and stepped inside the building. Steve beckoned to her from an open doorway and led her into a large room lined on two sides with cages of varying sizes. The doctor pointed to the row of kennels to her right.

Moose, looking too much like a discarded child's toy, lay unmoving in the center of the cage, surrounded by fleece blankets, with an IV taped to one front leg. He looked so small and helpless in the bottom-most cage. A sharp prick of fear pierced her, despite Steve's assurance on the phone.

"Moose?" She barely gave voice to his name. Immediately, his furry little head popped up, and his tail swished twice against his bedding.

"I'm here, buddy." She rushed to the small enclosure, sliding to her knees in front of the door as she worked the latch and pulled it open. Moose struggled to sit up, but he couldn't quite make it, so

Jade tugged his blankets to the edge of the cage floor and sat cross-legged next to him. He snuggled against her leg as she stroked his fur. "You're going to be okay. Good as new." She sucked her bottom lip between her teeth and bit down, hoping the sharp pain would keep her from falling apart. Moose's eyes gradually closed again, and he exhaled slowly as though finally content.

Striding to her side, Steve leaned one hand on the cage above Moose's, reminding her she wasn't alone. She dabbed at the corners of her eyes self-consciously. He'd done her a huge favor by seeing the dog immediately, but Jade didn't know him well enough to let him witness her falling apart. She cleared her throat and lifted her chin, giving him a watery smile. "Are you sure he's okay?"

Steve crouched beside her, so close their shoulders rubbed, and laid his hand on Moose's tiny body. "He's still pretty weak, but you got him here in time. Barring any complications, he should make a full recovery. I drew some blood and sent it off to the lab. That'll tell us if his internal organs are all working properly. We'll monitor him for twenty-four hours, just in case, but you'll be able to take him home after that." The doctor ran his hand over the back of his neck. "There's a cot in the back if you want to stay over."

It was a tempting offer. Not letting Moose out of her sight was an appealing option, but she still had work to do. "I appreciate that, but I need to get back to the kennel. There was a minor catastrophe there right before I found Moose. I need to do some cleanup and get the dogs settled."

"Is everything all right? Do you need help?"

"Thanks, but I can manage." With Coop determined to stay, she'd have enough alpha-male attitude. "Getting back to work will keep me from freaking out about Moose. I'll never be able to thank you. Seriously, I owe you one."

He straightened and offered a hand to help her to her feet. "I'll be out your way in the next couple of weeks. I was hoping maybe we could go to dinner. Unless your overprotective friend has dibs on all of your time?"

The almost-invitation seemed to hang in the silence that followed. Heat rolled across Jade's skin. She stepped back to put some distance between her and the sudden claustrophobia that jangled her nerves.

He seemed like a good guy, but she'd only met him once before when he'd made a house call to the kennel. His friendly flirtation on that occasion had given her self-esteem a boost, and Nic and Ryan's presence had kept her unease in check. Unfortunately, the sad fact was men made her uncomfortable on a good day. On a bad day, when her memories became too vivid, her life could spiral out of control in a heartbeat.

She pulled her hand from Steve's and threaded her fingers together. "I don't know." It was the truth, but she hadn't meant to say it out loud. Now he was looking at her expectantly. "Coop's an old friend. He's visiting for a few days. That's all."

Damn it. Moose's veterinarian didn't need an explanation. It was none of his business. And why the hell did the thought of Coop leaving cause her heart to stutter? Jeez! She was losing it.

Interest flared in Steve's eyes. "Yeah? Then maybe I'll give you a call."

Forcing her focus back to the man in front of her, Jade flashed a quick smile. "That's sweet of you, Dr. Prescott. Unfortunately, I'm not sure what my schedule will be since I'm filling in wherever Ryan needs help." She flipped her hair over her shoulder. "Perhaps we can at least get a cup of coffee."

"Excellent," he said, glancing through the open doorway toward the waiting room. "My next patient just arrived, so I should go. Don't worry about a thing. We'll take good care of Moose, and I promise to call you if anything changes. Stay as long as you like."

Steve grabbed a file from a rack across the hallway and strode away with a smile on his face.

She groaned. Dr. Prescott was a nice man, and under normal circumstances, she might be excited to get to know him better. Blowing him off made her feel guilty, but even saying *yes* to coffee had her apprehension levels on the rise.

What *was* going on between her and Coop, anyway?

Moose was sleeping soundly and, as much as she hated the idea of leaving him, worry for the animals at the kennel won out. She moved the dog away from the opening, tucked the blankets around him, and closed the cage door. *Thank God he's all right. Coffee with Dr. Prescott is the least I can do and probably won't kill me.* Besides, maybe it would be fun. After all, Nicole had said the handsome vet was just what Jade needed.

Leaving from the clinic's rear exit, she nearly opened the door into Coop and MacGyver as they jogged up the ramp.

"There you are." MacGyver greeted her with a lopsided grin.

Coop's expression remained distant. "Is he okay?"

"He's going to be fine. Dr, Prescott wants to keep him for twenty-four hours just to be safe, though." Her gaze skittered to Coop and then away. His irritation was evident in the deep scowl he wore. "I'll drive over and pick him up tomorrow afternoon."

"Drive or fly; you won't be going alone, so get used to the idea." The last part of Coop's statement was no more than a growl before he whipped around and stomped toward the helo.

What the hell? Anger reached the boiling point in a heartbeat. Her chin jutted, and her hands dropped to her hips. "Excuse me? You don't get to tell me what to do. Who the hell do you think you are?" As he kept going, not even glancing back, a string of expletives, reminiscent of the ones often uttered by the men in her squadron, whispered past her lips. The man was infuriating.

At MacGyver's chuckle, she glanced toward him. He was at least three inches taller than Coop and the other team members she'd known. His sheer size would have made him intimidating if not for the smile that seemed permanently etched in his ageless features. As she glared, his grin faded.

"You know he just wants to protect you, right?" MacGyver spoke slowly with the hint of a southern drawl.

"Really? Sounds as though he'd like to kill me himself."

MacGyver shrugged. "Come on, Jade. Give the guy a break. He's still in shock. Yesterday, you were dead."

She ducked her head, kicking at a clump of dirt on the graveled parking lot. "I know. I didn't say I'd blame him if he did." How much longer could she bear the weight of this guilt?

"I always liked you. I thought you were good for Coop because you seemed to *get* him. You know, as well as I do, it's either black or white with him. The guy sees no gray. That's what made him such a damn good SEAL. He doesn't know how to give up. He's loyal to a fault. Once a friend, always a friend. And if he loved you yesterday, he still loves you today."

The words slammed into her. Hell, it was what Coop had been trying to tell her since he stepped out of the darkness onto her porch last night. Dread coiled in her gut. Her attention returned to MacGyver. "He can't."

"I'm not the one you need to convince." MacGyver glanced toward the helo as it came to life, and the rotors slowly began to whirl. "We should get going."

She survived the flight from hell, though why it mattered, she wasn't sure. No one had said a word when she'd climbed in the front with Blake. The quiet she'd hoped for had eluded her, however. Blake turned out to be a talker, and he'd chattered non-stop about her father, the general, and his military career. It'd become obvious Blake was more knowledgeable regarding General McDowell's achievements than she was. Learning how his life and service had influenced another officer should have made her proud. Strangely, the emotion that rose to suffocate her had not been pride.

Once they landed, she couldn't wait to get upstairs, hoping for a few minutes of solitude to regroup. The strangeness of Moose's absence had contributed negatively to her nervousness and irritation. There was no alone time to be had, however.

A delectable aroma and the drone of male voices met her at the top of the stairs. Luke and Travis stood near the open oven, apparently conferring about whatever smelled so good. As she burst into the room, they both swung around. She stopped as her stomach registered the fact she hadn't eaten since this morning. "Hmm...that smells delicious. What are you two cooking?"

Travis leaned toward the sink and dropped a spoon into the sudsy water. Luke stepped back and tossed the mitt he'd been wearing onto the countertop. "Just a couple of pizzas. Nothing fancy, but my wife insists I learn to cook well enough to keep myself from starving."

Travis ducked his head to push the rack inside the oven and closed the door, refusing to look at her. She deserved his snub. He was stubborn and loyal—two characteristics that had served him well in special forces.

Luke and Travis must have shopped because she

hadn't had time to stock up on much of anything but eggs, dogfood, and beer. A grin tugged at her lips. "Wife, huh? Never thought I'd hear that word pass your lips."

"Things change. Keepin' ahold of the ones you love suddenly becomes more important when you think you might have blown your chance." Luke stared as though she was too obtuse to get that he was talking about her also. Everyone had an opinion.

She raised an eyebrow. "Glad to hear it's working out for you."

Downstairs, the front door opened again, and boisterous laughter signaled the SEALs had finished tying down the helo for the wind gusts expected later tonight. Undoubtedly, they all planned to stay in her house. *Oh, good. Testosterone central.*

As MacGyver and Blake filed into the small kitchen, she pulled her cell phone from her pocket and skirted around them toward the stairs. No doubt Coop would be right behind them, and she couldn't face him right now. "Since you seem to have everything under control here, I'm going to see what I can do for the dogs and then call my sister to let her and Ryan know what happened."

"Jade?" The deep, gravelly voice belonged to Travis and stopped her retreat as though her feet had suddenly stuck to the floor. "I'm glad Moose is doing okay. Leaving him there for the night had to suck. I'm sorry."

Someone must have called ahead to inform Travis and Luke of Moose's condition. She turned and searched Travis' face. His regret appeared sincere, though she hadn't expected him to care one way or the other. That he'd taken an interest summoned a burning sensation in her eyes. *Damn it.*

Suppose she hadn't found Moose in time, or the helicopter hadn't been there to rush him to the vet. If Dr. Prescott hadn't ushered Moose into the examination room and started life-saving procedures immediately, the results could have been deadly.

Her heart still felt battered and raw. The what-ifs were killing her. She needed time alone rather than the constant conversation that kept her fear alive.

She respected the effort Travis had expended to speak the words. He was offering an olive branch after his earlier greeting. She tried for a smile but wasn't surprised when it fell flat. "Thanks. I appreciate that." Abruptly, she turned and fled the room, grabbing a sweatshirt from the hook by the door.

The edges of the rolling door, where flames had licked halfway to the top, were blackened with much of the paint peeling away or missing altogether. The guys had knocked down the fire so quickly; the wood had suffered minor damage. Jade took a power washer to the wooden surface until it was as clean as she could get it, then left it to dry in the afternoon heat.

She used the bucket on the tractor and a shovel to remove every scrap of charred shavings from the kennel and dog runs, moving the offending material to a rocky section of the property where nothing grew. While she raked the entryway and pens and spread a layer of fresh-smelling shavings, she washed and dried a dozen dog beds. When all was clean and back where it was supposed to be, she walked the dogs in one at a time, allowing them to smell and check out the place that had been so scary only a few hours ago.

The three dogs who'd been closest to the flames were visibly nervous when they entered, so Jade put them in pens that were the farthest away. With fresh water in their buckets, extra food in their dishes, and worn out from several hours of playtime, they all eventually settled in contentedly.

She found Nicole's stash of leftover paint and applied a coat of cougar brown to the doors that were now clean and dry. By the time the sun was sinking toward the horizon, her body was physically and mentally exhausted and covered with dirt, sawdust, charcoal, and paint. The kennel looked good, and that's what mattered—that and keeping her mind off the group cluster awaiting her in the upstairs apartment. She wasn't looking forward to going inside where machismo would no doubt be ankle-deep by now.

And Coop is there.

She shook her head as though by the mere gesture of denial, she could make them all disappear. That wouldn't happen, of course, but she'd be damned if she'd let them chase her from her home, even if it was only a temporary refuge.

She straightened, stretching the soreness out of her back before closing the paint can and setting it aside. After putting away the last of her tools, she swiped futilely at the paint on her hands and reached for her cell phone as she started toward the house.

Joining the men, without even the grounding presence of Moose, wasn't the only thing she'd been dreading. She'd procrastinated as long as she could, but the time had come to call her sister. Nic was already having trouble dealing with emotions in the aftermath of her injury. Wait until she heard the news about the kennel fire and Moose's poisoning. For a few seconds, Jade weighed the pros and cons of keeping the incident under wraps for the time being.

With a heavy sigh, she rejected the idea. Nic and Ryan had a right to know their business had been targeted and to make whatever decisions they deemed appropriate considering the events.

The phone awoke in her hand with a rumbling vibration, and she nearly dropped the device. She smiled when a picture of Nicole filled the screen, and she accepted the call. "Hey, Nic. I was just about to call you. I've got something to tell—"

"Is it true, Jade? Did Graves and his minions set fire to the kennel and poison your dog? Why didn't you call me? Why did I have to hear about it from the district attorney?" The bitterness of accusation rang in her sister's voice.

"What? How did he find out?"

"He overheard two of Carl Graves' men bragging about it in front of the courthouse. Standish wants to put Ryan and me in protective custody until after the trial. He said we aren't safe!" Nicole barely paused. "How bad is it, Jade? Are the dogs all right? Is Moose okay? And you? I was so scared something had happened to you. I mean—what other reason would you have not to call me?" Nicole was clearly beyond anger, bordering on hysteria.

"Everything's okay, Nic. I'm sorry. You're right. I should have called right away." So, Graves *was* behind the fire and Moose's poisoning. His followers were so arrogant; they didn't care who knew. Nicole had every right to be mad as hell. Jade clamped her mouth shut on the excuses poised on the tip of her tongue.

"The dogs are all fine. Fire damage to the building was minor. They were happy to spend the afternoon in the play yard while I cleaned up any trace of the fire." She forged ahead, hoping to make amends for her delay. "Moose is spending the night at the veterinary clinic, but he's going to be fine too. I know you should have heard about it from me, Nic. I just wanted to put things back the way they were so I could tell you the kennel was just the way you left it, and there's nothing to worry about."

Nicole's sigh came through the phone. "Okay."

Why did Jade get the feeling things were far from okay?

"That bastard, Graves, isn't getting away with this. He can do whatever he wants to me, but when he starts hurting the people I love, that's too much. Who's he going to attack next? Ryan? I was thinking of sitting this one out and not testifying, but after what happened today, you better believe I'll be in that courtroom." Nic's volume continued to rise.

"Calm down, Nic. Ryan can take care of himself, and so can I. You're getting yourself all worked up for nothing. Things will look different in the morning. Talk to your husband. Where is Ryan anyway?" Why wasn't he diffusing his wife's anger?

"He had a couple of deliveries to make after he

closed the store. He'll be back after a while, but this can't wait. If I don't push back on Graves, he'll think he can get away with even more. I'm going to have a little chat with him."

"This isn't about pushing boundaries. Graves is bad news. Don't go anywhere near him. Wait for Ryan to get home. Okay?" Fear started to prickle the hairs on the back of Jade's neck. She hastened her steps, veering toward the garage where her Jeep Wrangler was parked.

"This is something I have to do. You should understand. You'd do the same thing."

"Wait for me, then. We'll go together." It was too late. Jade was pleading with dead air. Nicole had hung up on her. *Shit!*

She broke into a run as she redialed, but the call went straight to voice mail. Dread mushroomed with each stride as she sprinted the remaining two hundred feet. Nicole losing her hot-headed temper and doing something foolish was what Jade had feared. Nic was a force to be reckoned with when she got in someone's face.

Carl Graves was dangerous, however. Coop had insinuated the man had no scruples. Nic planned to walk in and demand he leave her and her family alone. She had no idea of the danger the man presented. Graves wasn't the type to be persuaded by words. Jade groaned though she wanted to scream. As soon as she'd returned from the vet, she should have called Nic and warned her about Graves. Jade could have kept this from happening.

Jerking open the side door of the two-car garage, she barreled toward her Wrangler. Luckily, the keys were still in her pocket from when she'd planned to drive Moose to the vet. She slipped them out, started the Jeep, and hit the button on her visor to raise the overhead door. As it ground upward, she yanked open the glove compartment and rifled through the contents for her 9mm semi-auto handgun, but it wasn't there. *Damn.* That's right—she'd taken it out and found a safe place to keep it in her bedroom where she could get to it quickly if it became necessary.

Should she take the time to go inside and retrieve a weapon? Maybe tell Coop or someone what was going on and ask for backup?

For a few heartbeats, she remained motionless, debating her course though she was wasting precious time. Any minute her sister might walk into a horrible situation. If Jade arrived in time, she could prevent the debacle that would likely ensue. No doubt Coop would help if asked, but was it wise to depend on him? There'd be no question if she hadn't accidentally run into him yesterday. She'd been taking care of herself for a long time, and that wasn't likely to change.

Intimately acquainted with loneliness, she preferred solitude to the company of swine like Mahaz Bashara, the vile piece of garbage who'd captured and enslaved her for eight long months. He'd taught her that brutality had no bottom and that the power of hate was a double-edged sword.

With a shake of her head, she snapped back to the present, forcing the nightmarish memory from her mind. Why had Mahaz appeared so vividly now, when she should only be concentrating on reaching her sister?

Shifting the Jeep's transmission into reverse, she backed out of the garage, accelerating slightly before stepping on the brake. The rear of the lightweight vehicle spun around until it was facing away from the garage. She'd call Coop when and if she needed him. Decision made, she moved the shift lever to drive and floored the gas pedal, spinning out and flinging gravel in her wake.

CHAPTER ELEVEN

"Roberts says he hasn't received a report about a hit and run in the area or an accident involving a woman. Are you sure you got the story straight?" Travis shoved his cell phone into his pocket and took a seat on one of the stools, elbows braced on the top of the breakfast bar.

Coop leaned against the kitchen counter across from his friend, fingers jammed in his front pockets. Noah Roberts, special agent in charge of the FBI investigation into public corruption and murder in the small community of Pine Bluff, was a good man. PTS Security had worked with him before, and Roberts had proven to be thorough and capable. If he said there was no report, Coop wasn't going to argue the point.

Assessing the doubt on his partners' faces, he easily read their reservations. *Could Jade be trusted?* He frowned, refusing to dig too deep through his churning emotions. *Hell no.* It'd be a cold-ass day in July before he trusted her again, but he believed her about her sister. The fear she'd exhibited that morning hadn't been fake.

"Humor me, will you? She has no reason to lie or embellish the truth. Let's assume it went down just the way she said. Her brother-in-law, Ryan, reported the incident to the county sheriff who, supposedly, notified the state police." Coop dropped his hands to his hips. "OSP knows there's a federal investigation going on, yet the report didn't find its way to the Bureau."

"Law enforcement agencies argue over jurisdiction all the time. Maybe someone doesn't want the Bureau taking center stage." Luke strolled into the kitchen and went for the coffee, pouring himself another cup before topping off the others' lukewarm brew. "Seems a little too convenient, but it's possible."

Coop stifled a yawn. It'd been a long night and an even longer day. Striding to the counter, he seated himself on the stool beside Travis. At least his gut had finally settled from the excess alcohol he'd imbibed. He was a little hungry, and the smell of Luke and MacGyver's pizza had earned his attention. Everyone else had eaten a while ago. He hadn't trusted his stomach, so he'd stuck with water, trying to flush the last of the whiskey from his system. Now, he was waiting for Jade to finish working in the kennel and return to the house. It didn't feel right to let her eat by herself in her own home.

He'd sensed she needed to be alone after they got back from the vet clinic. He hadn't been surprised when she grabbed an old sweatshirt and a pair of gloves and headed for the kennel. Reluctantly, he'd let her go, but that hadn't kept him from worrying about her all afternoon. Hell, a couple of times, he'd sneaked close enough in the shadow of other outbuildings and trees to prove to himself she was okay. *Damn it. I'll get a cussin' if Jade finds out I spied on her.*

MacGyver turned away from the window where he and Blake took turns surveilling the front of the house. He joined the others at the breakfast bar. "After supper, I'll do some digging on the local law enforcement. Maybe we'll get lucky and learn something we don't already know."

A vibration caught Coop's attention. He looked up to see Travis glancing around as though he felt it too. Coop frowned as the sensation became an audible rumble.

Travis held his hand up, commanding silence. "What the hell *is* that? Thunder?"

Whatever it was, it sounded as though it was right on top of them. Coop turned his head slowly, trying to pinpoint the source of the noise. An instant later, he leaped to his feet and rushed toward the window that overlooked the parking area. Travis was close on his heels. The growl of a vehicle's engine, the whine of rapid acceleration, and the ricochet of gravel off his Dodge Ram shot adrenaline straight to his heart.

"Jesus! Is that Jade? Where the hell's she headed in such an all-fired hurry?" Travis peered around him at the retreating taillights.

"Shit!" Coop darted for the stairs and loped down them two at a time. Jade was hauling ass, and why was anyone's guess. Three possibilities came to mind. Moose might have taken a turn for the worse, or something could have happened to her sister, or perhaps Jade had tired of being a victim and set her sights on revenge. The last one chilled his blood.

Once outside, he sprinted to his pickup, vaguely aware someone was keeping pace with him. When Travis jerked open the passenger door and hopped in with a lopsided grin, Coop arched an eyebrow and stared at him blankly.

Travis smirked. "I was getting bored."

I knew he'd come around. Coop's mood lightened for a heartbeat until he cranked the ignition, slammed the truck in gear, and spun the vehicle around on the loose gravel to follow Jade. He caught sight of her taillights as she veered a crazy ninety-degree turn onto the county road.

"Damn. We better boogie if you want to catch her." Travis quickly buckled his seatbelt as Coop gave the Dodge more gas on the straight stretch and fishtailed the truck's rear end.

He couldn't fathom what was going on in her head, but he could cross Moose off his list as the reason for her bolting. She'd turned right toward Pine Bluff—not Baker City. Whatever it was that had set her off, she was on a mission, and he had a bad feeling.

No headlights were coming in either direction when he intersected the county road. Working both the gas and the brake pedal, he followed Jade's example, whipping the wheel and sliding onto the pavement without stopping. Accelerating, he lost sight of her vehicle as she started into a segment of tight curves.

Travis grasped his cell phone from the pocket of his hoodie. "Do you have her number?"

"Good idea, partner, but the answer is no. I didn't see much of a future in exchanging numbers."

He glanced at Travis with a shrug before focusing toward the front again.

The skeptical look on Travis' mug plainly said he wasn't buying the act. Coop gripped the steering wheel harder. He couldn't face his best friend. He didn't have time to convince Travis—or himself—he was handling this after mourning Jade for three damn years. That part of his life was over and done. If he couldn't grasp that reality, there was nothing to keep him from sliding off the edge into the same abyss he'd narrowly escaped before.

They were gaining on the Jeep. With racing suspension and performance tires, the Dodge Ram hugged the curves Jade had slowed to navigate. When she tore through the first traffic signal in the city limits without stopping for the red light, they were only about three hundred feet behind.

He braked sharply and pulled to the curb.

Travis swiveled toward him, are-you-crazy painted all over his face. "What the—what's going on, bro? We almost had her."

Travis knew him better than that. Coop had left indecision behind in the first week of BUD/s when he'd watched three hundred young, single-minded recruits just like himself ring that bell and give up on becoming a SEAL. He wasn't a quitter, and he'd decided he'd die before he rang that bell.

He'd die before he gave up on Jade too.

"Coop? What are we doing here, bro?" Travis' voice dumped him back in the present.

He flipped on his blinker, even though there was no one else around, and moved into the driving lane. At the light, he turned left, away from where Jade's taillights had disappeared. Travis' growl told Coop precisely what he thought.

"If she's gone vigilante, she'll be looking for Carl Graves. I know where he is, so rather than being two steps behind, I figure we'll head over to the feed store and wait."

"Where do you think she's going now?"

Coop chuckled. "My guess is she's recruiting her big-ass brother-in-law to help. If there's a fight, your job will be to convince him we're on the same side."

Travis snickered. "While you take care of the woman? Sounds about right."

Coop only grinned and refused to take the bait.

Fifteen minutes later, parked in the next block away from the feed store, he peered through the front windshield of the pickup with a pair of night vision binoculars. No one had moved on either side of the street. Beside him, Travis typed a text message to Luke and the rest of the team.

The moon, nearly full, peeked through intermittent clouds for a few minutes at a time before disappearing again. The feed store sat in the middle of the block, immediately across from the brick courthouse. An appliance store, a barbershop, and a bank all sat silent and dark, closed for the day. Together with three vacant buildings, the street wasn't giving off a welcome vibe.

Early on, Graves had blacked out his commandeered headquarters' front windows, insuring privacy for their late-night meetings. Next, he'd disabled the streetlights, leaving the entire block in shadows from dusk to dawn.

"Anything?" Travis sent the text message and laid his phone on the dashboard.

Coop shook his head. "Nothing."

"Are you sure Jade will show?"

"Yeah." Coop hoped the hell he was wrong, but the hairs prickling along the back of his neck told him otherwise.

Travis' cell vibrated, and he grabbed the device as the face lit up. After scanning the message, he passed it to Coop.

Black Hawk inbound to field south of town. Ready for extraction to safe house if necessary.

Hell, he'd spaced the safe house, the coordinates for which had been programmed into his GPS ap before he left San Diego. Every undercover gig PTS Security worked had one just in case. His lapse was one more piece of evidence that Jade's unexpected appearance had rearranged his brain cells, and he was no longer thinking clearly enough to be an asset to the operation.

A movement in the dark drew his attention to the street, and he quickly handed the phone back to Travis. At first, the binoculars yielded no sign of anything having changed, but as he searched the shadows, he finally noticed a thin stream of light escaping from the feed store's doorway. Almost immediately, a vehicle turned down the street, its headlights cutting a swath through the darkness straight toward them. Coop and Travis both ducked, even though there was no way the occupants of the other car could spot them a block and a half away.

"Is that her?" Travis reached for the door latch.

"I don't think so. That's not Jade's Jeep. It looks like a late-model sedan."

As the car pulled to the curb in front of the feed store, the partially opened door was flung wide. Two men Coop recognized from Graves' crew half pushed, half carried a struggling woman toward the vehicle, her hands tied behind her back. He tensed. At a distance, in the dark, she could have been Jade except for her light-colored hair visible in the glow of his night vision glasses. It had to be Jade's sister, and this was no doubt why she'd sped away from the kennel. Damn it! Why hadn't she asked for help?

Hell, he knew why. He'd as much as told Jade she'd already caused him enough trouble.

Another man jumped from the front passenger seat and opened the rear door, slamming it shut after the first two shoved the woman inside. As soon as the passenger slipped back into the front seat, the car lurched away from the curb and sped down the street toward Coop's truck. This time he and Travis ducked until they went by.

He opened the door and stepped out, leaning to grab his jacket from the backseat.

"What's the plan, bro?" Travis eyed him as Coop shrugged into the dark coat.

"Take the truck. Follow the sedan. I'm sure that was Jade's sister, Nicole. They probably don't have anything good planned for her." He hesitated for a fraction of a second, studying his friend. Had Travis lost trust in him and his leadership abilities? It was fair to say, Coop's confidence in himself had suffered. Relief surged through him when Travis nodded and climbed across the cab to the driver's seat with no trace of doubt in his expression.

"I'll wait for Jade. She should be along any minute and walk into a similar trap unless I stop her. The safe house is the answer for both, although Jade won't be happy. Keep in touch. Coordinate with Luke and watch your six."

"Keep your eyes and ears open, bro, and don't do anything I wouldn't." Travis grinned, seemingly eager for the battle. He was always a little crazy once the adrenaline started flowing.

Coop started to issue a warning, but the door closing cut him off. He gave a quick wave instead before he stepped back, blending into the shadows. He didn't have to say it—Travis would do whatever it took to keep Nicole's captors from harming her. There wasn't a better man for the job.

His Dodge rumbled awake. Travis made a tight U-turn and hightailed it to the end of the block before flipping on his lights.

Coop surveyed the street to see if anyone had been alerted by the engine noise. All was quiet again. He had few options except to act as though he belonged there on the darkened street, so he shoved his hands into his pockets and walked briskly. At each recessed doorway, he stopped, watching and listening, until the silence pushed him onward to the next building, where he paused and repeated the process. Gradually he worked his way past the feed store on the opposite side of the street.

He slowly scanned the area. If he were Jade, he'd park out of sight and approach from the west, bringing the muscle-bound brother-in-law for backup. They'd both be armed, and Ryan would likely shoot first and then ask questions. Coop's success in averting another kidnapping would depend on the element of surprise and how quickly he could convince Jade to trust him. It wasn't much of a plan, but it would have to be enough.

He studied the storefronts ahead before he ducked out of sight between two buildings. The block's last structure was a bank with double-glass doors and a small alcove with an ATM. He'd be able to watch the entire block from there, just in case his assumptions were wrong. Doubt sought to blast holes in his tenuous plan. Sure, he was leaving other avenues of access open—the east end of the block and almost certainly an alley—to name only a couple. Still, his gut told him this was the safest approach to the feed store and, therefore, the one Jade would choose.

A cloud slid across the moon as he stepped back onto the sidewalk and strode toward the bank. The dismal lighting and shadows that lined the building made it seem uninviting. Coop headed for the darkest corner.

He'd gone about twenty feet when the sound of a pump-action shotgun froze him in mid-stride.

CHAPTER TWELVE

"Why are you here, Coop?"

"Damn it, Jade! I'm trying to catch up with *you*." He started to swing around when the pressure of a gun barrel in his ribs caused him to abort.

"Easy does it," Ryan growled. "Get your hands up where I can see 'em."

Coop swore under his breath as he gradually raised his arms.

"Now, turn around…slowly." From the sound of Ryan's voice, the man had wisely backed up a few paces.

Coop pivoted until the man and his shotgun came into view. Jade, her expression shuttered, stood at the big man's elbow.

"Okay, now remove the weapon JD tells me you're carrying, set it on the ground, and kick it away." Ryan motioned with the barrel of the shotgun.

Coop shook his head. "Sorry. I won't do that." Hopefully, betting on Jade to keep her brother-in-law from using that shotgun wouldn't turn out to be the worst mistake he'd ever made.

A scary smile spread across Ryan's face. "Then give me one good reason why I shouldn't shoot you."

At least he seemed willing to talk. "I have

information about your wife." Coop's focus shifted to Jade. "Why'd you run off like that? If your sister was in danger, do you think I'd refuse to help you? I'm on your side."

A humorless snicker escaped Ryan. "We're supposed to trust you on your say so?"

Coop lowered his hands to his hips, keeping them visible so the man would have no opportunity to mistake his intent. "You seem like a smart guy, Ryan. I get it. You don't know me and have no reason to trust me under the circumstances."

He studied Jade's furrowed brow, but still, her thoughts weren't obvious. She'd always been good at hiding them when she tried. "On the other hand, your sister-in-law knows me. She's a fair judge of character except maybe when it comes to—."

Coop zipped it just in time. Bringing his opinion of her father into this wouldn't be a wise move. He'd made that mistake once before, and he'd never seen her so fired up. He couldn't help but smile while the memory of their hot make-up sex injected new urgency into his query. "What do *you* think, Jade. Can you trust me?"

She took longer than he would have liked considering his question. How damn hard could it be? Either she did, or she didn't. "I know where your sister is."

He heard her quick inhalation just as Ryan lunged for him, pinning him against the building, the shotgun uncomfortably close to his throat.

"Where is she? If you've hurt her, I'll kill you."

Ryan was all muscle and sufficiently motivated, but he wasn't savvy in the ways of hand-to-hand combat. The anger that sparked in his eyes was, undoubtedly, the only thing keeping his panic in check. Coop could relate. If he were in the man's shoes, he'd take on an army to get his woman back. Unfortunately, his empathy presented a problem. He didn't want to hurt the guy, but Ryan was wasting precious time. Coop needed to gain the upper hand without crushing Ryan's larynx, breaking any bones, or causing permanent damage. He *was* Jade's family, after all.

"Please call off your guard dog, Jade, before someone gets hurt."

The steel edge to his voice must have alerted her. "It's okay, Ryan. We can trust him. He's going to help us. Right, Coop?"

Ryan growled and raised a beefy forearm to press against Coop's throat with the weight of his two hundred plus pounds. "You might trust the son of a bitch, JD, but I don't. I'll back off when he tells us where Nicole is."

Coop stared silently into Ryan's eyes. Unlike Jade's, with her unreadable features, Ryan's expression telegraphed what was driving him. Fear for Nicole, whom he loved with a fierceness that made him capable of killing if necessary. Coop's gut told him Ryan was a good man, provoked to violence by the threat to his wife.

"Listen to me. You want Nicole back unharmed. So does Jade. To make that happen, we need to work together. I'm going to help you find your wife." Coop could almost see the wheels turning as Ryan evaluated his words.

"He's telling the truth, Ryan." Jade got in his

face, her hand on his shoulder. "You were right about Coop and me. I've known him for a long time. If he says he wants to help Nic, he means it. Give me the shotgun. Okay?"

Ryan hadn't taken his attention off Coop, and now an ounce of vulnerability broke through his tough exterior. "Why? Why would you help us?"

Coop held the big man's gaze. "I'd do anything within my power for Jade. You're her family, so that includes you now." The truth of his words struck a chord somewhere deep inside.

For a moment, Ryan didn't move, but his desperate eyes revealed confusion and indecision as he weighed backing off with his understandable need to punch someone. Finally, he pushed away from Coop, grumbled something indistinguishable, and shoved the shotgun into Jade's hands. Raking shaky fingers through his hair, he turned his back and stomped to the edge of the sidewalk. She followed, resting her hand on his arm as she spoke in a low voice, obviously not intended for Coop's ears.

He gave them a minute, then broke into their conversation. "We better get off the street before we're spotted by the wrong people. Where are you parked?"

"A block over." She turned, tipping her head toward the south. Neither of them moved. "Where's Nic?"

"I might have exaggerated a bit about knowing where she is, but I know where she isn't. I saw two of Grave's musclemen drag her out of his headquarters, toss her in a car, and take off about ten minutes ago."

"Son of a bitch!" Ryan whirled around. "They took her? And you just watched them? If you wanted to help, why didn't you stop them?"

Ryan was furious enough to break something, but Coop let him vent and focused on Jade as devastation broke through her stoic façade. His first impulse was to fold her in his arms and kiss away her fears. Instead, he raised his hands as though he could stave off her anxiety.

"It's not as bad as it sounds. Travis took my truck and went after them. You know Travis." He let a grin stir the corners of his mouth. "He's probably made them wish they'd chosen another profession by now."

Clearly, she hadn't forgotten Travis' rep because she nodded as the hint of a smile eased the shadows on her face. She studied him as she spoke to her brother-in-law. "Nic will be all right, Ryan. We need to trust Coop and his friends. Okay?"

Ryan still stared, his hands balled into fists. Coop understood. The man wouldn't be okay until he held his wife in his arms. Coop had asked for and received Jade's trust, and he'd even gotten a smile from her—almost. *One step at a time.* Despite warning himself not to read too much into her cooperation, he felt lighter than he had in a long time.

"Let's go. As soon as we find your ride, I'll text Travis, and we'll know what we have to do next." This time, he didn't hesitate. He took off at a brisk jog in the direction Jade had indicated. Soon, he heard matching footsteps behind him and a heavier set farther back.

She caught up to him and kept pace. "Thanks for

being patient with Ryan. He wouldn't hurt a soul."

Coop snorted a laugh. "When someone threatens his woman, I wouldn't bet on that."

As they rounded the corner, her Jeep came into view, and they slowed to a walk to let Ryan catch up. Coop pulled out his phone and tapped out a message to Travis.

Status? Jade and company secured.

Only a few seconds went by before the reply came through.

What took you so long? On our way to the rendezvous point.

Coop grinned. "He's got her. She's safe."

Ryan turned away and leaned his arms on the vehicle. He bowed his head, and his broad shoulders slumped.

Jade dropped back a step, and a soft laugh issued from her lips. A genuine smile lit up her eyes, and they sparkled the way he remembered when she was *his*. Slowly, she approached him until she was close enough to place the palm of her hand over his heart. "Thank you!"

The gesture of love from so long ago, so familiar, ripped at the scarred edges of his heart and stilled his tongue. Every time their respective duties had separated them, her touch on his chest had been part of their goodbye, wrapping in all the worry that came with knowing something could go wrong and that this might be the final farewell. It meant she trusted him to return no matter what, and if she was the one leaving, she promised to do everything in her power to find her way back.

Does she remember? She stood so close; he

couldn't help but clasp her around the waist and haul her against him. The softness and the scent of her dulled the memory of the years that had come between them. It felt right when she burrowed into his neck. Immediately, his dick reacted as her eyelashes fluttered beneath his ear, and her proximity warmed his cheek. The relief of finally being where he belonged warred with the two-ton elephant in the room.

Against all odds, she *had* found her way back, but she hadn't returned to him. He wouldn't know she was alive now if PTS Security hadn't taken a job that landed him in the same town as her. This, right now, was gratitude for her sister's safety. Mistaking it for anything else would only make him the fool again.

Suddenly, he needed to hide how hopelessly he clung to the past. He stepped back until Jade stood at arm's length, choosing to ignore the look of embarrassment that replaced her smile. "No need to thank me. It was all Travis."

She frowned. "I'm sorry. I didn't mean to make you uncomfortable."

"That's not it. I'm just realistic." His reaction wasn't about her display of appreciation. It was strictly self-preservation, a response Travis would approve of, and one Coop was strangely ambivalent about adopting. His past and present had collided in a spectacular shit show. If he ever hoped to reclaim the pitiful life he'd pulled from the ashes, he had to hold on until the show was over.

The silence stretched while she dragged her gaze from his and turned away.

Well, that was smooth, asshole. Somehow, Coop resisted the nearly overwhelming urge to go after her and apologize. *For what? The truth?*

Ryan flew out of the front seat before Jade came to a complete stop. Coop climbed from the backseat and strode slowly toward his friends gathered around the helicopter. He was in no hurry to witness Ryan's reunion with the woman he so obviously cherished. *Jealous much? Any day now, I'm going to tighten down the screws on my life and move on.* Right. That was almost funny, seeing as how finding Jade alive had moved that day a hell of a lot further out.

MacGyver examined Nicole's injuries near the bird, but she struggled to her feet as soon as she saw her husband. Limping and cradling her casted wrist against her stomach with one arm, she came to meet him.

Ryan crushed the petite woman against him, then seemed to remember her injuries. He shoved her away for a moment, only to pull her in again for a long kiss.

I guess true love does exist for some people. Coop hadn't seen a PDA so genuine since Blake and Tori hooked up three months ago. Lately, his single friends had been dropping like ripe fruit in September. Before that, it was MacGyver and Kellie, and before that, Luke and Sally. Tori and Sally both had children. Six-year-old Isaiah and ten-year-old Jen. When they all got together, they were one big, happy family. They always included Coop in their activities, which he appreciated the hell out of, so he invariably swallowed his pride and tried to forget he didn't belong anymore.

Thinking of Isaiah and Jen made him grin, and when he glanced at Jade, walking beside him, she smiled in response.

"Thanks, Coop. I don't know what Ryan would have done if he'd lost Nicole." Exhaustion was apparent in her glazed eyes and jerky movements. It'd been a shitty day, and it wasn't over yet.

"Happy to help. Like I told Ryan, I'd do anything for you, and isn't that pathetic?" He frowned as he focused his attention on the aircraft ahead.

She kept pace with him in silence for a few steps. "I don't want to fight with you anymore." It was more of a request than a statement, and the defeat in her voice worried him.

He stopped and turned to study her. "I don't want to fight with you either." A truce wasn't going to happen any time soon, however. Not considering the argument they were about to have when he told her she and Nicole were on their way to a safe house. He resumed walking toward the group of people standing near the helo.

"Do you think we could have a cease-fire on snarky comments and try to play nice?" It appeared she wasn't ready to let the subject rest.

"No more snark works for me." He divided his attention between her and Luke, who had entered into a tense conversation with Ryan and Nicole.

Suddenly, Nicole's voice rose loud enough for him to hear. "No, I won't do that!" She backed out of the circle and would have walked away if Ryan hadn't caught her hands. They spoke quietly but earnestly as they huddled close a few steps from the other men. Could it be Ryan agreed with their plan to move the women to the safe house indefinitely?

Abruptly, Nicole jerked free. "No way! I'm not leaving you here alone. Don't you dare ask me." Tears rimmed her eyes.

Travis stepped toward her. "It's the only place that's safe for you right now. Graves won't stop just because a stranger took you away from two of his men tonight."

"I appreciate your help, but I'm not leaving my husband or my sister.

When Travis glanced his way, Coop gave a slight shake of his head. He hadn't had time to bring up their plan to Jade, nor was he ready for the argument that would surely follow. Unsurprisingly, the sisters weren't all that different.

Jade hurried the last few steps and put her arm around Nicole's waist. "I understand how you feel, but their idea has some merit. You'd be safe, and Graves won't be expecting you to disappear when the trial is about to start. I'd like to see his ugly face when he hears you're gone." She laughed, and Nicole offered a faint smile in return, but it was clear she was far from convinced.

"You scared us tonight, Nic." Jade slid her other arm around Ryan. "Promise me you'll never do something so foolish again."

Coop had to smile. She hadn't shared why her sister was somewhere accessible for Graves' men to snatch, but she assumed the role of a stern mother like a pro.

"That's for damn sure." Ryan crossed his arms

and fixed a glare on Coop. "Are you sure you can protect her at your so-called safe house?"

"Guaranteed." Judging by the distrust directed toward him, it didn't appear likely Ryan would ever forgive him for the altercation at his store.

The man laughed skeptically.

Nicole straightened with some difficulty and popped her hands on her narrow hips. "Ryan West, don't be thinking you get to decide where I go and don't go. Read. My. Lips. I'm staying with you."

"Please just think about this." A frown drew Jade's brows together.

Ryan scraped a hand over his face, scrutinizing each of the men, finally stopping on Luke. "You got room for two?"

"We'll make room," Luke replied.

"Okay, we'll both go."

Nicole appeared speechless only for a second. "What about the store?"

Ryan shrugged his massive shoulders. "I'll arrange for John & Larry Ames to fill in. They haven't been working, anyway, since Graves took over the feed store. It's about time we had ourselves a little vacation."

Nicole's eyes widened, and she flagged her hand in her sister's direction. "What about Jade? We can't leave her."

"What do you think, JD?" Ryan flashed her a grin.

Shit! Now he'll have both of them tossing out objections. Coop braced himself.

Jade studied Ryan for a moment, then turned toward Coop. "Can I bring Moose?"

He buried his surprise beneath a layer of relief. "Sure. We'll pick up the meatball tomorrow just like we planned." *Hell, somewhere pigs must be flying. Since when does Jade McDowell give in without a fight?*

CHAPTER THIRTEEN

Coop's pickup rumbled to life, and the lively lyrics and pop/rock vibe of Taylor Swift's newest release streamed from the speakers. He adjusted the heater, turned off the radio, and silence settled over them.

Leaving the kennel, with its small upstairs apartment, was more challenging than Jade had imagined. Her temporary home had become her safe place. Now, here she was, running away. Hiding. Not even waiting for Moose to get well enough to go with her. Taking off without her little shadow was like scooping out a piece of her heart and leaving it behind. Much like being freed from hell and then deserting Coop without saying a final goodbye. That realization made her want to hit something. She threaded her fingers together in her lap instead.

"Are you worried about the meatball? Don't be. We'll retrieve him tomorrow just like we planned." His confident grin did little to make her feel better.

She forced a smile and turned away when he pursed his lips as though he could see right through her. He'd been nothing if not considerate since she agreed to go with Nic to the safe house. With patience she hadn't known he possessed, he'd helped her pack a few essentials and some clothes for Ryan and her sister and then for herself. It would be all kinds of wrong to take out her frustrations on him.

They'd stopped at Coop's motel long enough for him to grab his duffle bag. It had been already packed and ready to go. He'd been telling the truth about leaving for home when the rest of his team arrived. Not that she'd doubted him. He'd never lied to her before. Once he got them settled at the safe house, would he retreat from the emotional gut-punch she represented? She was beyond grateful he was willing to help Nicole, but once the immediate danger had passed, she wouldn't blame him if he left and never looked back.

There were other, more pressing worries. Nicole might have died tonight if Travis hadn't ruined her abductors' plan. Thank God he'd been there. Jade's apprehension lightened marginally, knowing he was taking care of Nic and Ryan.

The helicopter, carrying her family, Travis, and Blake, had lifted off about two hours ago from the field south of town. From inside the cab of Coop's truck, she'd watched it go, staring at the red, green, and white anti-collision lights until they faded into the distance. Now that she and Coop were on their way, she could relax.

Despite the truce they'd agreed on, tension thickened around them. The silence in the cab finally became more than Jade could stand. "Won't Graves be suspicious if you're gone?"

He hesitated, then ducked his head and rubbed his hand across the back of his neck. "Graves expects me to stick with you. If you skipped town without me following, I'd have a lot more questions to answer."

"What are you? My stalker?" She laughed nervously. Even though she'd decided to trust him, his confession once again stirred her doubts.

"I didn't care for the threats Derek was making, so I told him you were mine and to keep his hands off."

She jerked toward him. "Threats toward me?"

He nodded. "Staking my claim worked for a while, but then he opened his big mouth at a meeting in front of Graves who thought it was a great idea that I get close to you. I'd be in a position to keep him in the loop if you decided to do something stupid." He glanced at her and shrugged. "If I'd let you and your sister slip through my fingers, it would've ended my usefulness in Graves' eyes. So, I could either bug out and go home or go to the safe house. I chose to go with you and help Travis secure the house after everyone's settled."

"Oh." *I sort of told him you were mine?* His words, echoing in her mind, warmed her heart, despite the certainty he hadn't meant them. He'd told Derek a lie to keep her safe. It was natural for him to look out for people. That was his nature, but maybe he didn't despise her.

She suddenly became aware of the expectant silence and wasn't sure how long she'd been in her head while he'd waited for her to—what? Get angry because he was taking care of her when she didn't need or want him? That's probably what the old Jade would have done.

"I should thank you. I'm sorry you blew your cover because of me."

He glanced toward her, a hint of surprise revealed in his raised eyebrows. "Don't be. I'm happy not to have to cover for Derek anymore. What a douchebag."

He grinned, and she couldn't help the laugh that burst from her lips. There was the easy-going Coop she used to know. Maybe, if she could keep him talking, their truce could work, and the ride to the safe house wouldn't seem so long.

"I'm surprised you left the SEALs. You loved that job." The instant the words were out, she wanted them back. She cringed as they hung in the crackling tension for a moment. Was the reason he'd quit interwoven with her disappearance?

He stared straight ahead, his grip visibly tightening on the steering wheel. Jade half expected him to lash out and tell her to stay out of his business. That wouldn't have been like him either, and there was no anger in the glance he gave her. "A few months after you…didn't come back, we got separated from Luke and Ian on a mission. Remember Ian?"

"Sure. A young guy from Idaho. Right? He was always joking around. Pulling pranks with Travis."

The air whistled between Coop's teeth as he inhaled, as though the recollection had been too vivid. "Yeah, that's the guy. He and Luke were captured and held hostage by a group that split off Al-Qaeda."

Dread rolled over her in waves. She couldn't possibly have heard right, but one look at Coop confirmed the horrifying disclosure. Memories she'd fought hard to bury deep sprang from the darkest recesses of her mind. Cold sweat sent a shiver through her, even though the cab of the truck suddenly seemed stifling. Desperate for air, she wanted to yank on the door handle, shove it open, and jump into the void outside that promised to swallow her.

No, don't go there. I'm okay. I'm safe. Luke is alive. He's coping. So am I, most of the time. Damn it! I need Moose.

Something warm grasped the fist she'd clenched on her lap. She hadn't realized she'd closed her eyes, but when she opened them, it was Coop's large, strong hand that covered hers. Without really thinking about it, she opened her fingers and twined them with his. An instant later, clarity returned, and she tried to pull free.

He held on until she turned her head to look at him. "You're safe with me. I won't let anything happen to you."

His words, soft as a whisper, were a lifeline, and she grabbed ahold. Shame followed swiftly. How could she even think about relaxing into the protection he offered so selflessly? After what she'd done? Now that she knew how much she'd hurt him? Unable to handle the compassion that shone from his eyes, she turned away. When she tugged on her hand again, he let her go. She forced her churning stomach into submission as she focused her attention on the lights of the truck illuminating the roadway ahead.

"Six months they were tortured every day, mentally and physically. Two weeks before we got solid intel on where they were being held, they killed Ian."

Jade gasped. *Oh God, no.* As she studied his profile, grief and horror rose to choke her.

"When the rescue team went in to get Luke, all hell broke loose, and he took a bullet to the chest. His heart stopped twice on the way back to base. He's damn lucky to be alive." Coop opened his mouth, then closed it, as though he had more to say but changed his mind.

"That's awful. I'm so sorry, Coop." Her voice broke on his name, but if he noticed, he let it go.

"After you disappeared and Luke nearly died, I'd had enough. It seemed like every time we took out a high-value target and got a little bit ahead, a dozen more fanatics stepped up to *kill the infidels*. I'd signed up and went through BUD/s so I could make a difference."

"You did, though. You have to know that, right?" It was a team of SEALs who'd rescued her. They'd made all the difference in the world.

He shook his head. "Maybe, but MacGyver and Travis were on the same page. Together, we came up with a plan to start a private security business, where we can help people and put the training Uncle Sam provided to good use. Even more important, we have each other's backs when transitioning to civilian life gets rough."

"Is Luke a partner too?"

"He is now. We kind of lost track of him while he was in rehab. We all ended up at Ian's brother's place in Idaho at the same time. Luke and his lady, Sally, had some trouble chasing them, so after we took care of that, we talked him into going in with us."

It was apparent the men still operated like a close-knit team. From the little she'd been around them in the past twenty-four hours, it appeared they deferred to Luke as the buck-stops-here guy. Jade had some idea of the hell he must have gone through in captivity. By all appearances, he'd handled the brutality better than she had.

Coop flipped the lights to the high beam, jarring her from her thoughts. He glanced toward her. "Are you okay? Warm enough?"

"I'm fine, thanks." She wasn't really. Learning about Luke's experience as a hostage had shaken her more than she'd ever admit. At the same time, she was curious. How was he able to seem so normal? "So much has happened. It feels like my mind is in overdrive. I can't stop thinking. Especially about what might have happened to Nicole tonight." She hugged herself to ward off the chill that tickled her skin.

"It's okay to relax, you know. You and your sister are both safe now."

"Thanks to you and the rest of your team." She owed them a debt she'd never be able to repay.

"I'm glad we were there." A gentle smile released the dimple on his cheek as he reached across the seat and pushed her hair back from her face. The brush of his fingers on her neck ignited desire that sent a jolt through her core with such force she pulled back.

He jerked his hand away as though he'd also felt the unexpected pulse of heat between them. "Shit, I'm sorry—old habits. I didn't mean to scare you. It won't happen again."

"I'm sorry too. You didn't scare me. It's just…sometimes I overreact when people—." Not sure where to go from there, she stopped. Human contact was often a trigger for a runaway heart rate, hyperventilation, or a full-blown panic attack. She was miles ahead of where she'd been. In the interim, she'd become an expert at not letting people get close enough to touch her, emotionally or physically.

She'd never come face to face with this particular ghost before, though. Fighting the longing to let this man envelop her in arms capable of shielding her from all the evil in the world was exhausting. It would be so easy to give in to the pull of his self-assurance. A definite sign he was getting under her skin. She needed to stop it cold.

Still, why couldn't she spend an hour or so in his arms or his bed? There was nothing wrong with accepting comfort when it was available. She could get the need for him out of her system. A man would never let an opportunity for no-strings sex go to waste.

Whew! It's hot in here. She barely resisted the urge to fan herself.

Suddenly, an irrational urge to laugh out loud seized her. A chortle escaped, sounding more like a snort. She turned toward the side window, wrapping her arms around her stomach as the heat of embarrassment clawed its way into her cheeks. *It's been a long time since I've thought about my needs.*

Out of the corner of her eye, she saw Coop watching her. "Um…Moose usually keeps me from making too big a fool of myself."

His confusion and concern slowly relaxed into a

grin. "I see. The meatball has a full-time job then?"

The sharp prick to her pride dissipated as soon as he started laughing. She turned to look at him, a tentative smile breaking free at the sight of the man she used to know. A younger, lighthearted Coop. Still tough as nails, ready for anything, yet intensely loyal with a heart of gold. Even with a split lip, black eye, and bruises covering the side of his face, he was the sexiest man she'd ever known.

When he leaned toward her and said, "Come on. You know that was funny," she lost her battle, joining him in a moment of surprisingly easy camaraderie.

Their laughter significantly lessened the tension in the truck. Coop's eyes sparkled with amusement. "Hey, it's good to see you lighten up."

"Yeah? I could say the same thing to you."

He nodded and focused his attention on the road. "It's good to talk. I've missed that. I was hoping we could fill in some of the blanks. Like…where do you live when you're not here, keeping your sister out of trouble? We're a little over an hour from the safe house. Plenty of time to catch up if there's anything you want to get off your chest." His vulnerability tugged at her heart and reminded her, yet again, how badly she'd betrayed him.

She sucked her bottom lip between her teeth as she gave him a sidelong glance. Would telling him part of the truth alleviate his pain? The need to share with someone was an ache so deep she couldn't identify where it originated. The silence that hung like a curtain between them grew heavier and heavier.

"It was only a recon mission. We were supposed to photograph a suspected chemical weapons facility a few clicks north of Damascus. I told Andrew, my navigator, we'd be home by dark. Somehow, we got off course." Jade shivered. Talking about her friend, Andy, never got easier.

Coop brushed his hand down her arm, purely a gesture of comfort. It startled her, and she jerked away, barely holding in the scream that filled her throat. *Okay, this won't do.* She had to remain detached. Close her mind to the memories and tell her story the way she and the general had practiced.

"Armed fighters with tanks and rockets spotted us and opened fire. We were too low, flying below the radar. I turned back, aborting the mission, but a drone came out of nowhere. Everything happened so fast. The Raptor took a hit, went into a spiral, and the controls weren't responding.

"Andrew was unconscious, or maybe he was already gone. I couldn't rouse him, so I initiated the ejection sequence. He was dead when I got to him on the ground." She wrapped her arms around the emptiness in her gut.

Today wasn't the first time she'd relived the unthinkable events of that day. The smoke and fire. The smell of death. The terror. The adrenaline rush. The general had required her to practice for her debriefing until every word was pitch-perfect and politically correct.

Jade glanced sideways at Coop, hoping he hadn't noticed the tremble in her voice. Thankfully, his attention alternated between her story, the dark road before them, and the rearview mirror. He hadn't asked how a seasoned pilot with a navigator had strayed so far off course.

"I knew the enemy couldn't be far behind me. I tried to camouflage Andrew's body in hopes the rescue team would find him before the Syrian soldiers stumbled across him." It had been a waste of precious time. She remembered Colonel Reiner's warning as though it were yesterday. *"If something goes wrong, the rescue operation will be focused on the southern hills according to your orders. They won't find you."* As her commanding officer had argued logistics and what-ifs, the general had remained silent.

"They caught up with me just after nightfall, so I took cover in some rocks and concentrated on improving the odds until I ran out of ammunition. I'd taken a bullet to the leg. It wasn't bad. The slug went clear through, missing the bone, but I'd lost too much blood to run any farther. I figured I was dead at that point, but it turns out I wasn't that lucky." Her cynical laugh did nothing to alleviate the tension emanating from Coop.

With white knuckles, he clenched the wheel and stared straight ahead. "Where did they hold you?"

"A munitions dump a few miles north of where the Raptor went down." She'd only been at that location for a few hours before Mahaz had claimed her for his own.

"Were you treated well?" Barely controlled rage vibrated in his voice as though he already knew the answer.

For a fraction of a second, she considered lying. But hadn't she lied enough? "The first few days, I was housed in a makeshift infirmary. A doctor cleaned and dressed my wound, and I managed to regain some of my strength before my captor came back for me. I spent the next several days alone in a dark, wet dungeon surrounded by concrete. I lost track of time. I thought I'd go crazy. It was so cold, dark, and silent. The complete absence of sound nearly drove me insane. There were no blankets, no food, and only dirty water that dripped down the walls and pooled on the floor.

"After a few days, I knew I was going to die, and I prayed for a quick death. It seemed God had other plans for me, so I prayed for someone—anyone—to come back. I should have been more discriminating in my request. I soon learned just how good I'd had it alone in that cell."

She turned toward the side window and stared at her reflection. "They treated me as though they hated women—American women worst of all—and everything else the West symbolizes." She squeezed her eyes closed as the memories pummelled her. Repeatedly raped, beaten, and tortured, she'd taken the hard road rather than let them break her. In the end, she'd gotten her revenge, sending Mahaz to hell with a bullet between his eyes.

"Bastards!" His voice, hardly more than a whisper, dropped into the well of silence with the finesse of a set of symbols, followed by his fist slamming into the steering wheel. She nearly jumped out of her skin.

The next instant, his cell phone vibrated, sliding across the seat between them. The buzzing, coming so close behind his angry reaction, caused Jade's heart to hammer painfully against her ribcage.

He snatched the device and frowned at the screen, then brought it to his ear.

CHAPTER FOURTEEN

"Hey, Blake. What's up? Everything okay at the safe house?" Coop strove for a light, carefree tone, despite the fact Blake wouldn't be calling unless something had gone south with the plan. He caught sight of Jade's concerned expression and gave her a smile he hoped would reassure her.

"No problems. Travis and Ryan secured the house and perimeter as soon as we arrived. Nicole is baking cookies. Says it relaxes her. She's a little jumpy, but she'll be fine once Jade arrives. I'm on my way back to town."

"Awesome, man. Nothing like the smell of fresh-baked cookies." *Shit!* Blake's strong suit wasn't idle chit-chat, increasing Coop's apprehension. He glanced toward the rearview mirror again, then pressed his knee against the bottom of the steering wheel and used his free hand to crack open the window.

There it was—to the west of them. He could barely make out the cadence of the bird's whirling blades. The sound filtered into the cab along with the crisp, pre-dawn air, tinged with the smell of damp pine needles and sagebrush. The aircraft sounded distant, but that didn't stop him from quickly scanning the sky for the red and green lights. He couldn't locate them, which added to his unease. Was Blake flying without running lights? What were the odds his friend was calling for the same reason Coop had become hyper-vigilant in the past few minutes? The growing agitation in his gut had been clanging alarm bells in his brain that something wasn't right.

"Looks like you picked up a tail," Blake said, lowering his voice.

"Affirmative on that." Coop caught a glimpse of the other vehicle's headlights through the trees as it came out of the curve he'd navigated a moment ago. Whoever drove the car that shadowed them was far too good at mirroring his speed—slowing and accelerating when he did—to be an innocent early-morning commuter. Still, he hadn't wanted to tell Jade and add to her nervousness.

"Afraid I've got some more bad news for you."

Ah hell. "Let's have it." A glance toward her suggested he'd done a lousy job of hiding the tension set free by Blake's announcement.

She laid her hand on his arm. "Is Nic all right?"

That much he could confirm, so he forced a smile and gave a brief nod.

"About two miles ahead of you, a couple of vehicles are blocking the road. Looks to be a half-dozen hot spots on the infra-red." Blake delivered his assessment in the same no-nonsense manner he would have briefed his SEAL team for a mission.

"Cops?" Coop already knew the answer, but he was still in wouldn't-it-be-nice-if mode.

Blake chuckled. "Well, the cloud cover makes it pretty dark down there, and I couldn't see any reflective lettering on the sides of the vehicles."

"What's wrong?" Jade paled as alarm strained her voice.

"I'm putting you on speaker, Blake, so you can bring Jade up to speed." She'd find out soon enough anyway. Still, he tried to downplay his concern as he and Blake filled her in on the pickup that'd been following them for the last few miles and the roadblock awaiting them ahead.

"What do we do now?" Determination glinted in her eyes as she tilted her chin.

There was the fighter he remembered, unafraid of conflict and confident in her abilities. He should have known those bastard jihadists couldn't break her. Bend her, maybe, but there was still steel in her spine.

He considered her question for a moment. "Did you get a chance to scan our tail for hot spots, Blake?"

"You know I did. You've got two back there."

Coop grinned at her. "Odds are better behind us. What do you say?"

"I say we pull over, leave the lights on and doors open and find some cover. When they stop to check it out, we'll politely ask what they want." The corners of her mouth tipped upward ever so slightly.

"I like the way you think." Not to mention, being on the same side as his woman against a common enemy sent heat rocketing through his blood. *His woman? Yeah, in another lifetime.* For a heartbeat, the time and distance between them ceased to exist.

"I don't mean to interrupt this heart-to-heart, but I might have a better idea."

Coop forced his attention back to the phone and what Blake was saying.

"Just around the next corner, there's a forest service road that cuts to the north. According to the map I googled, it dead-ends a couple of miles in, but I don't think you'll have to go that far. After a half-mile or so, the topography goes nuts. It's rugged country with lots of trees and brush. Perfect for hiding out until you draw them in close enough to be suitably impressed with a fully armed Black Hawk helicopter in their faces." Blake was proud of the transport he'd bought after crashing his old Bell 206 with a hot-as-hell reporter on board. Said reporter had made an honest man of him a few months ago and came with a six-year-old son who idolized Blake.

"What do you think?" Coop glanced toward her.

The smile she allowed was fierce but humorless. "I love seeing the looks on peoples' faces when they realize they've brought a pussy-cat to a dogfight."

Blake barked out a laugh, and Coop winked at her before checking the rearview mirror. The vehicle still trailed at the same distance, not trying to overtake them. Now he knew why. The occupants' only job was to herd Jade and him to the main event. Thanks to Blake, whatever endgame they'd planned wasn't going to be as easy as they'd hoped.

"Okay, we're all on the same page. We'll hold this speed until we make the turnoff and then haul ass to the hills. Leave this connection open and stay in contact." He spotted the gravel road ahead, took a left, and punched the gas pedal. The truck's rear end skated on loose rock, and he turned the wheel into the slide and gave it more gas.

The vehicle following them rounded a bend in the road about three hundred yards behind and couldn't miss their change of direction. Likely, they'd try to catch up and run them off the road, now that they weren't proceeding toward the ambush ahead. That was okay. The point wasn't to lose them but to draw them close enough to appreciate the Black Hawk's firepower. Maybe they'd decide trying to grab Jade or her sister was a bad idea.

The first two hundred feet of the forest service road was graveled, straight, and smooth. Unfortunately, it didn't stay that way. The moment they entered the tree line, it turned into a dirt path, the center filling in with tall grass and pine seedlings. Protruding rocks, alternating with ruts and severe washouts, slowed them down at the risk of breaking an axle. At least they were increasing in elevation and heading in the right direction.

Jade remained silent as she rocked with the motion of the truck, one hand gripping the dash and the other clasping the armrest. Her calm demeanor and willingness to stand and do battle filled him with pride. She'd always been gutsy, but this was somehow different. As though there was nothing the world could throw at her that she hadn't already survived. At that moment, he had to know what she'd endured and help her heal somehow.

"We're going to finish this conversation later." He felt her swing toward him. *Shit, did I say that out loud?*

In the glow of the dash lights, her beautiful eyes sparkled with life. "I know," she whispered.

Full-blown gratitude erupted inside him with a force he could barely contain. Those two little words had to mean she was starting to trust him. Maybe she wouldn't—or couldn't—tell him everything yet. Perhaps they needed to get to know each other again before all of her walls would come down, but it was a beginning. He could be patient.

Except, now, he wanted to reach for her and drag her onto his lap. Just hold her. Protect her. *Okay, so now's not a good time, but damn, there better be an opportunity later.*

"Maybe when you're done talking amongst yourselves, you could update me on your position." Blake's humor-laced voice jolted Coop from his self-congratulations.

He'd completely spaced that the line was still open, blown away by her response and vulnerability. He caught her studying him, a soft smile gracing her perfect lips.

"Thought you had a bird's eye view." She pulled the cell phone from the cupholder and held it closer to her mouth.

"Negative. I'm in a holding pattern on the far side of the ridge you're approaching, standing by for my grand entrance. You'll…my eyes." Static crackled over Blake's words, but Coop got the gist.

"I want the slope to our backs before we turn and face them. We're not making good time. The road looks like a B-52 used it for target practice."

"Copy…" Blake came back, but his reply cut out.

"Hey, Blake, you're breaking up." Coop steered the truck around another huge hole while waiting for his friend to answer. Suddenly, his phone's screen went black, and the last bar of service blinked out.

Oh hell. Coop's plan just lost its muscle. "See if you can get him back, Jade."

The headlights in his mirror bounced up and down erratically and steadily closed the distance between them. He accelerated as much as he could, but they wouldn't be able to outrun the pursuing vehicle.

Blake wouldn't let them down. Once he realized the phones were out, he'd find a way to adapt. Coop didn't doubt that, but their show's timing was critical, and they'd just stopped the clock. If the two in the trailing vehicle called ahead to alert the team at the roadblock, they'd be having more company than planned.

It was time to make a stand, and his priority was to get Jade out of harm's way.

"Hang on!" Their tail had sped up and was gaining fast. The trees closed in on all sides as Coop stepped on the gas and slid around a narrow curve.

Jade clung to the dash with one hand, clasping his phone in the other. "We're going in and out of service, but the signal isn't strong enough to complete the call." The growl of the churning four-wheel-drive nearly drowned out her words.

"We need to get higher." He scrunched down to see out her window. The ridge they'd been heading for, outlined by the gray shimmer of dawn, wasn't far to the north. Unfortunately, they were now going east, parallel to the elevation they needed.

She shoved her phone toward him while she still gripped his in her hand. "Let's switch. I'll climb the hill on foot until I get a strong enough signal to call Blake. Slow down and let me out."

He was already shaking his head. "No, we stay together." A helpless feeling crawled into his gut. The thought of her taking off by herself in unfamiliar terrain with what was sure to be armed goons on her tail scared the shit out of him. Expecting his stern glare to discourage her argument was wishful thinking.

He focused his attention back on the road just as they caught air over a small berm. The road jogged left sharply, and ten feet beyond that, a fallen tree blocked their way. He slammed on the brakes. The pickup slid sideways and tucked itself snugly against the giant, horizontal tree trunk, blocking the passenger side.

Throwing open his door, he jumped out. The other vehicle had stopped, its lights shining at a crazy angle into the thick trees. Had they gotten stuck, or better yet, tore the hell out of their rig? Maybe, but it was much more likely they were stalling, waiting for reinforcements from the roadblock. Jerking the back door open, he pulled his M24 sniper rifle from beneath the backseat.

As Jade scrambled from the cab, he caught her arm. Reaching into the front seat, he put her cell phone in his jacket pocket, pulled his SIG from the console, and pushed it into her hand. "Okay, you got your wish. We split up. You head uphill until you can call in the cavalry." Whatever was going to happen would likely be over before her efforts made any difference, but it would remove her from immediate danger.

"What are you going to do?" Was that worry that narrowed her eyes?

"I'll be right behind you after I slow these guys down." He'd do whatever it took to keep those assholes off her trail.

"If you're making a stand, I'm staying." The gleam of defiance in her eyes, so reminiscent of the stubborn woman he'd known before tragedy struck, brought a grin to the surface despite his best efforts. Anger sparked in those violet-blue depths, and his control snapped. He snaked one hand around her neck and hauled her flush with him.

"Wait. What are you doing?" She stiffened but didn't pull back.

"The one thing I know will shut you up." His mouth covered hers, raw, urgent need overwhelming him. Her sweet lips—lips he'd thought he'd never taste again—nearly made him forget the plan. He didn't have time, damn it! With a groan, he broke the kiss and stepped back.

She staggered but caught her balance, shimmering eyes staring into his.

"Go, now, and don't stop. I'll catch up."

Hesitating only a second, she turned, rounded the back of his truck, and sprinted into the trees.

DIXIE LEE BROWN

CHAPTER FIFTEEN

Fir trees closed in around her, dark and disorienting, the ground unfamiliar and uneven. Jade shook her head to clear the fog, knowing—yet not knowing—her mind was playing tricks on her.

Brush pulled at her pant legs. Windfall blocked her path, and rocks tripped her. In her haste, she fell, and pain ricocheted from shins to knees. As she scrambled to her feet and brushed the dirt and dry pine needles from her stinging palms, the ridge above taunted her. If only she could climb high enough.

Why was it so important?

Confusion stole her momentum, and she shook her head again, but her mind remained stuck between past and present. Smoke and jet fuel vapors permeated the air. Her clothes reeked of it, and her eyes watered. Voices nearby jacked her heartrate to the danger zone. Too close. Lungs ached with each panicked breath.

Run!

The heels of her boots kicked up sand that spattered rhythmically against the legs of her jumpsuit. They were closing in. They knew she was there—that she was alone. Memories whipped through her mind. The mission. The drone. Her Raptor hit. Oh, God! Andy!

Anguish nearly took her to her knees. It should have been her who died, but it didn't matter. She'd be dead soon enough. They wouldn't take her alive.

The handgun weighed ominously heavy, and she stared at her hand. When had she pulled her weapon?

"Hey, American, don't hide. We have food and water. We want to help you." His accent was thick—English, not his native language.

She whipped around, her gaze darting from shadow to shadow. Where were they? Their laughter seemed to come from every direction, delighting in her pain and fear.

He was right about one thing—she needed to find water. Her throat was parched, and her leg throbbed with each footfall. Blood ran down her leg and dripped on the toe of her boot. Her hand went automatically to the source of the pain, and she stared at the sticky substance that coated her fingers. Skin clammy. Unable to concentrate. She'd lost too much blood.

Her foot caught on a root, and the ground slammed into her. She gasped. Yellow spots floated in front of her eyes. Her fingers protested as she clawed to her hands and knees. The gun. Where was it?

Pain lanced through her shoulder as someone grabbed her from behind. She bit back her anguished scream and swung around to defend herself, falling back on her training.

Fight to the death.

A single shot from a high-powered rifle discharged, then echoed through the stillness. Jade's lungs heaved in and out as she peered into the shadows, trying to get her bearings. She crouched, ready to let loose all hell on her enemies only to find she was alone. No Syrian soldiers. No smoking wreckage of her Raptor.

It had seemed so tangible. Caustic fumes burned Jade's throat, her eyes watered, and her heart raced. She could still smell the men's sweat and feel the hand that had jerked her cruelly to her feet. Dropping to her knees again, she dry-heaved on an empty stomach.

She ducked as more gunfire rang out, this time from a smaller caliber weapon. Reality slammed into stark relief. Coop's salvo had rescued her from the waking nightmare. He was delaying the men in the vehicle that'd followed them from town. She was supposed to be hauling ass up the ridge behind her until she received a strong enough signal to call Blake. How long had she been out of her head?

Patting the pocket that held Coop's cell phone to confirm she hadn't lost it, she whirled and started to climb; his gun still clutched in her hand. The pops of weapons firing drove her on. Every time she stopped to rest for a few seconds, she checked the phone. The disappointment, crushing. The fear she'd let Coop down even worse.

He'd kissed her more than once now, and she hadn't protested. His strong, hard body against hers, his lips, demanding, confident, felt like safety to her. Since when did she need to be taken care of by a man? But she'd relaxed into his protectiveness, knowing she shouldn't need it. Knowing she didn't hate it, either. She'd been confused and conflicted—no wonder the ugly past had hit her like a battering ram.

Jumping for a rock ledge a few feet above her, she laid Coop's SIG on the hard slab and hauled herself up and over the edge. Rolling onto her back, she plucked the phone from her pocket and jabbed a fist in the air when two bars appeared in the signal icon. The air over her began to vibrate as she tapped *recents* and hit Blake's name on the screen.

"I was beginning to wonder what the hell happened to you." Even as Blake spoke, the Black Hawk appeared above her, running dark, and swooped down the ridge's steep slope, staying just over the treetops.

The air pressure caused by the rotor blades turning furiously so close overhead pressed down on her chest, or maybe it was the relief that suddenly inundated her. "We lost cell service." Laying on her back, she willed him to hurry as the aircraft disappeared over the trees to her left.

"Jade? Where's Coop?" Concern edged his voice.

She'd spaced the fact she was using Coop's phone. Blake had no doubt expected his friend's voice. She scrambled to her feet and watched the helicopter approach the firefight below. "He insisted on staying behind."

"Ah," he said, that slight sound seeming to indicate he understood Coop's reasoning. "And you thought he didn't care."

She opened her mouth, then closed it again. *Not*

true. Just the opposite. I'm afraid Coop cares too much. Afraid seeing me after believing I was dead will be the blow that does him in. Because, except for physical desire, every time we touch, nothing has changed.

"Okay, I see him on the infra-red. Stand by. Our little show of force should only take a minute."

She felt the blast of .50 cal ammo from the helo's guns through the rocks beneath her feet, glad she wasn't any closer.

"Yep, they're turning tail. That didn't take much." His chuckle sounded unmistakably smug. "Wait. I'll be damned. One of 'em thinks he's going to take me out with a portable rocket launcher. These small-town crusaders are certainly well-armed, and they must want you out of the picture pretty bad."

A chill wound through her. "Why? I don't understand." Was he right? Was all of this to get her out of town? That didn't make any sense.

The next instant, an explosion startled her, lighting up the gray morning with a brightness that forced her to shield her eyes. "What was that?"

"Just a little demonstration of superior firepower." He laughed. "They're going to need some transportation, though."

The vehicle. Blake must have blown up their ride. "You're crazy."

"You're welcome."

"Is Coop in one piece?" She owed Blake for sure, but concern for Coop was foremost in her mind.

"He was on his way to you last I saw him."

Relief surged anew. "Copy that. Thanks, Blake."

"All in a day's work. I'll hang around for a bit.

Make sure these guys clear out and take their roadblock buddies with them." The call ended abruptly.

She wasn't sure if he'd ended it or if her luck with those two signal bars had finally worn out. It didn't matter. Coop was safe. With any luck, she'd have time to figure out the emotional carnival ride she was on before she saw him again.

The snap of a branch jerked her attention toward the shadows of the forest below her rock ledge. She'd run through those same trees and thick brush on her climb up the slope. Downed logs and fallen branches had made her footing treacherous, and there'd been no shortage of noise as she rushed toward the top of the ridge.

Remaining still, she studied the area for a few seconds, expecting to see Coop approaching with a satisfied grin on his face. Nothing moved. Silence lay thick, like a layer of dew on a chilly morning. Okay. It had probably been a pinecone falling to the ground or something else as innocuous.

The helicopter's sound had receded; its pilot evidently assured their attackers were retreating in the face of the Black Hawk's dominance. She'd have given anything to see the looks on their faces. That would teach Graves to mess with her or Nicole.

Now that the danger was over, amusement and a minor case of nerves made her almost giddy. According to Blake, Coop was on his way up, no doubt to make sure she was okay. His protective streak had always run deep. Though she'd been annoyed by it more than once in Iraq, a sense of contentment warmed her heart. And trepidation.

The guy could kiss, and she enjoyed it way too

much. She'd wanted more, but nothing could come of the attraction she felt for him. Anyway, it was probably just her body's reaction to the stress of the situation. He'd undoubtedly be as eager to forget it ever happened as she was.

She pocketed his cell phone, retrieved the handgun, shoving it into her waistband, and started down the slope the way she'd come. A half-dozen strides later, the heavy brush below and to her right rustled as though something moved through its thick greenery. She stopped and examined the landscape, hoping to hear the wind stirring the leaves of other nearby bushes or the measured tread of booted feet. Not that she'd be able to hear Coop, even if—

She rotated a three-sixty as the truth sunk in. Coop moved silently. She couldn't count the number of times he'd scared the crap out of her by suddenly appearing when she'd have sworn there wasn't another soul around. No, it wasn't him leaving a trail a novice could follow.

She laughed softly. She was letting her imagination go crazy. It was nothing more than an animal—deer, elk, maybe a bear. The rough country was their habitat and the final minutes before dawn was their time to move. Wildlife she could handle. Still, the skin at the back of her neck prickled as she turned and started downhill again.

The stark outlines of lodgepole pine and fir trees closed in on her, standing sentry over the too-quiet forest. The smell of smoke and gasoline drifted on the occasional current of air. She picked up the pace until she was jogging over the uneven ground, keeping a close eye on the terrain.

One second she was hopping over the rotted trunk of a fallen tree; the next, she was face down on the ground, a substantial weight holding her immobile. All she could see was a denim-clad knee and the bottom portion of a muscled thigh on either side of her shoulders. Her ears rang from the wallop she'd taken, impacting the ground. She shook her head and spat out a chunk of dirt before rearing up, trying to shake off her attacker. Apparently, he'd prepared for an escape attempt. He tightened his legs around her and leaned his weight forward, effectively reducing her ability to force air into her lungs.

The troglodyte had the nerve to laugh. When he put his mouth next to her ear and whispered, the pounding of her heart made it impossible to hear. She threw back her head. Rewarded with a grunt when her skull smashed into his, she gasped for air and opened her mouth to scream.

"Shit!" A hand clamped over her mouth. "Jade, it's me. Be quiet." The man whispered again, but this time she heard him.

She stilled her thrashing immediately, and just as quickly, he removed his hand and slid off to one side of her. "Coop? What the hell?"

In the gray morning light, muted by the forest shadows, she squinted at him as he levered to his knees and peered over the fallen tree. When he turned toward her again, he raised a finger to his lips. "Someone's stalking you."

"How do you know? Did you see him?"

"He's making enough noise to alert anyone within a mile radius."

A skeptical huff escaped. "That doesn't mean

he's stalking me." Yet she'd felt it, hadn't she? Wasn't that why she'd run?

He took her cell phone from his pocket and handed it to her. "Halfway up here, I got a signal. It was weak, but I decided to try Blake anyway. It was a lousy connection, but I heard enough of what he said to know he'd spotted someone trailing you. Stopping when you did. Running when you ran."

"That doesn't make any sense. Blake said there were only two men in the vehicle following us. Besides, how would they have known I'd take off up the ridge on foot?"

"Good question. We're about to find out. Do you still have my SIG?"

She nodded, her hand going automatically to her back waistband.

"Keep it out of sight. I want you to head due east, downhill toward the sunrise."

She glanced at the horizon, where a tinge of orange was washing over dawn's gray. "Okay, so I'm the bait. Where will you be?"

"I'm going to get around behind him and make sure he doesn't get away with the bait." He grinned in that confident way he had.

"Good to know." A small sigh escaped. She felt safer just knowing he was there. *How odd, after all the months of never feeling safe.*

His knuckle stroked her cheek in the gentlest of touches that sent chills scattering over her skin. "Give me sixty seconds before you move." In the blink of an eye, he disappeared into the landscape.

She counted off the seconds, then jumped to her feet and set a rapid pace. From the corners of her eyes, she examined each shadow, each group of trees that might afford a hiding place. With a new sense of calm, she waited for her stalker to strike. Knowing someone was out there, watching her, didn't elicit the same fear now that Coop had her back. She was almost relieved when the man's broad shoulders detached from the shadows to her right.

"Captain McDowell." The newcomer wore camo, nearly blending into his background.

She stopped and turned slowly toward him. "Do I know you?" Her head cocked to the side as she feigned curiosity. No weapon was apparent, but she sensed part of the self-assurance that radiated from him came from the fact he carried arms and knew how to use them. He reminded her of someone, but she was sure she'd never seen this man before.

"I don't believe we've ever met, but I know all I need to know about you." He advanced a few steps before glancing around. Was he sensing Coop's presence?

"That sounds suspiciously like our meeting out here isn't a coincidence, Mr.…" The open invitation to fill in the blank went unanswered. "What do you want?"

He strode a few more steps toward her. "I have a message…and a warning for you."

"From someone afraid to meet me face to face?"

He smiled, the emotion failing to reach cold gray eyes. "Fear has nothing to do with it, Captain. The man who sent me—let's just say he prefers to remain anonymous for the time being."

She rolled her eyes. "By all means. What's the message? Or is that shrouded in mystery too?"

"My employer wants me to remind you that you swore an oath of silence, and your country takes your oath very seriously. Do you?" The man's gaze raked her body and returned to her face.

Nausea roiled her stomach, and all-too-familiar helplessness assailed her. She began to shake with equal parts anger and disgust. "Who sent you?"

"Don't you want to hear the warning?" The man's long strides cut down the distance that separated them to a half dozen steps.

The sound of a clip sliding into the grip of a weapon brought him up short, and he swung around as Coop stepped from behind a group of saplings. "I'd like to hear your warning." His handgun, leveled at the man's chest from thirty-five feet away, never wavered.

She drew her weapon. When the man whirled and started to take another step, she aimed for a spot between his eyes. "Close enough. Hands up and get on your knees."

For a moment, his expression spoke louder than any words as he stared, apparently weighing whether she would shoot him. Maybe he'd been telling the truth when he said he knew all about her. Or, it could be he'd seen something in her eyes that convinced him she wouldn't hesitate to pull the trigger. For whatever reason, his hands went up. Coop came from behind and forced him to his knees, then removed two handguns from holsters behind his back.

She started to shake and couldn't stop. Someone had sent a gunman to deliver a threat, the message itself giving away the anonymous sender's identity.

Dear old dad.

"Answer the lady's question. Who sent you?" Coop towered over the kneeling man.

"That's not part of the message." The man smirked, and Coop punched him, knocking him sideways into the dirt. Blood seeped from the corner of his mouth.

"That's enough. Let's just go." Jade didn't know what she was saying. All she could think about was getting away from this man before he said something Coop wasn't supposed to hear.

He cast her a curious glance but turned his attention back to the man almost immediately. "I'm sure the FBI will get you to talk, but first, I'd like to hear your warning."

The man swiped blood from his face, his expression severe. "The warning is for the captain's ears only, but I think I'll make an exception this time." He wiped the blood onto the leg of his camo pants.

"No, please don't." The gun shook in her hand. There was no way out of this. She couldn't let him speak. She couldn't shoot him, either. Suddenly, she dropped the SIG and slammed her hands over her ears.

He smiled, almost sympathetically, ignoring Coop completely. "The oath you took was on pain of death. My employer urges you to remember that."

Coop turned his head to study her, his probing stare boring a hole through her.

The man slumped forward and yanked up his pant leg. Suddenly, he held a small snub-nose weapon in his hand.

"Look out!" In agonizingly slow motion, she

pointed and leaped toward Coop.

He crouched and spun around, raising his gun as he turned.

A muffled shot sounded. At the same instant, blood and brain matter exploded from the back of the man's head. The gun beneath his jaw, and the hand that held it, dropped lifelessly, cushioned silently by the spongey forest floor. It seemed like forever before his torso hit the ground.

CHAPTER SIXTEEN

"What the holy hell just happened?" Coop looked away from the gory scene to Jade and back again. *Unbelievable!* What hired messenger in his right mind blows his head off to protect the identity of the man who sent him? Few things were worth taking your own life, and this seemed like egregious overkill.

One thing was for damn sure. Coop was missing several pieces of the puzzle. What's more, there was little doubt Jade was holding out on him in the information department. Operating in the dark was getting old.

He knelt beside the dead man and searched his pockets. "No ID. I don't recognize him from Graves' bunch. Have you seen him before?" Not likely. She'd given the guy an opening to introduce himself, but, still, he had to ask. When she didn't answer, he straightened and swung around.

Jade was visibly trembling and slowly shook her head. With a white-knuckled grip on the handgun, her focus never wavered from the bloody display in front of her. At some point in the middle of his confusion, he registered that the shock and horror frozen on her face was way more than skin deep.

"It's over, Jade." He stepped toward her and carefully pried the weapon from her fingers, slid the safety on, and stuck it in his belt. She finally blinked. Then she grabbed two fistfuls of his jacket and stepped into him as though she couldn't get close enough. Her shoulders shook as sobs wracked her, and chances were good she hadn't been aware it was him she'd turned to for comfort. He didn't care. Nothing could have kept him from locking his arms around her and pulling her in tighter.

Her body, molded to his, fit perfectly, just the way he remembered. That's where the sameness ended, however. She'd always been a woman in charge of her emotions. The idea she was hurting soul-deep pained him more than any grief he'd ever endured. Her well-being suddenly became his only goal. He'd move the sun and stars to defeat whatever demons stalked her, starting with finding out exactly what she was hiding, even if she hated him for it in the end.

He pressed his lips to her temple and rubbed his hand up and down her back. "It's okay, sweetheart. I've got you." He whispered the words more like a vow than for any reassurance to her, but she must have heard him. She burrowed into his chest, a whimper escaping on a teary hiccup. Wrapping her arms around his waist, she held tight as though the world was flat and she was too close to the edge.

Suspicion nagged him. Carl Graves' rabble-rousers were fanatics for sure, but whatever had drawn them here for their version of civil disobedience didn't jibe with killing yourself to avoid answering a few questions. That was a whole other sphere of activism. More along the lines of terrorism—except terrorists weren't happy unless they took a dozen or so innocent bystanders with them.

He kept coming back to the same questions: Why had someone hired a militant messenger to tell Jade to keep her mouth shut and then deliver a thinly veiled threat if she didn't? How had the guy even found her in the middle of nowhere? Most bothersome of all, why would she take an oath of silence? His fingers itched to get on his laptop and start searching for answers because expecting her to fill in the blanks was probably wishful thinking.

She finally stopped trembling, and he could feel the tension return to her body. Still, he was reluctant to let her go. When his phone vibrated, he had no choice. She straightened and pushed away, refusing to look at him. He grabbed his phone. "Hey, Blake. Thanks for the assist."

"Any time. Can I assume everything's under control there?"

"Yeah, almost. Hang on a second." Coop swiped his screen until the camera was front and center, then snapped a picture of what remained of the dead man's face. "I'm sending you a photo. Can you get it to Roberts? Let him know where he can find the body. And see if his FBI buddies can give me a name and a list of known associates."

Blake was silent for a few seconds, and Coop could sense his friend's revulsion when he finally came back on the line. "Damn, Coop. You didn't leave much to work with."

"I know. Unfortunately, I didn't get a choice in

the matter. The guy shot himself."

"Jesus! What the hell's going on down there?"

Coop turned his back to Jade and moved a few steps away. "That's what I'm going to find out. Is there a spot you can land close by?"

"Yeah, sure. Whatever you need."

"I'd like you to take Jade to the safe house. She's pretty shaken up, and I've got some unfinished business back in town."

Blake's hesitation was just long enough to tell Coop he wasn't entirely on-board with the idea. "Okay, but are you sure your *business* can't wait until you have some backup?"

Coop snorted a laugh. "Don't worry. I have all the backup I need." He ended the call.

She was silent and distant the rest of the walk down the hill. That was all right with him because his rage simmered just beneath the surface. It didn't help that one minute, he wanted to strangle her, and the next, he craved her lips and the softness of her body against his.

After the Black Hawk set down in a clearing, she climbed in without argument. At the last minute, she stretched out her arm to stop him from closing the door behind her. "What are you doing?" The concern that radiated from her angered him further.

"What I should have done before I left town. Make sure Graves doesn't bother you or your family again."

"What? No, wait. You can't go back there alone. It's too dangerous." She grabbed his coat sleeve and hung on.

He extricated himself from her grasp and

stepped back. "If you won't tell me the truth, I'm going to dig until I find out for myself."

She tossed her head and rolled her eyes. "I'm not lying to you. I don't know who that man was."

Maybe she wasn't lying, but she wasn't telling the whole truth, either. "What did he mean when he said you'd taken an oath of silence?" He studied her face, hoping she'd come clean, that she'd trust him enough to let him help her. He should've known better.

She looked away. "Please let it go." The quiver in her voice wrenched at his heart.

Disappointment landed like a lead ball in his gut. With an effort, he held on to his anger and forced a scowl. "I figured that's what you'd say. We'll finish this conversation when I get to the safe house." He backed away a half-dozen steps before turning and jogging toward his truck.

He had to put it in four-wheel drive to climb out of the good-sized depression he'd made in the soft earth when he'd slammed into the downed tree. He watched through the rearview mirror as the helicopter lifted off and gained altitude. The farther they receded into the distance, the easier it became to breathe. From his belt, he removed the gun he'd taken from Jade and laid it in the console. Finally, he forced his attention toward the front and retrieved his cell phone from his pocket.

It took him a minute or two to find the number. He hadn't called Colonel Mark Reiner since he'd left Iraq in a fog of grief. He'd met Jade's commanding officer a couple of times before her crash and had instantly liked the guy. After the tragedy, Colonel

Reiner had gone above and beyond to seek him out just to check on him. He'd respected Reiner for that and considered him a friend.

After she'd been officially declared dead, Coop had rotated back to the States with a promise to call the colonel if he ever needed anything. Now, three years later, to say he needed something was an understatement. He needed to know why the hell his friend, the colonel, hadn't notified him when Jade was rescued.

With a tenuous grip on his temper, he pressed the call button. Reiner answered after the second ring.

"Coop? How the hell are you? Damn, how long's it been?" The colonel sounded downright glad to hear from him.

Coop wasn't buying it, but he might as well play along. "Too damn long. I should have called a long time ago. How've you been, Mark?"

"Mostly good. Hell, I've wondered about you a hundred times over the years. I almost called you a few different times, but, well, I figured you'd contact me if and when you were ready. It's good to hear from you." Nothing in the colonel's voice indicated he was anything but sincere. Could he be that good an actor?

It took a stone-cold bastard to pull off a scam that nearly destroyed another man—all while pretending to give a shit. Coop swallowed the angry words perched on his tongue. "You still in the Middle East?"

"Naw, they've had me riding a desk at the Pentagon for the past year or so. What about you?"

"I'm in private security, working a case in Oregon right now."

"Sounds like a good gig. A lot of former special ops guys have gotten back on their feet that way." Reiner paused. "So, how are you doing, Coop?"

"I'm okay. At least I was until a couple of days ago when I ran into Jade McDowell. I'm not going to lie to you. Kinda knocked my legs out from under me." He forced his voice to remain level though he wanted to reach through the phone and pinch the colonel's head off.

A long pause and what sounded like air hissing from between Reiner's teeth was the only indication he was still on the phone. A chair, or something, scraped across the floor, and Coop could almost see the man dropping, deflated, into his seat.

"Aw shit. You know Jade is dead…"

"Don't even go there, Mark." He was hanging on to his fury by a thread. "I saw her. I talked to her. Now I'm asking you: what the *fuck* is going on?" The colonel's hesitation threatened to blow the lid off his control.

"It was her father's idea. Her last mission was top secret. Our recon flights weren't supposed to be anywhere near the no-fly zone. If the truth had gotten out, it would have destroyed U.S. credibility for years to come—not to mention General McDowell's five-star reputation."

"You son-of-a-bitch. You knew where Jade was, and you *left* her there?" A red haze of rage blinded Coop for a moment.

"I swear we all thought she was dead. It was months before we learned the truth. As soon as we located her, we sent an extraction team. It was all on the down-low, so our allies wouldn't discover we'd overstepped our authority."

Coop gritted his teeth. "Why didn't you tell me? Hell, why didn't Jade get in touch with me? What's this bullshit about an *oath of silence*?"

Another hesitation. "You have to understand—the general was in a tough spot. As much as he loves his daughter, the country always comes first with him. You know how he is. He falsified the records to keep her rescue and return to the States out of the news. I tried to talk him out of it—told him it wouldn't work. Hell, I tried to keep Jade from taking the mission from the start. By the time we got her back, we had no other choice."

"The hell you didn't! Did you think I'd do anything to hurt her in any way?"

"I understand you're mad as hell. I would be too. You need to know; she was all in on the mission. She understood the consequences going in, yet she gave her word as an Air Force officer that she'd keep her mouth shut for the sake of national security. I'm not saying it was right or fair. You know she would have done anything to make her father proud. He laid on the pomp and circumstance, and she fell in line."

Coop's hand tightened around the steering wheel as he maneuvered his truck from the rutted, pot-hole-filled trail to the paved county road. "That doesn't answer my question, Mark. Why didn't you tell me?"

General McDowell was an asshole. From what he could ascertain from stories she'd told him, her father had bartered his approval for Jade's cooperation all her life. It was the one subject Coop had tried to avoid because it was sure to make her livid.

"McDowell knew your reputation as a straight-shooter. He was afraid you'd blow the lid off, thinking it was your duty or some shit like that. That she might face a court-martial after everything she'd been through." Reiner sighed as though relieved to have the story off his chest.

Coop saw red for a heartbeat. "Wait. Are you telling me the directive to cut me out of her life and let me think she was dead for three years came directly from General McDowell?"

"Don't think she wasn't upset about that part. It damn near broke her. She needed you."

I wasn't there. The thought sliced through Coop, nearly tearing him apart. The question formed before he could think better of it. "What happened to her, Mark? How bad was it?"

"Jesus, Coop, I can't..." Reiner's reluctance was laid bare in every nuance of his voice. "It's her story—one she apparently hasn't shared with you. Frankly, I wouldn't blame her if she never wanted to speak of it again. What I *can* tell you is that she went through hell. Anything you can imagine wouldn't come close to reality. After her debriefing, I damn near puked out my guts."

Coop's stomach rolled, and it took all of his self-discipline to keep his last meal where it belonged.

"I hope you can find it in your heart to forgive her because she's done her penance a hundred times over," Reiner said. "Then, if you love her, you can let her go so she can put that chapter of her life behind her for good."

Something about Reiner's suggestion hit every one of Coop's that's-so-wrong buttons. If that was the right thing to do, why did it unsettle him? *Am I that selfish?* "None of this is on her. Given enough time, I might forgive you, but I won't be satisfied until I get five minutes with that prick she calls a father." He clenched his teeth to the point of pain and rode out the waves of fury that promised retribution.

He cut off Reiner's warning about the general's status and friends-in-high-places with a press of the *end call* button on his phone's screen. He'd heard enough. Too much, really. He needed time to wrap his head around everything Reiner had told him before talking to Jade again.

A smattering of clouds ensured a gorgeous sunrise was not too far off as he drove past the Pine Bluff city limits sign. The Sunday morning streets of small-town Oregon were just starting to see movement. Apparently, early church services appealed to a few residents.

He pulled over in front of the feed store and parked. As he rummaged in one of his bags in the back seat, he kept an eye on the storefront. Graves' Expedition, Derek's bike, and a handful of obvious farm pickups were parked next to the curb. Early for so many visitors, but then they'd had a big night of kidnapping and ambushing.

Two local farmers left the store, got in their vehicles, and pulled away. That left Carl, probably Ethan, Derek, and two or three others who weren't in it for the fight and would fold quickly. He could live with those odds.

Stepping from his pickup, he strode across the blacktop, adjusting the weight of the shoulder holster he'd grabbed from his bag. Without slowing, he threw the glass doors wide and stomped inside.

Carl, huddled with Ethan in quiet conversation, glanced up and did a double-take. His eyes widened an iota before he flashed his signature smirk. "Well, Coop. Here you are. You know, we looked all over town for you and your new girlfriend last night. Where were you?" Graves circled the table that held all of the group's propaganda until it was between them.

Coop spotted Derek as the two locals he was talking with backed away and headed for the door. His gaze returned to Graves. "Sticking close to the lady, like you said."

Graves glanced toward Ethan and nodded. "Good. I assume you know where she and that sister of hers are? Bring them in. We need to lock down those two troublemakers until the trial is over."

"I figured that after you tried to kidnap Nicole West last night." Coop's slow drawl often lulled people into a false sense of security, and he'd learned to rely on it in moments like this.

"Yeah? Where were you when we needed help?"

Coop snickered. "If two of your able-bodied thugs can't corral one little woman, you need more help than I can provide."

He caught movement to his left as Derek reached around to his back, no doubt for the semi-auto handgun he always carried there. The next instant, Coop's long knife lay balanced on his palm. He still focused on Graves. "Tell your boy to stand down, Carl. I didn't come here to kill anyone, but shit happens."

Graves' warned off Derek with a shake of his head. "You're a lousy cop!"

"Wrong again. But I do have friends in the FBI, and I can tell you two things that'll get them in here straightaway. One: A shoot-out at OK Corral." Coop raised his hand and twirled his index finger in a circle. "Two: Jade McDowell or Nicole West calling the number I gave them to report a kidnapping and attempted murder."

"Attempted murder? We didn't try to kill anyone!" Derek stepped forward but stopped when Coop looked his way.

"Let's forget for a moment that Nicole could have died when your men ran her car off the road."

Derek glared at Ethan. "That wasn't supposed to happen."

"Shut up, Derek," Ethan said.

So, the kid *had* been involved. Coop wanted to shake some sense into him, but no doubt he'd missed his opportunity. "Nicole is going to be fine. You dodged a bullet there. The thugs who followed my truck out of town and the other six waiting to ambush us at a roadblock? How did you think that was going to end? Oh, by the way, one of your guys blew his own head off."

It could only be stunned bewilderment that crossed Graves' face. "What the hell are you talking about? Nobody followed you. No one set up a roadblock. Hell, we didn't know you were gone until we started looking for you."

Coop weighed Graves' statement in light of

what he'd seen with his own eyes. Oddly enough, he believed him. Last night's event would have taken a significant measure of discipline in the ranks—something he'd not seen within the organization. The mystery man who turned his gun on himself? Not even Graves himself was that fanatic.

Sheathing his knife, he pulled out his cell phone and scrolled to the photograph he'd taken earlier this morning, then offered the device to Graves. "Was he one of yours?"

Graves strode forward and accepted the phone. Glancing at the screen, he frowned and shoved it back to Coop. "I've never seen him before."

The man's reaction to the gruesome image had been oddly clinical. Either he was lying, or he was a damn good actor. "Okay. Good enough. Leave the women alone, and I'll leave you alone." He turned to walk away and frowned as Derek stepped toward him. "Try to keep the damn kid alive," he said over his shoulder.

The drive to the safe house was pleasant in the daylight. With everything rolling around in Coop's head after last night, he had plenty to occupy his thoughts. First and foremost, the crew that waylaid him and Jade. Who were they, and what did they want? If someone was after him or his team, he could understand. PTS Security had helped to put away some nasty characters in the past year. It wouldn't be unheard of for a perp to seek revenge. The whole oath of silence thing was tossing pineapple on his Canadian bacon pizza. It didn't make sense. His gut told him whoever staged last night's events was far more dangerous than Carl Graves' militia.

When he parked in front of the fifteen hundred square foot log cabin safe house, Travis and Ryan sat at a picnic table in the front yard, drinking beer. He climbed from the truck and stretched. "Kinda early for that, isn't it?"

Travis saluted him with his bottle. "Yep. Want one?"

"Of course. In a minute. I want to talk to Jade first. Where is she?"

Ryan pointed a thumb toward the house. "She and Nic are taking a nap."

Travis laughed. "Yeah, they were kinda grumpy."

Ryan jumped up. "I'll go make sure they're not armed and tell Jade you want to see her. I'll bring you a beer on the way back." He disappeared inside.

Coop grinned. How many bottles had Travis let him have? "He's in a better mood."

"You're welcome," Travis said.

"I can always count on you." He slapped Travis on the back, then threaded his long legs into the picnic table and sat.

"Blake filled us in on what went down. Special Agent Roberts hasn't had any luck identifying your dead man yet. What the hell did he want?"

The sun felt good on Coop's back, and he pulled off his jacket, draping it over the edge of the table. "He said he had a message for Jade and then reminded her about an oath of silence. I think she knew who he was, but she wasn't into sharing. I had a chat with Graves, and he said the guy wasn't one of his. I believe him." The anger he'd forced down after speaking with Reiner stirred to life. "I learned something else, too. I called Jade's—"

The screen door banged shut behind Ryan. "Nic's awake, but Jade's gone, and so are her bags."

Coop met Travis' gaze. "Oh shit!" they said simultaneously.

CHAPTER SEVENTEEN

Damn it! I must have taken a wrong turn. Sweat trickled down Jade's back as she looked both ways from the top of the rise. She'd been heading for this high spot for the past half hour, sure once she reached it and looked beyond, she'd see some sign of civilization. Instead, the dusty, graveled road wound away into the distance and eventually disappeared into the trees.

Arriving at the safe house by helicopter in the gray light of dawn had short-circuited her navigation skills. The log home was secluded and surrounded by forest, set back off the county road a good half mile. The pavement, once she'd reached it, was two-lane and well-maintained. Walking west, because Pine Bluff *had* to be west, the paved road had turned to gravel about ninety minutes later. She hadn't seen another human. No cars. No houses. No water, either, which was going to be a problem soon.

It'd been an impulse decision, clearly not well thought out. Leaving without basic necessities was just plain stupid. Fury had overruled any kind of rational thought. She'd been so angry with Coop and his I'm-always-right bullshit. He wasn't going to bully her into answering his questions. His self-righteous indignation only made her shame harder to bear. Bottom line—he'd hurt her, and she *had* to run. Selfish? Childish? *Maybe, but, damn it, he pissed me off.*

She groaned and dropped her bag in the tall grass alongside the road. A steep slope covered with loose dirt lay between her and any shade. Sticking out her lower lip, she blew a blast of air that moved the bangs on her forehead. Hot, sticky, and tired, she needed to rest. Then she'd suck it up and go back to the house. The heat and the long walk had served to dull her resentment, and the incriminating specter of foolishness was on deck.

She ripped off her jacket and tossed it on the ground. Dropping onto her bag, she laid her head on the coat and closed her eyes against the brilliant sunlight. Her tank top bared her arms to the heat while a pleasant breeze tickled her skin as it dried her sweat-dampened clothes. *Ten minutes is all I need.*

Over the sound of a slight breeze swaying treetops on the hillside above her, the faint drone of a vehicle's engine disturbed any hopes of a catnap. *Damn!* It hadn't taken Coop long to come after her. Now, she wouldn't get credit for going back on her own. *I hope he at least brings water.*

Another thirty seconds went by before she sat up and scanned the road she'd walked only moments ago. She saw nothing but a swirl of dirt where the wind had kicked up a dust devil. She swiveled to look in the opposite direction. Barreling down the middle of the road, a dark-colored SUV left a thick stream of dust in its wake.

She felt exposed, and for a moment, considered

grabbing her stuff and clawing her way up the slope to the forest that lined the road. Uncertainty held her in place too long. The driver had to have seen her by now. She got to her feet, struggling to remember where she'd put her weapon. *Shit!* Coop had pried it from her fingers after she'd fallen apart that morning. Her heart lurched into a gallop.

The vehicle, driven so recklessly, made her nervous. It was likely some crazy kid out for a joy ride, but that did nothing for the apprehension churning her stomach. What if it wasn't? It could be one of Carl Graves' crew—or worse. An image of the man from last night, blowing his head off, flashed through her mind.

The instant replay of the bewildering episode amplified the dread in her stomach. The idea that her own father had sent someone to kidnap and threaten her was preposterous. Still, she'd have to confront him at some point. The idea blew chunks big time.

The SUV was close enough she could see two men in the front seat, and yet the driver hadn't slowed. Maybe they'd fly right by and keep going.

No such luck.

A few feet away, the driver slammed on the brakes. The vehicle slid sideways toward her. She yelped, kicked her bag farther up the slope of the ditch, and jumped out of the way. The car came to a stop on the spot where she'd been standing. The passenger, tall and lean, hopped out and started around the front, a lame grin showing beneath the dark sunglasses he wore.

Outrage roared through her veins. "Do you think that was funny?" She glared at the man, barely taking notice of his gray suit and blue silk tie.

"Yeah, a little," he replied, striding toward her. He reached inside his jacket and flashed a credential so quickly she had no time for more than a glimpse. "Jade McDowell, you're coming with us."

She backed away, batting away the hand that reached for her. "I'm not going anywhere with you."

"Yeah, you are." He lunged toward her, his grin turning to a sneer.

There was no time to contemplate how he knew her name. Ducking beneath his grasp, she spun and grabbed his little finger, applying pressure toward the back of his hand until he dropped to his knees. When the joint popped, he shrieked and spewed a volley of four-letter words.

As she released the first man, the driver rushed toward her. She whirled and kicked, connecting solidly with his jaw. Broad-shouldered and stocky, the man stumbled back, shaking his head.

With a cold and calculating smirk, he wiped the blood from the corner of his mouth. "I don't think *Daddy* would approve of you being way out here all by yourself, dressed in that little white tank top...just the way I like."

She dropped her fists. "What did you just say?" Was he admitting her father had sent them? She wasn't ready when his beefy knuckles slammed into her jaw.

Face-planting in the dirt and pine needles, stars exploded behind her eyes. She tried to push herself up to the blare of horns and John Phillip Sousa playing *Semper Fidelis* in her head, but the man was on her before she could rise from the ground. He rolled her over on her back and sat on her abdomen. The smell of sweat and alcohol wrinkled her nose in distaste.

She went for his eyes, but her vision was still blurry, and he easily avoided her thumbs. Grasping her arms, he captured them beneath his knees, and the weight of his body held her down. She struggled to no avail. The noise in her head was quieting except for the horn, which seemed louder.

"You should have come peacefully, darlin'. We could have made this a lot easier." He bent toward her, his foul breath putrid, and wrapped both hands around her throat.

Jade bucked and twisted, trying to throw him off, but he was too heavy. He was crushing her larynx, and her lungs screamed for relief from the terrible emptiness. She was helpless.

Time slowed. Blackness encroached at the edges of her vision. *After everything, this is how it ends?*

Suddenly, the man released her. Precious air rasped painfully through her throat and filled her lungs. She gasped huge gulps again and again. For what seemed like forever, she lay there, considering the possibility she was dead.

Then weight returned as someone leaned on her shoulders. She tried to jerk away, striking out with her fists, but her assailant trapped her hands against her body.

"Jade, it's me. Open your eyes, so I know you're okay."

Coop? His voice was shaking. Was he hurt? She forced her eyes open, and his chiseled features filled her narrow field of vision. Still bruised from his fight with Derek, fresh blood seeped from a cut on his lip. How had he found her at precisely the right time? A memory niggled at her brain. *The horn!* She smiled, and a tear rimmed over and fell.

He released a shaky sigh and caught the tear with his thumb. "We need to get you to a doctor. The FBI is on the way. They'll take care of these two and find out who sent them."

I know who sent them. But it hurt to talk. Jade would tell him later—she owed him that and so much more.

She let him pull her up, then staggered into him as her world tipped on its side. "Sorry." The croak that came from her throat was barely recognizable as her voice. Not to mention, it hurt to swallow or take anything more than shallow breaths. With one hand over her eyes to slow the spinning, she braced her other arm against his chest. "So lightheaded. Need…a minute."

"I've got you." The next instant, her world tilted again, and he was carrying her. She laid her head against his chest, where it fit beneath his chin. His masculine scent surrounded her. She relaxed into him. Letting go of the need to depend only on herself, she allowed him to take charge. She had no doubt she could trust him with her life. How had she lost sight of that? As the feeling of safety settled into her soul, it started to sink in—she was alive only because of him.

"Thank you," she whispered, hoping he'd know her gratitude was for far more than carrying her.

His warm lips brushed her forehead. For the first time since she'd recognized him in Ryan's store, the tension between them melted away.

"Grab the door, Jade." As soon as she pulled it open, he pushed it out of the way with his shoulder and deposited her gently on the seat. Disappearing from her sight, he returned a few seconds later with a bottle of water.

"There's the boy scout I remember—always prepared." She winced, and the scrape of sandpaper beneath her vocal cords brought a groan from deep in her chest.

"Don't try to talk." His expression was desolate as he twisted the cap from the bottle and handed it to her. "Go easy on that. Drink too fast, and you'll likely choke."

With both hands on the bottle, she took a small sip. The cold water went down smoothly, so she tipped the bottle up and drank more until Coop tugged it away. To her dismay, a whimper escaped her lips.

"You can have all you want, as long as you take one sip at a time." His voice was gruff, but only concern surfaced in his eyes.

She gave him a half-assed salute. "Got it."

He grinned, handing her the bottle again. "Okay, smart-ass, let's see if you do."

She didn't drink right away. Instead, she held the cool bottle against her cheek and stared past him through the open door. "What about them?" She nodded her head toward the SUV that still sat half on and half off the graveled road.

"They're out cold and all trussed up for my friend, Special Agent Roberts, who'll be here in an hour or so. They might get a little warm by the time he arrives, and the one who choked you is laying extremely close to a red ant hill, but they'll live—which is better than they deserve." A grim frown shadowed his features.

She studied him for a moment. He was a warrior, from his hard head to his combat boots. A capable, talented and deadly SEAL. A man so handsome and sexy, yet genuinely kind and compassionate. An irresistible package that she had no right to think about in those terms. He deserved better.

"I'm sorry I left without telling anyone. If it means anything, I was on my way back." He had no reason to believe her. "I know you probably came after me so you could yell at me on the drive to the house. So, I'll give you this one. Go ahead. Yell all you want. I've got it coming."

The hint of a smile tickled his mouth as he feathered his knuckle along her bruised jaw. "I came after you because I promised I'd take you to pick up the meatball today. If you still want to, that is." He quirked an eyebrow. "And, I just said *don't try to talk*."

Moose! Jade had forgotten about him. What kind of a dog-mom was she, anyway? Thankfully, Coop had remembered. Emotions she hadn't dealt with in a long time welled in her chest, putting pressure on her throat. Staring at the water, Jade fought to bury the feelings that threatened to sever her heart in two again. Not sure she could keep her reactions in check, she nodded.

"Okay, then. Let's roll." Reaching across her, he buckled her seat belt.

Strange, how right it felt to let him take care of

her. *Better not get used to it.* She took another sip of water, laid her head back, and closed her eyes as he shut her door.

Jade sat up straight when she heard his voice. When he appeared at the open driver's-side door, he caught her watching and winked.

"Thanks, Travis ... Yeah, I'll tell her. She'll be fine, but she probably won't be taking off by herself again for a while." With an amused grin, he eased the sting of guilt caused by his words.

"Since we're less than thirty minutes from Baker City, we'll go get the dog. I'll find an urgent care facility to check her out and make sure nothing important is damaged."

Jade shook her head. She hated hospitals and doctors, with good reason. Short of being on her death bed, she wasn't going to put herself through that.

His brow furrowed. "Whether she likes it or not."

That's the problem with letting a man take charge, even for a minute. She groaned, regretting it when her throat tickled and made her cough.

"Contact me the minute you hear from Roberts. I need to know who hired those men and why. It might be late by the time we get back. Tell Nicole and Ryan she's okay, and she's sorry for worrying them." He grinned like he knew her indignant huff was only for show.

She should apologize to her sister, and she would as soon as they got back.

He slid into the driver's seat, tossed his phone on the dash, and started the pickup. Reaching toward her, Coop skimmed his fingers over her tender throat. She was already bruising and would raise some eyebrows when she walked into the veterinary clinic.

"What did Travis want you to tell me?"

Coop chuckled. "He thinks you need a keeper."

"Based on the past few hours, he might be right."

With one finger, he pulled her chin around and looked back and forth between her eyes. "Are you still lightheaded?"

"A little." She was still croaking. Somewhere she'd read that in at least half of the cases of strangulation, the victim's voice changed permanently.

"Stopping the blood flow in the carotid artery can cause that. Do you have any blank spots in your memory? Pain in your spine or around your hyoid bone?"

"No, but my throat hurts." She touched the front of her neck lightly.

"Bruised inside and out. It'll be sore for a few days. The doctor will be able to give you something for the pain and swelling." His hand slid down her arm until he covered hers on her leg, eliciting an involuntary shudder.

"Yeah, about that doctor—I don't do the whole medical thing anymore."

He gripped the wheel, put the truck in gear, and pulled away from the side of the road. "Sorry. Not negotiable. Strangulation can cause injuries that result in delayed fatality. I'm not taking a chance on missing something."

She turned her head, surprised by the urgency in his voice. Torn between being irritated by his mandate and the irresistible urge to give over control and let him run with it, no words of protest escaped her lips. Telling herself it hurt too much to argue, she turned away, cracked her window, and let the wind blow across her heated face. Closing her eyes, she laid her head against the seat.

She must have dozed off for a minute. She woke up when Coop rescued the water bottle from her fingers and set it in the cupholder.

He unbuckled her seatbelt. "It'll be easier on your neck if you move over here and rest your head on my shoulder."

"I'm fine. I don't want to make this awkward."

"I'm willing to take that chance." He didn't stop tugging on her until she scooted across the seat and settled her head against his bicep.

He'd been right, of course. It was far more comfortable. The next thing Jade knew, he was coaxing her awake with gentle sweeps of his fingers down her arm.

"We're at the vet's office. Do you want to stay here? I can spring the little meatball."

She sat up and looked around, then winced when she swallowed. The entire incident flooded back with a jolt. She touched her neck gingerly. "How bad do I look?"

He scooped a lock of hair behind her ear. "You look beautiful to me, but if you'd rather not explain to the infatuated doc in there, I'm happy to take that task off your plate."

She grimaced. "Infatuated, huh? I was hoping I was reading something into his attention that wasn't really there."

"No, I'm quite sure you got it right. So, let me take care of this." His lips pursed as he opened his door.

She placed a restraining hand on his arm. "I'll go with you. And you *will* be nice. Steve didn't have to take Moose in right away, you know. I'm sure he had a full day of appointments without us." Not looking away, she waited. "Agreed?"

He grinned. "Sure. Whatever you say." Stepping out, he crossed in front of the truck to open her door, and they walked into the clinic together.

Moose was frantic to get out of his cage when he saw her, barking frenziedly, then stopping to claw at the latch until she freed him. Before she could stand straight, the dog leaped into her arms and covered her face with his happy tongue.

"He's glad to see you. He's been protesting his incarceration all day." Steve glanced at his watch. "I have to say; I thought you'd be here earlier." For the second time since they'd entered the clinic, he frowned as his attention returned to her throat. The vet shot a quick look toward Coop, who lounged in the doorway with arms crossed, then stepped closer and lowered his voice. "Is everything all right? If he's hurting you, just say the word."

As Moose finally settled in her arms with a contented sigh, she tried to smile reassuringly. "I meant to be here first thing this morning, Doctor Prescott. Things got a little complicated last night. There was a brawl at the Dirty Duck. We were with Sheriff Carlton when she got the call, so Coop and I went along for backup." Hopefully, Steve would buy her lie.

The upward quirk of Coop's eyebrows as he watched did nothing to alleviate her guilt for leaving Moose so long or for the lie that had spilled from her so easily.

Skirting around the doctor, she strode toward the door. Coop straightened and stepped aside, and she slid through, pulling her checkbook from her purse as she stopped by the receptionist's desk.

"Hey, Doc, we have another stop to make that might take a while, and it's already getting late. I don't suppose you could recommend a motel that allows dogs where we could get a room for the night?

His emphasis on a single room almost made her laugh out loud. She set Moose on the high counter and glanced over the invoice the receptionist shoved in front of her.

"Hey, sweetheart, okay with you if we spend the night and drive back in the morning?"

Jade's skin heated, and she could feel herself blushing. Coop was giving the doctor the wrong idea. With a silent groan, she turned a dazzling smile on him. "Sure, babe. That'd be great." It would've come off a whole lot sexier if she wasn't still croaking like a frog.

She finished writing her check, then stole a glance toward Dr. Prescott in time to see the disappointment mirrored in his eyes.

"Best Western is always a good bet, but almost all motels in town allow dogs. You shouldn't have a problem." To his credit, the doctor appeared to have shaken off the rejection and remained professional.

"Great. Thanks for taking care of the mutt." Coop shook the doctor's hand, but Jade suspected it was more a contest of strength than any sincere appreciation. *Men!*

She gathered Moose in her arms and turned. "Thanks again, Doctor Prescott. I appreciate your help. Dinner is on *us* if you make it to Pine Bluff."

Coop ducked his head to hide his smile, and she had to turn away quickly to keep a straight face. He caught up with her, sliding his arm around her shoulders. As the door closed behind them, they both laughed.

"Do you think he got the hint?" He kept his arm around her, and she gripped Moose with both hands.

"Yeah. Steve seemed a little disappointed when you mentioned getting a room. You shouldn't have teased him."

Coop stopped, gripping the door handle of his truck. "I was dead serious."

She stilled the laughter that had filled her a second ago and studied his face. "Surely, you don't think I'm going to share a room with you?"

"Yeah, I do. You've been attacked twice in the past twelve hours. I'm not letting you out of my sight until we figure out why."

Hell no was on the tip of her tongue when he slanted her chin toward him and covered her lips with his, silencing her. Immediately, she tensed. Warning bells rang in the top-of-the-line safety system she'd built around her emotions.

Despite her efforts, training, and the damn promise she'd given her father—the one that appeared to be worthless now—Coop's warmth and tenderness seeped through her defenses. Desire sparked across her nerve endings, short-circuiting her brain. A moan rumbled in her throat. He gave an answering groan as the kiss turned from gentle to probing and hungry. She parted her lips, and he plunged inside, stroking and claiming. Weak already, her knees turned to rubber under his delicious onslaught. With Moose caged between them, she pressed as close as she could, one hand fisting in the lapel of his jacket. She needed this—to her shame and the detriment of everything she held sacred—she didn't want to stop.

Her body was flushed with heat when he raised his head until his lips hovered over hers. "That's non-negotiable."

What was I saying? Oh, right, staying in the same motel room.

Moose whimpered and licked her face, eliciting a laugh from Coop. Two sweet parting kisses later, he released her, opened the passenger door, and waited while she climbed into the seat. Then he jogged around to the driver's side and hopped in, flashing the sexiest grin in creation.

She shook her head, partially clearing the haze of lust that possessed her. *Haven't I hurt him enough?* Coop had been collateral damage in a fiasco of epic proportions, and she'd just made it a hundred times worse.

CHAPTER EIGHTEEN

Way to go, dipshit! Coop rubbed the back of his neck as the brunette behind the registration desk ran his credit card. What the hell was wrong with him? He hadn't meant for the moment to get out of hand, but he'd let it anyway. He'd kissed the woman who'd torn his heart out and tossed it into a woodchipper. Not just a platonic, it'll-be-okay kiss. Oh, hell no. A full-on, chest-thumping, I-want-your-hands-on-my-body, hot-blooded kiss. Knowing full well, she'd made up her mind a long time ago. *Jesus! What a dipshit!*

To make matters worse, she'd seemed all in, returning as hot and heavy as she got, pulling him in closer, turning him rock hard in a nanosecond. Was he supposed to believe her words or her actions? Who knows how far things would have gone if they hadn't been standing in the parking lot of the veterinary clinic?

In his defense, he'd nearly lost her today. For the second time. The woman he'd planned to spend the rest of his life with and whom he'd, apparently, never gotten over. *Oh, hell.* A gut-deep groan ricocheted around in his chest, causing the motel clerk to turn and scrutinize him curiously.

Was it true? It sure as hell felt that way. He might as well own it. Either way, he was screwed, big time. Too far in now to walk away, he had no choice. Jade was in trouble, and he wouldn't leave her unprotected. His heart was already swiss cheese, but the chances of him getting through this with a sound mind were slim.

Boundaries. As in, he needed some—like not being alone with her.

"Here you go, sir. Room 242. Top of the stairs and to your right. There's an elevator around the corner. Enjoy your stay." The hotel had no available first-floor rooms—his preference—but at least this one was near a stairwell that led to an exit, just in case. The cheery clerk smiled her dismissal and moved to the next couple waiting to check in.

He picked up the key card she'd placed on the counter. *One* key. Was he sharing a room with Jade because he needed eyes on her to keep her safe? Or because he needed her? *Shit!* Best not to think too hard on that.

He stopped just inside the lobby doors, where he could see his truck and called Travis. "Change of plans. We're staying the night at the Best Western in Baker."

Travis' momentary silence was positively leaden. "You sure that's a good idea, bro?"

The last thing Coop wanted to do was explain himself to his friend, especially since he had no rational explanation. "I'm sure. What did Roberts find out about the low-lifes who hurt Jade?"

"You're not going to like it. They're spooks—both of them. Military assets. Roberts got his ass chewed by the Joint Chiefs, and then he chewed mine. Thank you very much." Sarcasm dripped from his words.

"Goddamnit! Did anyone happen to say why they're after a former Air Force captain and POW?"

"*Need to know,* buddy, and those at the top don't think we need to know."

Coop raked a hand through his hair. "I don't believe this!"

"How's she doing?" Travis' voice lost its cynical edge.

"The last couple hours in the ER were hard on her. The doc poked and prodded and asked questions 'til I thought she might deck him. Hell, if he'd looked at me one more time as though I was the A-hole that did that to her, I'd have knocked him on his ass myself." He was damned proud of her for hanging in there. "She's tough…and stubborn. I can't get her to stop talking and rest her throat."

"It could always be worse," Travis said.

"Don't remind me. Anything new with Graves' militia?"

"Rumor has it half his crew took off when they learned the FBI had gotten a man inside and was about to shut down the operation. Left Graves so shorthanded, he was more than happy to get a recruit who knows how to handle himself. According to MacGyver, he's toned down his rhetoric and is no longer openly intimidating the townsfolk. The trial starts tomorrow."

Hopefully, Derek had gotten out of town. If he had taken it upon himself to silence Jade's sister, he undoubtedly realized Graves wasn't going to be the fall guy. Considering Derek's fascination with Jade, Coop would rest easier if the punk was in another county.

"What the hell did you say to him this morning?" Travis interrupted his musing.

Coop grunted. "I simply suggested he and his goons stay far away from Nicole West and Jade McDowell."

"I assume it wasn't so much what you said as how you said it." Travis paused for a heartbeat. "Maybe you should remember that when you're talking to Jade. Just sayin', buddy."

Coop wasn't sure what his friend meant by that, but he strove to keep his tone light. "You taking her side, now? The day I take your advice about women hasn't arrived yet." It was a safe subject. He and Travis were hopelessly inadequate at trying to figure out women.

Travis laughed. "Right back atcha, partner."

"Listen, I have to go. In the morning, I'll check in before we head back."

"Don't worry about me. I've been summoned for a thrilling game of Scrabble later. Just shoot me now." Travis' grumble faded out before he ended the call.

A grin elevated Coop's mood as he shoved the phone in his pocket and pushed through the glass doors. Long strides ate up the distance to his rig. It was after seven, and the parking lot was filling up. He eyed the line of vehicles but saw nothing that raised any flags.

Jade smiled tentatively, her hesitation and the most likely reason for it, piercing his chest. They needed to talk, and sooner would be better.

He scooped up the dog and helped her step down from the cab, nudging her toward the sidewall of the pickup so she could lean if necessary. She reclaimed the meatball while he grabbed their belongings from the backseat. "Room 242." He handed her the key card. "Elevator is beyond the registration counter, to the left."

She held herself stiffly as she walked across the pavement. It was clear she was downplaying her body's aches and pains. Once inside, she ducked behind Moose's furry head, no doubt to hide the angry red marks on her neck as she passed by the front desk. In the elevator, she sighed and sagged against the wall.

"You okay?" A stupid question when it was apparent she was nowhere near okay.

"Fine...but I need to sit down soon." The admission seemed to embarrass her.

Gathering both bags in one hand, he snaked his free arm around her waist. "Have you always been so stubborn?"

She shrugged. "Woman in a man's world. You know how it works."

He did, and she'd earned her captain's bars the hard way. Just one more reason he respected the hell out of her. The elevator doors opened on the second floor, and he swept her from the car as she leaned against him. Halfway down the hallway, they found their room, and she unlocked the door.

Flipping the lights on, he dropped the bags just inside. "Hang tight a minute." A quick search of the room relieved his overprotective tension somewhat.

Still, considering Travis' new information, he checked the locks on the window before returning to the door to throw the deadbolt and hook the chain.

"Paranoid much?" One corner of her mouth twitched in a semi-grin as she set Moose on the floor and moved a few steps into the room. She performed a cursory inspection of their sleeping accommodations. "Which bed do you want?"

He laid his weapon on the nightstand. "I'll take the one closest to the door." Retracing his steps, he grabbed her bag and placed it on the other bed. Shrugging out of his jacket, he tossed it on a chair.

She hadn't moved from her spot just inside the door. Folding her arms across her stomach, she peered at Moose as the dog explored, sniffing out his new surroundings.

"Jade?"

She jerked to attention, darting a glance toward him before she focused on her bed and shuffled in that direction. Stiffly, she sat on the edge as though prepared to bolt at the slightest sign of trouble.

The tension between them was unmistakable. Was it the kiss that had made her so nervous? He turned toward her and slowly sat on the edge of his bed. "We need to talk." His words overlapped hers when she spoke at the same time.

"I have to tell you something, Coop." Wide-eyed, she stared at him, and then they both started to laugh.

It was good to see her let go, though he could tell by the way her hands went to her throat, it wasn't without pain. He should have thought of that sooner. Jumping up, he crossed to his jacket and removed the bottle of pain pills the doc had prescribed. She'd worried they'd make her less stable and had wanted to get to their room before taking them. He bumped the container against his palm until one pill fell out, then entered the bathroom and returned with a half-full glass. She winced as the drug went down. The subtle marker, reminding him of how close she'd come to death, brought a surge of fury and a crushing need for payback. His fists clenched and unclenched as he fought for control.

He took the glass from her and set it on the nightstand. "I'm sorry about the kiss. I mean, I'm not sorry I kissed you, but I don't want you to think I expect anything else. We're not sharing a room so I can get you in the sack."

She raised her head to look directly into his eyes. "You're an honorable man, and I sincerely appreciate everything you've done. I'm a big girl, and I'm just as much to blame for what happened. And, for the record, I'm not sorry either."

Say what? He sat, mute until a playful grin curved her lips. His heart thawed around the edges under her warm perusal. "Good. That's really good." Not that he intended to throw her down on the bed and have his way with her. There were still unresolved issues between them. It was a start—a damn good start.

"Tell you what. I'm going to order a couple of fruit smoothies from the juice joint down the street. If we're still hungry after that, I'll hunt up some milkshakes for dessert. While I'm gone, why don't you get ready for bed? Then we can talk. Sound good?"

Her smile seemed to illuminate the room, as well as a few of the dark places inside him. "Sounds wonderful. I'm kind of hungry…and dying for a shower. The fruit smoothie idea is really thoughtful. Thank you."

He winked. "Don't tell the guys. I have a rep to uphold." He grabbed his jacket, considered the handgun, and picked up the key card instead. "Lock the door behind me and don't let anyone in. I'm leaving the SIG just in case. I'll only be gone five minutes, ten tops." He raised his eyebrows. "Think you can be in and out of the shower by then?"

She looked from him to the gun. "You're scaring me." Her hands rested lightly on her hips. "Do you know something you're not telling me?"

He unlocked the door and placed one hand on the doorknob. "We're safe here for now, and I think we both know something we haven't shared. Don't forget to lock the door." He stepped into the hallway but only walked away after he heard the deadbolt sliding home.

The pain meds had kicked in. Maybe half a pill would suffice for her next dose. Coop took the smoothie cup out of her hands after her third attempt to suck the last drops from the bottom.

She stuck her lower lip out, pretending to pout, then giggled when he shot the cup into the garbage for two points. "Mmm mmm mmm…you are a sexy man, James Cooper."

He turned to see her ogling his ass. Only fair, since he'd enjoyed the view of her perky breasts in a flimsy, sleeveless, cut-off shirt that stopped three inches short of meeting her flannel pajama pants. Her wavy hair glistened, still wet from her shower. Olive complexion, scrubbed clean of the ground-in dirt from her life and death struggle, screamed for him to stroke her silky skin. The smell of soap and strawberry-scented shampoo messed with his control as she sat cross-legged in the center of her bed. Having finished off the sausage sandwich Coop had bought for the little mooch, Moose lay curled in a ball against Jade's thigh.

So far, he'd resisted a repeat of their kiss, but every time she spoke, her raspy voice went straight to his dick. "I think it's time for you to sleep it off."

The come-and-get-me-look in her eyes was hard to ignore, but he'd bet it was drug-induced, and she'd be embarrassed in the morning. He wasn't about to take advantage of her unless it was to get her to open up to him. He'd take that any way he could get it. Coop yanked his T-shirt off, unbuttoned his jeans, and flopped on top of his covers.

She snorted. "I haven't had anything to drink."

She might as well have. Taking the pain pill on an empty stomach probably hadn't been the best idea. He rolled on his side and studied her. "Okay, then talk to me. You said you needed to tell me something."

The sparkle faded from her violet-blue eyes, and he could almost see the shutters slam into place. She dropped her gaze to his bare chest and reached for the dog tags he wore—her dog tags. Almost reverently, she fingered the raised lettering as though she'd never seen them before. The silence stretched as he gave her time. Pushing her wasn't the answer.

A deep sigh rocked her shoulders. "I did say—I mean, I do, but...I need to work up to this conversation...so, maybe you could go first?" She raised her head. Her whisper, her body language, the desperate question in her eyes—her entire demeanor cried out for him to understand.

He wasn't looking forward to this particular exchange of information either, but he couldn't very well hold out on her if he expected her to share. "I checked in with Travis after I arranged for our room. Your sister and Ryan are safe and secure at the house. Travis is grumbling. Something about a Scrabble marathon." His lips quirked as a quiet laugh slid from her throat.

"Those men who attacked you today are military assets. Their existence is classified, and they don't show up in any database in the world. The other guy, the one who offed himself, is likely from the same kettle. Killing himself was a good indicator whoever sent him isn't exactly operating within military protocol." He paused as concern skated across her features.

"That means the FBI couldn't hold them. Right? They're out there somewhere, looking for me." Instead of the fear he'd dreaded, her eyes flashed with anger.

"Roberts will keep tabs on them. Whoever's behind this will want the commotion to die down before they try again. We'll leave early tomorrow and be at the safe house long before they've had a chance to regroup. No one will get to you there." Not while he was alive.

"You think the person who sent those men has

gone rogue." Her assessment wasn't a question.

He paused while he processed that information. "You know who it was, don't you? Maybe someone involved with your final mission? Who has the most to lose if you break your *oath of silence*?"

She stared over his right shoulder, her lower lip caught between her teeth. Her eyes constantly moved as though she was trying to calculate the answer and didn't like the bottom line. For a few minutes, no one spoke.

"I talked to your commanding officer this morning." Maybe a change of subject would inject new life into their conversation and break the impasse.

She tensed. "Colonel Reiner? You had no right—"

"I had *every* right to find out what *you* wouldn't tell me." Coop struggled to keep his voice level, but his words still sounded harsh. He swung his legs over the edge of the bed and faced her. "I'm trying to keep you alive, and it'd be a hell of a lot easier if I weren't operating in the dark." He fisted his hands in the comforter to keep from leaving his bed for hers.

A shaky breath seemed to calm her. "What did Mark tell you?"

He chose his words carefully. "That your mission wasn't sanctioned. Reiner said you were gathering intel in the no-fly zone, and the Syrian soldiers were waiting for you. You didn't have a chance."

"What else?" Her voice was gruff, and he suspected it was from the raw emotion that vibrated her entire body.

He forced himself to continue. "It was months before they got confirmation you were alive and sent in a team of SEALs." Goddammit, he should have been there. "Mark didn't share any private details about your captivity—only that it was hell. He didn't have to. I could use my imagination to know how those bastards treated you."

A lone sob shook her.

That was the end of his restraint. He rolled to his feet and slid to the center of Jade's bed. Her eyes red-rimmed, she reached for him, and he locked his arms around her. "I'm so damn sorry I wasn't on that tarmac when your rescue chopper landed. You have to believe I would have been if I'd known." His heart lurched as rage pounded through his veins. He wanted to kill the asshole who'd kept him away. Voicing that desire would be a mistake, however. That man was General Terrance McDowell, Jade's father, and she was highly protective of her old man.

Moose stirred with a whine and tried to insert himself between them. Coop eased back and let him slip onto her lap. Periodically, the dog whimpered and pawed at her leg.

Coop lost track of how long he held her while she cried, issuing promises from his heart she'd probably never let him keep. The dam had broken. The strongest woman he knew could take no more. His whispered words of comfort were nothing in the face of such despair. But he was there, and that had to count for something.

When she finally cried herself out, and the teary hiccups had almost run their course, he brushed the hair from her face, dried the wet streaks, and kissed her cheek. Folding back the bedding, he placed her on the sheets and tucked the covers around her. Moose stretched his body protectively along her side, opposite Coop.

She caught his arm as he turned away. "No...stay with me."

He squeezed her hand. "I'll be back in a flash." He padded to the door, checked the locks, and peered through the peephole. Crossing the room, he gazed through the gap in the drapes, satisfying himself there were no suspicious vehicles in the lot, then let the curtain fall closed.

His socks hit the floor before he crawled under the covers and drew her close again. The feeling of being home was both comforting and heartrending. How long would she want him by her side? Not that it mattered. He'd be there as long as she needed him.

She leaned on one elbow and rose to hover above him. Slowly, deliberately, she traced a circle on his chest, and he was hard in an instant. She smiled when he sucked in a sharp breath. Her soft lips feathered against his jaw, then teased his mouth. Despite her injuries and her compromised state, his body reacted to her touch. He placed one hand on the back of her neck and pulled her in, taking control.

Her kiss was urgent, so damn hot and full of promise. Because she wanted him? Or was it a small white pill on an empty stomach? Caught up in lust and how good she felt pressed against his chest, Coop almost lost sight of the difference. *Almost*. With what seemed like his last drop of integrity, he pushed her up and onto her back.

He tasted her lips one last time before raising his

head. "We both need to get some sleep."

Hurt flashed across her face. "I'm sorry." She turned on her side, away from him, and the meatball curled into the curve of her body.

Coop rolled to his back and stared at the ceiling, kicking himself for putting rejection and humiliation in her expression.

She was silent for a few minutes, but he knew she wasn't sleeping. Suddenly, she slammed her fist into her pillow several times, flipped it over, and heaved a sigh. "I feel like a fool, throwing myself at you. I thought…"

When she didn't continue, he turned on his side, slid his arm around her, and pulled her back tight to his front. He kissed a trail from her shoulder to the spot where her pulse thrummed beneath her skin. "You thought what? That I wanted you? To make love to you all night? You weren't wrong." He rocked against her flannel-covered ass.

A quick exhalation told him the moment she understood. "Feel how hard you make me?" He thrust against her again, eliciting another exhale. She tried to shift around, but he held her fast. "I've never wanted you this bad. I hope to hell it's not just the pain meds talking because it's going to happen—just not tonight."

She stopped wiggling against him as his hand found the bare skin of her abdomen and moved upward until his thumb lightly stroked the curve of her breasts.

"You're injured. Your body suffered a serious shock. Hell, you nearly died today. I'm in charge tonight, and I say you need eight hours of uninterrupted sleep. I'm here to make sure that happens." He would no doubt be wide awake for a while. His voice dropped to a whisper. "Tell me you understand how desperately I want to be inside you." He circled her ear with his tongue and smiled when she shivered. "Tell me."

"I do—I understand." Her hoarse voice made him even harder.

Okay, I might never sleep again. Coop released his hold so she could move, his heart warming when she stayed close beside him. "Go to sleep, sweetheart. I've got this watch." After a minute or two, she relaxed against him. Considering what she'd been through, he'd call it progress.

When he thought she was about to drop off, she leaned into him to look over her shoulder. "You asked if I knew who sent those men. Not for sure, but I think it was my father."

The sucker-punch slammed into his gut, and it was all he could do to keep from flinching. What kind of a father tried to kill his own daughter? Scratch that. Coop didn't need to know. One way or another, he was going to end the son-of-a-bitch.

CHAPTER NINETEEN

Jade woke, groggy, to a sliver of pale light through the nearly closed drapes and radiating heat from the man with his arm draped over her, holding her solidly against his hard body. He smelled masculine with a hint of wintergreen, the mix an erotic scent that fostered intimate cravings. Desire pooled between her legs, and she clenched her thighs together in response.

Pleasant dreams were few and far apart, so she burrowed into the warmth of this one and tried to recapture the thread. Until fingers swept over her puckered nipple, and a bolt of lightning shot through her body. She jumped and half-turned before someone caught her in a vice grip.

Awareness slowly replaced the remnants of sleep in her foggy brain, and she surveyed her surroundings. Beige walls enclosed the bed where she lay. Straight ahead, a small table with one chair and a reading lamp pressed against the drapes that almost hid the cloudy skies beyond. A reddish-blond fuzzball, which must be Moose, lay curled and sound asleep by her bag on the next bed. *Where the hell am I?*

"Good morning." Hot breath warmed the back

of her neck. Lips dropped erotic kisses from her throat to her earlobe while those fingers shifted downward, toward the throbbing wetness at the apex of her legs.

Not a dream. Holy moly! "Coop?" The electricity zapping her nerves caused an upward lilt at the end of his name.

He chuckled without stopping his exploration. "Who were you expecting?"

"No one, actually. Didn't you turn me down last night?" She had a partial memory of him expounding the idea *he was in charge*. Maybe he was since just his voice had her turned on and ready. She stretched her legs and brushed against his erection.

He groaned and pulled loose the tie of her flannel pajama pants with a purposeful flourish. "That was last night, and I explained why. Did you sleep well?" He slipped his hand beneath her sleep pants, caressing her skin, and stopped a good two inches from where she needed him to be.

"I did. You?" She was pleased to note her voice was clearer this morning, and her throat didn't hurt as much when she swallowed.

He nipped her shoulder, then soothed the sting with his tongue. "Not really. I was up all night." He thrust his pelvis against her ass as the hand on her stomach kept her in place. "I think we should fix that problem now that you've had your eight hours."

At some point during the night, Coop must have removed his jeans. Every solid ridge of muscle pressed against her from head to toe. Her thin pajamas were no obstacle to his heat. "Only if you're still up for it." She inhaled sharply, then moaned when his hand slid between her legs.

"Shh…we don't want to wake the meatball." With a soft chuckle, he nuzzled her neck. "Mmmm…you're so wet." He rotated her onto her back as he rose on his elbow and slipped his knee between her thighs.

His muscled body holding her down flipped a panic switch somewhere deep inside. Exposed and unable to move, fear invaded her heart. Ugly memories of being restrained as soldiers took her forcefully encroached on her reality. She whimpered and tensed for flight, even while trying to talk herself down off the cliff.

Coop would never hurt me.

"You're okay. It's just me." Concern laced his calm voice. He rolled to his back and pulled her toward him, so she leaned over him. "You can trust me. I promise you that." He kissed her ear. "Do you remember your safe word?"

That's right. Back in the day, they'd gone for adventurous, often spicing up their romance with role-playing and edgy sex. On occasion, Coop had gotten off on being in control in the bedroom, and she'd learned how sexually rewarding shaking up the status quo could be. She felt herself grow wetter, just remembering.

"Um…yeah. Leapfrog."

He laughed, a fierce, sexy sound. "Good. We're going to take it nice and slow for now, but if I do anything that makes you the least bit uneasy, use your safe word. Okay?"

"Okay." *For now?* Did that mean he wanted more than a one-time deal? Distracted by the prospect of a real future, she moaned as Coop slid his finger through her wet folds and plunged inside.

Excruciatingly slow strokes. With each thrust, the heel of his hand rubbed her sensitive mound. Pleasure to the point of pain built to a crescendo, only to have him back off, his hand sliding up to lavish attention on her swollen nipples.

"Does that feel good, sweetheart?"

"Need...more."

"What do you need? Tell me."

"You...inside me." She pressed against him, pleased when he groaned.

Suddenly, he grabbed her hips and lifted her until she straddled him. He positioned her apex over his throbbing manhood and ground against her. Awash in sensual pleasure, she closed her eyes and braced against his chest, aroused further by the pounding of his heart beneath her hands.

He jerked her top up and off, tossing it toward the end of the bed. "We'll get to that in a minute."

Her nipples hardened more with the heat of his gaze. His hands cupped her heavy breasts as desire flamed in his eyes. She wrapped her hand around his thickness and squeezed while working her way to the base. A sense of power surged through her when his eyes fell closed with a hiss.

Fingers skimmed her stomach until he tugged on the waistband of her pants. "Do you like these flannel things?" His nearly black eyes stared into hers.

"Yes. Why?"

"We better get you out of them before I tear them to shreds." Hands encircled her waist and lifted her sideways.

She landed on her back with a surprised squeal. Coop knelt beside her, lifted her hips, and pushed down her pants, peeling them from her legs. In an instant, she was naked and exposed, and fear returned. Her frantic mind searched for her safe word, but she'd lost it as the image of Mahaz loomed over her. She tried to curl into a ball, but her wrists were pulled tight and pinned. Rough hands grabbed her ankles and forced her legs apart. She drew air to scream.

"Open your eyes, Jade." Coop's calm demand shredded the illusion that had possessed her, and she obeyed.

He smiled through the strain of concern on his handsome face. "Look at me. It's just you, me, and the meatball if you want to count him.

A strangled laugh surfaced, but she wouldn't let go of his gaze.

"I swear to God there's no one in this room who will hurt you...or let anyone else hurt you...ever again." He kissed her with such tenderness it brought an ache to her chest. "I'm sorry. I'm pushing you too fast. It's too soon."

When he raised his head, she caught his face in her palms. "No, please don't pull away. I want this. I want *you*. I don't want *him* to have this power over me. It's just—I haven't let anybody get close since—."

A teasing grin reached his eyes. "Not even Doctor Steve?"

Grateful for him lightening the mood after her embarrassing confession, she huffed a laugh and waggled her eyebrows. "No, but he's got a certain appeal. Don't you think?"

Coop laughed. "Oh no, you didn't!" He claimed her mouth, gently at first, sweeping his tongue inside to tangle with hers.

She wrapped her arms around his neck, pulling him closer. He'd always been such a good kisser. That had been her downfall on their second date. Well, that and two giant margaritas in quick succession. He latched onto one of her nipples, and she felt the tug in her core. She couldn't help pressing into him.

While one hand caught her hair, the other meandered over her rib cage and abdomen until he palmed her mound. He groaned as he worked his fingers through her slickness, then inserted two of them deep inside, sliding in and out to some unknown rhythm. She pulsed around his fingers as he pulled out and sank in again. Slowly, he kissed a path down her body until she felt his breath on her softly throbbing womanhood.

"Are you ready?" His whispered words were wind to a flickering flame. He didn't wait for an answer, and, truthfully, she wouldn't have been able to form a cohesive thought at that moment.

Sweat beaded on her brow and between her breasts, and pressure built with every stroke of his magical fingers. Suddenly, the fullness of him was gone. A heartbeat later, his thumb rolled over her clit, lifting her hips off the mattress in an involuntary need for more. He pinched her sensitive bud sharply, the sudden sting dissolving into sparkly bits of bliss and reverberating through her nerve endings.

The next instant, his tongue laved the spot, then

his mouth closed over her, and he sucked hard. She gripped the bedding as molten lava poured through her veins until she rocketed into orbit, crying out his name, and stars exploded behind her eyelids.

Even then, he didn't stop, bringing her through each tremor that shook her entire body, drawing them out until her strength depleted, and she floated in a sexual haze. His talented mouth took hers in a scalding kiss, his teeth scraping her lower lip, his tongue darting inside at the first opportunity. Hands stroked her torso and teased her painfully swollen nipples while his tongue plunged deep, tasting, claiming as though he owned her soul. At that moment, he did.

When he shifted away from her, she missed his heat and closeness immediately, protesting with mumbled pleas not even she could understand.

"I'll be right back, sweetheart." Coop leaned off the edge of the bed, rifled through something on the floor, and produced a condom. His white teeth flashed as he bit and ripped the package open.

She snagged it from his hand. "Not so fast. It's my turn." She closed her hand around his thick penis, and it hardened even more beneath her fingers. With her other hand, she pressed against his chest until he laid his head and shoulders on the pillows. Holding his gaze, she slid her hand down his length in a slow swirl, then back up and thumbed the tip until he jerked and groaned. A thrill washed over her at the need and hunger in his eyes. Slowly, she leaned over him and took him in her mouth.

He lunged for her, lifting her to the side and under him in one movement. "Damn, Jade. I can't wait another second. I need to be inside you. Now." He found the condom package where she'd let it fall and quickly sheathed himself. He dropped to his elbows over her, spreading her legs with his muscular thighs. With one thrust, he filled her and captured her moan of pleasure with his mouth as he gently kissed her.

He lifted her legs until she wrapped them around his waist. Twining their fingers together beside her head, he settled his hard chest against her tender breasts. His brown eyes almost black, he stared as though silently demanding she not look away.

Slowly, he pulled out and rocked back into her, going still as he kissed her again with infinite tenderness. "Are we good?" His whisper tickled against her lips.

She laughed softly. "Now you ask?" She'd forgotten he was such a kind and compassionate lover. No wonder she'd fallen so hard.

He grinned. "I'll take that as a *yes*." He tightened his grip on her hands and powered into her.

Again and again, he filled her. With each thrust, the bone of his pelvis slapped her sensitive clit. The pleasure was tormenting, the pressure almost more than she could bear, yet it wasn't enough. He released her hands without missing a beat and tilted her hips, opening her wider and plunging deeper.

Jade fisted her hands in the sheets. Her need was so intense, she tried to hold back, savor it, but it was too much. When she broke, it was as though a bomb detonated somewhere close. Her world shook, and she shattered into a million pieces.

Driving home again, he pressed her into the

mattress as he strained to reach deeper. He came with a roar as tremor after tremor rolled through him. "Mine." The word was barely audible before he collapsed and gathered her into his arms as though desperate he might lose her.

She stiffened. Had Coop really said that word, or was it only the way the air escaped his lungs with his release? Either way, the implications of what they'd done would surely break her heart again.

CHAPTER TWENTY

Coop woke to daylight through the crack of the curtains and an empty bed. He had a full two seconds of *oh-shit* before the bathroom door opened, and a freshly showered and dressed Jade appeared. She ushered the smell of wildflowers and sunshine into the room, followed by an adoring Moose who shadowed her every move. Relief that she hadn't run—or worse, that he'd dreamed the whole thing—robbed him of strength for a moment.

He rolled to his side and propped on his elbow. "Mornin, gorgeous."

Dark brown hair, still wet, rested on her shoulders, leaving water patches on her hunter green tank top. Tight jeans molded to every curve, and he felt his body awaken in response.

"You always were a morning person." Fussing with the clasp on her watch, she refused to look at him.

His heart did a freefall into his stomach. *She regrets making love. Damn it! I should have known she wasn't ready.* He watched as she skirted the end of both beds and strode to the window. With a sweep of her arms, she yanked the curtains wide, allowing the feeble sunshine to invade the room. Despite the splotchy clouds he could see through the glass, he had to squint against the sudden brightness.

"Looks like it might rain." She turned and moved toward him, her face indistinguishable in the light arcing around her as though she was an angel straight from the presence of God.

He should tell her he was sorry—that he shouldn't have pushed her. She needed to know she was the best thing that ever happened to him, and he'd start from square one, earning her trust, if only she wouldn't say she never wanted to see him again. Words failed him, and he slumped against the pillows, a dull ache in his chest.

Jade walked between the beds and rifled through her open bag until she pulled out a well-worn jean jacket. She dropped it on the bed, and the dog jumped up, circled, and laid down on top of the coat. Running her fingers over the meatball's head, she turned, the beginnings of a smile pulling at her lips. Her body blocked the sun that had kept her face hidden. Her gaze locked on his, her smile faded, and a myriad of emotions cascaded across her attractive features. Curiosity, realization, regret, fear swirled in her eyes, bluer now because of the shade of green she wore. *God, she's so damn beautiful.*

She sat slowly on the edge of the other bed, then nodded as though agreeing with him about something. "It's okay if it didn't mean anything to you. I mean, we can forget it ever happened. We can be friends, or you can continue to hate me if you want. It's just...being thrown together like this—"

The silly woman kept talking, but he was no longer listening. How the hell could she think their love-making this morning hadn't meant anything? She needed to get that thought out of her head right now. He sat up, leaned over the edge of the bed, and grasped her wrist. With one tug, she sprawled across his lap as a surprised squeak interrupted her rambling.

Flipping her onto her back, he rolled halfway on top of her. "Enough." He covered her mouth with his as she started to protest. His lips moved over hers gently, but her squirming served to finish the job of turning him on, begun when she stepped from the bathroom. Slipping his hand beneath her shirt, he teased her nipples, already puckered and tight for him. He longed to run his tongue over those sweet peaks, but he had to set some things right first.

With a growl, he raised his head. "I must be losing my touch." When she started to speak, he silenced her with a finger over her lips. "You had your chance. Now, it's my turn." His hand went back to roving over her body, stopping at the button of her jeans. With two fingers, he popped the button loose and lowered her zipper.

"Coop—"

He took advantage of her open mouth to silence her with lips and tongue, plunging inside, claiming all of her. She tasted sweet and minty, and he couldn't get enough. Finally, she relaxed and melted against him, one arm going around his neck.

He released her mouth and nuzzled his way to her ear. "As I was saying, I must be losing my touch if you think making love to you didn't mean something to me." He purposely whispered in her ear and smiled when she trembled beneath him.

A small sigh left her as his hand slid beneath her panties.

"There's no way in hell I'll ever forget. I could never hate you, and I most certainly won't be just your friend. We're staying right here for as long as it takes to get that foolishness out of your head." He wiggled his fingers as he pressed on toward the prize. He found her sensitive spot and teased the delicate bundle of nerves until she was writhing and pressing into his hand. A firm flick of his thumb sent her over the edge, and she clung to him as she came apart in his arms.

He grinned down at her and gathered her closer. "You realize you've got too damn many clothes on, right?" Coop kissed the corners of her mouth where they turned up in a smile.

She laughed. "That didn't seem to hinder you."

He pushed to his knees, grabbed the waistband of her jeans, and stripped them off along with her panties. A grin spread over his face. "It might for this next part."

She snorted a laugh. "You want more? Don't you think we should hit the road?"

He lunged for her as she squealed and tried to roll off the bed. She wasn't nearly fast enough. Grabbing the hem of her shirt, he tugged it over her head, sending it flying toward the foot of the bed. Desire burned through his blood as he pulled her bra straps down her arms enough to free her breasts. *So beautiful.* He had to clench his teeth to keep from ending this prematurely.

Reverently, he cupped the creamy mounds, kneading, occasionally brushing her taut pebbles to make her lungs work harder. When he couldn't hold out any longer, he filled his mouth greedily, licking and sucking. Jade's nails scraped his back every time he licked the tip with his tongue. He ran his teeth gently across the swollen bead, then released it and turned to give attention to her other breast.

With a moan, she pulled his head down, encouraging him to take his fill, which he was more than happy to do. Her legs parted, and he filled the gap with his thigh, rubbing along her slickness.

"Coop...I need you." A tremble vibrated in her voice.

He released her breast and moved up her body until they were face to face. "Are we done pretending this doesn't mean anything? That *you* don't mean everything to me?" Brushing the hair from her face, he looked into her eyes.

Doubt resided there for a moment until she tilted a determined jaw, and he could almost see her walls coming up one by one. "What about the past three years? I knew it would hurt you, Coop, and I did it anyway. How will you ever forgive me?"

He understood why she'd returned to the States without contacting him after being rescued. Her former commanding officer had spilled the beans. She'd admitted she believed her father had sent the men who tried to kill her—a shocking accusation. He'd get to the bottom of it as soon as they returned to the safe house. Forgiving her was easy. She'd been a victim, and she'd suffered far too much. He would never forgive her father for what he'd put them both through.

Wrapping a strand of her wet hair around his

finger, he tugged gently. "Already done." He dropped a kiss on her jaw and captured her mouth. Tenderly meeting her lips, he longed to assure her he'd protect her from the ugliness of her past, including that perpetrated by her prick father.

She pushed against him and tried to wiggle out of his arms, but this was one time he wasn't backing off. He tapped the side of her head. "Tell me what's going on in there."

"You don't mean that. You couldn't possibly..." A strangled laugh interrupted her.

He tipped her chin and forced her to look at him. "I mean every word. I swear to God I'm not just trying to knock boots with you."

She rolled her eyes, a trace of humor in those violet-blue orbs. "You're *so* romantic."

He laughed. "Yeah? You knew that about me when we first hooked up."

A watery smile brightened her eyes. "True."

Covering her lips, he kissed her deeply, with all the hunger and yearning he possessed, then pushed the hair back from her face. "I don't want to scare you, but the truth is I want a hell of a lot more from you than a roll in the hay. Like I told you when we met, I don't do one-night stands." He teased his thumb over her soft cheek, watching as fear sprang into her eyes, and she tried once more to push him away.

"Hold on. Don't panic. I don't mean I expect things to go back to the way they were before. I know that won't happen. What you went through changed you, and losing you changed me. We're two different people." They would have to start over, learning if they still wanted to be together.

"What do you want from me, Coop?"

"A chance...to be in your life. To learn to trust each other again." He brushed his hand over the swell of her breast, and her breathing hitched. He grinned. "I think there's still a sexual attraction."

"Ya' think?" Her eyes sparkled with something more than tears.

He rocked his hard length against her hip. "You have to admit; this is pretty damn hot. We can start here," he tweaked her nipple, "and see where it goes."

"What if it all falls apart?" Jade studied his face intently as her hand moved to his penis, and her mere touch made him jerk and hiss between his teeth.

A gut-deep groan wound through him. He kissed her lips as he hardened more beneath her hand. "That's not going to happen—but if it does, or if you want out for any reason, all you have to do is use your safe word...and I'll walk away. Okay?"

She squeezed his rock-hard shaft, working up and down its length. He'd take that as a *yes* any day. In one motion, he pushed to his knees, shoved his arm under her hips, and flipped her over.

"You could give a girl a little warning." She propped her head on her elbow with a sexy grin and watched as he leaned over the edge of the bed to grab his discarded jeans. Fumbling for his wallet, he removed a condom and sheathed himself.

He leaned forward and pulled her hips off the bed until she was just where he wanted her. As she tried to redistribute her weight and balance, he pressed against her ass, spreading her legs, his dick at her opening. One arm locked around her waist, making sure she stayed on her knees, and the other hand pressed down between her shoulders. As her elbows bent and her head lay on the mattress, the movement tipped up her hips, and he used the extra momentum to plunge in deep, clear to his balls. Pleasure, sharp as pain, crackled all around him. Sweat broke out on his forehead as he fought the compulsion to come right there. Holding still was excruciating, but he forced himself.

She moaned and rocked against him, clearly trying to make him start moving, but he held her tight. "Coop, please...do something."

"Do we have a deal?"

"What? Now you ask me that?"

He adjusted his arm around her waist, drawing her tighter against his hips. The sheets muffled her whimper. He grinned. "Do we...have a...deal?"

"*Yes!*"

Coop pulled out half-way and plunged in, the force sliding her toward the top of the bed. "Slow and easy?"

She shook her head vehemently. "Hard...and fast." The words came out on a groan.

He smiled. There was the woman he'd loved. "Brace your arms against the headboard. Hold on tight." Once she was in position, he removed his hand from her back and started working her clit.

Moaning, she pressed against him. He drew out slowly, all but about an inch, and slammed in again. Setting the rhythm from there, he pounded her perfect ass with each thrust, his fingers never letting up on the sensitive place between her legs. The little sounds she made spurred him on. Pressure within him grew exponentially, stroke after stroke propelling him closer to the brink.

She was tight and hot, and he tensed every muscle to hold off his orgasm for as long as he could. She broke with a muffled cry seconds before him. Her walls pulsed around him, driving him toward the precipice. Two more thrusts, and he exploded, the agony of pleasure shattering what remained of his control. His lungs stopped working for the space of several heartbeats as he clasped her against him and strained deeper. He pressed her down, and they both collapsed on the bed.

It was a few minutes before he could speak. Except for gasps of air, Jade hadn't budged either, sparking concern within him. She'd asked for hard and fast, and he hadn't held back. With hindsight, maybe he should have. He pulled out and levered to her side. "Are you okay? Did I hurt you?"

She opened her eyes and smiled. "I'm good."

Relief let loose of the hitch in his chest. He kissed her. "Holy hell, you're better than good. Amazing. Fantastic. Incredible."

She poked his side. "Stop." Her smile had widened.

Surely, she hadn't doubted herself. Coop landed another kiss on her cheek, patted her slightly red ass, and rolled off the bed. "Don't go anywhere. I'll be right back."

He relieved himself, cleaned up, and splashed water on his face before he left the bathroom. Jade still hadn't moved, and now she was sound asleep. He debated waking her, but she needed the rest, and they could head back in a couple of hours. He'd still have plenty of time to dig up the information he needed on General McDowell.

She didn't make a sound when he tucked the blankets around her naked body, ignoring the incessant stirring of his dick. *She's so damn gorgeous, just like an angel.* He had to force away the fear she might be a figment of his imagination—that if he closed his eyes, she'd disappear again.

The deal they'd made was epic. Coop had an opportunity to keep her in his life. Seventy-two hours ago, he'd thought she was dead. Now they had a chance to start over and the possibility of a relationship he'd cut off his right arm not to mess up.

CHAPTER TWENTY-ONE

Jade parked in front of the rustic log home and removed the truck keys with her left hand. After Coop had begged off, saying he needed some shut-eye, she'd driven the last thirty miles with him holding her right hand firmly on his thigh while he dozed in less-than-five-minute increments. It probably hadn't helped that every time he fell asleep, she tried to slide her hand from his grasp and back to the steering wheel in the two o'clock position. It hadn't worked.

Neither of them had gotten enough sleep. *Imagine that.* While the memory of him whispering *mine* in the throes of passion had sent her heart on a crazy roller-coaster ride, excitement and apprehension co-mingled in her stomach. How was she supposed to feel about him and the deal they'd struck while she was in those same throes? *Hopeful? Confused? Scared?* Apparently, the answer was all of the above.

She shifted toward him only to find he was watching her. "Hey, we're home." Her sing-song voice was still a little raspy but much better than it had been. She tugged on her hand, but he held it effortlessly. "What? Aren't we going in?"

An easy grin quickly spread to his eyes. "Sure. I'll get the bags. Where's your bedroom?" Moose, curled in Coop's lap, raised his head and yawned. It was easy to see who his new favorite person was. *Some service dog you turned out to be.*

"That's okay. I'll take care of my bag." She cracked her door open and started to step out.

He stopped her, still holding firmly to her hand. "Okay, but I need to know which room is yours so I can put *my* things in there."

She glanced toward the cabin, expecting her sister to come piling out any moment. Finding everything quiet, she turned back to him, sure the wave of heat that swamped her was turning her face red. "I can't just invite you to stay in my room. What'll I tell Nicole? Even if Ryan told her I knew you from Iraq, she's not going to expect us to sleep together. I don't even want to know what Travis will say."

His smile faded. "We're all adults here, Jade. How about telling your sister the truth? Who gives a damn about Travis or anyone else? This is between you and me."

She saw the hurt in his eyes, and it ripped the scab off old wounds she'd thought long healed. "You don't understand. They don't know anything about what happened to me in Syria. No one does. My father made sure the cover-up came with a detailed history—places, people, a life fabricated to fill those missing months. Nic will know I lied to her. Then I suppose you'll want me to tell her I think our father is trying to kill me? I can't bombard her with everything at once. I need some time."

"They're here!" Nic stood on the porch, holding the screen door halfway open while yelling to someone behind her. Her blonde hair caught the sun just right and made her appear to glow.

"Please?" She would beg if that's what it took. It was inevitable she'd have to explain him to her family, but she wasn't ready. One life-changing crisis at a time was all she could handle.

He regarded Nicole thoughtfully as she shuffled toward the truck. A frustrated sigh told Jade he understood, but he wasn't happy. "Okay." He released her hand and checked his watch. "You've got twenty-four hours."

"A whole day?" *That's helpful.*

He winked as his trademark grin spread from ear to ear. "Or...*I* could give them the highlights. Course, there's a lot I don't know, and I'm sure your sister will have questions. Your decision." He scooped up the dog, stepped out, and set Moose on the ground.

As he bent over, firm muscles rippled along the back of his shirt. Jade wanted to be irritated with him for assuming she was his to do with as he chose and for having the audacity to impose a deadline. Instead, her mouth went dry at the thought of his hard body wrapped around hers. The closing of the passenger door jolted her back to reality.

She barely had time to climb down and put a smile on her face before Nic came around the driver's door and gave her a bear hug. Over her sister's shoulder, Jade tracked Travis' progress as he came to meet Coop with a handshake that morphed into a bro-hug. The two spoke quietly for a few seconds, then disappeared into the house.

"Don't ever do that again, Jade." Nic was clearly trying to be stern, but the affection in her eyes directly contradicted her tough words.

Jade tugged her close for another hug. "I'm so sorry I made you worry, Nic. No more walking away angry. I promise."

Ryan appeared behind Nicole. "Sure, you say that now, but you've got the same issues with your temper as me, and chances are neither of us will ever be in control." He slung his arms around them both. "Seriously, JD, not cool. We were worried."

"I know, and I truly am sorry." Her brother-in-law was right about her temper. If he only knew how many anger management classes she'd needed to get where she was.

"Yeah? Sorry enough to tell us what's going on with you and Coop?" Nicole leaned in and lowered her voice. "He looked positively inscrutable when he got out of the pickup, and the sexual tension sizzles between you two." Her eyebrows hitched upward, and she flashed an expectant smile, obviously inviting Jade to spill her guts. "Ryan told me you knew Coop before you ran into him here. You're not going to leave me hanging, are you?"

Jade snorted a laugh. Her sister had always been a fan of romance novels. As a teenager, Nicole had suffered broken hearts again and again until she'd accepted Jade's truth that life was rarely a happily-ever-after storybook. When Nic met Ryan, it was as though he'd stepped from one of her novels and swept her off her feet. Jade had agreed her sister and Ryan were the real deal and damned if she hadn't opened her heart to the prospect of a soulmate of her own.

Is it too late?

She pushed the blatant self-pity from her head. Coop had asked her to start over, and she had agreed to give it her best shot. Negativity regarding the likelihood of finding the love written about in fairytales somehow seemed disloyal and selfish. Coop deserved better than that.

At least Nicole had given her an opening to broach the subject of her feelings for Coop—if she could only figure out where to start. She slid her arm around Nic's waist, and they strode toward the house. Ryan walked beside them, and Moose trotted ahead. "How about if we talk later? There *is* something I need to tell you, but it has nothing to do with sexual tension."

Coop reappeared from the house and met them on the worn dirt path that led to the door, a glint of something hard as steel in his eyes. "I told Travis I'd brief him on what went down. Luke and MacGyver will join in on an encrypted server. I'd like you there, too. Thirty minutes? In the kitchen?"

"Sure." Jade appreciated the opportunity to learn firsthand what Travis had discovered about her attackers. As much as she hated the idea of being disloyal to her father and, possibly, her country, she needed to air her suspicions and get input from Coop's team, men with no preconceived notions about General McDowell.

Coop searched her face before settling on her lips. The heat of his inspection nearly scorched her and stretched far longer than necessary. She fidgeted under his examination. Finally, his jaw relaxed, allowing the barest hint of a smile. A feeling of safety and belonging encircled her. If Nic and Ryan hadn't been there, she would have stepped into him and submerged herself in the sensation.

His sudden wink broke the spell, and he nodded toward her family. "You're welcome to sit in too. Luke and MacGyver will give us an update on the situation in Pine Bluff."

"We'll be there," Ryan said.

A slight breeze ruffled the hair at Coop's forehead as he turned and strode back to the house.

"There, you see! Did you see that?" Nicole pointed her finger at the screen door as it banged shut. "Sexual tension."

Jade rolled her eyes for her sister's benefit, but Nic wasn't wrong. More to the point, Jade wasn't immune to the charms of the devastatingly handsome man. What he did with only a smile and the hint of promise in his brown eyes had set her body on fire and given her an incentive to make good use of the next twenty-four hours.

When she and Nicole entered the kitchen, MacGyver, Luke and Blake had already joined the discussion. Coop's laptop showed them arranged in a semi-circle around the breakfast bar in her apartment above the kennel's office.

Coop caught her eye and motioned for them to come around in front of the screen. Ryan jumped up, giving Nicole his seat, and stood behind her with his hands on her shoulders. Jade went to lean against the kitchen counter beside Travis.

"Hi, Jade. Nicole. I trust you're comfortable at the safe house and have everything you need." Luke reached forward, apparently to adjust something on his laptop.

"It's really great. I feel safe for the first time in weeks. Thank you." Nic glanced over her shoulder and smiled at Ryan, no doubt remembering it was her husband who'd sealed the deal for moving her away from Pine Bluff. "How's everything in town?"

"It's been quiet. Carl Graves and his men are laying low while the court selects the jury." Luke leaned back in his chair.

MacGyver shook his head. "Trust me; there's plenty of hostility left in that bunch. That they're still in town says it all. I feel as though we're waiting for someone to lob a grenade through the window. They'll finish with jury selection in a day or two, and we'll know more."

Luke nodded in agreement. "Blake and I will keep an eye out for jury tampering while MacGyver sticks close to Graves. Don't worry. Everything's under control."

"Thank you. I'm so glad you're there, taking care of the town. We owe you so much." It was just like her sister to speak for all of Pine Bluff, even though no one outside of their group was aware of benefactors in their midst.

Blake's brow furrowed as he massaged the back of his neck. "DA Standish dropped by this morning. He wanted to remind Nicole he's counting on her testimony."

Ryan tensed, and Nic reached toward her shoulders to touch his hands. "Did he threaten to issue a subpoena?" Anger flashed in Ryan's eyes.

"It was mentioned," Blake replied.

Ryan's jaw firmed. He loved his wife with all of his heart and wasn't willing to put her in danger. Jade didn't like it either, but she'd back whatever Nic chose to do. She opened her mouth to speak the words out loud but stopped when Travis touched Nicole's arm.

"You know we can get you in and out of there, slick as can be, right? No muss, no fuss." Travis' gaze swept to Ryan. "No danger. Guaranteed."

Jade groaned silently. That sounded so much like something she would have said—cocky, arrogant—back before she'd learned the hard way that sometimes things go horribly wrong.

Nicole peered over her shoulder at Ryan, and with apparent confirmation by whatever silent language eleven years of marriage allowed them, Nicole smiled and turned to Travis. "I know. Thank you."

Soft laughter filled the room, breaking the tension. Jade was bursting with pride for her sister, and from the looks of Coop's wide grin, he felt the same.

Blake kicked back in his chair. "Okay, that's settled then. What else do we need to cover?"

"How's it going at the kennel and the store?" Jade worried about Nic's new business having to shut down in their absence.

"Couldn't be better," Blake said. "Larry and John have the store running smoothly, and they're keeping out the riff-raff—the ones who enjoy shooting up the place."

Jade huffed a laugh, caught off guard by Blake's humor-filled scrutiny and obvious reference to her unloading buckshot into the ceiling. Luke, Blake, and Ryan chuckled, and Coop's speculative grin started her heart thumping again. John and Larry Ames had been in the store the day she'd run into Coop, and apparently, they liked to gossip. She probably deserved it, overreacting the way she had, but that bottom-dweller, Derek, had ticked her off. *And there's that anger quotient again.*

"Vince and I handle the kennel. The dogs aren't suffering any ill effects from the fire. We're keeping them fed and exercised. All three of the guys you asked to help out are good hands, and they think highly of all of you." Blake leaned forward and crossed his forearms on the bar.

"They've been good friends to us. Haven't they, honey?" Ryan pulled Nic back and dropped a kiss on her head as she nodded.

Luke cleared his throat. "Okay, unless anyone has questions, that's all we've got for now. We'll check in again tomorrow at the same time. Coop, if you and Travis would hang around for a few minutes, we'll talk some business before we get back to work."

Low-level conversation hummed as Jade pushed away from the counter, then hesitated when Coop stood and strode toward her. He reached her the same time as Nic, who was no doubt anxious for the conversation Jade had promised.

Coop's hand caressed her lower back. "Can I talk to you for a minute before you go?"

She glanced toward Nicole, who tried to hide her

smug grin while giving a dismissive wave of her hand. "You go ahead. We'll catch up with you later. I think I might need to rest for a while, anyway."

"Are you okay?" Jade searched her sister's face for signs of fever or headache, symptoms her doctor had warned them to take seriously.

"Just tired. I think I'd like to sit on the porch swing with my man." Love shone from her eyes as she slid her arm through Ryan's.

He patted her hand. "What the lady wants, the lady gets. Excuse us." Arm in arm, they walked away.

Jade bit her bottom lip to squelch the shot of envy that made her insides ache. She might be jealous of what they shared, but her sister's happiness meant the world to her.

Coop caught a lock of her hair and swept it behind her shoulder. "I like your sister. She reminds me of you when we first met, except I haven't heard her swear like a sailor yet."

A laugh burst from her lips. He was right. Jade had been a lot like Nicole back then. Confident. Idealistic. Certain where the line was between right and wrong. A dreamer out to make a difference in the world. She'd done all right for herself too, back when black was black and white was white—before everything went to shit.

"Even Ryan is growing on me." He took her hand and rubbed his thumb over her knuckles. "Are you okay?"

At least I don't swear as much anymore. She shook off the memories, suddenly aware of Moose's tiny feet scratching her pant leg.

Coop reached for the dog and set him in her arms, where he licked her face and settled against her chest.

She scratched his head, then smiled at Coop. "What was it you wanted to talk about?"

"Yeah, that was an excuse to get you to stay and your sister to leave. Luke has something he wants to tell us about those men who hurt you. I assumed you wouldn't want Nicole or Ryan to hear it this way if it turns out the General sent them."

"Oh. Right." Her knees felt weak, and she grabbed for the counter to steady herself.

His arm came around her shoulders, and he led her to the chair Nicole had vacated. As her head spun, someone said, "Is she okay?" Then Coop was there again, with a bottle of cold water, that he pressed in her hand. She held it against her face until he pried it from her fingers, twisted the cap, and put it to her lips. Two swallows slid down her throat before she choked and started coughing.

When she finally stopped hacking, her face was wet with tears. Someone handed her a wad of tissues. Her throat hurt like hell again, but her world had stopped spinning. She blew her nose, dried her cheeks, and then noticed five sets of eyes focused on her. *Perfect!*

Coop knelt in front of her, still holding the water, his brown eyes dark with concern. "Better?"

She nodded and forced a painful swallow. "Sorry," she said, only for Coop's ears. "I'm not sure I want to hear what Luke has to say about the general, either." The verdict was in—the new Jade wasn't anything like the woman Coop had met three years ago. How long would it be before he realized she no longer existed?

His smile was tender as he stroked his thumb along her jaw. "That's okay. I've got your back. Whatever it is, we'll deal with it together."

"That goes for me too." Travis squeezed her shoulder as he took his seat on her right.

"I think it's safe to say we all have your back." Blake's voice came from the laptop's speaker, and the two men with him nodded in agreement.

Coop's smile widened, and he rose to his full height. "Ready?" At her nod, he pulled his chair closer and sat, holding her hand as though he didn't care who saw them.

CHAPTER TWENTY-TWO

"Do you know a Major Paul Bingham?"

Jade's eyebrows flew upward, telling Coop, as well as everyone else in the meeting, Luke's question had taken her by surprise.

"Paul? Sure, he's been a fixture in my life since before I could walk." A tiny smile played across her lips, then slowly faded. "Why?"

"Does Nicole know him too?"

"Of course. Whenever my father was home, Paul always came to see us. Our father didn't relate well with two daughters, but Paul always went the extra mile. He made us feel special and managed to draw Dad into whatever we were doing. Paul's visits were some of the best times I remember spending with Dad." She smiled, but sadness shadowed her features. "Paul knew how to get us to spill our guts about what was going on in our lives…school…boys. In short, he was the father we never had."

"He served with the general?" Luke stood and moved out of view, returning with the carafe and topped off all three of their coffee cups.

"They met at the Pentagon years ago, hit it off, I guess, and Dad kind of took Paul under his wing."

Coop heard the suspicion in Jade's voice, mildly surprised Luke had gotten as far as he had without blowback. "Why the fishing expedition, Luke? What does the major have to do with the attacks on Jade?"

Luke frowned. "There's no connection that Special Agent Roberts could dig up, but the major showing up in town the day after she was ambushed makes for an interesting coincidence."

"Wait. Paul is in Pine Bluff?" She sat straighter, and Coop sensed her tension.

"Has he ever been here before?" Blake brought his cup to his lips and took a gulp.

"I don't know. You'd have to ask Nicole."

"When the major came by the store, he specifically asked for you." Blake let that soak in for a few seconds. "How would he know you were here…unless General McDowell gave him your location?"

She shook her head, irritation simmering in her eyes. "You're missing the big picture. My father and I haven't spoken in nearly two years. How would the general know where to find me?"

Coop squeezed her hand gently. "Nicole or Ryan?"

"I doubt that. Dad isn't one to keep in touch with the family. Anyway, I think Nic would have mentioned it if she'd heard from him." Jade crossed her arms over her chest, and it was clear how vulnerable she still was when it involved her father. "He must have had me followed…or maybe he's tracking my phone. I'm learning nothing is beyond his reach."

Coop couldn't stand seeing her in pain. He

started to turn—to pull her onto his lap but stopped just in time. That wasn't what she needed right now, especially with an audience. "You told me you believe your father sent those men who attacked you. Why do you think it was him?"

She seemed to consider her answer for a minute, though for all he knew, she might be trying to decide if she could trust him with her reasons. Black circles lined her eyes. Exhaustion rounded her shoulders. *Shit!* He should have insisted she sleep on the drive back to the safe house. The meatball whined and licked her chin. She turned away, but Coop tugged on her hand, drawing her focus back to him.

"I'm right here. I want to help. Tell me what's going on in your head so I can."

She looked down at their joined hands. "The guy in the woods said he was sent to remind me I'd sworn an oath, and *my country takes that very seriously.* Those words are exactly what my father would have said. Plus, there were only a handful of people who knew about the oath." She pressed her lips together and raised her chin. Her beautiful blue eyes, sharp with determination, searched his.

"The man who choked me said *your daddy wouldn't want you out here all alone.* I know that might be a stretch. Maybe he was just an asshole making conversation before he killed me, but it felt personal like he was trying to tell me something. My father and Colonel Reiner were the only ones who knew what happened to me or why no one else could ever learn about the mission. The general treated me like so much collateral damage. Like a stranger rather than his daughter. If it hadn't been for Colonel

Reiner—." She pulled away and stood so suddenly, the meatball had to leap for safety. "I have to find Paul. He'll know if my dad is involved."

She strode for the door as everyone started objecting at once. Coop caught up before she'd gone ten feet, placing his much larger frame between her and the door. "No. You're not going after the major. Think about it. If it is your father behind the attacks, maybe Major Bingham came to finish the job?"

Her eyes widened. "Paul wouldn't do that."

He laughed cynically. "Don't be naïve." He backed off a step as anger flashed across her face. She was too tired to think straight—but not too far gone to react swiftly and harshly to condescending comments like the one he'd blurted out. He raised his hands to ward off what was sure to be her biting retort. "Maybe you're right, but going back to town without knowing for sure whose side he's on is not the way to go. We have to be smart."

Still shooting daggers at him, she took a deep breath, and then another, in an obvious effort to control her temper. Thirty seconds ticked by slowly before she abruptly whirled and stomped past Travis to stand by the table. Facing Luke, Blake, and MacGyver on the screen, she threw her hands in the air. "If I don't talk to Paul, how will I know if he's the general's errand boy, come to finish me off?"

Coop approached from behind, somehow resisting the urge to lace his arms around her waist and pull her against him. Instead, he shoved his hands in his pockets and spoke to the back of her head. "Of course, you should talk to him. I'm only saying it's too dangerous for you to be walking the streets of Pine Bluff or anywhere else right now."

She slowly pivoted until she faced him again. "If you have something in mind, stop being a jerk and spit it out."

Ouch. Yeah, I guess I deserved that. "I'll bring Major Paul Bingham to you."

It wasn't hard to find the major, especially after John Ames told Coop the man had hung out in front of the store for most of the day, apparently waiting for one of the McDowell girls to appear. It was clear Bingham had a high degree of determination, which was interesting in an unpleasant way. Coop was even more certain he'd been right to insist Jade stay at the safe house.

He parked his pickup across the street from the store and studied the man in civilian clothes who sat on one of the benches out front, reading a newspaper. Jade had described Bingham as mid-fifties, 5'9" or 5'10", slim build, black hair going to silver, and a receding hairline. *Bingo.* The man appeared relaxed, one leg crossed over his other thigh, forming a handy spot for the paper. Nothing about his body language set off any warning bells.

Before stepping from the truck, Coop checked up and down the mostly deserted street. Undoubtedly, Graves already knew he was in town, but he couldn't help thinking an encounter with the man would go smoother at a time and place of Coop's choosing.

He strode toward the store without hesitation and claimed the other end of the bench beside his target. "Major Bingham?" Coop surveyed the empty street but sensed when the man raised his head.

"And…you are?" Bingham spaced out the words in an I-couldn't-care-less manner.

"My name's James Cooper, but I doubt you've ever heard of me. We have friends in common, though."

"Really? Who might that be?" The Air Force officer resumed his perusal of the newspaper as though he wasn't overly interested in the answer.

If it wasn't for a slight tick in the muscle of his jaw, Coop might have thought he had the wrong man. "Jade McDowell and Nicole West. I heard you were looking for them."

That got the major's attention. He folded his paper and laid it on the bench between them. "News travels fast in small towns. You can't help me unless you know where they are."

"I can help you. The question is, do I want to? That depends on why you're here." Coop rested his arm along the back of the bench, relaxing, as though he had no place else to be.

"Not that it's any of your business, *Mr. Cooper,* but I'm an old family friend. Just passing through and thought I'd stop and see two of my favorite people."

"Well, any friend of Jade's is a friend of mine. Call me *Coop.* Everyone does." He gave the major his best down-home drawl and an aw-shucks grin.

Bingham offered a slight nod as he studied Coop's face, and the barest hint of an I-didn't-think-so grin of his own appeared for the space of a heartbeat. "Okay, *Coop*, now that we have the bullshit out of the way, what do you want to know?"

"Did General McDowell send you?" Coop held

up his hand to halt Bingham's reply. "One lie. That's all you get, so think before you answer."

No emotion showed as Major Bingham seemed to consider Coop's warning. Then he waved his hand the length of his torso. "Do I look like I'm here at the command of an Air Force general? On the contrary. I'm here because of *Jade's father,* but, no, he didn't ask me to come."

The way Bingham emphasized the relationship caught Coop's interest. He weighed the man's appearance, from the rolled-up sleeves of his button-down shirt to his faded jeans and beat-up Adidas. Bingham had a point, though the distinction might mean nothing. "Why?"

Bingham wagged his head. "I'm afraid I can't get into that. For Jade's ears only. I'm sure you understand."

Coop rose abruptly, towering over the man. "As I'm sure *you'll* understand if I don't waste any more of my time." He turned and took two strides.

"It's important."

He stopped, waiting for something to make turning around worthwhile.

"Life or death."

Coop cocked his head and spun around. "If it's so important, why didn't McDowell come himself? Why are you here?" If only the general stood before him, he wouldn't waste any time getting to the truth.

Bingham turned partway. "The general and Jade have never had a good rapport. They haven't spoken in two years. He didn't think she'd agree to see him."

Coop snickered. "His chances might have been better if he hadn't already made two attempts against her life."

"Shit!" Bingham sat forward, knocking the paper to the ground. "I'm too late then."

"For what?"

"To warn her. Look, you have to take me to her. She needs to hear what I have to say." Bingham unfolded his legs and stood. "I can get her someplace safe." He paced one way and then the other in front of the bench.

Coop studied his face. "What do you think I'm trying to do—get her killed? You've yet to convince me you're not part of the problem." He swiveled and resumed walking toward his truck.

He heard Bingham hit the pavement running. The man's hostility was a pervading force of its own as he neared. At the last second, Coop crouched, balancing on his hands while he kicked in an arc that swept Bingham's legs from under him. The major landed with an *oomph* and rolled to his back.

Coop was on his feet and standing over Bingham before he came to a stop. Reaching down, he grabbed the man's shirt and yanked him off the ground. Forcing him backward across the street, they stopped abruptly when Bingham's back met the tailgate of the Dodge Ram.

Coop flipped him around and slammed him against the truck again, then zip-tied his wrists behind him and jerked him to the passenger door.

"Where are you taking me?" Bingham eyed him warily as Coop stuffed him roughly into the seat and latched his seatbelt.

"You wanted to see Jade. That's where I'm taking you." He hadn't made up his mind about

Major Paul Bingham, but it wasn't in her best interest to trust him just yet. Luckily, he still had some time. He shut Bingham's door, removed his sunglasses from the neck of his shirt, and slipped them on his face. Then he wrenched his door open and hopped in.

"You won't regret this." Bingham squirmed, no doubt trying to get comfortable with his hands bound behind him.

"You'll talk while I'm driving. The same rule applies. If you lie to me, even once, I'll zip-tie your feet, too, and drop you in a ravine somewhere." He started the ignition and turned to stare at the man beside him. "Whether you get to see her or what kind of shape you're in when you do…is entirely up to you."

DIXIE LEE BROWN

CHAPTER TWENTY-THREE

What was she supposed to make of Paul Bingham showing up in Pine Bluff to see her? Now? When her life had literally been upended? Coop's answer had been a definite *no* when she'd said she was going with him to retrieve her old friend. Under normal circumstances, she would have told him where to put his cave-dweller routine, but the guy *had* saved her life. Twice. He'd provided ample evidence he was on her side. As hard as it'd been to swallow her pride, she'd given the big-headed ape a pass.

Moose followed on her heels as she strolled into the kitchen. She stood still, watching Travis wash, peel and chop what looked to be at least twenty potatoes. Offering to help was on the tip of her tongue when he plunked down a bag of carrots on the counter. She jumped as he plunged the point of a knife into the cutting board not six inches from her fingertips.

He grinned. "Dinner prep will go a lot faster with two of us."

"Didn't anyone ever teach you the word

please?" She worked the tip of the knife from the wood and used it to cut open the bag.

"Please? SEALs don't usually have to say *please*." Humor sparkled in his eyes.

"Well, there's that." Diving into the bag, she brought out a handful of carrots. "You got a peeler for these over there?"

He yanked open a drawer, rummaged around, and tossed the requested utensil on the counter.

"Something smells great. What are you cooking?" She made short work of the first carrot and started on another.

"I found a big elk roast in the freezer. Whoever brought in supplies for the safe house knows how to stock a cabin."

"I didn't realize you had a domestic side." Even Moose sniffed the air and licked his chops.

Travis smirked. "I don't, but I like to eat."

"Good point." She wasn't much of a cook either, usually taking the easy way out by throwing together a salad or tossing steaks on the grill. Coop had loved to cook when they'd been a couple, and she'd stayed out of his way in the kitchen. It'd been a long time since she'd thought about that period of her life without grieving. Was it possible they could have that again? She might even learn how to follow a recipe this time.

The butterfly wings in her stomach at the mere thought of a future with him gave warning of the painful consequences if their rekindled relationship fell flat. She squared her shoulders. She'd handle it somehow, just like she'd managed the past three years.

"Moose?" Looking around for the dog—her lifeline, she found him stretched out on the floor under the table. His head lifted, and his tail thumped once when he heard his name. At the same time, she became aware of the silence and glanced toward Travis.

He rested a hip against the stove, his arms crossed over his chest. A cunning gleam tinged his eyes as he studied Jade. "You look like shit, ya know?"

She chuckled. "That'll work wonders for my ego." Finished peeling, she grabbed the knife and began cutting the carrots into one-inch chunks.

"Aw, hell, I didn't mean it like that." At least he had the decency to be contrite. "You're still an attractive woman, but you're too damn skinny. When was the last time you did more than pick at your food? Or sleep, for God's sake? Those black circles under your eyes are a dead giveaway. Your everything's-under-control routine might fool your sister. Maybe even Coop. But you're not fooling me. Or Luke. Or MacGyver. We worry." Travis dropped his chin and squeezed his eyes closed for a heartbeat as though he had no idea how this conversation had suddenly gotten so personal.

She ducked her head to hide her grin at his obvious discomfort. The concern in his expression revealed a softer side he clearly tried to keep hidden. Not likely it was for her, though. He was anxious for his friend, as he should be.

The last thing she wanted was to hurt Coop again. She released the knife and sank into one of the kitchen chairs. "I'm worried about him too. I didn't mean for this to happen—for him to get involved." How had everything gotten so complicated?

Travis pushed off the counter. The chair next to her scraped across the floor as he pulled it out and seated himself. "You're not hearing me, darlin'. I'm worried about *you*. Hell, I worry about Coop too. Finding you threw him for a loop, but he's doing okay. The best way to keep from hurting him again is to take care of yourself. By the looks of you, a strong wind could topple your ass."

She tried to laugh, but it came off sounding pathetic. Suddenly, Moose landed in her lap, his silly tongue lapping at her chin. She latched on to him and hugged him tightly, his slight weight grounding her.

Crap! He's right. For a long time, she'd only been existing, not really living. She'd been trying to get through each day the best she could.

He scratched behind Moose's ears. "Well, you got the fuzzball here, and assuming you decide to stick around, you've got Coop and the rest of us. We're a package deal, whether you want us or not. Lucky for you, we're so easy to get along with." He grinned at his joke.

"Eventually, you'll meet MacGyver's fiancé, Kellie, and Blake's wife, Tori. Blake adopted her son, Isaiah. He's crazy about that kid. Luke and his wife, Sally, had a baby boy a few months ago. Sally's daughter, Jen, is ten, going on twenty-five. Get us all together, and we're one big, happy, slightly dysfunctional family." He fiddled with an empty coffee cup on the table.

"What about you? No special woman? Or man?" She'd never known him to talk so much, but his touching introduction to his family, such as it was, had put a smile on her face and made her slightly jealous.

"Hey, now. I only swing one way. I'm not ready to settle down with just one woman yet. Besides, there aren't too many women out there that'd put up with me. Though I admit, those guys make it look easy." He rubbed his chin. "Anyway, you get the idea. You need something, you just ask."

She shook her head, amazed by the man's concern. "Thanks. That means a lot. After what I did, I never expected to hear that from you."

He rose and smiled at her. "That doesn't mean I won't kick your ass if you pull a stunt like that again." Striding to the counter, he rustled noisily through the cupboards until he brought out a large, flat roasting pan and set it on the island.

"I'd expect nothing less." She got to her feet and moved to the sink to wash up. After drying off, she rested her hand on his arm for a second, hoping somehow, he'd understand how much she appreciated the second chance he was giving her. His only reply was a non-committal grunt, but that was good enough.

"What else can I help with?" She laid the knife down and pushed the cutting board, covered with carrot pieces, toward him.

"Nothing to do now but wait." He spread the vegetables in the roasting pan and set it aside. "There's an old-time rocker on the back porch that's calling my name. A checkerboard, too, if you feel like getting whupped."

Tempted, she laughed at the challenge in his

eyes. "I'll take a raincheck. I'd like to get cleaned up a bit before Coop gets back. First, I need to clear up some things with my sister."

"Suit yourself," he replied.

Moose jumped up and followed her from the kitchen. With one hand on the banister, she paused to peer through the front windows. Thunder clouds were building, and the wind was beginning to kick up. A breeze and a good rain would be a nice change to the mugginess that pervaded the air. Feeling sticky and hot, she jogged upstairs, looking forward to a relaxing shower. Maybe it would help her chill out before Major Bingham arrived.

Nicole had said she was going to lay down after Coop left for town. Ryan had accompanied her to their room, and Jade hadn't heard a sound from them since. Good. They'd both had a chaotic couple of days. Rest was just what they needed. She'd catch up with Nic after she spoke to Paul and learned why he was there.

Twenty minutes later, she stepped from the shower, still on edge. As she dressed, she accidentally bumped her phone beside the sink, and the screen lit up.

Three missed calls? From Mark Reiner.

She hadn't spoken with her former commanding officer for months. Oddly coincidental that he'd call her now, the day after someone had tried to kill her. She swallowed hard against the apprehension building in her chest. *Don't get all paranoid.* Mark was her friend. He'd been the one person she could count on through everything. Still, two Air Force officers trying to contact her on the same day?

Highly unlikely.

Reiner and Bingham didn't travel in the same circles to her knowledge, but they both knew her father. If either of them had information that would help her, she needed to speak to them as soon as possible.

She hurried to finish dressing, pulling on her last pair of clean jeans and a lightweight, button-up shirt with long sleeves that she rolled to just below her elbows. She brushed her teeth, captured her hair into a ponytail, then grabbed her things and returned to her bedroom. Moose raised his head from his spot in the center of the double bed, stretched his legs, and happily accepted her attention for a few seconds.

Sitting on the edge of the bed, she stared at her phone. She couldn't put it off any longer. Though a case of nerves made her stomach tighten, she had to know why Mark had called. She didn't bother with the voice mails he'd left, tapping his name on her screen and going right to the source.

He answered as though he'd been hovering over the phone, waiting for it to ring. "Jesus, Jade! It's about time you got back to me. Are you all right? I was afraid I'd be too late." The stress level in the colonel's voice was off the charts.

Her heart rate leaped into a gallop. "What do you mean? What's wrong?"

"Listen, we don't have much time. I'm on my way to you. You're in danger."

"Two men tried to kill me yesterday. Coop saved my life. I'm in a safe place for now, but I need to know why this is happening."

"I've been listening in on the underground

chatter at the Pentagon ever since Coop called."

She grimaced and squeezed her eyes closed. "He told me he spoke with you. How much did you tell him?"

"Coop thought he saw a ghost. The guy was at the end of his rope. I had to tell him the truth, that you'd been held hostage in Syria. That after your rescue, the records were sealed, and General McDowell ordered you to stay away from him. I can tell you he wasn't happy. I hope he doesn't run into your father any time soon."

She groaned. Coop had known since the day after their encounter at the store.

"He knows it was bad and that you were in no shape to see him when you came back."

She pulled herself up straight. Coop knew the enemy over there—he'd fill in the blanks himself. Right now, there were more pressing issues. "What did you find out? Why am I suddenly a target?"

"Those men that came after you? They're highly trained government assassins. Many of the Crimson Guard were surprised you survived your captivity." The way he lowered his voice when he named the group sent a chill through her body.

"The Crimson Guard? What are you talking about? I thought they were a myth. Are you saying they exist?" A secret brotherhood. The deep state. People called them many different things. The Crimson Guard was either performing valuable services for the U.S. government or lining their own pockets off the horrors of war, depending on who you asked.

"They exist, and they're sending another

assassin for you and Coop. This guy has never failed. There's no time to waste. We have to get you into hiding. If I can find you, so can he."

This was crazy. Jade stood and paced across the room. "Why are they after me?"

"It has something to do with your last mission. I don't have all the details."

"Who did you overhear?" There was a moment's hesitation, enough to tell Jade she hadn't heard the worst yet.

Mark sighed. "General McDowell."

She swayed and spread her palm against the wall to hold herself up. *Holy hell*. She'd been right, but the confirmation hit her harder than she'd expected. Her father *had* tried to kill her. Not only him, but a mysterious group of covert operatives. Pressure ballooned in her chest as she fought to control the panic that threatened her ability to think clearly.

"Jade?" Concern threaded through Mark's voice.

Moose was beside her, whining. His little feet pawed at her knee. She twirled away from him and rushed to the window. Coop should have been back by now. Her hand flew to her mouth. What if Major Bingham was the assassin?

"Oh my God! I have to warn Coop! He went into town to meet an old friend of my father's." She started to press the end-call button, but Mark's shouted command froze her.

"No, wait. Let me help you. The assassin will keep Coop alive until he has you. In five minutes, I'll be parked at the end of your driveway. Meet me. We'll figure out what to do."

"What? How did you find me?" A split second of uncertainty troubled her.

"I put a trace on Coop's cell phone after he called. Once I found him, he led me to you. I know he and his partners are protecting your sister. She'll be fine, but if you tell anyone you're leaving, they'll try to stop you. We must move now if we're going to get to Coop in time. Come alone and hurry." The call ended.

Jade had so many questions. She stared at her phone helplessly. Why hadn't she asked Coop for his number? Mark apparently had it. So did Travis. She slipped her feet into a pair of sneakers and grabbed a jacket as she stuck her phone in her pocket. Commanding Moose to stay, she closed the bedroom door in his face. Poor little guy. He was almost as frantic as she was.

Nicole and Ryan's room was quiet when she snuck by. She took the stairs two at a time and headed for the kitchen. Halfway there, she stopped. Mark was right. Travis wouldn't be happy about her leaving the house alone. At the very least, he'd argue and slow her down. If Nicole and Ryan woke up before she made her escape, there'd be hell to pay.

She hesitated. It felt wrong to leave without telling Travis. Hadn't she nearly lost her life yesterday by doing precisely that? This time, she wasn't going anywhere—just to the end of the driveway. Once she and Mark had a plan, she'd come back and tell Travis everything. Enlist his help. Ask him to call in Blake and the Black Hawk. The general's assassin wouldn't stand a chance against all of them.

Feeling lighter with her decision made, she pivoted and strode out the front door. She broke into a jog as soon as she cleared the grass. The drive was a curvy, downhill half-mile, and when she rounded the final corner, a black SUV waited on the side of the county road. A man leaned against the passenger side, legs crossed at the ankles as though he had all the time in the world.

It must be nice to be so calm. Slowing to a walk, Jade willed her heart and lungs to at least act the part of a highly trained Air Force officer prepared for battle. She wasn't even partially successful.

As she approached, the man pushed away from the vehicle and took a couple of steps toward her. She recognized Colonel Mark Reiner by his profile, though he'd dressed as a civilian in jeans and a blue polo shirt. His short, brown hair had begun to recede since she'd seen him last, and his strong, trim core was a bit more rounded. Mid-fifties would do that to a man working a desk at the Pentagon.

Twenty feet away, his brow furrowed. Jade hesitated, the same unease she'd felt on the phone, making her second guess herself for a fraction of a second.

Then he smiled and strode toward her. "Damn, it's good to see you, Jade." He stepped close enough to give her a chaste kiss on the cheek before stepping back and motioning toward the vehicle.

She was being ridiculous. The colonel was the same man she'd respected as her commanding officer. Nothing had changed, except maybe the dark circles under his eyes. "You too, Mark." She pulled her cell phone from her pocket. "Do you have Coop's cell number? I want to call and warn him."

"Sure. You don't?" He gave her a quizzical glance. "I'll text it to you. I've dialed him a half dozen times since I hung up with you. He must have his phone shut off." Mark tapped at the screen of his phone, and almost immediately, hers dinged. "You can try him too, but if he turns it back on, he'll have several messages waiting."

As much as she wanted to hear Coop's voice and know he was all right, she couldn't dismiss the fact Mark had done everything possible to get the message to Coop. All she could do now was wait for him to call.

"Meanwhile, we'll head into Pine Bluff and see if we can intercept them before they get here, where your sister might get caught in the crossfire." He opened the passenger door of the SUV and waited expectantly.

A chill shuddered down her spine. She wouldn't allow her father to hurt Nicole or Ryan. "I can't leave yet. I mean…one of Coop's friends is at the house, and I have to tell him what the plan is so that we can get more manpower." As Mark's frown appeared again, she fell back a step, another twinge of disquiet reverberating through her.

Mark glanced around as though deep in thought, then suddenly shut the door. "Sure. We can use all the help we can get. Just a minute." He opened the back door and dug through some notebooks and papers until he held up a map. Unfolding it, he walked around the back of the vehicle, opened the rear hatch, and spread it on the flat cargo area. "There's a scenic lookout here where we could set up surveillance and a few spots where we could pull off and surprise them." He pointed at each location on the map. "With enough people, we could cover the whole area."

"What if surprising the assassin gets Coop killed?"

Mark scoffed. "I think you're underestimating your boyfriend. If this guy gets the drop on Coop, he'll be looking for any opportunity to turn the tables. With your friend at the house following us and a couple more of Coop's buddies dropping in behind them, we'll squeeze the shooter before he knows we're on to him." Mark indicated a place on the map that looked ideal for their ambush. "As you said—manpower is the key."

Optimism filled her. It had to work. She couldn't even entertain the idea of anything happening to Coop. "Okay. I'll run back to the house and talk to Travis. He can make arrangements for backup." Should she tell Mark about the Black Hawk? Maybe they wouldn't need it. She'd leave that to Luke and the others.

"Get in. You might as well introduce me." He closed the liftgate and skirted the SUV to open the passenger door.

She had to tell Travis the whole plan anyway. There was no reason he shouldn't meet Mark. A nervous stomach greeted her silent acknowledgment of how angry Travis was going to be that she'd snuck away to meet her former commanding officer.

He'd get over it once he understood the urgency. Jade hopped in. Mark lobbed the map over her shoulder to land on the rear seat, closed her door, and slid into the driver's side.

Before he started the car, he grabbed his phone, tapped the screen, and held it to his ear. "Voice mail again." He drummed his fingers on the steering wheel. "Coop...it's Mark Reiner. Call me, goddammit!"

Worry settled deeper into her bones as the big engine rumbled to life. She watched her side mirror in case they got too close to the barrow pit as Mark backed up to make the turn into the driveway. Suddenly a stinging pain pinched the left side of her neck. She swung around as he tossed an empty syringe into the cupholder.

Her words, demanding to know what he was doing, halted on the tip of her tongue. Her mouth was no longer obeying her commands. Neither could she lift her hand to grasp the door handle. It was all she could do to force air into her lungs.

"Relax, Jade." Slamming the transmission into park, he jerked his door open. Gravel crunched under his feet as he left her line of sight.

Suddenly, he was at her door. He removed her seatbelt and tossed her over his shoulder. She watched, helplessly, as her phone slipped out of her pocket, bounced on the dirt shoulder, and disappeared into the drainage ditch beside the road. Then she sprawled on the back seat, her head spinning from the abrupt landing. His face floated above hers, and he studied her eyes. Rage nearly choked her as his betrayal hit home. More than anything, she wanted to ball her hand into a fist and break his jaw. *Damn!* Why couldn't she move?

"What you're experiencing is paralysis induced

by a neuromuscular blocking agent. You won't be able to move for a few hours. It probably feels like your lungs are frozen, but I was careful with the dosage, and you're breathing on your own just fine. To make you more comfortable, I'm administering oxygen." He positioned a nasal cannula in her nostrils, looping an elastic band around her head.

The oxygen flow was reassuring, though she still had to concentrate on inhaling and exhaling. It would be easier if she could manage to calm down, but that didn't appear to be in the cards anytime soon.

He held a vial of drugs and slowly drew the liquid into a syringe. "I'm giving you a sedative so you can relax. I have to keep you alive until I find Coop. You're the bait. Now that he knows the truth about you, he won't stop until he figures out the rest, and we can't allow that to happen." He lifted her arm and injected the drug.

It burned in her vein. Her vision clouded, and she floated above the scene. She watched as Mark placed his hand over her face. His touch was warm, almost caring. She wanted to scream. When his hand slid away, she was blind. He'd closed her eyelids. *How thoughtful. The bastard.*

She didn't know he'd moved until she heard the door close, and a moment later, the vehicle rocked side to side over the uneven ground, then smoothed out as it hit the pavement.

Jade fought to stay awake. To pay attention to where they were going. Count the curves and hills. Part of her was afraid if she fell asleep, she'd forget to breathe. It was a fruitless endeavor. As her cognitive ability slipped further and further away, she hung on as long as she could by concentrating on how she was going to kill Colonel Mark Reiner.

CHAPTER TWENTY-FOUR

He plotted his course, opting for the longer, scenic route back to the safe house. To Bingham's credit, he remained silent while Coop navigated the small-town streets until they left Pine Bluff in the rearview mirror.

Setting the speedometer at forty-five, he relaxed his white-knuckled hold on the steering wheel. "Okay, let's try this again. You came to warn Jade about a matter of life and death—your words. Explain."

Bingham dropped his chin and snorted a laugh. "How do I know you'll use my information to help her?"

"You have my word." About halfway through, he realized his word meant nothing to Bingham. If Coop wanted the whole truth, he'd need to give the same. He held up his palm to stop the other man from talking over him. "I was in love with Jade when her plane went down in Syria." He kept his eyes on the road, but he could feel Bingham's interest. "We never made it official, but I think she felt the same. When I saw her four days ago, she'd been dead to me for three years. Three long, hard years, part of which I spent trying to figure out good enough reasons to get up in the morning.

"I was shocked, relieved, and enraged all at the same time. I demanded to know why she'd left me hanging. No goodbye. No contact. No nothing. She wasn't talking, not even to defend herself against my accusations. So, I decided to talk to Colonel Reiner, her former commanding officer."

Bingham's entire body jerked as the space between them in the cab crackled with hostility. "*Is Reiner here?*"

His adverse reaction caught Coop by surprise, but he managed to tone down his instant curiosity. "Not that I know of. I called him on his cell. He said he'd been assigned a desk in Virginia, and I assumed that's where he was. Do you know something I don't?" He'd had no reason to suspect the colonel was anywhere close. Had that been a mistake?

Bingham shook his head. "What did he tell you?"

Coop clenched his jaw. "He said Jade had survived the crash, was captured and held hostage. Eight months in the hands of animals who hate Americans and consider women property. It took the military that long to locate her and bring her home."

"*Right.*" Bingham growled the word, and Coop turned an accusing glare on him. "The assholes didn't find her because they didn't *look*."

Every internal warning light Coop possessed started flashing red. Gravel flew as he maneuvered his truck to an abrupt stop at the side of the road. "What are you saying? That they knew she was alive and did nothing? Why? *Who left her there?*" The last question exploded with a roar as he reached for a handful of Bingham's shirt and yanked the man as close as his seatbelt would allow.

With gritted teeth, he turned on the bound man beside him, battling an overwhelming need to use his fists. Anger burned in Bingham's eyes almost as fiercely as fury simmered in Coop's blood. It was the look of a man who wanted revenge. Coop could relate. Maybe he had more in common with the man than he'd thought. Still, he needed to be careful. Bingham hadn't proven himself yet.

With a groan, Coop shoved him away. He faced the windshield and slammed both hands on the wheel. "Jesus! How could a man have so little compassion for his own daughter?" The general was to blame. He knew it as certainly as he knew what day it was, and he would make sure McDowell paid dearly. Laying his head against the seatback, he closed his eyes, but he couldn't rid himself of the image of a beautiful, dark-haired woman, enduring untold atrocities, praying for her countrymen to rescue her.

Suddenly, he shoved the door open, stumbled to his hands and knees, and lost the contents of his stomach alongside the road. He wanted to scream his frustration to the wind—smash General McDowell's face until there was nothing left but a bloody pulp. Coop didn't care that Bingham might be escaping while the agony of Jade's reality slashed new, deeper wounds in his chest. He'd been so self-righteous, demanding to know why she hadn't stepped back into his life. Hell, he was just one more person who hadn't bothered to come for her.

Self-loathing forced him to his feet. He raked

both hands through his hair and stomped across the two lanes of asphalt. He paced—trying to put his ricocheting emotions back in their box and separate his shame from the much more shocking guilt of Jade's father. The asshole would suffer if it were Coop's final act on this earth. New purpose put him in the *zone*. That place in his head where the imminent battle was paramount, and he could detach himself from the reasons and the possibility of failure. There was no failure in the zone. His gaze narrowed on the front seat of the pickup as he crossed the pavement again. By sheer willpower, he forced his churning guts into submission as he crawled into the driver's seat.

"You're still in love with her." Bingham stared at his lap, his words an acknowledgment rather than a question.

"Tell me the rest." Coop sat rigidly. One hand, braced on the wheel, vibrated with the idle of the engine.

"Ever heard of the Crimson Guard?" Bingham's voice was as quiet as the wind through the trees.

Coop glanced at him, not sure he'd heard right, but Bingham returned his look and waited.

"Everyone has heard those stories. Like hunting snipe." Coop's laugh oozed sarcasm.

A hint of a grin appeared at the corner of Bingham's mouth and disappeared just as quickly. "Except the Crimson Guard is real. And not a force for good, as some of the legends would have you believe."

"Come on, Bingham. You'll have to do better than that if you want me to believe in a—"

"It's true. I'm a member."

Coop stared at the man, weighing the shimmer of truth on his face with the stories he'd heard over the years and dismissed as tall tales. He cleared his throat. "Let's pretend for a minute I believe you. What does this Crimson Guard have to do with Jade?"

"It's a long story. One I can only repeat on penalty of death. I'm pretty much dead at this point anyway, so what the hell. On one condition." Bingham shifted in his seat, stretching his arms and bound hands.

"You're not really in a position to be making deals." Coop checked for traffic and pulled his truck onto the road.

"I'm aware." Bingham settled back in the seat. "A few minutes ago, you offered your word you'd help her. Is that still on the table?"

"Of course. I'll be there for Jade whether you give up any information or not. Are you telling me you're suddenly ready to bank on my word?"

"Let's just say my choices have narrowed." Bingham leaned forward and wiggled his fingers. "Since we're getting all chummy, how about cutting me loose? I'll give you my word, and you can bank on that." Damned if he didn't grin as though he'd just bested Coop at poker.

Shit. Maybe he did. There was something about this guy Coop couldn't quite put his finger on, yet his gut registered a fledgling trust. He retrieved his pocketknife and sliced through the plastic tie.

"That's better. Thanks." Bingham shook his arms and massaged his wrists where the binding had left red indents.

"Don't make me regret it," Coop said.

"You asked what the Crimson Guard has to do with Jade. General McDowell is the top dog. The membership caps out at twenty-five, all handpicked by the general."

Coop regarded him skeptically. Not that McDowell wasn't an asshole, but to be openly involved in illicit activities was a whole other story. "You still haven't convinced me."

"Colonel Reiner too."

"That son of a bitch!" For some reason, Coop had no trouble believing Reiner was dirty. Why was that? Maybe he should just shut up and listen.

Bingham cocked an eyebrow, seeming to indicate he agreed.

"They started small. Smuggling drugs. A few automatic weapons. Don't get me wrong. There's a reason very few people talk about this operation. Snitches don't live long. Lots of ways for military grunts to *accidentally* die. I'd guess they're out there somewhere, looking for me right now." Bingham glanced through the side window.

"So, why break your silence?"

"I didn't join the Guard by choice." Bingham went on as though Coop hadn't spoken. "McDowell brought me in to launder money because—how'd he put it? 'Your ill-advised and deliberate interaction with a family member of a United States Air Force officer has had a deleterious effect on all concerned.'"

"You screwed an officer's daughter?" Coop snickered, then tensed when Bingham faced him with a you-think-that's-funny stare. "Shit! Was it Jade?"

"No, hell no!" Bingham's reaction was almost as vehement as Coop's question. "It was years ago. I was a captain—maybe twenty-two. McDowell saw a use for my talent with numbers, and he wanted to keep a close eye on me. Forcing me to get my hands dirty with their criminal conduct meant the next time I screwed up, I'd be facing a court-martial if I was lucky and one of their *accidents* if I wasn't."

"So, you kept your mouth shut."

Bingham nodded. "I'm not proud of it. For years, I did what I was told."

"Was Jade involved in your military mafia?" They were within five or ten minutes of the turnoff to the safe house, and he still didn't know how she'd ended up in the middle of this cluster.

"No. McDowell kept her out of it…until three years ago."

"Her top-secret mission?" Coop's patience was growing thin.

"That bastard set her up." Bingham's face twisted as he spat the words. "McDowell announced the Guard was shipping a *special load*. He meant girls from nearby villages. They were sending them north to a Taliban stronghold near the Turkish border as sex slaves."

This story was going to end badly. A growl rumbled through Coop's chest, but he pressed his lips together and forced himself to listen.

"I didn't know, but the men had rounded up twelve young Kurdish women and were holding them in an unused bunker at the edge of the compound. We were all there when the truck rolled in just before dawn. Reiner and a few of the newer guys brought out the girls and loaded them up like cattle."

Two deep breaths later, Coop congratulated himself for maintaining his cool.

"While we waited, McDowell laughed and went on about how much those *religious zealots* would pay for virgins. But the real money, he said, was in special orders. Like when one of the leaders requested a particular American woman."

Coop slammed on the brakes, and the pickup tires squalled as they skidded to a stop in the center of the road. He sat, stone still, glaring through the windshield, his hands locked around the wheel because that was the only thing holding him in place. He had an idea what Bingham was going to say next, and he didn't want to hear it. There was no alternative. So much for keeping his shit together.

Several heartbeats of silence pounded inside his head as Coop waited. "Finish it." It took all of his strength to rasp the words.

Bingham shifted closer to the door, no doubt sensing Coop's tenuous hold on reason. "Muhammad Ali Naqvi, a Taliban field commander, had pulled off a successful offensive that brought Kandahar back under Taliban influence temporarily. He was a hero whom Allah had blessed with victory, and the prime minister wanted to reward him. Naqvi asked for an American woman to rape and slaughter live on video. Not just any woman. This one was a captain in the Air Force stationed at Al Asad and had led a successful bombing mission on one of their chemical weapons plants—that killed Naqvi's brother.

General McDowell heard about it through his Taliban contact. Of course, he shut them down immediately, or so he said, but he couldn't keep from bragging about the money he was getting for this *special shipment.*

"When he told me what he'd done, I couldn't believe it." Bingham slid the palms of his hands down his jeans as though wiping away his sweat. "He planned to send her on a classified mission into the no-fly zone, where two Russian Migs would intercept and force her to land at a Taliban-controlled airstrip. Naqvi would be there to collect his reward."

"Why didn't you stop him?" Revulsion formed a ball in Coop's throat.

"I threatened to blow the lid off the whole operation if he didn't halt the mission. He said I was too late. Jade had taken off at dawn. I called the tower anyway and begged them to order her back to base. They refused. Said General McDowell was the only one who could instruct her to abort the mission. I wanted to kill the bastard." Bingham's hands curled into fists. "That wouldn't have helped her. There was only one course of action I could think of that might make a difference, but it could just as easily have killed her.

"I had to make a split-second decision. We'd had a successful operation a few months before, where one of our intel guys posed as a Russian special operative and ordered a drone strike on one of their own planes. I figured it could work again. I speak passable Russian. All I needed was a radio."

"So, Jade was shot down by Syrian militants on your orders? That should have given our guys time to launch a rescue mission. What went wrong?" It was a halfway decent plan on the fly; if you didn't count the legitimate possibility she could have died. But she would've suffered a brutal death if Naqvi had gotten ahold of her. Bingham had given her a fighting chance and probably saved her life. Still, he had taken a hell of a gamble, and the navigator who'd died? Well, he was dead either way, wasn't he? Coop ground his teeth together and forced himself to keep his hands off the major's throat.

"There was a group of insurgents in the area where she went down. I had no way of knowing. They reached the drop site first and were gone before we got boots on the ground. Since it was a classified mission, no one involved could talk about what happened. General McDowell was there to fill the gap, as well as the official records, with his bullshit." Bingham fell silent, staring through the side window.

"He knew she was alive?" Coop's chest constricted, and he tried to ignore the images that assailed him.

"First Lieutenant Moore's body was found near the crash site. Someone had tried to get him out of his parachute and camouflage his remains. Who else would have done that?"

Coop raked a hand through his hair, remembering Jade's words. "She knew the insurgents were close. She led them away from the body on purpose."

Bingham didn't respond.

"I'm going to kill that son-of-a-bitch." How the

hell could he have done that to his flesh and blood. Coop couldn't look at Bingham. He wasn't exactly innocent either. "So, you collected your share of the spoils, and life went on."

"Every cent I got went into a bank account in the Cayman Islands. I never spent a dime of it on myself. You're right—life *did* go on to a certain extent."

Coop's tense muscles objected as he put the Dodge Ram in gear and rolled a hundred feet to the driveway that led to the safe house.

Bingham sent him a curious glance and a raised eyebrow. "Every spare minute I had, I dedicated to locating Jade. The money came in handy for that. After I found her and went to the commander of ground forces in Iraq with the information, I figured I was a dead man if I stuck around. So, I went AWOL. Completely off the grid. I spent more money tracking her, Reiner, and the general. Eventually, I changed my will, so she gets what's left when I'm dead. I didn't know about you until she ran into you here, and all hell broke loose."

Coop pulled up to the house as the sun went down behind the hill standing watch in the back forty. He threw the truck into park and turned the ignition off. Something wasn't making sense. He turned his head to study the man in the passenger seat. Bingham's blue eyes surveyed him without wavering.

"Why?"

"Why what?" Bingham's question was clearly an avoidance tactic.

"Why risk your life for her? Or make her the heir to your fortune?"

"The general would always drag me with him whenever he went home. His wife had cancer and passed away when Jade and Nicole were teenagers. Their grandmother raised them after that. They were great kids, despite not having a mother or a father." Bingham's disgust practically dripped from the last word.

"Not good enough. Try again."

Bingham's mouth quirked into a half-assed grin. "Because my 'ill-advised and deliberate interaction with a family member of a United States Air Force officer' was a weekend I'll never forget. Of course, I didn't learn until later that the beautiful young woman I met that weekend was then-Colonel Terrence McDowell's wife. She wasn't looking for a relationship. She merely needed someone to treat her like a desirable woman for once in her life. I was young and naïve and more than happy to do my part. Neither of us intended for her to get pregnant."

"*Jade's your daughter?*" Coop blurted the question, struck for the first time by the dark blue of Bingham's eyes and how much they reminded him of her.

CHAPTER TWENTY-FIVE

Jade's arm shook as she leveraged her torso slightly higher than the rest of her body and braced her hand on a rough, splintery surface. She groaned, only able to squeeze her eyes shut against the nausea her movement had awakened. When her stomach showed no signs of settling, she eased down to the floor again, with no idea where she was or how she'd gotten there.

Everything hurt. Especially her head. Had she fallen? That would explain why she sprawled on her stomach on an uneven, wooden floor. She shifted her head slightly to ease the strain on her neck. The displacement of air stirred up dust particles, and she inhaled just enough to cause a round of wracking coughs. After that, it was a vicious cycle until the logical solution made it through the pain.

It seemed to require all of her strength to roll onto her back, and she was unable to stop the whimper as her head hit the floor. Each additional cough radiated waves of misery through her skull. She couldn't remember when she'd had a worse headache. Or why her thought process was operating in slow motion. And the question of the hour: *where the hell am I?*

When her coughing subsided to labored rasps, scraping across her sand-paper throat, she opened her eyes a crack. With infinite care to hold her head still, she slowly swept her gaze around. She was in a small, square room with one tiny window, which allowed a glimpse of a patchy blue sky overhead and barely enough light to recognize the utilitarian metal desk wedged in one corner. A dust-covered four-drawer file cabinet by the wall and an ancient computer on the desk seemed to indicate that no one used the space regularly. In the corner, on the opposite side, sat a metal chair with a padded seat and armrests of green vinyl. Scraps of baling twine littered the floor around its legs.

The unfinished wood of the ceiling and walls looked old and time-weathered. The floor was worn smooth in places beneath her fingers but grimy with dirt and debris. The whole area lay hidden under years of neglect. The smell of pine and molasses stirred memories of her grandparents' barn, where she and Nicole had spent most of their time after their mother died.

Swallowing hard, she shifted her head to the right. Sacks of grain stacked the length of the wall nearly reached the ceiling. *The feed store?* Why would she be there, where Graves and his hoodlums held sway? Her skin prickled with the tightening of her gut.

Encouraged that her head hadn't screamed with agony, she tilted her chin so she could see the wall behind her. She gasped when she focused on the man standing silently in the open doorway.

Upside down and with a leering, self-satisfied

smirk, Colonel Mark Reiner regarded her with cold eyes and nothing short of hostility.

In an instant, her memory flooded back.

Her fingernails dug into her palms as she clenched her fists in anger. Mark had lied to her and drugged her. The bastard had betrayed her. She sat up slowly, her back to him, allowing her stomach a moment to adjust to her new position before she swiveled around to face him.

Hatred burned through her veins. Luckily, she'd had eight months to learn how to bury those emotions deep within her. She never took her eyes from the colonel as she slipped onto her knees. Silently, the vow she'd made just before she'd lost consciousness ran through her mind. *I will kill him.*

Mark's smirk became a snicker. "It's about time you woke up. Has civilian life made you soft?"

Don't engage. Jade needed to focus on finding an opportunity that would get her the hell out of here. The only avenue of escape was through the SOB who blocked the doorway.

Behind him was another room. Several chairs, arranged in a semi-circle, faced a folding table strewn with papers. Beyond that, the Main Street Feed Store's colorful buckets, horse tack, and veterinary supplies beckoned in an oddly cheerful display.

It took every bit of concentration she had to stop the shaking of her legs as she rose to her feet. She squared her shoulders and allowed contempt to curl her lip. "How did you know where to find me?"

"That was genius. You thought I was giving you that mutt. Actually, I planted a government prototype tracking device, one of a kind, just under the dog's skin. You've been helping the CIA test it for the past year. It worked like a charm. Once I had your location, it was simple to track your phone."

"You used Moose to keep tabs on me? Why, Mark? I thought we were friends."

"Just following orders." An expression that could have been regret skipped across his face. "I never wanted it to come to this. Everything would have been fine if you'd stayed away from Coop. How much did you tell him?"

"Stayed *away* from him? I didn't seek him out. Our running into each other was an accident. What was I supposed to tell him with my deception standing right in front of him? He deserved the truth."

Mark laughed. "If you only knew how many times I wanted to tell him the truth. Hell, you don't even know the truth."

"What's that supposed to mean?" Her mind raced, searching for answers.

He opened his mouth, but no words came out. Instead, he winced and rubbed his chest as though Jade had struck him.

She recognized remorse when she saw it. Mark wasn't all in with whatever he'd started. If there was any chance of convincing him to let her go, she had to focus. "It's not too late. You can do the right thing. You know I'll help you. My father was the one who falsified the records. You're not responsible for his actions."

At the mention of her father, his shoulders slumped. He shook his head slowly. "You have no idea how late it is. I'm in too deep." He regarded her with sadness, then straightened. "So are you…and so is Coop. Now, if you'll excuse me, I have to go find him." He turned his back and stepped into the bigger room.

"And what? Are you going to kill him? *No!"* Coop was innocent. He hadn't done anything wrong, except maybe falling for the wrong woman. Fear and rage mixed until the injustice of Mark's intention roared in her ears.

He gave no indication he'd heard her and kept walking through a long, narrow room lined with stacks of hay and bags of grain. Halfway to the store shelves, piled high with merchandise, he hooked his thumb back toward her and appeared to speak to someone. She couldn't hear him. The noise in her ears was too loud—her fear for Coop too great.

"*No,"* she screamed again and sprang through the doorway, focused on his retreating back.

When six feet separated them, he must have heard her. Or maybe someone else shouted a warning. As his upper body swiveled and he made eye contact with her, she slammed into his kidneys with everything she had. The momentum knocked him into the edge of a shelf hard enough for blood to fly. She landed on his back.

Dazed, she tried to roll away from him. There was no way she could win a fight with the man. It was run or more than likely die. She had to stay alive to warn Coop.

Mark grabbed her ankle, and she smacked face down on the floor. Sharp stinging in the bridge of her nose brought tears to her eyes. She ignored the discomfort. Kicking with all her might, she jerked free, landing a blow to his already-bloody face. He bellowed in rage and scrambled after her.

Weak and dizzy from the drug still in her system, the only thing holding her up was adrenaline. Barely registering that she was in the feed store, surrounded by fencing supplies, horse feed, and farming tools, she focused on the front door and the street beyond. Putting one foot in front of the other took all of her strength.

He caught her before she'd gone three steps. Pain erupted anew in her head as he wrapped his fist around her hair and yanked her backward until she collided with his chest. His hands banded around her upper arms and squeezed. She fought for all she was worth, spurred on by the knowledge he could easily break her bones without even trying. A lucky kick to his knee made him stumble back a step.

"You *bitch*!" Mark's grip on her held. Suddenly, he roared and flung her away as though she were a dishrag.

She flew into the wall to her left with such force, several items on display crashed to the floor. She landed in the same pile, shaking her head to banish the darkness encroaching from all sides.

"You're making this harder than it has to be," he growled.

She could barely see, but his voice told her where he was. He'd stopped moving, no doubt waiting for her to get up so he could knock her down again. She pushed up on her hands and knees and flipped over so she faced him. He stood with his weight on one leg and his arm hugging his ribcage.

The left side of his forehead was split open, and blood poured over his eye and down his cheek. Near his chin, it mixed with more blood from his broken nose. She would have smiled if her head wasn't pounding like a jackhammer. It was clear she was probably going to die, but she'd made him fight for it, and she'd done some damage in the process.

She returned his glare and shrugged one shoulder. "Mark, you don't know the meaning of hard."

He laughed and limped slowly toward her. From one of the shelves he passed, he selected a hammer and weighed it in his hand. She balanced on one knee, positioning her other foot flat on the floor, and rocked forward to force herself to stand. When she couldn't make it, she fell back to a crouch, catching herself with a hand against the wall. How could she have been so wrong about the man who'd been her commanding officer? Everyone in her squadron had liked and respected him. He'd given her Moose, probably saving her life. Yet his dead eyes reflected no human compassion as he wielded the hammer.

In the face of certain death, she'd finally found the fearless place within her. Her runaway heartbeat slowed. Everything except Colonel Reiner receded into a miasma of white noise. She welcomed the stillness. No fear. No panic. She'd felt this way before, in battle, with her mission clear and her mind centered on the target. It'd been a long time since she'd been that person. *I've missed you.*

With each menacing step, he drew closer, a half-crazed expression on his face. Gone was any trace of regret.

She pushed forward again and tried to straighten her leg to stand. Once more, she dropped back. Every muscle tensed. Strength and peace flowed through her. Two more halting steps and he'd be within striking distance. She had one more chance.

He took another hobbling step, raising the hammer above his head.

Jade rocked forward, pushing off her knee and toe, feeling the power in her calves as she lifted upward. Simultaneously, she bent at the waist, both hands grabbing the handle of one of the tools that had fallen from the wall. With one movement, she ducked under his attack and lunged forward, plunging the prongs of the pitchfork into his torso just below his ribs.

Mark shrieked and lurched backward, his eyes wide with shock. He lost his balance, and she let go of the pitchfork as he staggered and sprawled on his back. The handle stuck straight up, the sharp points embedded deep in his abdomen like a ghoulish Halloween display. Blood trickled from his gasping lips.

Voices and footsteps intruded into her abhorrence. She tore her gaze from the wounded man and searched the store. Two men appeared from behind her, spread out, and advanced toward her. No doubt they were the cohorts Mark had spoken to while pointing at her. She'd seen them both before but couldn't sort their identities from her blurred memory. It didn't really matter. Stalking toward her with ax handles and shovels in their hands, she doubted they were coming to help.

She swung toward the nearest exit sign. The

front of the store was empty. Her path was clear, and she sprinted for the door, determination keeping her upright. Heavy footsteps gave chase. Suddenly, the bell over the exit door went crazy. The wooden and glass barrier flew toward her, forced open by a gray-haired man. When he closed the door behind him and locked it, she slid to a stop.

"Dad? Why are *you* here?" He was out of uniform. She'd only seen him dress as a civilian a handful of times her entire life. The general lived and breathed the Air Force. Deep in her gut, a warning blared.

Her automatic distrust of him confused her until Mark's revelation about her father leading the infamous Crimson Guard resurfaced in her mind. Mark had lied to her. Had he lied about her father too? "Help me, Dad. Colonel Reiner tried to kill me." Behind her, hurried footsteps moved closer.

For a fraction of a second, guilt flitted in the general's eyes. Then his expression hardened, and he stood straighter. "You've caused me enough trouble. You'd think I had time to drop everything and fly across the country to stop you from making the worst mistake of your life." He joined his hands behind his back, and his scornful glare bored into her. "Only to learn I'm too late. You've betrayed your country. You've betrayed me. Now, I must determine what to do with you."

The general's role was the only thing about which Mark hadn't lied.

Someone grabbed her from behind, but she didn't look away. "So, this is what you do in your spare time? No wonder you had no room in your life for a family."

The general snorted disdainfully and dismissed her, turning his attention to the men who restrained her. "Where is Colonel Reiner?"

"She stuck him like a pig. He's probably dead by now."

Jade recognized that voice. *Derek.* Coop's friend and one of Graves' henchmen. She almost smiled, imagining what Coop would say about referring to the sniveling coward as his friend.

Her father scowled, apparently unhappy that Mark was currently indisposed. He gestured to Derek. "Take her in the back and secure her."

Derek jerked on her arm, and she used the momentum to add power to her kick into the side of his knee. At the point of contact, his joint bent at an impossible angle, and Derek screamed. She pulled from his suddenly loose grasp and twisted toward the other man, already raising her knee toward his balls. Something hard crashed into her head. Her vision blurred as she hit the floor. Her body went blessedly numb. The ringing in her ears muffled every sound.

"*You hit her too hard.* I told you I need her alive for now." Fury dwelled in the general's voice from a great distance above her. "Get her in the back before anyone sees her."

Someone hoisted her over their shoulder and carried her while Derek's faltering steps followed along behind. The general's measured tread trailed them also until he veered away after a few steps.

"Help me," Mark hissed from somewhere to her left. "That bitch tried to—"

"You've become a pain in my ass, Reiner." The

general's words chilled her, accompanied by the unmistakable racking of the slide on his handgun.

The sudden gunshot reverberated through her head as someone jerked the waistband of her jeans and tossed her carelessly into a chair. Her neck rolled back, then forward, and the blackness reached for her.

CHAPTER TWENTY-SIX

"Where's Jade?"

Ryan and Nicole, their arms linked, stopped halfway down the stairs as Coop barked out the question. He caught a glimpse of Travis through the kitchen doorway. His friend wiped his hands on a towel, balled it up, and tossed it toward the sink.

"She headed upstairs about an hour ago. Said she needed to talk to her sister." Travis strolled toward them, his hands resting on his hips, and his critical regard swept over Bingham.

Nicole shifted her scrutiny from the major to exchange a glance with her husband. "We just came from her room. She's not there." Her intense stare swept to Coop. "What's going on? Why is Major Bingham here?"

The major's expression softened. "I'm sorry to show up out of the blue, Nicole, but I must speak to Jade."

Nicole's brow furrowed in confusion. "How did you find us?"

"We'll fill you both in, but right now, we need to find Jade." Coop's churning gut was a sure sign something was wrong, and he'd learned not to ignore the warning. "Bingham and I'll take the front."

"I've got the back." Travis was already on the move.

Bingham went right, and Coop went left once they exited the house. Twenty minutes later, he gave up calling her name. He'd searched every deer trail and blade of grass for signs, including a hundred feet beyond the tree line on the uphill side of the house. Except for some mashed down grass in the front yard, there'd been no indication she or anyone else had been in the vicinity. He joined the other two men near his pickup as the major and Travis exchanged names and a handshake.

"Anything?" Coop's mouth was dry, and he nearly choked on the word.

"Nothing." Bingham shielded his eyes against the sunlight as he peered down the driveway.

"We're missing something." Coop pivoted a half circle as the fear taking root in his heart slowly seeped into his taut muscles. "She didn't just disappear. Travis, recheck the house. See if anything's been disturbed in her room." A sudden thought jarred his memory. "And find the dog."

"On it." Travis jogged toward the front door.

"What are you thinking?" Bingham's worried gaze caught Coop's.

"She wouldn't have walked away—not after what happened yesterday."

"What happened yesterday?"

"I almost lost her." It pained Coop to say the words. If he'd let her go with him today, he'd know where she was right now.

Focus, damn it! He'd have the rest of his life to blame himself unless he got with the program and found her. "If somebody wanted to grab her without being seen, they would've parked out on the road and hiked in." He strode onto the graveled parking area. "That's where we need to look." He broke into a jog. Two strides later, he was running flat out, not surprised when Bingham caught up to him.

There were no tire tracks on the winding driveway except those his truck had left coming and going. He didn't slow his pace until he reached the county road and the spot wide enough to park next to the rural mailbox. Bingham saw it at the same instant and slid to a stop beside him.

Goddamnit! Clear impressions in the loose dirt indicated a vehicle with a wide wheelbase had not only parked there but had maneuvered back and forth to get farther off the paved road. The footprints in the loose dirt told the rest of the story blatantly, and it seemed impossible he'd not seen it when he turned into the drive. If only he hadn't been stunned by Bingham's confession and the general's unforgivable betrayal of Jade.

"Looks like a man in boots met a woman in sneakers here not too long ago. Hell, we probably just missed them?" Bingham pointed to where the woman's footprints ended. "No sign of a struggle. It looks like she willingly got in the vehicle."

Coop could read the signs as well or better than Bingham. If his stomach hadn't lodged in his throat, the same conclusion might have come from his mouth. As it was, he turned away to tamp down the emotions that threatened to put him on his knees. Thankfully, Bingham took the hint and shut up.

Coop had to clear his throat before he trusted his

voice. "It had to be someone she knew and trusted. Jade wouldn't have met a stranger alone, much less agree to go with him." Unfortunately, the footprints in the dirt left them exactly *nowhere*. Angrily, he whipped around to head back to the house.

As the major walked the edge of the road, still studying the ground, a miniature avalanche of loose rocks slid over the side into the barrow pit. A flash of color caught Coop's eye. He jumped down the slight incline and bent to pick up an abandoned cell phone nestled in a clump of dried grass. The small rockslide had jostled the screen enough to rouse a photo of the meatball in a backdrop of red tulips.

"It's hers." Thankfully, there was no password to hack, but he'd need to have a talk with her about on-line security when this was over. The absurdity of the thought almost brought a smile to his face. He tapped the phone icon and went to her recent calls. "Shit! *Reiner*."

Bingham stepped closer and peered at Jade's call record. "Three calls from the Colonel in about fifteen minutes." He backed away and ran both hands over his face. "I didn't get here in time. She had no reason not to trust him."

"Let it go, Bingham. The game starts over now." One by one, Coop played Reiner's calls on speakerphone.

The first two messages were brief and basically the same. *"Jade? Where the hell are you? Call me back as soon as you can."* The third one dangled a new carrot. *"Damn it, Jade. You're in danger, and so is Coop. We need to meet as soon as possible. Call me."*

"She returned his call without listening to the messages." Coop couldn't grasp how the colonel had convinced her to meet him alone. "She knew she was in danger." He ground his teeth as anger simmered. "It would have taken more than that to get her to break every damn rule I left her with this morning."

"I agree." Bingham laid a hand on Coop's shoulder. "She wasn't concerned for *her* safety—she was afraid for you."

Horror exploded through him at the idea she'd endangered herself because of him. Followed almost immediately by a rush of satisfaction that she cared enough to worry about him. He stuffed the feeling down as quickly as it raised its head. It would make no difference if he didn't get to her in time.

"Where would he take her?" Thankfully, Bingham was staying on track. He started hiking back to the house.

Coop straightened and jogged to catch up. He slid Jade's phone in his shirt pocket and retrieved his, tapping Travis' number. "I don't know, but I'm going to find out." He put the call on speaker as his friend answered. "Did you find Moose?"

"Sleeping safely on Jade's bed."

"Excellent. Jade will need her service dog when she gets back."

"You found something?" Travis sounded hopeful.

"Yeah, but we don't have much to go on yet. We're on our way back, and we'll fill you in. Then, I need my laptop to see if I can find some answers. In the meantime, would you call Luke and let him know she's missing? We might need the whole team once we locate her."

"You got it," Travis said.

Coop ended the call. It was a big load off, knowing his friends had his back. Now all he had to do was figure out where Reiner would have taken her. Of one thing, Coop was adamant. He wasn't leaving her to rot in some man-made hell again. He would never stop looking for her until he brought her home.

*****

The blow slammed into Jade's jaw, nearly spinning her head clear off. Pain exploded with a thousand little twinkly lights. She allowed her head to loll forward onto her chest, not bothering to pretend she could hold it up. Blood poured from her nose. The inside of her cheek felt like raw meat from the impact with her teeth. Maybe it hadn't been such a good idea to bite Derek when she'd come to with him feeling her up and his sloppy mouth grinding against hers. No way was she sorry.

"That'll teach the bitch." Derek's whiny voice penetrated the ringing in her ears.

"Damn it. Don't screw this up, Derek. McDowell is paying us good money to make her disappear once they don't need her anymore. If he finds out she'll be entertaining us for a while before that happens, he won't like it. So, keep your hands off of her and stick to the plan."

Jade recognized the speaker's voice. His name was Aaron or Elon. No, Ethan. That's what Carl Graves had called him. His second in command.

Why were Graves and his men suddenly taking orders from her father?

"Yeah, yeah. The bitch owes me, and I'll collect any way I see fit."

"Fine—as soon as General McDowell is out of this. Let's go dispose of Reiner's body before Graves gets back."

Two sets of footsteps receded. Relief washed over Jade when the door closed behind them—until a click and the thump of a padlock against wood let her know escape wasn't going to be easy.

She lifted her head, closing her eyes for a moment against the dizziness and blinding pain. When she could move again without reeling, she tried to wipe the blood from her face on the shoulder of her shirt. She sat in the center of the room, her arms and legs bound to the metal chair with white zip ties. Any movement caused the hard plastic around her wrists and ankles to pinch her flesh.

A glance around the room confirmed there was nothing to use as a weapon and no sharp edges that would aid in freeing herself. *Damn it!* She'd trusted Reiner because he'd been there for her after her rescue. Without him, she wouldn't have made it home. Even now, it was hard to grasp the fact he'd tried to kill her. For some reason, that bothered her more than her father's betrayal.

Worse was the guilt for letting down Coop again. He'd asked her to do one thing—stay with Travis. What an ignorant fool she'd been. Frustration morphed into rage. With a roar, she threw her weight forward until she stood on her spread feet, her hands grasping the arms of the chair, and shuffled forward a step. The ties around her wrists cut into her skin. The metal seat's weight messed with her balance, and she barely managed to plop down without upsetting the chair.

She'd hardly made any forward progress, yet it took her a minute or two to recover her strength after each try. Giving up wasn't an option. If she could get close enough to the wall, she could make noise. Knock her hard head against it if she had to. She wasn't going down without a fight.

With each heave forward, dragging the weight of the chair, she got closer to her goal. Her wrists bled freely as the bindings cut deeper. The top of her head threatened to explode at every step. She ignored the pain and focused on the mission. *Reach the wall, bang the chair against it, attract someone's attention, escape.* There was a lot that could go wrong between the first item on her list and the last. She'd worry about that later.

When she was within a couple of feet from her goal, a noise drew her attention to the door. Quiet sounds as though someone was trying to be stealthy. She stilled. The key jiggled in the lock, the handle rattled, and old hinges squeaked as the door slowly opened. Her vision blurry, she squinted, noticing for the first time how dark the room had become. Only a dusky light filtered through the small window, the day turning to night without consulting her.

Is it Derek sneaking in alone to teach me another lesson? Mesmerized, she watched the dark form slip through the door, swing it closed, and snap on a flashlight. When the beam hit her full in the face, she squeezed her eyes shut and turned away.

Immediately, the light went out, and footsteps approached. A hand touched her knee, and she jerked away.

"Easy." The muffled voice wasn't completely unfamiliar.

She strained to make out the man's features. "Who are you?"

His only answer was the unmistakable *snick* of a knife blade sliding open.

She *hated* knives—had never conquered her fear of them. Panic overwhelmed reason in two seconds flat. She tensed and sucked in air to scream.

The man's hand shot out and clamped over her mouth. "Huh-uh. None of that." He slipped the knife blade along her arm, and Jade felt a tug as he cut the tie. Relief engulfed through her as he did the same to the bindings on her ankles and finally her other wrist. He removed his hand from her face. "Are we good now?"

She nodded, leery of making any sound, but curiosity won out. "Who are you?"

He snickered. "Well, honey, I'm about the only friend you've got right now. So, I suggest you stick close to me."

Jade's heart tripped in recognition of the man's arrogant, overbearing manner. "Carl Graves." The man who'd left her sister for dead and poisoned Moose. What was he doing here?

He laughed, grabbed her elbow, and pushed her toward the door.

CHAPTER TWENTY-SEVEN

Travis handed Coop his laptop the minute he and Bingham walked in the house. "Luke and the guys are on standby. He's turning the FBI loose on Graves and his crew, so we don't have any distractions. What'd you find?"

Coop headed for the kitchen doorway. "Jade's cell phone in the ditch by the mailbox. It was Reiner. He drew her out to meet him by insinuating I was in danger. He must have had a damn good story because she went with him with no sign of a struggle."

As he stepped into the kitchen, he stopped short. Nicole whacked her broken wrist against the table in her haste to stand, and the color drained from her face. Ryan jumped up to steady her. For a heartbeat, Coop half expected her to collapse. He hadn't meant for them to hear him, but it was too late to shove the words back in. The next instant, Nicole pulled herself up straight and started toward him with something close to murder in her eyes.

He raised a hand to stall her. "It'll be okay. We're going to get her back."

"That's for damn sure." Travis stepped in front of him, grabbing Nicole's fists from the air before they pummeled Coop's chest. "You and Ryan can help." Travis led the woman toward the living room, and her husband followed. "Get on the phone. Call everyone you know. Tell them to keep an eye out for Jade.

Coop set his laptop on the table, turned it on, and then watched Travis settle Jade's family on the couch while his voice droned on comfortingly. As big a badass as his friend could be, he had a compassionate streak a mile wide. Thankfully, he'd been there to divert Nicole because Coop only had one mission.

He dropped into a chair and tapped his password into the laptop. Behind him, Bingham's pacing was driving him crazy, even though Coop understood, only too well, what caused the man's anxiety. He glanced over his shoulder and nodded toward the coffeemaker. "We're going to need some java."

Clearly relieved to have a project, Bingham almost smiled as he hurried to the counter.

Coop turned back to his keyboard and did a quick search for car rental places. He handed Bingham a list when the major set down a steaming cup of black liquid beside his computer. "See if you can find out what Reiner's driving."

Bingham snatched the list, dug his phone from his back pocket, and stepped out the back door.

Coop took a swig of coffee and winced. *Guess I deserved that for not making it myself.* He pushed it away and concentrated on the screen. Five minutes later, he had Mark Reiner's cell phone records in front of him. His three calls to Jade stood out, as did her return call a few minutes later. After speaking with her, he'd immediately dialed another number. What were the odds it wasn't related?

Punching the unfamiliar number into his phone, he ground his teeth as it rang twice and abruptly stopped.

"General McDowell," said the gruff voice on the other end.

Coop pressed the *end* icon. *That son of a bitch.* Though Bingham had told him of McDowell's role in Jade's ill-fated mission, it still made him sick that her father and Reiner were neck-deep in the same cesspool.

A few more keystrokes, and he'd know where to find Reiner. Usually, he'd call Special Agent Roberts and let the FBI get a subpoena to obtain Reiner's location legally, but that would take too long. Besides, Coop wasn't concerned about a conviction in a court martial. Roberts could worry about that detail on the off chance the colonel lived through the night.

Reiner had turned his cell phone off shortly after his call to McDowell. *Strange.* The last ping recorded was between the safe house and Pine Bluff. Coop typed in another URL on a hunch and quickly learned the provider for McDowell's cell service. Once he had that, it was simple to locate the general's phone.

Well, look at that. Pine Bluff is a popular place. Hiding is going to be a problem, though.

He jumped up. "Travis, I've got them." He swung around as Bingham slammed through the back door.

"He rented a 2017 Chevy Suburban. Black. License number 118 BND. Here's the kicker—they rented another one just like it to an Air Force general about an hour ago."

Travis appeared, with Nicole following closely. She peered around him. "Vince Neilson has been working at our store all day. He said there's a black SUV sitting in front of the feed store. He wouldn't have paid any attention, but another one pulled up a little while ago, stayed twenty minutes, and then left." She glanced between Coop and Travis and back again. "Did you just say something about an Air Force general?"

Shit! Coop did not want to have that conversation with Jade's sister. Telling Nicole her father was a traitor and a slimeball and, *oh, by the way, Jade is only your half-sister*, was at the top of his least-favorite-things-to-do list.

Suddenly, Ryan pushed forward and put his arm around her shoulders. He studied Coop for a heartbeat longer than necessary. "Go get Jade." He tipped his head subtly toward the front door. "Everything else can wait until she's safe." For a moment, it looked as though Nicole would protest, but he dropped a kiss on her cheek. "Come on, Nic. If your dad's in town, we'll see him later." He took her hand and turned her away from Coop. "Don't worry. You know how tough Jade is. Hell, I just hope she doesn't hurt anyone too bad."

Nicole snorted a laugh as she draped an arm around his waist.

After a relief-filled glance in Coop's direction, Travis followed the couple from the room. Coop knew he was giving them the spiel about staying inside and locking the doors. He was certain no one would be looking for them tonight with the FBI rounding up Graves' militia.

Bingham started to walk by, and Coop held up a hand to stop him. "You sure you want in on this? If something goes wrong—if Reiner or the general stay alive long enough to face a tribunal, they'll make sure you go down too."

The major focused on the floor and raked a hand through his dark hair. Finally, he looked Coop in the eyes. "Let them do their worst. It's not like I don't deserve it. Right now, the only thing that matters is finding Jade. I'm in."

Coop grinned and slapped him on the back. "Let's go."

Travis met them at the pickup. Coop opened the rear door and slid a long, narrow case from under the back seat. Inside was his standby M24 sniper rifle and a spare handgun. He selected the Glock and checked the safety before handing it to Bingham. "You may need this."

The major accepted the weapon, shoved it in his belt, and climbed in the back seat. Travis hopped in the front as Coop started the engine.

At the end of the driveway, he turned right on the county road. The wide spot by the mailbox seemed to mock him as it disappeared in the rearview mirror. He'd failed Jade twice. His grip on the steering wheel tightened. By sheer force of will, he shoved the guilt into a dark corner of his mind. Conscience would demand he deal with it at some point, but his purpose was clear. He wouldn't let her down again.

His phone vibrated, and he leaned forward to slide it from his back pocket, hoping it was Jade. The name on the screen was the last one he'd expected.

"Shit."

Travis swiveled to look at him. "Who is it?"

"Carl Graves."

"What the hell does he want? If SA Roberts is doing his job, he should be on his way to jail by now. Let it go to voicemail."

Coop considered Travis' suggestion for the count of two, but his gut told him to answer the call. He swiped the screen. "Didn't expect to hear from you again, Graves."

"You probably didn't think you'd owe me a favor before the night was over, either. Did you?" Graves' voice was low and clipped.

Coop chuffed a laugh. "What could possibly make you think I'd ever owe you a favor?" In the hesitation that followed, he heard footsteps.

"I'm putting you on speaker so you can talk to your girlfriend about that but keep your voice down. We're not out of the woods yet."

"Coop?" Her whisper sent a shiver through him as though she'd breathed his name against his lips.

"Jade? Are you okay? Did he hurt you?" Fury coiled in his gut.

"No. I'm safe for the moment. Graves saved my life. He's with ATF, undercover." Her voice cracked, and she cleared her throat. "It was Colonel Reiner and my father. They're behind the attempts on my life."

What the hell? Coop glanced toward Travis, disbelief coursing through him. He placed his phone on the console and pressed *mute*. "Graves claims he's a fed, an ATF agent." Travis yanked his phone out and started texting. No doubt it was to Luke seeking confirmation of Graves' claim. If the ATF had an agent undercover on this op, they damn sure should have shared the information with the FBI.

Coop pressed *speaker*. "I know. Reiner and the general will get what's coming to them." *For everything.* "First, I need to know you're safe. Where are you?"

"Reiner is dead. I had to—he was going to kill me." The words spilled from her as though she couldn't hold them in any longer.

"Good girl. You did what you had to do." He was sorry he hadn't been there to save her from taking the life of someone she'd considered a friend.

"That's not exactly factual." Graves sounded like he was standing close by. "Jade only took him down. The general had the kill shot. Guess he doesn't take failure well. Did you verify my credentials yet?"

Coop glanced at Travis again, and his friend nodded. A fresh wave of anger tore through him. "Yeah, but that doesn't mean I trust you." He gritted his teeth to keep from hitting something.

"Whatever. Listen up if you want to help Jade. With you threatening to call in the FBI to shut them down, Ethan and Derek decided to leave town. Unfortunately, they stopped for a drink at the same bar where McDowell and Reiner were having a discussion. Ethan overhead them say they should have brought more men. Not the sharpest tools in the shed, he and Derek offered their services. They're not far behind us."

"Where are you?"

"About a mile east of town, there's a dirt road that turns north and heads up into the mountains. Stay on that for another mile or so, and you'll see an old warehouse that's had better days. We'd have gotten farther, but it turns out Ethan was a sniper in the Rangers. He blew out both front tires on my pickup, and we were on foot for the last half mile. If I had to guess, they're probably dispensable to a man like the general, but I couldn't convince them they were making a mistake." As Graves spoke, the sounds of objects scraping across the floor also came through the phone.

"I think the general may have promised them something more than monetary reward." There was an edge of fear in Jade's voice that tore at Coop's heart and fueled his hatred.

That son of a bitch!

"So, we're barricading ourselves in the back office as best we can until the cavalry arrives." Graves paused as the sounds of pounding came through loud and clear. "When do you think that might be?" It was apparent, the man was trying to sound unconcerned, probably for Jade's benefit. If only he knew the woman was tougher than either of them.

Travis' phone chirped, and he held up four fingers. "The Black Hawk is on the way."

Coop smiled. "Can you hold them off for four minutes?"

"We'll do our best." Gunfire blasted through the phone. Louder shots answered.

There wasn't a damn thing Coop could do. He was seven or eight minutes from town and another three to the warehouse. Whatever was going to happen would likely be over before he arrived. His powerlessness made him almost physically sick.

"Coop?"

At Jade's low voice, he grabbed his phone and took it off speaker. "Stay with me, Jade. Okay?"

"I want to tell you...just in case. I love you, Coop. I think I have from the first night we met, and I never stopped. I know there's tons of baggage between us, but I just wanted you to know." Her voice broke on the last word.

Damned if his eyes didn't start burning. Happiness crept into his heart despite the gunfire that had interspersed Jade's declaration. "I know. I feel the same. The baggage is behind us. We're starting over. Remember?"

"I hear a helicopter. Is that Blake, making a grand entrance?" She laughed, but he could hear the stress in her voice.

"Yep. Luke and MacGyver are with him. Travis, Bingham, and I will be right behind them. Keep your head down until I get there."

Suddenly, she gasped. "I smell gasoline!" A crash followed, and everything went silent.

"Jade? Jade?" The call had ended. He dropped his phone in the cupholder, pressed his foot on the gas pedal, and watched as the speedometer needle vibrated into the red zone.

CHAPTER TWENTY-EIGHT

Jade fumbled the phone, tried to catch it, and sent it spinning beyond the barricade of abandoned equipment, broken furniture, and mangled metal shelving they'd quickly improvised. Graves caught her arm as she tried to crawl past the edge.

"Stay down," he growled.

She jerked back. "There's smoke coming in under the door!" She'd gotten far enough to see that much. "Something's on fire."

"Give me your coat." Graves squirmed out of his jacket, grabbed the one she handed him, and started crawling toward the door.

She peered over the top of the barrier, watching as he rolled the fabric and stuffed the clothing tightly against the threshold. On his way back, a random bullet fired blindly through the wooden door caught him in the shoulder. Swearing non-stop, he continued to drag himself toward their last line of defense.

By the time he reached her, one side of his upper body was drenched in blood, front and back. The bullet had gone through, which was good, but he was losing a lot of blood. She looked around, swiftly concluding her shirt was the only thing available to staunch the flow. *Oh well. Modesty is over-rated.*

She quickly unbuttoned the garment, eliciting a lopsided grin from the wounded man that ended with a wince.

"Serves you right. Do you have a pocketknife?" She took the one he dug from his jeans and split the shirt into two pieces. "Lean forward." She bunched one section and placed it against the wound on his back. "Put as much pressure on that as you can." She folded the rest of the fabric and pressed it against the front of his shoulder.

"If you're trying to take my mind off how much that hurts, it's not working." A shudder went through his body, but he tried to smile. "Looks like you know what you're doing."

"You don't spend a lot of time in the Middle East without learning a few things."

He leaned his head back and closed his eyes. "Is that where you pissed off that colonel and the general?"

"You could say that." She hesitated. How much did she want to tell this man about her personal life? Somehow it seemed only fair to answer his question. He'd blown his cover to save her life, after all. "Colonel Reiner was my commanding officer and a friend...I thought. I've known the general all my life." She shrugged one shoulder. "He's my father."

His eyes popped open. "Holy shit!"

"What about you? Why are you in Pine Bluff, pretending to be someone you're not?"

"I infiltrated Ethan Trudell's organization two months ago, right after he made the domestic terrorism watch list. He's got powerful connections who've helped him raise a lot of money for arms and explosives and recruit some unsavory companions like the ones you've seen around town. We need to know who he's working with and what their plans are for the money and firepower."

A sudden pounding on the wall startled Jade. "Hey, Carl! We'd rather have the woman alive, and we're willing to let you go to get her. What'dya say?" She recognized the voice as Ethan's.

Jade couldn't hear the helicopter anymore. The cavalry should've been there by now. What was keeping Blake?

A few seconds ticked by before a volley of gunshots sprayed the wall where Ethan's voice had been. "I told you it wouldn't work. We have to cut our losses. Burn it down, and let's get the hell out of here."

"*Goddamnit! That bitch is mine!*" Derek's whiny voice gave her images of a petulant tantrum and made her snort a laugh, despite the tension.

The next instant, the smell of gasoline became a lot stronger, and her humor faded. The sound of liquid sloshing against the walls and door made her cringe.

"I'm gonna count to three. If you don't come out with your hands in the air, you're gonna fry," Derek yelled. "One…"

Her gaze went to the broken windows high up on the walls. There was no way to reach them.

"Two…"

She exchanged a glance with Graves. "Coop's friends *will* be here." Was she trying to reassure him or herself?

"Three!"

Something hit the wall. The whoosh of accelerant feeding flames was unmistakable. Jade jumped to her feet as smoke began to pour under the door. "Come on. We have to get out of here." She reached for Graves' good arm and helped him to stand.

He leaned against the barricade. "You better take this." He handed her his weapon. She gripped it as they exchanged a glance, then started toward the door. A fresh volley of gunshots that tore through the paper-thin walls drove them to the floor again.

The knob rattled as someone tried to gain entrance. She clutched the weapon with both hands and trained it on whoever was coming through that doorway.

"Get away from the door, Jade."

Wait! She knew that voice. It was Luke. She let out the breath she'd been holding and lowered her arms. Beside her, Graves grabbed her leg and pulled her down, then groaned and held his shoulder.

"You're going to be okay. It's Luke." Another blast of gunfire shredded the door, and it flew back against the wall. Then MacGyver was there, helping her up. Blake tossed Graves over his shoulder, and they all ran, flames on every side.

Luke was already outside, pushing two men onto their knees, their hands bound behind them. Derek and Ethan were both bloody and undoubtedly in pain. Someone should have told them working for her father wasn't a healthy occupation.

As MacGyver half-carried her to safety beyond the flames and the worst of the heat, coughing overcame her. When he finally let her stop, she fell to her knees and hacked smoke from her already raw throat and lungs. Swallowing glass couldn't have been any more excruciating. When her spasms receded, she rolled to her back and braced herself on one elbow. Savoring deep breaths, she gaped at the surreal scene before her.

Luke strode toward MacGyver, who knelt beside Graves not far from where Jade rested, a frown scrunching his brow. "How's our covert ATF agent?"

MacGyver glanced up as Blake joined them. "He'll be okay, but he's lost a lot of blood. Let's get him in the helo."

"On it." Blake broke into a trot toward the aircraft.

Luke dropped to his knee beside her. He scrutinized her briefly before he removed his shirt and held it out to her.

She groaned as she glanced down at herself. *Jeez!* Rare embarrassment quickly heated her face, and she shoved her arms in the sleeves, fastening the first three buttons before looking up again.

"We won't tell Coop…or my wife." He smiled and winked. "Are you doing okay?"

"I'm alive, so there's that." She was grateful for the quick change of subject. "Thank you." *For so many things.*

He laughed. "You're kind of family now, whether you like it or not. We watch out for our own."

She mulled over the notion of being surrounded by people who cared. It had been a long time since she'd had friends willing to go to bat for her.

Surprisingly, she didn't hate the idea. Plus, she'd always have Nic and Ryan. Who needed a father who'd never really been part of her life anyway? Sadness shrouded her, despite the unforgivable actions of the man she should have been able to trust above all others.

"Where's Coop?" He was ten times the man her father was, and she needed to tell him.

Luke nodded toward the winding dirt road as the growl of a powerful Hemi engine echoed through the trees. "That'll be him now." The sound of tires sliding on gravel rose above the roar of flames lapping at the tinder-dry building. He offered a hand to help her stand.

Jade watched as the green pickup fishtailed to a stop thirty feet away, sending a plume of dust into the air. Coop's broad shoulders pushed the driver's door open, and he broke into a jog the second his feet hit the ground. Luke stepped aside, and she took two shaky strides toward Coop.

She knew the instant he saw her. He stopped. His trademark grin spread across his face as though a weight lifted from his shoulders. Travis exited the passenger door and said something she couldn't hear. Coop shook his head and started toward her again, his long legs eating up the distance.

He halted with a foot still separating them. She closed her eyes as gentle fingers whispered over the new bruises on her jaw and cheekbone. Then she was in Coop's arms, not sure which of them had taken the final step. She wrapped her arms around his waist and burrowed into the safety he offered.

Sirens wailed in the distance as helicopter blades

began to rotate. A black sedan pulled alongside Coop's truck. Two men, wearing bulletproof vests with *FBI* emblazoned on the back, piled out and joined the group gathered by the aircraft.

"I'm pissed at you." Travis appeared at her side. The big grin he wore took the sting from his words.

"I deserve it. I shouldn't have left the house without clearing it with you. If it makes a difference, I'm so sorry."

His eyes widened as though surprised, and he patted her shoulder. "Hey, I'm just glad you're okay."

"Where's Bingham?" Coop kept one arm around her waist as he swung around to look at his pickup. A firetruck careened into the parking area, stopped a safe distance from the flames, and killed the siren. A half dozen firefighters jumped into action, unrolling hoses to fight the blaze.

Travis swept a glance over the area beyond the truck. "He said he was going to check out something down by the pond." He shrugged. "I think, once he saw that Jade was all right, he decided to avoid the crowd and…you know…anyone that might recognize him."

Coop nodded as though that made perfect sense to him. She was about to ask *why* when Luke appeared beside her again.

He slapped Coop on the back, then turned toward her. "Graves is stable. We're taking off for the hospital in Baker City. We've got room for one more, and I think it should be you."

Jade shook her head and moved closer to Coop. "No, I'm fine. I mean, bruises and cuts will heal. I don't need a hospital." Luke glanced questioningly at Coop, and she turned to meet his concerned perusal. "Really, I'm okay. A little headache—that's all. I want to stay with you."

The critical consideration in his eyes softened, accompanied by a hint of humor that said he knew she was playing him. "You guys go ahead, Luke. I'll drive her to the hospital." He put a finger against her lips when she started to protest. "What about Derek and Ethan?"

"They're not hurt bad. SA Roberts will take them in." Luke tipped his head toward her but continued speaking to Coop. "You sure?"

She huffed. "I'm right here, and I'll decide—"

"Yeah. We'll meet you there." Coop ignored her. "That'll give us time to talk."

"Oh, hell no!" Travis raised his hand. "I'll just take that extra seat in the bird." He followed Luke toward the helicopter.

She couldn't help chuckling at Travis' expression. The guy was drawing the line at yet another personal discussion involving her. Coop pulled her into his side as they watched his friends load up. The helicopter lifted off and was soon out of sight.

The two FBI agents led Derek and Ethan to their car, and the back doors closed one after the other once the prisoners were inside. The driver strode toward them and handed her a business card. "Special Agent Roberts, ma'am. I understand you're on your way to the hospital. We're going to need a statement from you as soon as you're able. In the meantime, Luke filled in some of the gaps. We'll be issuing a BOLO for General McDowell. If you see or hear from him, contact me immediately."

"Thank you. I will." She slid the card into her back pocket.

"We'll call you when Jade's up to giving her statement. Then you can explain to me how the supposed leader of our armed militia turned out to be a federal agent." Skepticism radiated from Coop.

"As soon as someone explains it to me," Roberts grumbled and spun around. He returned to his car with a curt wave, made a three-point turn, and drove away.

Coop relaxed as soon as the agents were out of sight. His arm fell away from her waist, and he gripped her hand, threading their fingers together. "Come on, let's get out of here. We'll pick up Bingham on the way."

Jade glanced at the flames still leaping from the building. Evidently, the firefighters had opted to let it burn. Their concern seemed to be keeping the blaze from spreading to dry grass and nearby trees.

Coop opened the passenger-side door and helped her onto the high seat. He leaned across her lap to grab the seatbelt and buckle her in, then cupped her chin and pressed a lingering kiss to her forehead.

When he straightened, his intense focus made it impossible to look away. "Did you mean what you said on the phone?"

A half-smile tugged at the corners of her mouth. "Every word." She reached to touch his cheek as the tenderness in his eyes welcomed her home.

The sexy grin she loved spread across his face. "Hospital first, then let's get you home to the meatball." He leaned in for one more kiss before he stepped back, closed the door, and jogged around to the other side. After starting the engine and shifting into drive, he reached across the console and covered her hand with his.

She loved him. The ease with which the words formed in her mind scared her a little. He'd forgiven her for the cruel way she'd hurt him. Now, if only she could forgive herself. Their happily-ever-after depended on it. He'd never done things halfway, and he was all in to make their relationship work. Could she give anything less?

It was not quite a mile downhill on a narrow forest service road to reach the county pavement. Jade and Graves had sprinted from the main road and taken cover in the old warehouse after gunshots had disabled his pickup.

She'd paid little attention to the tranquil waters of the pond they'd passed, surrounded by cattails and wild blackberry bushes. Now, through the driver's side window, she watched a flock of geese take off, even as more were landing. It was beautiful in a way. Willow trees grew in clusters of two or three. Beyond the pond, a gentle slope rose into thick pines that seemed to swallow the early morning sun. Inexplicably, a shiver rolled through her.

She admired the scene through the rear window until, suddenly, a sharp crack and the sound of glass breaking made her heart lurch into her throat. She swung toward the front just in time to shield her face as the truck's windshield shattered. Coop grunted, and the pickup veered to the right.

"Get down!" Confusion and shock immobilized

her until he stretched to shove her below the dash. He stood on the brakes, and the pickup slid to a stop. Ramming the transmission into reverse, he stomped on the gas pedal. Dust billowed all around them. With his upper body swiveled to see out the rear window, he braced one arm on the console. The vehicle flew backward down the dirt road.

The front window sagged inward in a million mosaic-type pieces of glass that somehow held together against all odds. A small hole, surrounded by jagged edges, stared at her from just left of center. Slowly, the jigsaw puzzle came together. Someone had taken a shot at them. *Right where Coop was sitting.* She rocked toward him as he spun the steering wheel to the right. Blood poured down the side of his head from a wound near his temple.

Before she could find words for this new horror, the ground fell out from under the rear tires. One second, they were sliding down a sharp slope; the next, they bottomed out jarringly, still upright on four wheels.

"Get out! Take cover in the trees!" He hissed the words as he clung tightly to the steering wheel. His head down, blood dripped onto the leg of his jeans.

"No! You're hurt. I'm not leaving you." She unbuckled her seatbelt and reached for him.

He caught her shoulder in a harsh grip before she could touch him. "Jade, do what I said. Please. I know what I'm doing. Trust me." His dark brown gaze bored into hers as he issued the words through clenched teeth.

There was no better man to put her trust in, but, damn it, she didn't have to like it.

When she hesitated, he leaned across her and shoved open her door. "Go…and stay out of sight. That was a sniper round from a fair distance. Whoever it was, he'll come for us. I couldn't be there for you when you needed me three years ago. But I'm here now, so get the hell out of the way and let me do my job." He gave her a shove toward the edge of the seat.

She still had the handgun Graves had given her after he was wounded. The shooter wouldn't be expecting that. She leveled her glare on Coop. "I'm going, you big jerk." She stepped from the truck, harnessing all of her anger to convince him she was complying. "Don't make me sorry I trusted you." Abruptly, she turned, studied the terrain, and sprinted toward the nearest ponderosa big enough to shield her from view.

After glancing around, she raced to a gnarled juniper, then did it over again until, by her estimation, she was about eighty feet from the pickup. At this distance, she was seriously pushing the limits of her weapon's accuracy. Even if she couldn't hit anything, at least she could get their attention. It might be enough to give Coop an advantage.

Crouched in the shadow of a grand fir, she divided her time between watching the pickup and monitoring the curve in the road where she expected the sniper to appear. Frustration grew when she couldn't spot any movements inside Coop's truck. Repeatedly, she had to tell herself that was a good thing. *The man moves like a friggin' shadow.* If she couldn't see him, then neither would the shooter.

Watching the road didn't bring her any satisfaction either. No matter how hard she concentrated or how silent she was, the area remained devoid of human activity. Smoke from the warehouse fire had settled into the forest, making her eyes water and giving the air a charcoal flavor. The sun was fighting with patchy clouds for equal time while a slight breeze stirred the air now and then. The whole world had gone still and eerie.

She had no idea how much time had passed as she waited. At some point during the night or early morning, she'd smashed the face of her watch, and the hands had ceased their movement, much like everything else.

Was Coop okay? How severe was his head wound? Maybe she should check on him. What if something had scared off the shooter and Coop died while she was waiting? A whimper rose in her throat before she bit it back. Cold sweat covered her body. She'd never forgive herself.

Why was she pretending she didn't know who the shooter was? It had to be her dear old dad. Or someone he sent to do his dirty work. *Strange.* She couldn't muster an ounce of sympathy or love or even regret. He was a stranger to her. As far back as she could remember.

She sighed and stretched her right calf to ease the ache building from tension and forced inactivity. Her attention drifted back to the cab of the truck. *Where is he?*

A *pop* to her right made her jerk around. Her heart leaped into a gallop. She searched the sun-dappled forest for movement. Suddenly, a squirrel voiced its objection to her proximity. She traced the chatter to a tall tree about fifty feet away, over her right shoulder. A pinecone bounced noisily from branch to branch until it landed with another *pop* at the base of the tree. She exhaled with relief. *Jeez!* A querulous rodent had thrown her into a panic. She was losing her touch.

Jade turned back to the curve in the road and the surrounding area, her thoughts straying to Coop's truck every few minutes. It was too still. Something was wrong. A chill shook her as it ran the length of her spine. The unmistakable sense of being watched was like an icy breath on the back of her neck.

Still crouched, she swung around, gun hand outstretched, searching the terrain for the source of her foreboding. A blur of motion at the corner of her eye made her flinch, and she fell back on her butt. A booted foot smacked into her hand, sending a blast of pain up her arm and the gun spinning away. She scrambled to her feet and stopped short, staring into the barrel of a rifle.

She dragged her focus from the weapon to settle on the man whose finger rested on the trigger. Though she'd expected him, the reality still twisted the knife in her gut. "I figured you were around here somewhere." Scorn dripped purposefully from her words.

"And you, Captain, never learned when to quit." Slowly, the general lowered the rifle barrel and produced a 38 special from his coat pocket.

"Why are you doing this? I'm your daughter—your flesh and blood. Did you ever love Nicole or me?" Coldness encased her heart.

"I'm *not* your father." His face contorting into a mask of rage, he stalked a few steps closer. "Your mother was a whore, and you were the unholy result of one of her affairs. How could I have any feelings but contempt for you?"

Shock at his revelation left her speechless with her mouth hanging open. He was crazy. His eyes darted wildly, never remaining on her for more than a second. She stood her ground, refusing to show fear. "Even if that's true, what about Nicole. You were never a father to her either."

"Why would I believe Nicole was my daughter? I couldn't trust your mother. I played the part all those years. Even after she died, I continued to put a roof over your heads, fed you, and paid for your education. I did more than enough under the circumstances. You should have been grateful."

She straightened. "You left me to die in that compound in Syria. Didn't you?"

He had the nerve to shrug. "If it's any consolation, I never wanted you to suffer. You should have stayed dead. I can't allow you to talk to that SEAL and his friends. They could ruin everything I've worked for." A nervous tick beneath one of his eyes added to his crazed expression. He raised the 38 until she stared into the muzzle.

Jade eyed her fallen weapon. It was too far away, but it was her only hope. Breaking right, she leaped toward the gun, rolling as she felt the metal slide into her hand. The blast from the general's weapon deafened her as she gained her feet. The sound slammed into her like a baseball bat. She staggered back a step.

Another sharp crack startled her. The general fired again as his arms flailed, and he lurched forward. She glanced at the weapon clutched in her hand. Confusion followed the realization she hadn't pulled the trigger.

"Jade?"

She squinted toward the voice. Her vision was blurry, but she made out Coop's form jogging toward her, his SIG held in one hand. He was okay. He was here. She didn't mean to drop her weapon, but she heard it hit the ground. Then her knees slammed into the dirt, and stunned, she rocked back and forth before she toppled over on her side.

He was beside her, gently turning her onto her back. She struggled to retain consciousness. "I don't know...what's wrong with me." She tried to sit, but her body was too heavy.

His hand pressed her down as he undid the buttons of her shirt. "*Shit!* You're wounded."

"How bad is it?" Was she slurring her words?

His grin seemed forced. "I'm going to stop the bleeding and get you to a hospital. You'll be okay." For some reason, his voice didn't sound all that confident.

She turned her head and peered at the wound he was probing. All she could see was blood. There was no pain. She couldn't feel anything. "That's probably a good thing," she mumbled.

Something moved over his shoulder. "Coop..." Why was it so hard to get the words out? The general shuffling toward them, raising the gun, broke through her daze. Desperately, she pointed. "Behind you..."

Coop whirled around, then dropped down in front of her. He was protecting her, sacrificing himself.

The blast sounded far away. His body fell on hers. "*No...*" The emptiness of life without him swallowed her whole. She couldn't bear it. She didn't want to. How could her heart still beat?

She started to hope again as he pushed himself up until he crouched beside her. He stood as a whistle shrilled from the direction of his truck. Forcing her eyes open took the rest of her strength.

He smiled and waved as a man's voice shouted, "You're clear!"

"Who...was that?" She barely heard her raspy whisper.

Coop dropped to his knees beside her again, and she felt his weight on her chest. "That was providence—*your father.*" His brown eyes sparkled as he kept her gaze until she couldn't hold her eyes open any longer. It wasn't like he was making any sense anyway.

The blackness swirling around her promised respite and shelter from the devastating loss. Jade reached for the gift, and the darkness took her.

CHAPTER TWENTY-NINE

Fingers slick with blood, Coop gripped his cell phone and pressed the name of the one person who could save Jade's life.

"Hey, man, we just got good news." Blake raised his voice over the sounds of celebration from the other occupants of the helicopter.

"I need you to—"

"Ethan took a plea deal to save his ass. He'll testify that Lloyd Bueller bragged about killing his wife right before the bastard hired an army to invade the town. The FBI is rounding up the rest of them as we speak."

"*Blake—*" Coop yelled into the phone. He didn't give a damn about Bueller—not with Jade bleeding out in front of his eyes. "*He shot her. I can't stop...there's too much blood.*" Panic reached for him, and he fought to detach and compartmentalize his feelings for her.

"Who? Jade?" Blake was all in now, concern radiating through the phone.

"I need you to turn around, or she's going to die."

"Way ahead of you, man. MacGyver wants to know where she's hit."

Coop could finally breathe as the vice around his chest released marginally. They were on their way back. "Upper left chest area just below the clavicle. Bullet went through." Responding to MacGyver's questions gave him purpose and hope.

"ETA six minutes. Keep pressure on." MacGyver's calm voice came through the speaker. "We've got medical supplies on-board. She'll need IV fluids. Is she conscious? In pain?"

"She's been out since just before I called you."

"Breathing okay?"

"Rapid and shallow. Pulse is thready."

"That's to be expected. Jade will be okay, Coop."

She has to be. He looked skyward as the distant *thrum, thrum* of the helo drifted in and out on the breeze. *Just a little longer.* He studied her pale face, her lashes dark against ashen skin. "Don't leave me, sweetheart."

"What's taking so damn long?" Coop paced right up to the swinging doors, where hospital staff had stopped him when they wheeled Jade's gurney through hours ago. He whipped around and glared at Travis as though his friend was withholding the answer.

On a long-suffering sigh, Travis pushed off the arms of his chair and stood. "I'm going to get some coffee. You want some?"

Aw, hell. He shouldn't be riding Travis. He'd stayed behind when Blake, Luke, and MacGyver took off for Pine Bluff to lend a hand sweeping up the rest of Ethan's men. Despite Coop's foul mood, growing darker as the afternoon wore on, Travis hadn't left his side. Until now. Apparently, his friend had had enough of Coop's grousing.

When he didn't answer, Travis sighed again and started for the corridor.

Coop rubbed the back of his neck. "Travis."

His friend stopped and turned partway.

"I'm sorry. I shouldn't be taking out my frustrations on you."

One corner of Travis' mouth hitched upward. "No apology necessary. I know what she means to you, and that buys you a little slack. But you don't need to worry. She'll make it. The question is, what will you do to keep her from walking away once she's back on her feet?" He raised an eyebrow before turning and sauntering down the hallway.

Would she do that—leave me again? He could still hear her saying, *I love you.* Does it count if she thought she was going to die any minute when she spoke the words?

"Mr. Cooper?"

He whirled to face a man in scrubs. "How is she?" His voice shook, but he didn't give a damn.

"Ms. McDowell is out of surgery and in stable condition. The bullet nicked the left subclavian artery and fractured the second rib. There's extensive tissue damage. The injury precipitated atelectasis of the left lung exacerbated by the anesthesia. Fairly common post-surgery, but I want to leave the endotracheal tube until she's ready to transfer from ICU to a medical ward."

All the words ran together after *stable condition.* "Can I see her, doc?"

"She's heavily sedated due to the intubation. I'm afraid she won't know you're there, Mr. Cooper. Go home. Get some rest and come back tomorrow."

Coop ran one hand over his face and the whiskers that hadn't seen a razor in several days. With that and blood all over his T-shirt, he must look like a serial killer. "I just need to sit with her for a while." He shook his head. "I can't leave until I see, with my own eyes, that she's still here." What if he came back tomorrow and she was gone without a trace, just like three years ago? He'd camp in the damn waiting room before he'd let that happen.

The doctor studied him for a couple beats before a slight smile eased the lines around his mouth. "Fifteen minutes. I'll have one of the nurses come and get you once Ms. McDowell is settled."

Coop felt alive for the first time since he'd registered the blood spreading across Jade's chest. "Thank you."

The doctor nodded and disappeared through the swinging doors just as Travis strolled into the waiting area holding two cups of black coffee. "What'd I miss?"

Afraid he'd lose it if he tried to speak around the lump in his throat, Coop merely slapped his friend on the back and threw him a lame-ass grin.

Travis' smile stretched from ear to ear. "See. What did I tell you? Your lady's going to be all right."

After the longest twenty minutes he'd ever sat through, a matronly, no-nonsense nurse emerged to lead him to Jade's ICU bed. His first glimpse of her pallid face and nearly colorless lips almost knocked his legs from beneath him. He had to remind himself she'd been in a battle for her life, and she'd survived.

He walked to the bed, reached over the railing, and grasped her hand. "Hey, gorgeous. It was a tough fight, but you did great. I'm so proud of you for never giving up." Monitors beeped steadily. The ventilator whooshed, sending life-saving oxygen to her lungs. Yet the silence was thunderous, so great was his need to hear her voice.

"I won't lie to you. This next part will be hard too. I'd guess you've got months of physical therapy ahead of you. That's probably just what you wanted to hear, right?" He laughed at his bad timing. "You're the strongest person I know. You can do this. *We'll* do it together. I promise you from now on, when you need me, I'll be right there beside you." He squeezed her hand.

She'd been so still, his heart kicked in his chest when her eyelids fluttered.

She's only dreaming.

He reached to brush her hair off her forehead but stopped short when her eyes moved again, then opened partially. Her fingers twined with his and returned his caress with more strength than she should have had.

A heartbeat later, her eyes closed. She'd heard his promise, and she was going to hold him to it. The tears that defied his will rimmed over and rolled down his face, first one and then the other. *Happy tears,* she'd called them. He got it now. He was still standing at her bedside, sandwiching her hand in both of his, when the nurse came to kick him out.

*****

"I'm going home." She was alone in the hospital room. Soledad, who'd covered the day shift since Jade arrived in the ward, had just given her the news. Thanks to the nurse's exemplary care and Blake's frequent visits over the past several days, she was fully aware of how lucky she'd been. If Coop hadn't been there when General McDowell shot her—if he hadn't called Blake for an air-evac, she'd likely have bled out on the ground beside the general.

A shudder gripped her, and her hand went involuntarily to the wound just above her left breast. It hurt like hell whenever she accidentally twisted her upper body. Her left arm rested uselessly in a sling, which was going to complicate her efforts to dress. The pile of clean clothes Travis had brought this morning mocked her from the chair beside the bed. Changing without bending or twisting, with only one hand, was going to take a while, so she might as well get started.

"Looks like we arrived just in time."

Jade swung around at the sound of her sister's voice, then froze until the knife-like pain lessened to a bearable level.

"Oh…sorry." Nicole was beside her immediately, chewing her bottom lip.

Jade forced a smile to alleviate Nic's worry. "You'd think I'd have learned not to do that by now."

"I've heard the McDowell women like to do things the hard way." Ryan strode across the room, a crooked grin accentuating the laugh lines on his face. He gave her a careful hug. "Hey, you're looking good, JD."

"Yeah, I bet. Thanks for coming to spring me." An ache started in her abdomen and spread outward. She'd hoped Coop would come to pick her up. Vague memories nagged her. Him hovering over her bed, squeezing her hand. His comforting voice in one-sided conversation when she woke from her drug-induced sleep. Since leaving the ICU and being allowed visitors, there'd been someone with her constantly, but the face she longed to see hadn't appeared.

Neither Blake nor Travis would look her in the eye and answer her questions about where he was, other than to say he had some things to take care of and he'd be back. She'd finally accepted that the drone of his deep voice at her bedside had likely been the result of a morphine drip.

Blake tapped on the half-open door and pushed through without waiting for an invitation. His arm draped loosely over the shoulders of an attractive brunette with striking blue eyes that sparkled with the intensity of her smile.

"Hey, you're up. Jade, I'd like you to meet my wife, Tori."

The woman extended her hand. "Hi, Jade. I've heard so much about you. I'm glad you're on the mend." Tori's smile was genuine, and Jade liked her immediately.

"Nice to meet you." With her good arm, she gestured toward Nic.

"Oh, we've met. Nicole and Ryan have been helping me, uh, spruce up the cabin." Tori grabbed the neatly folded clothes and motioned toward the door. "Why don't you boys find the cafeteria and have a cup of coffee? Jade's going to need a little help and some privacy. Send Kellie up when she and MacGyver arrive. Okay?"

"You got it. Come on, Ryan." Stopping in the doorway, the men exchanged greetings with someone in the hallway. Then Blake looked toward Jade. "When you're ready, you've got a visitor out here."

"Coop?" Her traitorous heart did a little flip.

Blake shook his head. "No, but he said he'd stop by later." He abruptly swiveled as though eager to drop the subject, disappearing with Ryan close on his heels.

Disappointment sliced through her, and mortification followed quickly. She could tell by the awkward silence that Coop's name from her lips had given away her deepest desire. It was apparent, Nic and Tori knew he wasn't coming, at least not for the reason she'd hoped, and neither of them wanted to tell her.

Nic snatched the clothes out of Jade's hands and laid them on the bed. "First, let's get that sling off."

Tori's heels clicked across the floor. "I'll guard the door so that you can change out here. It'll be easier than trying to maneuver in that tiny bathroom."

She hated feeling helpless, but Jade forced herself to let Nic help her dress. Her gut told her she should probably get over it. It was more than likely she'd need help with many daily activities she'd taken for granted up until now. Her sister seemed to be healing well from her injuries. Soon, Jade would have no reason to stay. She dug deep for a smile. "I can't wait to get out of here."

"Carl Graves left this morning. The ATF wanted him back in Portland for his next *undercover* assignment." Nic made air-apostrophes to emphasize his covert activities.

A smile touched Jade's lips. She still had a hard time believing the man she'd despised down to her bones was a federal agent who'd ended up saving her life. Ryan and Nic had filled her in on Ethan's role as the real mastermind behind the militia's attempts to subvert justice in Bueller's murder trial. He'd gotten greedy when he learned the general planned to eliminate one of the McDowell women who was currently making his job harder. Ethan and most of his men, including Derek, were in jail, awaiting trials. Pine Bluff was slowly getting back to normal.

Jade looked closely at her sister. The lack of sparkle in her eyes spoke of the toll recent events had taken on her. "How are you doing, Nic?"

As she glanced toward Jade, a sad smile curved her lips. "I'm fine. Why wouldn't I be?"

Jade shook her head, seeing in her sister the same horror and disbelief she'd experienced when the general had told her the truth. "Nic, you're allowed to grieve, you know. He was your father, whether he was good at it or not."

Nicole huffed a cynical laugh. "No, he was a sperm donor. That's all. He never cared about either of us. After what he did to you—why would I grieve for a man like that? How do you?"

"I don't," Jade admitted, "but I'm not going to hold on to bitterness either. If I do, he wins. I won't let him win, and neither should you."

Nic sighed and blinked back tears. "I know you're right. I'm just feeling a little lost right now."

Jade wrapped her good arm around her sister's shoulder and pulled her close. "We've got each other, just like after Mom died. Remember? We'll be all right."

Nicole smiled as she shook the wrinkles from Jade's clothes. "Of course, we will. And we've got two good men in our lives."

"That's right." At least one of them did. Jade tamped down a twinge of envy for Nic's rock-solid marriage to her soulmate. So what if Coop had left for parts unknown.

Her jeans, knit top, and light jacket went on quickly if you didn't count buttons. The worst was her bra. That was a two-person job. One she would avoid once there was no one around to judge. Life was about to change drastically, again.

Someone tapped on the door, and she glanced up, pathetically hoping to see Coop walk into the room.

Tori cracked open the door and peeked in, then swung it wide to admit a blonde woman with stunning emerald-green eyes, pushing an empty wheelchair. "I took this off some guy out there who seemed way too eager to crash your party."

Tori let the door fall shut and tugged the newcomer toward the bed. "Jade, Nicole…this is Kellie Greyson. MacGyver's fiancée."

Kellie approached and shook their hands warmly, then positioned the wheelchair in front of Jade. "Your chariot awaits, milady."

"Jade, you and Kellie have a lot in common. You're both former military."

Kellie smiled and gave a quick salute. "Marine, short term. Not career like you. What's it like flying a fighter jet?"

"Better than sex." It was a familiar question, and Jade gave her standard answer without thinking. It was the truth, though—*almost.*

"I always suspected as much." Kellie held her hand up, palm out, and Jade slapped a high five while everyone laughed.

More tapping on the door, and Jade was able to catch herself before unwarranted expectations raised her heart rate. Tori stuck her head through the opening and spoke to someone in a low voice. Stepping toward Jade, Nic laid a hand on her shoulder. Jade glanced at her, perplexed by the concern that shadowed her eyes. She started to ask what was wrong, but just then, Major Paul Bingham slipped through the doorway, his gaze landing on her.

Tori glanced at her watch. "I told Blake I'd come and get Isaiah when we were done here. That's my six-year-old son. I better go before my husband sends out a search party. We'll have time to get to know each other later."

"I'll go with you." Kellie rushed out on Tori's heels, both nodding to the major.

Jade raised her eyebrows. "Wow. That was abrupt. Why do I get the feeling something's going on that I don't know about?"

Sadness and worry reflected in Nic's eyes before she turned to grab the bag she'd finished packing for Jade. "You've always had my back when I needed you. I want you to know your big sister will always be there for you if you need to talk." She nodded to the major. "I'll see you both downstairs."

Jade watched her leave in stunned silence, then studied Paul. He stood just inside the door, his brow furrowed. The fact that he obviously didn't know what to do with his hands and finally shoved them in his pockets verified his nervousness. She cocked her head. "You really know how to clear a room."

Paul chuckled, moved the chair from beside the bed to within five feet of her, and took a seat. "How are you feeling?"

She readjusted her arm in the sling. "Pretty sure you didn't come all this way to inquire about my health."

He leaned back in the chair and crossed his arms. "Okay, I get it. No small talk. I've been trying to figure out how to tell you this for years. I practiced on Nicole, and she wasn't impressed. She thinks I should—how'd she put it? *Drop the flowery shit and just rip off the Band-Aid.* So here goes."

He ran a hand over his face, looking at the floor. "I'm your father, Jade."

What? She opened her mouth to call *bullshit* and closed it without saying a word. Childhood memories invaded her mind. As far back as she could remember, Paul had been a part of her life. When she was five, he'd kissed and bandaged her scraped knees. When she was fifteen, he'd dried her tears and told an embarrassing story about *his* first dance that made her laugh and eventually feel better about hers.

How many times had she wished her father was more like Paul? There'd been days she'd pretended he *was* her father, but the harsh reality had always come back to bite her. Had it been true all along? The general had told her she wasn't his, and she'd believed him without hesitation. It was almost as though she'd always known. Paul's black hair and dark blue eyes, so like her own, blurred as moisture clouded her vision.

"I wish you'd say something." He was leaning forward, his elbows propped on his knees, his expression grave.

She smiled with trembling lips. "Uh...I'm going to need some of the *flowery shit*."

He laughed, relieving some of the tension in the room. For the next forty-five minutes, he talked, and Jade asked questions. He told her what a beautiful spirit her mother had been, not mincing words as he accepted the blame for their indiscretion. His broken heart when he learned of Jade's birth. The general's coercion into a life of deceit and criminal activity, and Paul's role in her rescue from the hellhole in Syria. And finally, how he was turning himself in to the military police for his crimes during his tenure with the Crimson Guard.

When he finally fell silent, they simply looked at each other. She was drained and filled with contentment at the same time. She felt as though she was seeing him for the first time. Her *dad*. Wow, was that ever weird. Wait until she told Coop. *Oh, right. Coop's not here.*

She hadn't seen him since the shooting, except in her hazy dreams. The last thing he'd said to her was nonsensical—something about providence and her father.

Wait a minute.

"You were the one."

Paul's eyebrows lifted.

"You shot the general that day and saved Coop's life and mine.

His eyes clouded. "I'm sorry. I was hoping you wouldn't remember that."

She stood as Paul got to his feet. "I'll never forget. Thank you." Her functional arm wound around his shoulders, and she pulled him in for a hug.

They broke apart when Soledad pushed through the doorway. "Good. You're all ready to go." A bright smile lit her kind face as she held out some papers. "A prescription for pain meds if you need them and instructions for care of the wound. Dr. Ramsey's number is there if you have any questions or concerns." She winked. "I added mine in case you can't reach the doctor. We're going to miss you around here."

"I'm going to miss you too, Soledad. You've forever changed my opinion of hospitals." Jade hugged her warmly.

The nurse steadied her while she regained her seat, then reached for her pocket. "I almost forgot. Housekeeping found this wrapped up in some sheets they were getting ready to wash. They returned it to the nurse's station, but I guess it got buried under paperwork. I didn't find it until this morning." She handed Jade a white envelope with her name scrawled across the front.

Coop's handwriting. He'd left a note to say goodbye. An instant ache reverberated through her chest. There was no way she could handle that now.

Folding the doctor's instruction sheet around the prescription and the card, she laid it in her lap.

Paul stepped behind her chair. "Are you ready?"

Summoning strength, she gave Soledad's hand a final squeeze. "Onward. Ready or not."

Soledad held the door open while Paul wheeled her into the corridor and to the elevator. They joined four other people for the ride down in silence.

As the elevator doors opened, the lobby erupted in semi-restrained cheers and applause. A big 'GET WELL SOON' banner hung over the exit, surrounded by balloons. Jade adopted her best smile as Ryan and Nic fell in beside her wheelchair. The glass exit doors slid open, and Paul pushed her outside into the sunlight.

Blake stood on one side, holding Tori's hand and grinning. MacGyver and Kellie were next to them. On the other side, Travis smiled broadly and winked when she cocked an eyebrow in his direction. Beside him, Luke had one arm around a petite brunette, and the other held a baby of eight months or so. In front of them stood the cutest little dark-haired girl. As Travis turned his attention to his cell phone, Luke urged his family forward.

"This is my wife, Sally, our daughter Jen and our son Kyler."

"So glad to finally meet you." Sally ignored her outstretched hand and came in for a hug.

"Oh, okay. You too." Jade stuttered a reply.

Sally laughed. "I know. We're pretty overwhelming when we all get together."

"Don't worry. You'll get used to us." Jen shook her hand politely.

The baby smiled and clapped his hands, and everyone laughed at his antics. Jade was grateful for Kyler stealing the limelight, if only for a minute. She wasn't sure how much longer she could hold it together. Glancing over her shoulder, she silently pleaded for Paul to take the hint and wheel her away from this family moment where she didn't belong. His attention focused farther out in the parking lot, where a vehicle grumbled to life.

She shivered, the cool morning breeze blowing through her light jacket. Small talk flew back and forth around her, and she tried to keep up, replying when spoken to, laughing when others did. She sucked at it, though, and prayed for whoever was driving her home to get their car.

A few seconds of silence made her glance around; afraid someone had asked a question she hadn't heard. Everyone had disappeared, probably inside the hospital since she hadn't seen them walk away. Paul was still behind her chair. She could see his hands. Maybe now she could make her escape and regroup before she had to face people again.

Her heart lurched as a vehicle pulled up to the ADA-approved curb. A green Dodge Ram pickup. She couldn't help but gape at the tall, blond hunk who stepped out, rounded the hood, and strode toward her. His grin did little to warm the cold void surrounding her heart. She couldn't keep a smile from erupting when he unzipped his hoodie to reveal a wiggly, reddish-brown furball who hit the ground scampering when Coop set him down.

"*Moose!*" She barely had time to lean forward and reach out with one hand before the little dog launched onto her lap. A flurry of licks and tail wags left her laughing and exhausted.

As Coop reached her chair, Paul stepped forward, and the two men grasped hands as though they were long-lost friends, then hugged and exchanged back slaps. After which Paul walked away, leaving her alone with the man who owned her aching heart. *What could he possibly have to say?*

She grasped Moose and tried to stand, but Coop knelt in front of her, blocking her attempt. Pursing her lips, she resolved to hear him out. She would not cry.

Facing her, now at eye level, his smile finally wavered. "Damn, it's good to see you." He reached to brush a lock of hair behind her shoulder and got his hand licked for his effort. She flinched away from his touch, and uncertainty tinged his deep brown eyes.

He ducked his head for a heartbeat as though reconsidering why he was there. His jaw firmed. "I'm in love with you, Jade. I have been for so long, I can't remember life before you. When I thought I'd lost you, I nearly lost myself. Now, here you are, so beautiful sometimes it hurts my heart to look at you. We have a second chance, and I don't want to waste another minute. I hope you've thought about us, and I hope you feel the same."

Suddenly, there was a small box in his hand. When he flipped it open, a beautiful diamond ring sparkled in the sun. "Jade McDowell, I want you in my life forever. Will you marry me?"

She hugged Moose close to still his excitement, looking from the ring to Coop's earnest face and back again. "Where have you been?" The sharp question escaped as confusion filled her mind.

His eyes widened. "You didn't read my letter?"

She pulled the papers in her lap from beneath Moose's feet and held up the card. "I just got it today." A frown greeted her lame excuse.

Without a word, he grabbed the knife from his belt and sliced open the envelope, handing her a single sheet of paper.

She had to blink a few times to bring the words into focus.

Hey, gorgeous. Sitting here watching you sleep, it's hard to quantify how much I love you. Just know I want you in my life, and I want to be part of yours if you'll have me. I've had three long days to think about this. It occurred to me our lives have been so crazy the past three years, two months, and seventeen days you might not have had enough time to think it through. So, I'm giving you time. Until you're discharged. Fair warning—when I see you again, I'll have a BIG question to ask you. I hope you'll say 'yes.'

**All my love,
Coop**

Jade dropped the paper and covered her mouth. A laugh slipped out, drowning in a blubbery sob.

He leaned toward her and pulled her hand away. "Aw, damn...please don't cry."

She sniffled. "I'm not crying." With a watery

laugh, she threaded her arm around his neck. "I don't need any more time. *Yes, I'll marry you!*"

He snatched Moose from her lap, wrapped his arm around her waist, and stood. Lifting her off the ground, he twirled her around with a big grin. Paul jogged up, grabbed the dog, and retreated again. Coop set her on her feet, but she stayed close while he slipped the ring on her finger. Cheers, laughter, and applause sounded from behind her. They had an audience, but she didn't care. When he covered her mouth with his, she forgot there was anyone else around.

When they came up for air, she wasn't about to let him go. "We have so many decisions to make. You live in California. I live in Oregon. What are we going to do about that?"

He kissed her quickly but soundly. "I've arranged for us to stay at the safe house for a few weeks until you're better. Tori and Kellie have brought in a few items to make it feel more like home. It'll be easier for your sister to check on you there. We'll figure out the rest."

Well, if that isn't a typical male response. Jade laid her hand against his chest. "What if we can't agree?"

He pulled her closer, careful not to hurt her, and nuzzled her neck. "I'll move the moon and stars to be with you."

She smiled. "Me too. And we've got all the time in the world."

"That we do," he whispered just before he kissed her again.

Other books by Dixie Lee Brown

The Hearts of Valor Series

Rescued by the Ranger
Published by Avon Impulse

Heart of a SEAL
Honor Among SEALs
For the Love of a SEAL
Published by Lyrical Liaison

SEAL of Silence

The Trust No One Series
All or Nothing
When I Find You
If You Only Knew
Whatever It Takes
Tempt the Night
Published by Avon Impulse

ABOUT THE AUTHOR

Dixie Lee Brown lives and writes in Central Oregon, inspired by gorgeous scenery and three hundred sunny days a year. Having moved from South Dakota as a child to Washington, Montana and then to Oregon, she feels at home in the west. She resides with two dogs and two cats, who are currently all the responsibility she can handle. Dixie works fulltime as a bookkeeper. When she is not writing or working, she loves to read, enjoys movies, and if it were possible, she would spend all of her time at the beach. She is also the author of the Trust No One series, published by Avon Impulse. Please visit her online at www.dixiebrown.com.

Printed in Great Britain
by Amazon